A VAMPIRE'S DESIRE

Elizabeth James

Thrall of Darkness

CONTENTS

Title Page

Copyright

Prologue

Chapter One: Job Search   1

Chapter Two: Interview   8

Chapter Three: Celebration   15

Chapter Four: Translations   21

Chapter Five: Warning   31

Chapter Six: Good Friends   38

Chapter Seven: Fleeting Fantasies   46

Chapter Eight: Farewell   54

Chapter Nine: Office Intimacy   60

Chapter Ten: Denied   68

Chapter Eleven: Park Assault   74

Chapter Twelve: Cathedral Plot   83

Chapter Thirteen: Later   91

Chapter Fourteen: Explosive Encounter   98

Chapter Fifteen: Blood Tax   103

Chapter Sixteen: Master   111

Chapter Seventeen: Darkness   118

Chapter Eighteen: Fraught Messages 126

Chapter Nineteen: Employment History 133

Chapter Twenty: Allotment 141

Chapter Twenty-One: Refused Offer 151

Chapter Twenty-Two: Future Plans 157

Chapter Twenty-Three: An Early Visit 164

Chapter Twenty-Four: Persuasion 173

Chapter Twenty-Five: Second Thoughts 179

Chapter Twenty-Six: Reason to Stay 185

Chapter Twenty-Seven: Bound 192

Chapter Twenty-Eight: Friendship 198

Chapter Twenty-Nine: Pure Blood 205

Chapter Thirty: Surveillance 213

Chapter Thirty-One: Interrupted 218

Chapter Thirty-Two: Tense Game 224

Chapter Thirty-Three: Surprising Answers 231

Chapter Thirty-Four: Friendly Visit 239

Chapter Thirty-Five: Bold Demand 246

Chapter Thirty-Six: Bleeding 253

Chapter Thirty-Seven: Discovered 259

Chapter Thirty-Eight: Weekend Away 266

Chapter Thirty-Nine: Under Watch 272

Chapter Forty: Deadly Apology 279

Chapter Forty-One: Burning 285

Chapter Forty-Two: Destroying Evidence 293

Chapter Forty-Three: Under Pressure 300

Chapter Forty-Four: Second Thoughts 306

Chapter Forty-Five: Testimony 313

Chapter Forty-Six: Intimidation   322

Chapter Forty-Seven: Mixed Blood   330

Chapter Forty-Eight: Transition   336

Chapter Forty-Nine: New House   343

Chapter Fifty: Sharing News   351

Chapter Fifty-One: Adaptations   357

Chapter Fifty-Two: Waiting   362

Chapter Fifty-Three: Loss of Control   370

Chapter Fifty-Four: Verdict   377

Chapter Fifty-Five: Next Steps   384

Chapter Fifty-Six: Together   391

About The Author   401

Thrall of Darkness   403

Books By This Author   405

PROLOGUE

"Are you enjoying this, Kairos?" asked my master softly as he ran his hand through my hair.

I couldn't answer; my back arched and I gasped for breath as his other hand stroked along my cock lightly, teasingly. My hands were bound behind my back as I knelt in the darkness around us. Vampires fed in the darkness, and my master was no different.

Rope tickled along my torso, wrapped around me tightly enough so I could feel the pull but loose enough that I didn't feel trapped. He always knew exactly how to tie me up. I'd noticed that he was getting tighter as I got used to it. Everything about this was new and frightening still, but I was desperate for him. I wanted to please him.

His hand carded through my hair again and his lips landed on the tattoo on my neck, the tattoo that marked me as belonging to a vampire house. His tongue lapped against my skin and I wondered, as I always did, if this time he would bite. I longed for him to bite me, to let my blood fill his body the way he filled me.

I tried to make out some sight of him in the darkness, but it was impossible. I wasn't blindfolded; the darkness of the vampire's lair was absolute. There was no light. He could see perfectly, of course, and loved looking into my fearful eyes.

"Well, Kairos?"

I managed to murmur yes as he stroked me almost playfully as if he knew how difficult talking was right now, with the sensations cascading through me. I could feel him moving behind me, feel his hand stroking down my back as I shivered, waiting to feel him pressing against me. He pulled the rope around me and I moaned as it pulled against me, constricting me in the most delightful way. Then I felt something against me and I tensed with anticipation.

Just then, a buzz sounded against the wall. Adze cursed softly and I heard him walk to the other side of the room to check his phone. He had it off for all but emergencies. I wondered what was happening that the other vampires would be contacting him in the middle of the day like this. Normally, all of their activity was at night when the vampire city came alive. Days were reserved for sleep. And play. This lair kept everything so dark that the sun was never an issue, and I had spent several hours here each day while the manor slept.

He spoke quietly in another language, then I heard the phone click down on the table again. He returned to me and I hoped it wasn't anything too important. I was on fire and wouldn't be able to stand it if we stopped now.

"Your services are required," he said, starting to untie me.

"No," I gasped. "You can't leave me like this."

I knew he would, though. He wasn't known for his empathy, and had left me hungry on many occasions, whenever it was inconvenient for him to give me relief. He reached forward to stroke my length and I sighed in relief.

"If you serve our House well today, I'll give you everything you want when we return," he said. "Control yourself until then."

I bit my lip but held still as he finished untying me and helped me to my feet. I looked around in the pitch black, unable to see anything. I stood nervously as I listened to him move around, then he touched my waist and I flinched slightly. It was unnerving being in such darkness. He helped me dress, then led me out of the room into the hallway, where a few dim lights began to get my eyes adjusted. It would be at least five minutes slowly adjusting before Adze let me go upstairs. It was well past noon. I wished, not for the first time, that I could spend all of my time in the vampire's lair. But he valued me for my intelligence and work ethic, not just my body, and I couldn't lose his interest. That meant our time together was often fractured with work, and I didn't get as much of him as I wanted. Still, he made every minute count, and I wouldn't trade it for the world. As I went to see what the other vampires needed, I looked back and saw Adze staring at me with just the slightest hint of a smile.

"You'll be back soon," he said. "Lilith only needs you briefly. And when you do come back, I'll be waiting."

CHAPTER ONE: JOB SEARCH

Two months earlier...

Janae and I waited for the movie to start and munched on popcorn as we discussed our post-college plans. She had a job lined up; I didn't and was starting to worry. I had a temp job working at a nearby fast-food place that had served me well during classes, but now I needed something full-time and jobs were scarce, especially for a History major like me and especially one with a specialty in Human Culture.

"Maybe you should work for a vampire," Janae said, and I laughed.

"I'm serious, Kairos," she insisted. "You studied them, why not put your knowledge to work?"

"They weren't my focus," I pointed out. "Humans were. And I've never even met one. Don't you have to grow up around them to work for them?"

"Usually," she acknowledged. "One of my friends works for one, though, and she had never met one. You could try. You know it pays really, really well."

"Maybe," I said. It was a possibility I had never considered. Vampires almost never hired outside their cities and I didn't even know anyone who knew a vampire. As the lights dimmed and the movie started, though, the idea kept floating through my head.

Vampires were a class apart; they lived almost entirely in their own cities with little contact with humans aside from the humans that served them. I had taken several classes on vampire history and was fascinated by them, but I hadn't grown up anywhere near one of their cities and had never met one, so it had never occurred to me to look for a job with one. I wasn't exactly qualified. I had almost no marketable skills and had planned on finding a generic job for a few years to save up money and go to grad school. Once I had my PhD, I could get a job teaching, but until then, my degree was almost worthless. Maybe I could find a job with a vampire. They were usually hiring, and Janae was right: the pay was insanely good.

Part of the reason for the pay, though, was due to the risks of living among vampires. While most vampires respected the humans who worked for them, some didn't and there were occasional casualties. It was always a risk around them. The vampires had a society of hunters among them who maintained order and killed any vampires who needlessly fed on or killed humans. Maybe one of them was hiring. I should be safe around them. They of all vampires wouldn't kill their servants.

I kept thinking about the possible opportunity throughout the movie and when I got back to my apartment, I looked up openings I might possibly be qualified for. There were the usual jobs requiring considerable physical strength, as vampire cities required massive imports and movers were always needed. But I wasn't especially strong and a job moving boxes wouldn't be worth the money. There were a few other menial jobs, but I wasn't interested in doing chores. Maybe if I got desperate.

I had almost given up when I noticed a job at the bottom of the listings. It was a single line long and I had nearly missed it as the other listings were quite lengthy.

"Intelligent assistant, vampire or human, knowledge of human culture required."

Nothing else. No indication of what exactly that assistant would do, but it was interesting that anyone could apply. I selected it and it went straight to an application, with no more information given. I considered. My specialty was human culture, which was a fairly obscure field given that humans

2

tended to assume their culture was the default culture and not worth studying. It was one reason my degree was so worthless, though since few people studied it, I was almost certain to get a tenure-track job teaching in the field once I had my PhD. I had never thought to find a job where my knowledge came in handy before that, though. This job was perfect, but I hesitated. I didn't like the lack of information. It didn't say which vampire this was for, or even which house.

Of course, I didn't know any of the houses, or what those houses did, but I could look them up. Each house had anywhere from around five to thirty vampires in it, all specializing in the same field. I vaguely knew the historical houses, but almost none of them were still in existence after the Species War last century. Most of the ancient vampires had been wiped out. But vampires were usually quite proud of their houses and it was odd that the house wasn't mentioned for this job. Unless it were a human looking for an assistant, a human who lived in a vampire city. That would be unusual, but not unheard of. Maybe I should apply just to see who it was. I could always turn the job down if I didn't like it, after all.

I brushed up my resume, emphasizing both my human culture specialization and also the classes in vampires I had taken, to make up for the fact that I had never met a vampire. The application asked for two human and one vampire reference and I stared at that for a long time. The human references were easy; two of my professors had already offered to be references for any job I picked. I was the best student in the field, they said, and they wanted to help me get to grad school. But I didn't know any vampires. I left that section blank, attached everything else, and submitted the application, fully expecting it to flag the area and demand input. To my surprise, the application went through. I hadn't realized the references were optional. I received a message that I would hear back within two days. Short turnaround, and it looked like I would actually receive a response. A lot of employers simply ignored the applications they rejected, not bothering to send a rejection.

With my application in, I went to sleep and dreamed about blood dripping from a crescent moon. The next day I had one final late in the evening and spent the day studying. It was a class in modern human culture and I studied especially hard in case I got a job interview. I had honestly never expected to use my degree so soon, though it was unlikely I would get an interview without a vampire reference. The final went well but as I turned it in, my teacher gestured me aside. She was smiling so I wasn't too worried, and I had wanted a chance to thank her in person anyway.

"You applied for a job with a vampire?" she asked. "I'm glad you listed me as a reference. I know many vampires."

"Did they contact you? Already?" I asked, surprised. "I didn't think I stood a chance."

"They asked about your degree," she said with a smile. "Vampires value this specialization very highly. They don't bother learning our culture so anyone who does study it is in demand. I didn't think you were interested in working for a vampire, so I didn't think to suggest it."

"I never considered it," I admitted. "But a friend suggested it. I've never actually met a vampire."

"It can be a shock," she said. "You're certain to get an interview, so try not to be overwhelmed when you meet them."

"Who contacted you? The job offer didn't have a lot of detail."

"An assistant," she said. "He was human. I'm not sure who he was representing but if you put me and Gary as your references, you'll get an interview."

"Thank you so much," I said.

She grinned. "No problem, Kairos. You'll learn a lot, make some good money, and get your PhD in no time."

"I have to get the job, first," I pointed out, and she laughed.

"Any vampire would be lucky to get you. They don't advertise the type of job you'd be good for usually, since it's

4

often in-house hires, but once they find out someone qualified is looking for work, you'll get requests. Be as picky as you like, and don't work for a vampire you don't think you can handle. Pay attention to their other servants. If any of them seem unhappy, don't take the job. But I think you'll land on your feet."

I thanked her again for the advice, the reference, and the great class. I promised to keep in touch and left in a good mood. When I saw a message from the job the next day, I held my breath as I opened it. Then I grinned. An interview. I had actually gotten an interview. Then I noticed the time and date of the proposed interview. They had given me two options: one in an hour and one in two hours. The city was forty minutes away. I checked when the email was sent, but it had just been sent. My address was on my application; had they bothered checking where I lived? I had to hurry, that was for sure, and I responded with a request for two hours, hoping that was all right. If there were traffic, I didn't want to be late. Then I hopped in the shower and got ready as quickly as possible.

As I drove to the vampire city, I tried to keep calm. There was indeed traffic and I fretted as I inched into the city. Once in the city boundaries, I couldn't help but look around, wondering who was vampire and who was human. It was day, so only rich vampires would be out, if any. The potion that granted temporary immunity from sunlight was extremely expensive, so it was likely most of the people walking around were humans, but there were so many of them. I hadn't realized the cities were so crowded.

The address was on the other side of town in a wooded area and when I reached the spot on the map, I stared. It was an enormous mansion and I stopped at a large gate leading to the estate. There was a call box and I rolled down the window, looking for something to push to indicate my presence. Then there was a buzz, and a voice asking for my name.

"Kairos," I said, adding that I was there for an interview.

After a moment of silence, the gate opened. I glanced at the clock. Fifteen minutes early. Better early than late, I assured myself. I wasn't unreasonably early.

I parked in the small lot and went to the immense front door, feeling intimidated. As soon as I stepped in front of the door, it opened. A man stood on the other side in a pristine uniform, looking exactly like a butler from the movies. He couldn't be the vampire, could he? Very unlikely. I wondered if I would have to wear a uniform like that as well. I knew vampires were strict about appearance and manners, and while I was always neat and polite, I suddenly realized that my standards might not be good enough for a vampire. Well, I had gotten the interview. That was enough.

The servant let me in and gestured for my coat. He didn't say anything, though, and I felt awkward taking off my coat and handing it to the man. As the servant left with my coat, leaving me standing in a large entry hall, I straightened my collar and was glad I was in a nice outfit. I was in khaki slacks, a white dress shirt, and a navy blazer, my favorite outfit when I had to dress up. I had even taken some time with my hair, trying to corral my blond curls into a decent style. I hoped it was enough; I needed to make a good impression.

There was an arch leading to another room in front of me and I could make out a grand piano at the other side of the room. I had never been in a house as nice as this. The servant returned and I wondered if he were the only servant here. I scanned the man's neck for the tattoo that I had heard all servants had on their necks to ward against vampire attacks and spotted it. The tattoo was a simple symbol, almost like a clover, and hardly noticeable.

It wasn't a real tattoo, I knew, and it indicated the house he served. When a servant was admitted to a job, the house granted him the symbol as a way to identify their servants and protect them from vampires outside of the house. Vampires within the house could still feed on them, and that's where the trouble was, but those outside of the house were unable to drink a servant's blood. But this man didn't look like he'd been fed on. He was studying me carefully and I worried that I was already failing the interview.

"You're Kairos?" the man asked.

"Yes," I said, and the man gestured for me to follow through the door. I obeyed and we entered a small study with a mahogany desk and white leather chairs. The man pointed to one of the chairs and then sat in the chair opposite it, and I was nervous as I sat down. I had never actually done a job interview, I realized. The fast food place had just asked for basic information before hiring me. They didn't really care. But I hadn't had any time to prepare for this or even look up the types of questions potential employers asked.

"Is this your first time in Redmond?" the man asked, and I nodded. The man hesitated. "First time in any vampire city?"

"Yes," I said.

"Have you ever met a vampire?"

"No," I said, wishing I had a different answer because the man looked annoyed.

"Do you realize how difficult these jobs are to find?" he asked. "It's rare enough that we're considering a human, but one with no experience with vampires is highly unusual."

I shifted uncomfortably. Why had they invited me here if I were unacceptable? Just to yell at me for daring to apply?

"Enough," another voice said from behind me. I jumped. That had to be the vampire. There was something in the voice, something powerful and smooth and, for some inexplicable reason, sexy. I shut my eyes briefly and wondered if I had failed the interview completely because hearing that beautiful voice, I realized just how desperately I wanted this job. Then I turned to look at the vampire and my eyes widened. He was absolutely stunning.

CHAPTER TWO: INTERVIEW

I turned to the man who had just entered from a hidden door. He was a vampire and I stared, unable to help myself. There was no question he was a vampire and I was ashamed that I had even considered the other man a vampire. The aura of power and danger was unmistakable, and also sexuality. I licked my lips, drinking in the sight of the vampire. I'd heard that vampires were attractive, but never imagined anything like this beautiful man with his light chocolate skin, glowing ebony eyes, and finely chiseled face. He was in an elegant suit, finer than any I had ever seen, and it fit his muscular form perfectly. Everything about him exuded power and sensuality and I felt drawn to him as I had never been drawn to anyone in my life. There was no emotion on that beautiful face and I wondered what he looked like when he smiled. Did he smile? Maybe not.

The vampire stared at me in return, then took a step forward and looked at the servant.

"There's no need to harass him," the vampire said. "His qualifications are suitable."

That didn't exactly bode well. I desperately wanted this job. I didn't even care what the job was. I wanted to be near this vampire. I wanted to look at him every day, admire him and serve him. I needed this job.

The vampire gestured for the servant to leave. The servant looked frustrated but obeyed, shutting the door behind him and leaving the two of us alone.

"Stand up," the vampire said, and I obeyed, though my legs felt shaky. The vampire examined me from head to toe and I wondered what he thought.

I was attractive, I knew from my friends. My friends were always a little upset about my sexual preferences and teased me about how many girls I could get if I wanted, but I was only interested in men. Still, I attracted plenty of those. My last boyfriend had always admired my slender body, my wide eyes, my pouting lips. I suspected my lips were my best feature as many people seemed drawn to them. But the vampire studied me impartially, his ebony eyes never lingering as he scanned my body before circling me, seeming to examine me from all angles before returning in front of me. Then the vampire met my eyes and I felt as if I were melting.

"You'll do," the vampire said, and my eyes widened. Surely that didn't mean I had the job.

"What?"

"Do you want the job?"

"Yes," I said. "But you haven't even talked to me."

"You know enough to begin," the vampire said. "You'll learn on the job."

"I don't even know what the job is," I admitted.

The vampire stared at me with those smoldering eyes.

"You'll learn," he said simply. "Do you accept?"

My mind whirled. I didn't know the specifics of the job or the pay or even the vampire's name, but I knew I would take the job. Should I negotiate? Find out more? Or would that risk the job offer? I wasn't going to risk it, I decided. I could always quit if the job were impossible.

"Yes," I said. "I'll take the job."

The vampire approached me and placed a hand on my neck. I shivered; the vampire's skin was cool against my neck as he pushed my collar down and touched just over my vein where I knew vampires liked to feed. Was he going to feed on me? I found I wouldn't really mind. There was a stinging and I flinched, and then the vampire removed his hand. I rubbed my neck and realized that the vampire had marked me. I now belonged to the vampire and was protected from other vampires. The job was really mine.

"You'll live here," the vampire said. "Move in as soon as possible. You'll have everything you require. I'll expect you to work every night, though only a couple of hours on the weekends. My name is Adze."

"I can't live here," I said, shocked.

The vampire stared at me again. "Were you planning to commute?"

I was silent. In all honesty, I hadn't expected to get the job and hadn't thought this through. I certainly hadn't expected to get the job this quickly. But of course I would have to move.

"I can move this weekend," I said uncertainly. "I haven't actually finished school yet."

That was on my application, luckily, but the vampire narrowed his eyes.

"You shouldn't accept a job you aren't prepared to take," he said. "Move in this weekend, but I expect you here every night in the meantime. You have a lot to learn."

"Of course," I said, grateful. I did not want to lose this job even as I was shocked at getting it. "Thank you."

"Dmitri will arrange the details. Ask him if you have any questions," Adze said. "I expect you here at midnight."

"Yes, I'll be here," I said, barely even processing that information. The vampire left and I sat down in the chair, completely stunned. I had gotten the job. What kind of job was it where my exact qualifications didn't matter, and a real interview wasn't necessary? Even the fast food place had asked me more questions than that. Slowly the times Adze had given made sense and I realized the vampire must be on a night schedule and had made an exception to see me right now. Most vampires were on night schedules, I knew, and it sounded like I needed to shift to that schedule quickly.

Another door opened and I jumped, but it wasn't the vampire. It was the servant, who must be Dmitri. He didn't look pleased, but he forced a smile. His thick black curls and tan skin were quite lovely, and any other time I would think he was extremely handsome. But compared to the incredible vampire, his beauty seemed dim. I wondered if he thought of me the same way.

"Congratulations," Dmitri said. "I hope you appreciate how lucky you are."

"I do," I said. "Um, I actually have some questions."

"I'm not surprised," Dmitri said, glancing in the direction the vampire had gone. "Master Adze interrupted before I could even tell you the job."

"Yeah, um, what kind of job is this?"

Dmitri sat in the chair across from me and began explaining the details of the job, and I was relieved as I listened. I would be assisting with paperwork for the most part, but they were correspondences from various humans and I needed to translate the hidden requests that humans always thought were obvious. Luckily, I had taken classes on Human Assumptions and knew the types of things humans didn't feel like they had to spell out. My lack of knowledge of vampires might hinder me, though, as there might be things even I took for granted that a vampire might not understand.

Occasionally – once Adze trusted me – I would accompany the vampire on business visits. I would also assist Dmitri in anything he needed and I gulped, because Dmitri sounded a little too happy about that. I wondered if that were actually part of the job or if the man had just thrown it in knowing I had no real say in the matter. Then we moved on to pay, and my eyes widened. I was going to be making a fortune, nearly three times what I planned on making as a professor. I would have enough money for grad school in a year or two, I realized in shock. I had expected to work at least five years and then have to keep working through grad school, but I would be able to fully fund it very soon.

"How long do you expect to work here?" Dmitri asked. "We've had some in this position who leave rather quickly."

"At least a year, though I'd like to stay longer," I said cautiously, not knowing if that was considered leaving quickly or not.

"Good," Dmitri said, and I let out a sigh. "What do you plan to do after this?"

"I want to get a PhD and become a professor," I said.

"Hmph," Dmitri said dismissively. "Well, do your best here. If he thinks you'll do, then you should last at least a year."

I wondered what about my future plans was disqualifying. Becoming a professor after getting the degree I had was almost a requirement, but I remembered what my teacher had said about the degree being in demand in vampire cities and wondered why no one had ever told me that before. Maybe there were other options than being a professor and I had just never heard of them before. Maybe, after a year working in a vampire city, I wouldn't want to become a professor anymore. And maybe I would want to keep working here if I liked it enough.

Dmitri got out some paperwork and showed me the contract I would be signing, going through each of the terms very briefly as he'd already explained all of them. Helping him was indeed in the contract, I was surprised to see. Everything was exactly as Dmitri had described it, but I hesitated before signing, wondering where exactly I would be staying, where I would be eating, and how those costs would be paid for.

"You've already accepted the job," Dmitri said impatiently, gesturing to my neck. "It doesn't even matter if you don't sign."

"I want the job," I said quickly, and signed before Dmitri reported my unwillingness to Adze. "I just had more questions."

"You'll probably keep thinking of questions," Dmitri said dismissively. "You know nothing about vampires or vampire cities."

"Adze told me I'd be living here," I said. "I just wondered where. How much will that cost?"

"Master Adze," Dmitri said sharply, and I gulped. Apparently there were rules in referring to vampires that I didn't know, and I made a mental note to add Master to the vampire's name from now on. Dmitri seemed shocked at my ignorance and I wondered what other seemingly obvious things I didn't know. Would Adze hold it against me if I messed up? I hoped not. I realized I still didn't know what house Adze belonged to, what house I now belonged to, but I was afraid to expose even more ignorance. I would look up the symbol on my neck when I got home.

"You really don't know anything, do you?" Dmitri said, then sighed. "You belong to him now. All of your expenses are covered. I'll show you your room."

He stood and gestured to me to follow as I wondered what counted as expenses. Food and a room, probably, and if I weren't paying for those, then I had almost no other expenses. I would have a fortune in my bank account before long. I followed Dmitri through a long hall to an elaborate kitchen with a square table along one wall.

"Meals will be in here," he said. "We're usually on night hours. At night there are two other servants. Dianne is in charge of the house and grounds. Don't make a mess. Margaret will cook for us. You can set your own schedule if you let her know in advance. She'll take any of your preferences into account."

I nodded and Dmitri led me through another hall. While the previous hall had been brightly lit and well-decorated, this hall was quite simple. There were three doors along the hall and Dmitri gestured to the first door.

"This will be your room. That's mine, and the bathroom," he said, gesturing to the two other doors. "Go in."

I opened the door nervously. It was a simple, bare room. It was smaller than my current bedroom and that was all it was: a bedroom. I would have to find storage for the rest of my furniture, since I wouldn't even need to bring a bed. I sat on the bed, which was a double like mine, and decided it would do. I could probably ask to use my own mattress instead, but this one seemed like a good combination of plush and firm. I wasn't very picky about beds. There was a bedstand, a desk, two lamps in addition to the overhead light, and a small window looking out on the beautiful yard. The view made up for the small size of the room, I decided. There was a closet, and then Dmitri showed me the shared bathroom. It had a large bath and separate shower and was spotless. I would have to make sure to be neat. There was a cabinet for me to use and a set of towels for me as well. I would barely have to bring anything.

Dmitri led me around a few more rooms: a library where Adze did much of his work, an open area that led to a wraparound porch with a path to the yard, and another study, this one with a desk piled with paperwork that Dmitri introduced as mine. I gulped and wondered how long it had been since someone had been doing this job, or if there would be that much work every day. Finally, Dmitri gestured to the stairs leading to the basement.

"Master Adze's rooms are down there. It's off limits to humans. Understand?"

I agreed and Dmitri gave me a few more instructions, then showed me where to park when I came back.

"Be early again," he advised. "Your timing today was perfect, and no doubt played into getting the job. Be prepared to stay at least four hours."

I nodded. I would need to take a nap before midnight to stay up that late. I was already driving home when I realized I had my last final in the morning. What was I going to do about that? I had to start work and I couldn't ask to leave early on my very first day. Well, I already had a solid A in the class. Even if I failed the final, it wouldn't affect my overall grade, just my teacher's opinion of me, and my teacher would hopefully understand. Mr. Grayson was my other reference, after all, and should be delighted that I had gotten the job.

After getting through the traffic and reaching my apartment, I collapsed onto my couch. Then I pulled out my phone. Janae wasn't going to believe what had happened.

CHAPTER THREE: CELEBRATION

Even though I needed sleep, Janae insisted on going out for dinner to celebrate my job. I got an hour of sleep and then got ready to go out. I was wearing jeans and a t-shirt but I brought a change of clothes – my black slacks and a crimson dress shirt – in case I didn't have time to stop home before leaving. I knew the traffic would be worse at night. My phone warned that it would take almost three hours, so I might have to leave right from dinner. I didn't mind, though, because I knew once I moved to Redmond, I would hardly ever see Janae. I had known that at some point we would move apart, but she was my best friend since high school and I hadn't expected it to be so soon.

She greeted me with a hug and an excited squeal as the waiter eyed us curiously and led us to a table. Janae kept staring at my neck and it took a moment before I remembered the tattoo. It didn't feel like anything and was easy to forget, but I had noticed it every time I passed a mirror. It was rare for someone to have a tattoo outside of a vampire city and I noticed several people staring at me as we sat down and wished I had worn a shirt with a collar. But I preferred casual dress and this wasn't a fancy restaurant, so I had a regular collar.

"I can't believe it," Janae said as the waiter asked if we wanted drinks. "We're getting drinks. He's getting a drink," she added to the waiter. "What do you want? It's on me."

"No, this is on me," I said with a smile. "You haven't heard my salary. Um, I'll have a beer. What do you have?"

The waiter rattled off several and I picked one at random. I liked beer in general, but was terrible at telling the different types apart. They all tasted vaguely the same to me with only slight alterations. Janae knew this about me and seemed amused. It probably looked like I was picking one on purpose, but she knew how random it was. She ordered a margarita with sugar, not salt: her favorite. Then the waiter left and she dipped a chip into the salsa and grinned.

"So tell me everything."

I did, starting with the unusual job listing and the quick response, and what my teacher had said about working for vampires. I described the beautiful mansion and the odd servant, and faltered when I reached Adze.

"He's really handsome," I said, blushing. "Like, really handsome. I don't think I've ever met anyone as gorgeous as him."

"That's not why you took the job, is it?" Janae asked a little skeptically. She wasn't thrilled at how little I knew about the job and I knew she had concerns about vampires. She had two friends from her classes who either worked for or grew up around vampires, so she wasn't too worried, but there were always some concerns when dealing with vampires. "Don't you know that all vampires are really beautiful? What's his name? What house is he?"

"Adze," I said, then paused. I had gone to sleep immediately and hadn't looked up the house. "I, uh, haven't checked the house yet. I didn't want to ask. I already didn't know so much."

"Let me see," Janae said, and snapped a picture of my tattoo. "I'll do a search. Keep talking."

The drinks arrived as I told her about Dmitri's explanation of the job before telling her I accepted the job, wanting her to think I knew what I was getting into when I agreed. She was searching while I talked but when I mentioned my salary, she blinked and stared at me.

"Wait, are you serious? And they're paying for your room

and board, too? What will you possibly do with all that money?"

"Save it and go to grad school, obviously," I said.

"Yeah, but not everyone has that plan," she pointed out. "What about the other people who take the job? What do they use that money on? Why is it such a high wage? Is there danger in the position?"

"Not that Dmitri mentioned," I said slowly, but now I wondered. Why was I getting paid so much to do paperwork? "But I don't think people work there long. Probably enough to make some money and then they leave. He asked how long I planned on staying. I said at least a year and he seemed happy about that."

"Found it," she said. "Oh, interesting. Wow."

She stared at her phone in surprise and I reached out, careful not to knock her drink over. While hers was still quite full, my beer was half-empty. I wouldn't get another, though. I had to be my best for my first day. I plucked the phone from her hands and looked at what she'd found. There was the clover symbol and the name of the house: Elviore. It sounded vaguely familiar and I scrolled down to the description. My jaw dropped. No wonder it sounded familiar. This was one of the ancient houses that had survived the war. There were only six members of the house and all of them were ancients. Adze was an ancient. I was stunned as Janae took the phone back and seemed to compare the symbol to the one on my neck.

"Yeah, there's no mistake," she said, sounding awed. "No wonder they pay you so much. They must have a fortune."

"What's their specialty?" I asked, wracking my brain for everything I knew of the house. Not much, unfortunately. I just recognized the name.

"Um, it doesn't say," she said. "Weird. Most houses advertise, but actually it looks like the ancient houses don't. Hmm. Yeah, none of the ancient houses say what they do, just the newer ones. Must be a cultural thing. Are you going to fit in? I mean, an ancient?"

17

"He accepted me to the job," I said slowly. "He knows I'd never met a vampire before. I put my vampire classes on the resume but they have to know I don't have any practical experience."

"Oh, wow," she said, still looking at her phone as she kept scrolling. "They didn't just survive the war, they fought it."

"Didn't all the vampires fight? I mean, weren't the humans trying to kill all of them?"

"No, House Elviore commanded the fighting in the war, and all of the vampire generals came from that house," she said, sounding shocked. "Adze must have helped lead the war. That's incredible."

I stared at her in even more shock, then took her phone again and scanned the history of the house. It was true. The house had always been small with only eight members, even before the war when vampire houses tended to be larger, and all of them had served as generals and commanders in the war. Two had been killed. No names were given, as very few vampires liked their names associated with history, and nothing was said about the six survivors since then. It was possible for a vampire to join a different house, but unlikely. Adze was almost certainly one of those survivors.

I thought of Adze and tried to make my mental image of the attractive vampire fit with the images I had seen of the war in class, when the humans had tried to eradicate the vampires and found themselves woefully unprepared. Although the vampires were outnumbered and almost none of the ancients survived, they had spawned an enormous generation of vampires who finished the war for them. Most vampires alive today were created during the war, since it was rare for vampires to spawn. I could imagine Adze leading an army, those smoky eyes gazing across a battlefield and coolly deciding on the best course of action. I could imagine that powerful form covered in the dense armor common to vampires in the war. He would have been beautiful.

"Well, I'd love to visit," Janae said. "I'd love to meet an

ancient. Whenever you want."

"I'd love to have you," I said. "I guess I'll have to get permission, won't I? I mean, it's not my house. But you can come visit."

Our food arrived and we dove in. I wondered if Margaret knew how to make enchiladas, because I was definitely going to be requesting them a lot. I doubted they would be this good or authentic, though. There was only a light smattering of cheese over the poblano sauce drenching the tortillas and chicken. I wasn't a fan of too much cheese and one reason I loved this restaurant was the scarcity. A lot of places dumped cheese on enchiladas but unless I was actually having cheese enchiladas, I wasn't interested in it. I savored the mild tang of the poblanos and the occasional flare of jalapeño from the pico de gallo. Before long my plate was empty, just a little lump of beans that I hadn't distributed properly. I had never been good at planning how much rice and beans to eat with each bite of enchilada and usually had one of the two left over.

As Janae finished her fajitas, I finished my beer and munched on the chips. I wasn't hungry by any means but they were there and delicious. I wasn't sure what my night would be like and if I'd get hungry or have a break for food. I'd never been on a night schedule before. I assumed it was like a normal schedule, just with the hours shifted, so there should be three meals, but at what times? When did a night schedule start, and when was it over? I had no clue.

We wrapped up the meal – I paid, of course – and Janae hugged me tightly after we headed out. I would indeed have to leave from here and I was glad I had brought my clothes.

"I know your new boss is hot, Kairos," she said, looking at me seriously. "But remember he's a vampire. And an ancient. If you don't like the job, quit. Not all houses have good working conditions and there's no point having money if you're miserable."

"I will," I promised, then kissed her cheek. She blushed and waved, and I got my clothes and went back to the restaurant to change. As I left the second time, the waiter stopped me. I paused, unsure whether or not I was allowed to change there the way that I had. Or maybe something was wrong with my card? No, the waiter would have noticed that instantly.

"What is it?" I asked.

"I just, um, have never met anyone who worked for an ancient before," he said. "Are there any positions open in your house?"

I blinked. "I don't know. I was actually just hired."

The waiter handed me a card. "If anything opens up, let me know, okay?"

"Sure," I said, looking at the card.

It was a plain business card, the type I myself had. I had brought one to the interview but hadn't needed to leave it since I had been hired on the spot. The waiter smiled brightly and went back to his tables and I went to my car pondering the exchange. Apparently my symbol was well-known, or else the waiter had heard us talking about it. I remembered what Dmitri had said about how lucky I was to even be considered for the job and realized how true that must be if strangers were approaching me for possible jobs. Why had they put up a listing if people were so eager to work for them? I wasn't sure, but I was grateful.

I knew that despite my promise to Janae, I was willing to put up with a lot to keep this job. The memory of Adze was starting to fade, but not the memory of being utterly enthralled by him. I would stay with Adze no matter how terrible the job ended up being. I hoped it wouldn't be too bad, though. Well, I would find out soon.

CHAPTER FOUR: TRANSLATIONS

Dmitri let me in and I glanced at my watch. I was about twenty minutes early and Dmitri didn't comment, so it must be a good time to show up. The city had been considerably busier at night and as I had looked at the people, I could tell some were vampires now that I had seen Adze. They were unmistakable and tended to move in a large bubble of space as no one appeared to want to get too close to them. In the bustling crowd, the people moving in the gaps were noticeable and all of them were exceptionally beautiful, though none as gorgeous as Adze.

Dmitri took my coat again without a word, then took me to the kitchen where I met Margaret, a slender redhead who smiled at me brightly. She asked if I was hungry and seemed a little put out when I explained I had eaten a late dinner, and promised to bring me a snack while I was working. We went towards the study that Dmitri had indicated would be mine and on the way, I saw a tall woman dressed in an outfit that fit every stereotype I had of a maid's dress. Not a sexy maid dress as Janae had worn for Halloween once, but a serious, down-to-business maid's dress that looked as impeccable as Dmitri's suit did. I straightened and hoped I looked presentable. Margaret had been in clean slacks and a blouse similar to my outfit, so maybe my appearance wasn't too out of bounds.

The woman stared at me as Dmitri introduced me, then she extended her hand and introduced herself as Dianne. She seemed as silent and unimpressed by me as Dmitri was and the two exchanged a long look.

"When are you moving in?" she asked.

"This weekend," I said nervously. "Friday, I guess. Or Friday night if that's easier."

"Come during the day," she said. "I'll come and help you get settled. Give me two hours notice."

"Thank you," I said. "I probably won't bring very much, though."

"You don't have much?"

"Well, it seems like everything is taken care of here," I said, wondering if my perception was off. "I'll be putting most of my things in storage."

"They'll go into storage here," Dianne said, and Dmitri nodded as if that were the obvious solution. "We have a large facility far nicer than any in town. It's on the other side of the estate but I'll help you move everything in. Do you need people to help you move? That can be provided as well."

I was a little surprised. I wanted to immediately assure her that I didn't need help, but if she were offering, maybe I shouldn't reject it so quickly. I knew a lot of jobs offered bonuses and help when the employee was required to move, so this probably wasn't as unusual as it seemed. Maybe my moving costs were part of the expenses that Adze covered.

"I can get everything packed okay, I think," I said. "I have some friends who will help. But I may need help unpacking once I get here. I have some bulky furniture I want to keep, though. I don't mind paying for storage."

"You'll have all the space you need," she said, waving a hand dismissively. "Not a problem. I'll arrange for some help when you arrive. Perhaps give me three hours notice."

"Thank you very much," I said. "I really appreciate it. I hadn't even started looking for storage places yet."

"Anytime you need anything, Kairos," Dmitri said. "Check with me or Dianne first. It's probably covered by your contract. Master Adze covers all reasonable expenses and I doubt you'll have any unreasonable ones."

"Okay," I said awkwardly. "Thank you."

Dmitri finally brought me to my new office and I stared at the imposing pile of papers and letters. There were hundreds of sheets of paper – all correspondence – and a pile of letters still in the envelopes, though they were opened. He sat me in the chair.

"You must wear gloves when handling everything. Do these in order as much as possible," he said, handing me thin latex gloves and pointing out which piles to do in which order. "You'll take a picture of it, input it here, and then in this box you'll write a description of the content, including human oddities."

He showed me around the software and it was very intricate, though easy to use. There was a place to describe the physical characteristics of each letter, since humans often used physical characteristics to indicate things, a place for the overall appearance including letterhead and signature, and a place for the actual content.

"Even though there's an attached picture of the letter, write everything out anyway," Dmitri instructed. "If a sentence means exactly what it says, write 'when it says this – write it out – it means this, and revise the meaning in your own words."

I nodded. That would check my own assumptions, since rewriting a seemingly obvious sentence would be more likely to reveal if it was actually obvious or if I mistakenly thought it was obvious. Dmitri gave me some more instructions and I wondered why he didn't just do it himself, but then again, I was the expert. I had never thought of myself as an expert before and it was an odd thought. Then he told me to get as much done as possible and see him after three hours. Margaret would bring a snack during that time, he said, and gave me the number to the kitchen to call for anything to eat or drink.

"Don't leave this room without permission," Dmitri said. "If you need to leave for any reason, call me and I'll give you permission."

A little odd, but it didn't seem like he would refuse any requests, so I nodded. He left and I took one of the letters from the first pile. I took a picture of it in the envelope, then laid out the letter and took a picture of that. Then I got to work.

By the time Margaret brought me a plate of cookies nearly two hours later, I had formed a fairly good conclusion of what the house did, but there were a few oddities. I smiled at Margaret as she set down the cookies and told me to take a break for a few minutes. She looked at the desk curiously. I hadn't really moved the letters after reading them; I put them back in the same stacks when I finished each stack so it probably looked like I wasn't making progress. She stayed in the room as I munched and was friendlier than the other humans here, so I ventured a question.

"I know I should probably know this," I said, hoping she wouldn't judge me. "But is House Elviore vampire hunters?"

"What makes you ask that?" she asked lightly, though I noticed she didn't deny it.

"Just some of the letters," I said, not knowing how much I could share. Some of the letters seemed fairly personal and I knew I couldn't talk in specifics, but a few vague comments were probably fine. "There's just stuff that seems like hunters would care about it. Are they?"

She shrugged. "You can ask the Master."

I stared at her oddly. She had to know whether or not they were hunters. That type of specialization would be obvious, wouldn't it? She just smiled brightly as I finished, and I didn't press. At least she didn't seem to mind that I didn't know the house very well. She seemed to expect it. I requested a diet soda and she took my plate, returning a few minutes later with a cold glass and a can of what I wanted. It was the right brand and everything and I thanked her before getting back to work.

I was about halfway through the stacks when there was a knock at the door and Dmitri came in. I glanced at my watch and realized it was about twenty minutes past when I was supposed to get him. He didn't look angry, though, just curious. He stared at the stacks and I blushed. Maybe I should be moving them around more. I typed the last few words and put the letter back in its pile. He stared at the pile.

"Are you doing them out of order?" he asked.

"I'm only halfway done," I said, a little embarrassed. "This is still pretty new to me. I know I'll get faster. I'm keeping them in the same stacks," I added. "That's why it looks the same."

"Show me the records you've entered," he said, and I zoomed out to the list of completed letters. They were sorted by send date and author and it seemed like I was doing the newer letters first. He stared at them, then asked me to open one. I opened one at random, not sure what exactly he wanted, and he leaned forward to scan the notes I had taken. I glanced at them as well, hoping I was doing this right.

"When you finish each letter, you need to let me know," he said slowly. "See this here? You attach it and then send it to me from here. Every letter you finish."

"I'm sorry," I said. "I must have forgotten. I don't even remember you telling me that."

"I didn't," he said. "I didn't expect you to get this far. From now on, send me everything you finish. Margaret said you had some questions. Master will be in to talk to you shortly. You can leave after he finishes with you. Is midnight a good time or would you prefer coming earlier? Our official hours start at nine."

"Midnight might be best," I said cautiously. "Tomorrow is the last day I have anything during the day but my friends like to stay out."

He nodded, scanned my notes one more time, then stood up. "Perhaps you will do all right here," he said grudgingly, and left the room.

I grinned, looking at my notes on the computer. I had gotten further than he expected and I had done well. I was extremely proud of myself and the feeling continued as I wondered if I were just supposed to wait for Adze or if I was supposed to keep working while waiting. I could do one more,

I decided. I analyzed it carefully and when I replaced it in its pile, I jumped. Adze was sitting across the desk from me. How long had he been there? I hadn't heard him come in or noticed him at all. His eyes were glowing and I wondered if he would be impressed by what I'd accomplished.

"You had questions about our house," he said. "You can ask."

The thought of his history suddenly overwhelmed me and my mouth went dry. He was an ancient. He had led the war. And he was sitting right in front of me, hands crossed over his knee as he studied me and waited for me to speak.

"Um, I don't really know a lot about House Elviore," I said nervously.

"You didn't know who my house was the last time we met," he said calmly. "I'm glad you did some research. Little is known about us."

I blushed, embarrassed that my lack of knowledge had been so apparent. It was true though; if I had recognized that the house was ancient, that he was an ancient, I would have reacted differently.

"I wondered if you were hunters," I said cautiously. "Some of the things in the letters I read fit with that, but some of them don't."

"Explain that to me," he said, still expressionless.

"Well, a lot of the letters were about vampires who had been killed," I said. He could know the exact content, I was positive. I worked for him, after all. "I assume hunters killed them, but that's the odd part. There's no mention of that. And most of them were about things that had already happened; only a few were about the future. If people were warning you about vampires who were attacking people, who needed to be killed, they wouldn't be reports of past attacks. Would they?"

"Which letters were about future events?" Adze asked, coming to my side.

"I marked them," I said. "They seemed to stand out so I made a note on them. You can sort for them using this."

"Very good," he murmured. "Send those to Dmitri right now. Flag them."

He was holding an envelope, I realized. He put on a pair of gloves and withdrew a letter from the envelope carefully.

"Put gloves back on and analyze this for me," he said.

I obediently pulled on another pair of gloves and took the letter from him.

"Take a picture and then analyze it out loud," he instructed. I obediently took a picture and then considered the letter, and especially the letterhead compared to the cheap paper the letter was on. It was quite a mismatch.

"Can I see the envelope?" I asked.

"Do you need to?"

"Sort of," I said, not wanting to push. "This paper seems odd and I want to see if the envelope matches."

He held it closer to me. "You can't touch it, but you can see it. Tell me if you need another angle."

"How heavy is it?" I asked. "Does it feel like a normal envelope?"

He looked at me blankly. I sorted through the letters next to me and selected one, handing it to him. He took it in his other hand.

"Is it heavier than this or the same?"

He hefted both of them. "The same," he said. "Almost exactly."

I nodded and took the other envelope back, replacing it carefully while eyeing the envelope he still held, wondering why I couldn't touch it. He was holding it oddly, too, and as I looked at how he held it open, I gasped. He had opened it without permission and planned on closing it again and leaving no trace. He was not supposed to be reading this message; it was intended for someone else.

"Analyze the letter," he instructed. "I will explain later."

"Well, um, whoever sent this doesn't want anyone knowing they sent it," I said nervously. "Anyone with a letterhead like this should have heavier paper. If it were just the letter or just the envelope with lighter paper, it would probably be a mistake, but both of them are lighter than they should be, so it's probably deliberate."

Adze glanced at the envelope in his hand, then gestured for me to continue. I scanned the letter quickly, then again, slower, looking for the unconscious cues humans put in their words.

"The content is misleading," I said slowly, scanning it again. "I noticed this with several of the letters I read. The letter is about a trip to Paris she took last year, but when you look at just the words it's a description of a building she's heading to soon. And there are several oddities. The number six appears four times. Humans think in threes so if appeared once or twice, it might be an accident, three times might be significant or might just be habit, but four times is deliberate. But six is used in four different ways so I don't know why it's significant."

"Can you tell what building is being described, or when the person will be there?" Adze said, and though his voice was calm, there was a hint of urgency in it.

"Some of the language is oddly religious," I said, considering. "Are there temples or cathedrals in Redmond?"

"It's in this city? You're sure?"

I glanced at the letter, and at the address on the top.

"The word home is used several times so I think the place being described is this person's home, and given the address, I assumed it was here. I might be wrong."

"And can you tell when?"

I studied it, looking for anything that might indicate a time. Everything was in a strange tense, describing past events but in a way that made it clear it was describing the future, but the timing was uncertain.

"She'll move through a courtyard to the left," I said, tracing along the movements in the letter. "There'll be something with religious significance to the right and she'll pause. Something with six. There will be shadows and when they reach a certain length, maybe six again, she'll act. Everything else just seems like filler to hide that message."

"Is it a description or orders to someone else?"

"It could be orders," I said, reading it one more time. "That makes more sense. I hadn't thought of that. Oh, that explains a lot of the letters I read."

I blushed, embarrassed that I hadn't realized such an obvious thing about the letters. They weren't descriptions or predictions, they were orders and reports on whether those orders had been carried out, or how to carry them out if they hadn't. All of my interpretations were correct but I wondered if I needed to resort everything with that in mind.

Adze extended his hand for the letter and I handed it to him. He carefully refolded the letter exactly as it had been and put it back in the envelope, then pressed it back down carefully. I had a feeling it would be impossible to tell it had ever been opened. I felt guilty and wondered whose privacy I had invaded, and whether or not this was legal. Were all of the letters I had read stolen, or had they been forwarded for interpretation as I had assumed?

"You have many questions about this job, and this house," Adze said. "Questions are good. But answers will have to wait until you live here. One of your references was a man. One of your teachers, I believe. Is there any chance he'll see you between now and when you move in?"

"Oh, I have a final in his class in the morning," I said, an edge of panic fluttering in my throat. I had completely forgotten. I needed to get home and sleep as much as possible. Would it be better to just stay up and sleep after the test? No, I needed sleep.

"You cannot go," Adze said.

I stared at him, confused. "What? It's a final. I have to go."

"He cannot know that you're working for House Elviore. Make up the test another way. He seems charmed by you; persuade him."

"I can't persuade him if I can't talk to him," I said. "I just won't tell him. I'll wear a high collar or something."

He stared at me emotionlessly. I was starting to wonder if he ever showed emotion. Then he glanced down.

"You may go," he said reluctantly. "If he notices my mark, do not tell him my name. Do not tell him you've started working for me yet. You've toured the house and that's it. Understand?"

"Of course," I said. "But why?"

He stared at me again and I gulped. I had forgotten that he was in charge and an ancient, and I was just a servant and a human.

"I'm sorry," I said. "I'll do what you want."

"When you finish, come straight here after seeing him," he said, turning to go. "Do not stop anywhere else. It doesn't matter what time it is. Dmitri will be waiting and will have further instructions. You may sleep here for a few hours before you return."

I knew better than to argue and simply agreed, and he dismissed me for the day. I was puzzled and as I drove home, I tried to figure it out. Why wouldn't he want my teacher to know where I worked, and why him in particular? Would Adze ever tell me? I was going to have to talk to my teacher anyway to apologize for the test I was now almost sure to fail and make sure it didn't affect my overall grade, and maybe I could learn something then. It was certainly a mystery.

CHAPTER FIVE: WARNING

Mr. Grayson stared at me as I scooted into class five minutes late. He handed me the exam without a word, though he did glance at my neck. I was wearing a high collared shirt, as I had told Adze I would, and the tattoo wasn't visible. I was dressed up far more than usual for class, partially to hide the tattoo and partially because I would be going to House Elviore after class. I would just be taking a nap, but I still wanted to look nice. Everyone and everything there was so impeccable.

I started writing my essay, struggling to remember the obscure names and terms from the class. The essay itself was fine, but I was worried I was mixing up two similar theories. I did my best, and took longer than I normally would. I finished next to last and when I handed him my essay, he gestured for me to stay. Good, because I needed to apologize. The last student finished and turned his paper in, and I smiled at Mr. Grayson nervously as he tapped the stack of papers and studied me, glancing again at my neck.

"I was called about your job," he said. "You're quite dressed up, and you're never late. Is it safe to assume you got the job and spent the night working?"

"Sort of," I said with a blush. "I mean, I got the job. I haven't started working yet, though. It was just a tour of the house."

"Who are you working for?"

"I don't know," I said, hating to lie but obeying my new employer was more important than telling the truth in this case. I hoped.

"You've been hired and you don't know your employer?" he asked, amused.

"I don't actually know that much about vampires," I said. "I don't know any of the houses or anything. It didn't seem to matter, though, I mean, I still got the job."

"Sometimes ignorance is a gift for them," he said. "Especially the ancients. What exactly is your job?"

"I don't know yet," I said, wondering how much I needed to lie. "I'm so sorry about today, sir. I was up late and then I slept past my alarm. I don't think I did well on the final, either. I didn't have time to study as much as I should have. I don't think it'll affect my grade much but I did want to apologize to you."

"Your grade probably doesn't matter much now, does it?" he asked. "You're graduating and you have a job, so GPA doesn't matter."

"I still have to get in to grad school," I pointed out.

"Then your plans haven't changed?"

"No," I said. "I'll be going to school a lot sooner than I thought, though. I'm making way more money than I expected. I might be asking for a letter of reference for grad school, would you be willing?"

"Of course. But how much are you making?" he asked with a laugh. "Which house is it that pays you so much?"

I laughed and didn't answer. He was eyeing my neck again and I ducked my head. I hated lying to him, hated hiding things from him. He had been a mentor at college and it hurt that I couldn't tell him the truth, but I had to obey Adze. There had to be a reason he didn't want my teacher to know.

"Kairos, there is something you should know about vampires, now that you're working for one," he said seriously. "Some houses are dangerous. Very dangerous. Not because of the vampires in the house, but the ones outside it. Some houses have a lot of enemies and servants of those houses might be targeted. You have to be careful."

I was surprised. I had only thought about the dangers of the vampires from the house, since they were the only ones able to feed on servants. It hadn't even occurred to me that other vampires would still be a danger or that servants might be specifically targeted. Was that why Adze didn't want him to know? Was he worried about Mr. Grayson targeting me?

"It's only the ancient houses," he continued. "If you find out you're working for an ancient house, you should quit. You're too talented to waste on them."

"What do you mean?" I asked, wondering why he thought an ancient house didn't need talent. This did explain why Adze didn't want him to know, though, since my teacher clearly had a grudge against the ancients. Was he trying to protect me or was there some other reason he didn't want me working for them?

"You could work for any vampire," he said. "I didn't think you were interested, but if you are working for an ancient and you want a new job that pays the same with a safer work environment, I can easily find you something."

"What houses would you recommend?" I asked. "I don't think I'm in trouble but maybe I'm already working for them. I'll find out tonight, I'm sure."

"House Salvite would be ideal, but I know you're not working for them," he said. "I checked with them after I gave you the reference. They haven't hired anyone, nor did they know anyone who was hiring. How did you find out about the job?"

"A listing," I said. "It had no detail at all. I really didn't expect to get it."

"Well, let me know when you find out your house, and especially which vampire it is. I know most of the prominent vampires and can find out about any of them. I'll make sure you're in a good place."

"Thank you," I said. "Um, I do have to go. I'm so exhausted. I'm sorry again about the test. I did my best. If it drops my grade, I'll live with it. It's my fault, after all. I shouldn't have applied for a job when I still had finals left."

He bid me farewell and I hurried to my car. I took a long moment to relax but when I felt sleep haze into my awareness,

I started the engine. I needed to get to my job, then I could try out my new bed. I didn't have any sheets, I realized. Well, I didn't mind a mattress.

As I drove, I wondered at what my teacher had said. Was I going to be targeted because of my job? Janae had mentioned I might be in danger, too, based on the salary. How much of that money was hazard pay and how much for actually doing the job? And who was House Salvite? I'd never heard of them, so they weren't ancients – though that was obvious from his negative view of the ancient houses. Janae had indicated that the newer houses advertised their specialties. I could look it up once I got to work.

The path was starting to be familiar as I made my way through Redmond again, heading through the downtown to the outskirts. There weren't really any good ways to skip the downtown area so I was stuck in more traffic, but I made it through. Soon I was pulling up at the house. I went to the back door that Dmitri had indicated I should use and as I was shutting it behind me, he appeared.

"Welcome," he said. "I hope your test went well."

"Not really, but it's over," I said. Then I realized it really was over. College was over. I still had to get grades, still had to graduate, but I was done.

"Did your professor ask about your job?"

"Yeah," I said. "He doesn't know what house I work for or what I do. Why did I have to lie to him?"

"Did he say anything to you?"

I paused, then explained the warning he had given me about the ancient houses and the job with House Salvite that he assured me he could secure if I wanted to switch jobs. Dmitri's lips tightened at the name of the house. Maybe the two houses were rivals. Maybe I actually would be targeted. Dmitri shook his head when I finished.

"You did well," he said. It was an unexpected compliment. "And you're far safer with us than you are with Salvite. I assume you're tired. Dianne made up your bed. You can keep the sheets if you like or bring your own when you move, or both. Everything in this house is available for you and we will provide everything you don't have."

"Thank you," I said, and followed him to the room. I used the bathroom, then collapsed onto the bed. The sheets were a white satin, unlike any sheets I'd ever slept in, very cool and smooth as I got under the covers and fell completely asleep.

I vaguely became aware of something, some pressure on my body, and opened my eyes. It was pitch black and I knew I was dreaming. Everything about this felt utterly unreal. There was something or someone over me, leaning into me as I lay on my back, stretched with my hands over my head. But I couldn't see anything, and I was starting to panic.

A pressure on my lips, and I realized someone was kissing me. It started as a vague impression and then, without warning, I felt my body completely and I was on fire from the soft lips caressing mine, the tongue that invaded my willing mouth. I arched against him, longing to feel more of him, longing to see him, and I could start to make out a blurred shape. He stroked down my bare chest, running fingernails over my nipples teasingly, then lapped his tongue against my nipple as I moaned softly. This felt too good to be a dream and I shifted against him, eager for his touch, for his tongue. He kissed up my chest to my neck and kissed right where vampires were said to bite, where I now had a tattoo of House Elviore. My vision returned just as he lifted his head above mine again and I gasped. It was Adze. He gazed at me with those glowing eyes, his hands stroking across my body, coming dangerously close to my hard cock.

"This is your dream," he murmured. "What do you want to happen?"

I couldn't speak. I didn't even know what I wanted to say, but my mouth wouldn't work properly. I couldn't move my arms to pull him closer. I couldn't move at all and I felt myself drifting awake, away from him, away from my beautiful vampire.

I awoke with a start. There was sun streaming in from the window. My body tingled with remembered pleasure and I was half-hard. What an unusual dream. I hoped I would be able to look at Adze without blushing. He was so incredibly attractive, but I hadn't stumbled last time I saw him, so I could probably manage not to make a fool of myself again. I remembered him kissing my neck and rubbed the spot, then checked the tattoo in the mirror. It was such a beautiful pattern, and as I studied it, I realized it was more intricate than I had originally thought. It was like a clover for the most part, but each leaf of the clover was in fact a series of thin lines that combined to make the shape. They were so fine, though, that it was hard to tell from a distance. It was almost like a bar code up close. I knew the tattoos were used to identify people in vampire cities; could they be scanned like a bar code?

I stretched and went to the bathroom to freshen up. Dmitri's door was shut and I was quiet, since he was probably sleeping. I wasn't sure if I could just leave or if I needed to wait for someone to excuse me, but as I went out into the kitchen, I saw Margaret. She would know. She smiled at me.

"You didn't sleep long," she said. "It's barely two."

"I didn't know you were here during the day," I said.

"Not usually," she said. "But I'll be tagging along with you until you move in."

"Why?" I asked, then realized how rude that probably sounded. "I mean, I would love to hang out with you. But I'm going to be packing and with friends and stuff. I'm sure you'd be bored."

"It's no problem," she said. "I want to make sure you get everything taken care of and help you pack. If you need anything, I can provide for that as well. Dmitri warned me that you might not realize what all is covered in the contract."

"That's really sweet, but-"

"It's not optional," she said, though she was still smiling. "If you want to work here, you'll take me with you."

"Why?" I asked again, trying to think of the real reason she

36

needed to come. I thought back to my teacher's words. "Am I going to be targeted? Are you trying to keep track of me so I won't get hurt?"

Her smile faded and she glanced in the direction of Dmitri's room as if wondering if she had permission to speak.

"I want to know if I'm in danger from this job," I said. "I won't quit. I just want to know."

It was true; even if I found out that I was in danger, I wanted to work here, for Adze. The memory of his body against mine in my dream flashed through my mind. It would likely never happen in real life, but when I was with him, near him, at least I could imagine.

"It's your teacher," she said reluctantly. "He doesn't work for a house but he does help one, and the house he helps doesn't like our house. He had you followed so he knows which house you work for now, and he'll tell them. You don't live here yet, so you're not fully under Master's protection. But if one of his true servants is with you, they won't touch you."

I shivered. "He had me followed?"

"That's why we needed you to come here after," she said solemnly. "If you had gone home, they might have tried something."

"But I'm safe tomorrow and Friday while I pack?"

"As long as I'm with you," she said, and smiled brightly again. I was glad that she was the one to come with me if someone had to come, since she was by far the friendliest. Dianne and Dmitri were like ice, though Dmitri did seem to be warming to me a little. But Margaret had always been kind. Maybe that's why she was chosen. Either way, I didn't mind as she changed into jeans and a t-shirt and brought a large purse to my car. I didn't have any plans yet, but I did need to say goodbye to all my friends. Having her around was going to be awkward. Still, there was nothing I could do about it, so I braced myself and drove home.

CHAPTER SIX: GOOD FRIENDS

Margaret dozed on the drive and was snoring slightly as I pulled into my apartment complex. The first speedbump must have woken her because she blinked sleepily as I drove to my building, going over two more speedbumps. She yawned and stretched before getting out and looking around.

"This place is pretty," she said, squinting at the grassy field across the parking lot from my building. "Are those deer?"

"Yeah," I said proudly. "There's a whole herd that live here. I have a view of some walking paths and they're always nearby."

I took her up to my apartment and was glad it looked presentable. It wasn't exactly clean and there were some dirty dishes lying around, but it was decent. She walked through the apartment and admired the layout and my furnishings.

"You have such modern things," she said, admiring my desk. "If the desk in your room isn't big enough for your computer, you can always use this one."

"It should work," I said, glancing at my setup. I had a laptop and desktop, both hooked up to the same monitor. I switched inputs back and forth frequently since I kept my schoolwork on my laptop and my gaming on my desktop. Having separate computers was supposed to keep everything separate but using the same monitor pretty much destroyed that idea. It was just a flick of a switch to move between computers so it almost didn't matter that they were different devices.

She went through the rest of the apartment, complimenting as she went, though I noticed she didn't comment at all when she saw my messy closet, not even to admire how large a closet it was. She was tactfully complimentary, I decided. I would have to be very clean in House Elviore with Dianne in charge, because I could tell Dianne didn't tolerate any mess at all. Finally, after I used the bathroom and she finished exploring, we returned to the living room and sat on my couch.

"What are your plans for the day?" she asked.

"Well, I need to start packing," I said, looking around with dread. "I'm meeting some friends at six for a graduation thing. Just a small dinner, probably drinks, nothing big. None of us are party people."

"Do you mind if I come?"

I hesitated. I knew I couldn't refuse. She had already made that clear and was probably just asking to be polite. I didn't really want her to come. I wanted to spend the time celebrating with my friends who had worked through college with me, struggled in the same classes and complained about the same problems. They knew me better than anyone and could appreciate how far I'd come from the lovesick teen I had been at the start of my college years, newly single after breaking up with my last serious boyfriend, too young to do anything except spend my nights gaming, skipping classes because I hadn't found anything that interested me yet. They had been with me as I started dating again, as I began broadening my social life, and as I discovered how fascinating human culture was and triumphantly declared my major halfway through my sophomore year. They had been there for all of it and I had seen them grow in the same way, and I just wanted to be with them tonight. But I couldn't.

"It's fine," I said.

"I'll try not to attract all the attention," she said. "Humans are always curious about servants but I know this needs to be about you and your friends. You won't even notice I'm there."

I smiled hesitantly, grateful that she understood my hesitation. Then she looked around.

"You've got some cleaning to do before packing," she said.

"How do you want me to help?"

A tactful way of putting it, I decided as I started planning my attack. I had her start packing up my books as I cleaned the apartment and soon she had three boxes filled and I realized it was nearly time to leave. I was still in my nice outfit, I realized in shock. I had taken off my jacket, but my shirt had water on it from the sink and I hadn't even realized I was getting the knees of my pants dirty when I had knelt to clean the floor. Margaret had come in casual clothes and looked great, but I definitely needed to change. She kept packing books as I quickly changed into jeans, but I kept a collared shirt. I didn't really want to draw attention to my tattoo. She approved of my outfit when I returned, the same way many of my female friends felt they needed to approve of my clothes, and we headed to the Library, our favorite bar.

Janae and Scott were already there when I arrived and I hugged both of them, then introduced them to Margaret, introducing her as a new coworker. They seemed puzzled why she was there and Janae – the only one who knew about my job – was extremely curious, but was biting her tongue since she could probably tell I didn't want to make a big deal of Margaret. We went to our usual table in the back. There were floor-to-ceiling bookcases lining the walls of the bar and our favorite booth snuggled in a corner and was nearly surrounded by books. The books were always interesting, though we had seen most of the ones near our table. Several were books on personality and included quizzes that we gave each other, trying to manipulate our answers to get the best results.

Scott must have arrived first because he had a drink and as we sat down again, the waitress came up with a margarita for Janae and asked for our orders. I got a gin and tonic, deciding to skip the beer and go straight to my favorite, but Margaret demurred and asked for a soda, quietly offering to be my ride home. Since it was likely I would need a ride otherwise, I was more than happy to agree, but I wondered how long it had been since Margaret had been out drinking. Probably quite a while, but she was slipping into the background as she promised.

Lee and Angie arrived together and once their drinks arrived, we toasted our successful completion of college. Well, Angie still had another year – she was an engineering major and there were too many required classes to fit into the traditional four – but the rest of us were done with college. Lee and Angie had started dating a few months ago and I was relieved that it was going well. If they broke up and I had to pick sides, I honestly didn't know who I would choose, so I was heavily invested in them staying together. Janae had shared the same concerns with me, since Lee and Angie were both very argumentative and half the time we hung out, one of them would leave fuming. But they always apologized and it was working, so I was happy for them.

We shared stories and I practically forgot Margaret was there. She was nearly invisible as we talked and ordered food and more drinks, even though she was drinking and eating as well. In fact, I barely noticed her at all until we started bickering about who was going to pay for what. It was a tradition and we passed the costs around depending on who had the most money, and since I had by far the most money, I was a little pushier than normal. But when I was met with almost universal resistance, I realized I hadn't told anyone except Janae about my job and they all thought I was entering unemployment. Even though I had introduced Margaret as a coworker, they likely hadn't realized she was from a new job and not my current one at the fast food place. The waitress arrived with the check and I snatched it from her before the others could take it.

"My treat," I said. "I have a new job."

"What job?" Scott asked skeptically. "I thought you'd barely started looking."

"He's working for a vampire," Janae interrupted. "A really hot vampire."

I blushed and looked at Margaret, who seemed amused by

41

Janae's comment. But Janae seemed to remember Margaret's presence as well and she blushed, too.

"What vampire?" Lee asked. "What job?"

"Um, paperwork and stuff," I said, not knowing how much I was allowed to share, especially with Margaret next to me.

"What house is it?" Angie asked, wrapping an arm around Lee's waist. He snuggled back.

"Um, House Elviore," I said, since it wasn't a secret.

"I've heard of them," Angie said, puzzled. "Aren't they an ancient house?"

"Yes," I said, but before she could ask another question, Scott leaned towards me and tugged at my collar.

"You must have a tattoo then," he said, and I unbuttoned my collar enough for them to see. Then their eyes went to Margaret.

"Do you work for House Elviore too?" Scott asked.

In reply, she pulled her collar slightly so they could see her tattoo. Scott laughed.

"Wow! I've never met someone who works for a vampire! What are they like? So your boss is hot? Who is he?"

I blushed again and glared at Janae, but she just shrugged. It was fair, though. I had gushed quite a bit about how beautiful he was.

"His name is Adze," I said, hoping that was all right to share.

"Is he from Africa?" Angie asked.

"You've heard of him?" Margaret asked. She hadn't joined in the conversation so far but now that we had acknowledged her, I didn't mind.

"No, I mean yes, well, not him, but I know there's an African myth of vampires called Adze. Don't vampires take their names after myths?"

"Some do," Margaret said. "And some don't."

"That's cool, Kairos," Scott said, reaching out to massage my shoulder. He was definitely drunk, or at least borderline. While Scott and I had never done anything, he had a major crush on me and would love to do something. I'd always put him off, not wanting to ruin our friendship. I didn't want to put my friends in the same awkward position that Angie and Lee were putting us in.

Then I looked at my watch and realized it was just after nine. And I suddenly realized that I had to work in a couple of hours, and I was half a glass away from drunk.

"Shit," I said, staring at my watch. I looked at Margaret in horror. "I have to work soon."

Margaret laughed. "I wondered if you'd forgotten. You'll be fine. I already said I'd drive you. We know you're on a day schedule."

I said goodbye to everyone quickly after that. I even persuaded them to help me move so we could all meet up again. Janae got a little teary eyed but she also shoved me out the door, telling me to be on time. I kissed her cheek and noticed Scott eyeing the gesture jealously. He gave me a very handsy hug and I had to gently untangle myself from him before heading to my car. I handed Margaret the keys.

"I need to change, and then we need to leave. We're going to be late."

"I know how to get there quickly," she said. "How do I get back to your apartment?"

Soon we were on the way to work and she urged me to nap in the car. I obeyed and shut my eyes, sinking against the cushy seat and resting my forehead against the cold window. Everything went silent as we approached the highway and I opened my eyes. It didn't sound like we had stopped and while it was dark and I couldn't really see outside, I knew from the blurred lights that we were still moving, and moving fast. I shut my eyes again and before I knew it, the gate was opening in front of us. I looked at my watch. It was twenty to midnight. That was impossible. It had taken nearly three hours at the same time yesterday, yet we had done it in less than two. Whatever shortcut Margaret knew, I would have to learn, because it was quite the time saver.

But now we were here and I was still a little wobbly. I could pull myself together, but everything was just a little fuzzy on the edges and I wasn't entirely stable on my feet. The world seemed to tilt just slightly to the left, tugging on me incessantly. I wasn't drunk, but I was pretty close. And I was at work.

Dmitri took one look at me when Margaret led me in and shook his head, but he didn't look surprised.

"You'll need to adapt to a night schedule soon," he said. "Drinking before midnight is looked down on."

"I'm sorry," I said, not knowing what else to say.

"Do you need to rest before you start? You can stay as long as you like and leave with Margaret in the morning."

"No, I can work," I said, then considered. "I might need to sleep after that, though."

"Don't push yourself," Dmitri warned, and I considered again.

"Maybe I'll just sleep an hour," I said cautiously.

"As long as you need," Dmitri said. "Nothing you are working on tonight is pressing."

"Thanks," I said, flashing him a smile. I hadn't expected him to be so understanding. Then again, there wasn't much he could do except fire me, and he wasn't in charge of that. What would Adze think when he found out I'd been drinking? Would he fire me? Would he understand my need to get some rest and try to sleep off a bit of the drink or would he want me to push through and get my work done? It was better to sleep now and do my job properly later, I decided. I would set my alarm for an hour, which ought to be enough time to get me back on my feet again. I might have a bit of a hangover but the direct effects of the drink should be gone.

Margaret helped me to my room and even tucked me in. She still looked very amused.

"You have good friends, but you really shouldn't drink before work," she chided. "Still, you did graduate college. It's nice to have friends like yours to celebrate with."

"It is," I said sleepily. "Thanks, Margaret."

She wished me a good night and shut the door softly. I set my alarm, closed my eyes, and was out.

CHAPTER SEVEN: FLEETING FANTASIES

A pressure again my lips, the sensation of being held and pressing up against a sexy male body. I was dreaming again. Would I always dream about Adze here? I wouldn't really mind, I decided as I snuggled closer and let him dominate my mouth. His hands caressed my naked body in lazy circles, drawing closer and closer to my ass. I wanted him so badly, but as with before, I couldn't see anything, couldn't move. I was paralyzed, but I enjoyed being frozen in his grasp. His mouth closed over my neck again and I wondered if this time he would bite. I hadn't really fantasized about him biting me – yet.

His tongue flicked against my neck and I could feel my blood pulsing under his touch. I wanted him. I wanted to feel him inside me, no matter how he got there. If it meant his fangs inside of me, so be it. I just wanted him.

His tongue moved to my throat, kissing and sucking up my throat to my jawbone and again to my lips. Everything was still black, but as with before, I was starting to make out vague shapes. This time I didn't want it, because I was afraid that as soon as I saw him, I would wake up. I wanted to lie here forever, my body on fire from his touch, his lips locked on mine as his hands caressed the outer curve of my ass, tantalizingly close to where I really wanted him.

I moaned softly as his hand brushed inward towards my cock, again tantalizingly close as he stroked along my inner thigh. I could see his blurred figure but I was still paralyzed. He kissed my forehead and everything cleared. I was staring into those ebony eyes and I was drowning in pleasure. His hand made unexpected contact with my cock as he slowly stroked me and I gasped in surprise. His head lowered and he closed his lips over my neck again. My body was returning to me and I struggled to move my arms and embrace him without waking myself up. I wanted to hold him. I moved my hand-

The room was empty, my hand raised as if to embrace a phantom. I was awake. I had woken myself up by moving. Cursing, I let my arm fall back and shut my eyes, trying to recreate the beautiful dream, but it was gone. There was a buzz and I noticed a bug flying around. I was tempted to swat it but then it glowed. A firefly. They were common in the field across from my apartment and I loved seeing them flash and glow in the darkening sky. It was late for a firefly, though. It must be confused from being trapped inside. I opened my window a little so it could go out but it landed on the wall and stayed still, nearly blending into the pale almond paint despite its dark shell.

The alarm was about to go off and I turned it off before it could start the soft melody I liked to wake up to. I stretched and went into the bathroom, realizing I hadn't brought a change of clothes. I was in a nice outfit, but I hadn't expected to sleep in it. My slacks were wrinkled, as was my shirt, but maybe no one would notice when I put my jacket on. I didn't know who I was trying to fool, since everyone knew I had been sleeping and everyone probably knew why. I splashed water on my face and made myself as presentable as possible, and then retrieved my jacket from my room. The firefly was gone, so I shut the window before heading down the hall to the kitchen.

Dianne and Margaret were sitting at the table and I ducked my head awkwardly, not knowing how to act. Margaret grinned at me and I was a little relieved.

"You're up," she said. "Do you want to eat anything now, or wait a little? I'll bring you something if you want to wait."

"I should probably start working," I said. "I'd love

47

something in a couple of hours though."

"I'll walk you to your office," Dianne said, rising and escorting me. She glanced at me. "You remember how to do everything?"

I nodded. "I didn't finish so I'll just be finishing that, right? Is there anything new I have to do first?"

"I'll show you the order," she said as we entered the room. There was indeed a new stack, though it was fairly small. If I worked all night, I could probably finish everything. Dmitri hadn't ever specified my start and end times, I realized. Adze had referenced working a couple of hours on weekends, so presumably I worked more during the week, but I had no idea what my hours were. I sat down and got the computer ready as Dianne lingered.

"Remember to call Dmitri if you need to leave for any reason," she said. "It's not a problem if you do need to leave. Just call him first. Master might be in to talk to you if there's anything important. He understands the delay in your hours tonight."

I blushed. "He's not mad, is he? I'm so sorry. I completely forgot. I'm just so used to going to work in the morning, and having all night to sleep, that I forgot it wouldn't be the same."

"You still have your job," she said. "You had a good first day, and he seems to like you. Don't disappoint him."

I nodded and she left, and I put on gloves and got to work. I had a headache, but it wasn't bad. I could ignore it. Dianne's words were harder to ignore. Adze liked me? What did that mean? Dmitri had said it was unusual for me to get hired so I must have done something right, but during the interview the vampire had just looked at me. He hadn't even spoken to me. Did that mean he was attracted to me? I hushed the thoughts in my head. Of course he wasn't. Why would he be? He was a vampire. He wouldn't think a human was attractive. There must have been some other reason I had gotten the job and he was putting up with me showing up drunk on my second day of work. I had done a good job last night, I reminded myself.

That was why they liked me.

I worked quickly and this time I moved the letters I finished to the other side of the desk because I had room. I tried to be as careful and thorough as possible, but I also wanted to finish tonight. I forwarded all of the analyses to Dmitri and twice he sent a response asking me to check one of my conclusions, so he was clearly reading them and taking them seriously. I wondered again why he didn't just do this job.

I took a break after a couple of hours, calling Dmitri and feeling weird asking for permission to use the bathroom. I was vague, just saying I needed to leave for a minute, because I felt so awkward about it. He gave me permission without question and didn't ask anything: why I was leaving, how long I would be gone. But he did tell me to wait a minute or two before leaving, raising my suspicions. Was there something going on that I wasn't supposed to know about? Was there someone here I wasn't supposed to see? Something was going on, but I didn't see anything out of place as I went to the bathroom and returned. I wasn't sure if I was supposed to call Dmitri and let him know that I was back, but he would realize I had returned when I sent my next completed analysis, so I just started working.

Margaret brought me a plate of crackers, cheese, and fancy olives after a while and sat with me while I took off my gloves and munched. She quizzed me about the foods I liked and what my usual diet was. I was tempted to make myself sound healthier than I was to impress her, but that would probably backfire since she was going to be feeding me from now on. I wanted to have snacks available, after all, and it seemed like she was responsible for stocking the fridge.

Soon I was back at work. I was on the next to last letter and glanced at my watch. It was nearly five in the morning. I wondered again what a normal workday was on the night shift. I finished up the letter and reached for the final letter when I realized with a start that Adze was there. He was leaning in the doorway watching me without a word. He was incredibly quiet and I didn't like how easily he could show up. I instinctively ran a hand through my hair and straightened, hoping I looked presentable.

"Nearly finished?" he asked, walking over to me with a smooth glide. I thought of his body pressed against mine in my dream and fought a blush.

"Um, yeah," I said. "Last one."

"You work quickly," he said. "Do you have any questions for me?"

My first thought was obviously to ask what he thought of me and hope he responded with a kiss. But I blocked that thought and tried to think of something, anything. I was drawing a blank. He was too handsome. All I could think of was how good my dream had been and I knew I needed to block it from my mind and focus, but it was hard. Still, I had some questions that hadn't yet been answered and I felt like I should ask something.

"I guess I still don't really know what House Elviore does," I said hesitantly. I hadn't thought to ask Margaret earlier. Looking it up wouldn't help, as the information didn't seem to be public. I realized I hadn't looked up House Salvite, either, though I had meant to do so.

"You wanted to know if we were vampire hunters," Adze said, pulling a chair to sit across from me. He was absolutely impeccable and those eyes were addictingly dark. "We are not, though we do occasionally assist in those matters. We do research."

He stopped and I wondered if he would explain, or if I were allowed to question him further. When he didn't continue, I decided to take a risk.

"What kind of research?"

"What kind do you think?" he asked. "You've read enough by now."

I blinked and looked at the stacks of letters. How did those possibly relate to any sort of research? They were all about various attacks on humans and vampires, though the content was usually hidden. My brow wrinkled.

"Do you research vampire deaths?" I asked hesitantly. "Or human deaths in vampire cities?"

"Both," Adze said, and I let out a sigh of relief. My guess was accurate and he wasn't disappointed with me. "We study the patterns to learn who is behind the killings."

"But you're not hunters?"

"No."

I stared at him, puzzled. As far as I knew, vampire hunters were the only ones with the authority to kill vampires and they only killed vampires who had been targeting and killing humans. There didn't seem to be any pattern in which vampires started attacking and I couldn't see any way someone would be behind it. Or did he mean the person behind the vampire hunters?

"You'll learn more," Adze said. "You're quick. But you don't need to know everything right away."

I smiled, pleased at the compliment. He reached into his jacket and handed me a letter as he had last night, asking me to analyze it. As with last night, I could tell he opened the letter illegally. It was quite similar to the previous letter and was clearly meant to go undetected. The letter, as before, was about something other than the true content. This letter was giving orders about something to happen on Sunday. Or I assumed Sunday. It referenced the full moon and that was Sunday, and Adze nodded when I explained my reasoning. It used the number six again several times and halfway through my analysis, I remembered that there were six vampires in House Elviore. Was this a specific reference to them?

"What is it?" Adze asked, and I realized I had stopped talking.

"Um, there are six vampires in your house, right?"

"Your house, too," Adze chided. "And yes."

"These letters, are they about you? Are you in danger?"

"What makes you think there's danger involved?"

"I mean, all of this is about sneaking around and then acting at certain times, and whatever the six means is usually the target of the actions. Are these orders to attack you?"

He studied me for a moment, then gestured me to continue. I bit my tongue and went back to my explanation, trying not to let my new worries and knowledge impact my analysis. When I finished, he took the letter back and resealed it. Then he stood and came next to me. I turned to face him, wondering if I should get up, but he put his hand on my head.

My mouth went dry. His fingers curled through my hair as he tilted my head up to look at him. I hoped he didn't notice how incredibly turned on I was by this, but the way he was holding my head, leaning in front of me, staring down at me, was irresistible. I wanted him, and the memory of him against my body flashed through my mind.

"Yes, the letters I've shown you are about our house," he said, and the words barely processed through my lust-filled brain. "You've already saved my life, and the lives of the others in our house. You may have done so again tonight. You are a valuable member of this house."

His hand carded through my hair and all I could process was that he was complimenting me, that he wanted me in his house. I was valued. He valued me. Nothing else seemed to matter, especially as he stroked my head and gazed at me with those glowing eyes. Then he petted me and withdrew his hand. I almost moaned at the loss of his hand, but kept it together. I didn't want him to know what effect his touch had on me. After all, he was my boss. My master. I shivered at the sexual connotations of that term.

"Finish here and get some sleep," he said, heading to the door. "You move in today, don't you?"

"Yes," I said, hoping it was true. Was it true? Yes. Yesterday was Thursday, today was Friday. Tonight I would spend my first real night here. Although I supposed it was more accurate to say that Saturday would be my first day here, since I would be working at night. My first long sleep in my new bed would be Saturday. I wondered how long it would take to adapt to the new schedule but I would work without sleep as long as it took to feel Adze's hand on me again.

"Good. Tell Dmitri when you're ready to start working tonight. I'll have new assignments for you," he said, gesturing to my nearly cleared off desk.

He left and I stared after him for several long moments before putting gloves back on and completing my final letter. I kept glancing at the closed door, hoping he would come back, but he didn't. There was no need to. He wasn't attracted to me outside of my dreams, after all, and after I finished, I did sleep for a little longer in hopes of another dream. But there was nothing, and soon the sun was up and Margaret and I were headed back home to move out completely.

CHAPTER EIGHT: FAREWELL

I ended up getting quite a bit of help moving, and not just from my friends. Margaret arranged for two moving vans, though I argued that we could pack everything in one, and she brought in three large, muscular men and one large, muscular woman to help me move everything. My friends came over to help, of course, but all we had to do was put things in boxes and decide whether they would go into storage or whether I would need them. Margaret helped with that as well, as it turned out I was free to put my things outside of my bedroom. My books, for example, would go to the house's library. It turned out that there wasn't a single television in the mansion so we were bringing my tv, though Margaret assured me she could upgrade it if I wanted. All of my items would get a small, nearly invisible sticker to mark them as mine and I could either keep them in my own room or intersperse them throughout the mansion. Other things were similar, though for the most part she recommended against taking them. Janae was also a good influence on me as I packed, frequently urging me to throw out the things I didn't need.

"I know they *will* store everything for you," she said several times, "But do you really *want* them to? You're never going to use this."

I generally followed her advice and soon had a series of boxes to be donated to local charities. Lee helped with that, since he volunteered and knew which charities needed what, and which items were accepted and which weren't. I was almost tempted to leave all of my furniture to charity and just buy new things when I moved into a new place, but Angie reminded me that I shouldn't rush into big decisions like that and I could always change my mind and donate things later. She and Janae were competing forces as I packed, Janae trying to get rid of things and Angie urging me to keep them.

Scott showed up after his shift ended and somehow kept finding ways to touch me, putting his hand on mine when he took something from me, placing a hand on my back to stabilize me when I picked up too big a box, sitting so close to me our thighs brushed. Maybe it wasn't the drink last night that had caused his flirting. This was likely the last chance we would be together like this and maybe he wanted to make something happen before I started my new job and left this life behind. I might have considered it even a few days ago, but not after seeing Adze. When Scott tousled my hair, all I could think of was Adze's hand in my hair and how incredibly arousing it had been.

Finally, everything was packed up and the vans had left. The charity items were packed into Lee's car to be distributed, and the things I was keeping were packed into my car with just enough room for me and Margaret. Margaret politely went to do a final check of the apartment to give me privacy while I said goodbye. Janae and Angie had to get to work and I gave them both tight hugs, and reminded Janae that she could visit and I would visit her. She was by far my best friend. Lee gave me a hug and headed to his car, and then it was just Scott.

"I'm going to miss you," Scott said, pulling me into a hug. He stroked my back and his breath tickled my ear. "You can visit me anytime. For any reason."

"Thanks, Scott, I'll miss you too," I said, trying to back away. He let me pull back just enough to look at me, and then he leaned into me and kissed me.

I was so shocked, I didn't react as his lips locked on mine and he wrapped around me, grabbing my ass and pressing his thigh against my groin. I pushed against his shoulders, trying to get him off, but he clung to me. He broke off the kiss but kissed his way along my jaw to my neck, right where Adze always kissed me in my dreams, right where my tattoo was.

"I wish I were a vampire," Scott whispered. "I would make you mine forever."

His lips closed over my tattoo and I felt his teeth against my skin. Was he seriously going to bite me?

"Stop it, Scott," I said, shoving him away as hard as I could. It didn't do much as he held tight, but his teeth were replaced by his tongue as he caressed my skin and then met my gaze again.

"You could spend a few hours with me, right?" he asked in a husky voice. "Before you move?"

I was quite irritated at how oblivious he was being. Couldn't he tell I wasn't interested at all? Why would he possibly ask when he should have known I would never say yes? How was he this blind?

"I'm sure I'll come visit you at you some point," I said, pushing him back. He finally let go and I took several steps away. "You're a great friend, Scott. Let's not ruin that."

"We're not ruining anything, we're making it better," he said, still in that husky voice.

"I want to be your friend, Scott," I said. "Nothing more."

He stared at me for a long moment and I wondered what he was thinking. Then he smiled and patted my shoulder.

"Right, friends," he said. "Tell me when you want to hang out. I'm going to miss you."

I said goodbye and he headed to his car. I wasn't sure what that meant. Was he actually okay being friends or was he going to try again if I saw him again? I would have to hang out with other people present, I decided. I did want to see him again, after all. He was a great friend and had only started hitting on me in the last couple of weeks. He had offered to let me live with him while I looked for a job, since I needed to move out to save my money. It was a generous offer and one I had considered. In fact, I probably would have done it if I hadn't gotten a job right away, and that likely would have led to a relationship. He probably knew that and was disappointed, because my job meant I would never be his boyfriend. I liked him, I did, but it would have been a relationship of convenience if I moved in with him. He would give me a place to stay, I would give him a little something at night, and we would be friends.

I sighed and went back in the apartment, where Margaret was on the small patio looking at the lush woods. I stood next to her. I really had lucked out with this place. Most of the complex faced other buildings or the street but this one corner bordered a park with deer and hiking trails and plenty of greenery. The rent was decent and the maintenance guy and I were friends. I had told the manager I wouldn't be renewing my lease over a month ago and I would have had to move out in a week anyway, but I had let her know earlier in the day that I was leaving. She had hugged me and Tom, the maintenance guy, had even stopped by to say goodbye. I had been here the entire four years I had been a student and had probably been a great resident since I was quiet and pretty much kept to myself.

"Ready?" she asked. "You should try to get some sleep before work starts tonight. I'll drive if you want to nap."

I took a long look around and nodded, mentally wishing this part of my life goodbye. Then we got in the car. Margaret drove, since she seemed to know a good shortcut even though she wouldn't specify what it was. I didn't notice it this time, either, because I shut my eyes and only woke up when we were pulling into a different garage further into the grounds. The two trucks were near a large building off to the side and the workers from earlier were moving everything inside. I had never realized how large the place was, because in addition to the multi-story storage facility hidden among the trees was an entire other house. It was out of sight of the main house but it was probably the size of the house I had grown up in: not large, but hard to miss.

"What's that?" I asked, pointing to the house. "I didn't know there were so many buildings."

"Dianne and I live there," Margaret said as she handed the

keys back to me. "She keeps everything in order. I help as much as I can, but her job never ends."

I should have realized that Margaret and Dianne lived here. I wondered briefly why they lived in a different house but if there were multiple houses, it was probably easy to live anywhere and this let the women live separate from the men. That was likely the reason, and if I had been female, I would probably live with them. I was glad I lived close to Adze, though. As we headed to the main house, the sun was starting to set. I would get maybe an hour or two of sleep. When I checked my watch, I blinked in surprise. Margaret had gotten us here in thirty minutes. How was that even possible? There was less traffic, but she must have bypassed the city completely. Next time, I would stay awake and learn the shortcut, I vowed.

Dmitri and Dianne were waiting at the back entrance to the main building and Dianne gave me a very formal hug.

"Tell me if you need anything," she said. "Anything at all. We take care of you now."

"Um, thanks," I said awkwardly.

Dmitri gave me a more complete tour of the main building and as we walked through hall after hall and saw massive dining rooms and vast ballrooms and all sorts of rooms that I couldn't imagine using, I was grateful that I only needed to know a few rooms. I was allowed to go anywhere unless it was in use, but I doubted that I ever would. Dmitri then gave me a map of the grounds, which were as much larger as I had thought than the house was. There were several distinct gardens, a small pond, tennis courts, a swimming pool, and nearly a mile of trails. I could go anywhere and use anything, though if I wanted to play tennis, I needed to let Dianne know so she could give me rackets. There were seven full-time people in charge of the grounds but I got the impression they switched often, as none were introduced to me. I was part of the permanent staff; they were not. I was a little pleased that I was considered permanent and hoped I lived up to their expectations.

Finally, we returned, but even though I had hoped for sleep, it was almost nine and I decided trying to get half an hour of sleep would only backfire. Margaret gave me a delicious breakfast, though it was odd to eat pancakes and eggs this late at night, and then I headed to my small office to start working. Dmitri had left while I ate and when I came in and saw my cleared off desk, I wondered what I was supposed to do. He would come and tell me, wouldn't he? I went to the desk. Just as I was sitting down, I heard a soft footstep and looked up to see Adze in the center of the room looking at me.

My heart leapt at the beautiful vampire and I wondered what he looked like when he smiled. So far he hadn't shown any emotion, even in my dreams. He approached me and reached out to caress my head as he had before and it took all of my strength not to turn into that touch and cuddle against him. He stroked my head as his eyes glittered.

"You'll start in my office tonight, working with me," he said, curving his hand to brush along my cheek. My heart fluttered and I couldn't speak. He stroked my cheek once more and then removed his hand. He went to the door and glanced back at me. I was stunned.

"Are you coming?"

I blinked and shook myself, then hurried after him. I didn't know what I would be doing with him and it likely wouldn't be what I really wanted to do, but I was delighted at the chance to spend more time with him. The touch of Adze's hand had lit a fire in me that not even Scott's groping could compare with, and I would do anything to be at his side.

CHAPTER NINE: OFFICE INTIMACY

Although I had peeked in Adze's office on my first tour, I hadn't been in it and it was incredibly lush. There was a large desk with a streamlined computer and monitor. Instead of a brand, it had the Elviore house symbol on it and I wondered what the specs were. There wasn't a keyboard or mouse but maybe they were hidden. I'd wanted to upgrade my computers for a while; maybe I could get them through my job as work expenses and personalize them to my heart's content. Or maybe they were just for vampires. I would ask Dmitri.

Adze set me down in a leather chair in a corner of the room next to a small table and a lush potted plant. Once I was sitting, he reached out to stroke my head again and I melted inside. I was worried, though, because if he kept touching me this much, I might get a little too aroused for work. I did not want him knowing this turned me on.

"I'm having a meeting with someone," he said. "You'll sit here and listen. Take notes. When he leaves, you'll explain what he meant and if I missed anything. He's a friend of the house so there are no penalties for failing. Understand?"

"Yes," I said, disappointed when he removed his hand and got me a pad of paper and a slim black pen with the house symbol on it. I was surprised, though, because Dmitri had indicated that I would only sit in on meetings with him when he trusted me more. But maybe this was a test. I was allowed to fail, after all. Maybe he would check what I said and if I did a good enough job, he would start trusting me. I remembered suddenly that he had said I saved his life once already, possibly twice. I had been so distracted by his touch that the words hadn't processed until now. Maybe he did trust me already. There was no penalty for failure, but maybe this wasn't a test.

"Do not say anything while he's here, and do not draw attention to yourself. No matter what happens, you must be as invisible as possible."

I nodded and he returned to his desk, then pressed a button on the sleek phone and asked Dmitri to send the visitor in. A few moments passed and then the door opened. Dmitri escorted a young man in. He had a stocky build and an exquisitely tailored suit, with a shock of red curls and pale skin with freckles. He and Dmitri bowed to Adze and the man's eyes never even went to me. It was as if I didn't exist and I was a little offended. Dmitri left and closed the door and the man came to stand in front of Adze's desk. I realized there were no places for the man to sit and wondered if it were because he was human or if Adze always made his guests stand. The man didn't seem surprised by it, though, simply arranging his feet into a comfortable stance and linking his hands behind his back. He was confident, and I made a note of his body position and what it meant.

"I bring greetings from my master, sir," the man said. "He wishes you well."

"I hope that's not the only reason you're here, Rory," Adze said with a trace of annoyance in his voice. "You were just here last week. What brings you here today?"

"My master wishes to know if you're in need of any assistance."

"What assistance would I need?"

"He heard you were hiring," Rory said. "We have several qualified humans we could part with, and depending on the job, our house's vampires are open to helping you."

"The job has been filled," Adze said, but didn't gesture towards me or indicate me in any way. Rory didn't look at me either, so he clearly didn't think I had filled the job and

61

I wondered why. There were very strange vibes from this conversation and I was trying to note everything. I would make sense of it later.

"Your hires tend to be temporary," Rory said. "We could offer you permanent assistance."

"When I'm looking to fill the position again, I'll be sure to approach your house," Adze said, and I was grateful. He wasn't being as diplomatic as I would have liked, because there was a definite edge of a threat in Rory's words and stance.

"I'm sure my master will be pleased to hear it," Rory said, bowing slightly. "Unless you're in need of other assistance, I'll take my leave."

"Your house is a strong ally, and I don't forget it," Adze said. "If I do need assistance, I will ask."

Rory bowed again and went to the door. I saw Dmitri waiting on the other side and when they were gone and the door was shut again, Adze looked at me. I looked at my notes, trying to put into words the strange things I had sensed.

"Why was he really here?" Adze asked.

"Um," I said, glancing through my notes. I had only written one page but I had tried to get everything. "Well, he actually was here about the job. He really wanted his house to fill it. He seemed almost threatening about it, like something bad would happen if you didn't give it to him, but when you said you'd do it in the future, he backed down."

Adze glanced at the door, nodding. "What else?"

"He seems to think you need other assistance. It seems more like a warning than anything else. He thinks you're in danger, or something is about to happen, and he wants his house to be the one to help you. He seems to think you understand what the danger is and didn't like being refused."

Adze tapped a finger against his lips. "So he knows we're in danger? That poses a problem. Anything else?"

I looked through my notes. "No, that was pretty much it. But he didn't seem to think that I had the job. Why is that?"

"He didn't realize you were there," Adze said. "I used a

glamour to hide your presence."

"A glamour?" I repeated. I had heard the word in all sorts of tv shows and movies whenever a vampire was present, but I didn't know many details. It was like a spell only vampires could use. There were all sorts of glamours, but I had mainly heard it used in the context of how attractive they were. That was how the term started. They exuded glamour and mesmerized the humans who looked at them. They could control how alluring they were and I suddenly wondered how strongly Adze used his glamour on me. Did he know how attracted I was? Did he want me attracted?

"I assume you've heard of them," Adze said, and I nodded. "As long as you didn't move, my presence was enough to distract all of his attention. You were invisible to him."

He stood up and approached me. I looked up at him, setting my pad of paper down on my lap nervously. His eyes were glowing and while there wasn't a smile on his lips, his face seemed relaxed.

"You were not invisible to me," he continued, and reached out to stroke my hair.

In anyone else, that would have been a definite come on, but what did it mean when he said it? Was he hitting on me, or just making a comment? He seemed to enjoy touching me; maybe he was flirting. But he was a vampire. Why would a vampire like him be interested in a human like me? I was completely flustered and I could feel my cheeks heating up. I was also very aroused, and hoped it was well-hidden under my notebook. Having him leaning over me like this, touching me, seeming to flirt with me, was a little too much and I leaned away from him slightly.

"Do you know that you're resistant?" he asked softly.

"What?" I asked. Did I know what that meant? It was hard to think clearly, but I didn't think I'd ever heard that before. What did that mean? Was it a good thing?

"You don't react to glamours as most people do," Adze mused. "You're resistant to them. It's unusual for a human. In the war, we killed resistant humans."

My eyes widened and my hands trembled. His hand continued to stroke through my hair but now it seemed threatening. Was I mistaking a threat for flirting? Was he threatening me? Because this felt like flirting, despite his words. I didn't feel resistant right now. It felt like everything in my world revolved around him in this moment. His touch, his caress, everything he did was more important than anything I had ever felt before and I wanted him even as he frightened me.

He ran his fingers across my cheek and without thinking, I lifted my hand to take his, to pull his hand to my lips and kiss those beautiful, long fingers. They were sweet and cool under my lips and I shut my eyes as I finally felt him, as I imagined where this could possibly go.

He pulled his hand away and suddenly it felt like everything fell out of focus. Disoriented, I looked around and realized what I had done. I had grabbed him and kissed his hand. I stared at him in horror. He would have to fire me for this. This was totally inappropriate. But he didn't seem angry as he stared at me.

"Not immune, then," he said softly, almost to himself. "Just highly resistant."

I blinked. Had he used a glamour on me to get me to kiss him? Had he made me do that? If that were true, then I might not lose my job. If that were true, I considered, did that mean he wanted me? Or was he just testing me?

"I'm so sorry," I said, rising to my feet. I kept my notebook pressed against me so he wouldn't see my arousal and sidestepped around him, hoping to get out of the room before anything else happened.

As I slid next to him, his arm caught my waist and twisted me until I was pressed against his chest in an embrace. The notebook fell to the floor and I braced myself against him as he pulled me tighter, leaning me backwards as he pivoted his leg between mine. I gulped as he made contact with my overly sensitive cock. He loomed over me, then drew close and whispered into my ear.

"There's no need to apologize," he murmured. "You're free to refuse, if you wish."

He stared at me with those beautiful glowing eyes and I wrapped my arms around his neck. I would never refuse him. He could do anything to me and I would always let him. I didn't know if it were his glamour or just him, but I knew without question that I belonged to him and wanted nothing else. I shut my eyes and tilted my head back, and his lips locked on mine just as his hand grabbed my ass and yanked me close.

I felt helpless as he ravished my lips, ground against my body, squeezed and caressed me. Helpless and utterly aroused. He sucked on my lower lip, then plunged his tongue into my mouth and my knees went weak. He twisted me and then I felt the desk against my hips. He lifted me and pushed me back until I was sitting on the desk, then his hands went to my belt. My heart leapt into an even higher gear. Was this actually happening? This had to be a dream, didn't it? Surely it did. Surely a vampire, my vampire, wouldn't want me like this. I was nothing; he was everything.

My belt came off and he unbuttoned my pants, kissing me the whole time. I was too busy clutching his back to help him, or stop him, or do anything really. I didn't know what I wanted but this was so fast, and then he shoved me and I was flat on my back as he slid my pants and boxers to my knees. Before I could react, he leaned forward and kissed me again, and I felt him pushing against my entrance. He had undone himself at some point and I was disappointed I hadn't seen him, but thrilled he was turned on by me, wanted me, and a little afraid too because he felt enormous as he pushed against me. His tongue darted into my mouth just as he burst into me and I stiffened with pain and would have cried out if not for his mouth on mine. He entered me swiftly and I wriggled against him as the quick slide was agonizing. There was a strong edge of pleasure, though, and my heart was stuttering with conflicting desires.

He gave me no time to adjust before he began thrusting into me and I squirmed and writhed against him, the pleasure growing stronger and stronger until the pain was only a memory as he filled me, thrust deep inside me, made me whole in a way no one ever had before. I was close to coming, so close, just one little touch would tip me over. I had been grabbing him, pulling him tight, but now I let a hand start to slide to myself. He grabbed my wrist and pinned it to the desk, his thrusts not slowing at all, then grabbed my other wrist and pinned it, too. Completely helpless now, I arched my back as his lips went to my neck, hovering over my pulsing blood, and I wanted him to bite me. I wanted him to taste how wonderful I felt. I wanted to give him a deep, intimate part of me. I wanted his fangs in my body. His lips closed on me but no fangs, not even a prick, and then he thrust hard and exploded inside me. I gasped and rode out the end as he slowed, then withdrew.

I lay on the desk panting as he let go of my hands and gently eased me until my legs returned to the ground. My body – and my cock – was throbbing and aching but he made no moves to touch me and when I moved my hand, he pinned it again. Was he just going to leave me like this? He couldn't, could he? Precum was dripping from my cock and he stared at me emotionlessly. Was he going to suck me off? My cock twitched at the thought. Instead, he helped me sit up.

"Not in here," he said, then pointed to a small door on one side of the room I hadn't noticed. "There's a bathroom. Clean yourself up."

I was stunned and just stared at him. He really was going to leave me like this. Sure, he was letting me jerk myself off, but he wasn't going to help. I staggered to my feet, my pants pooling around my ankles, and made it to the bathroom. It didn't take long before I peaked; I just had to remember the feel of Adze against and inside me. I took several long moments, splashed water on my face, and made myself decent before returning to Adze's office. He was sitting at his desk calmly looking at his computer. I was glad I hadn't knocked anything off his desk, since I hadn't been paying attention at all. He probably had been aware of my positioning and made sure I didn't damage anything.

I felt lost and confused as he looked up at me. His eyes were warm, but it was impossible to interpret that expressionless face. What had just happened? Did it mean something? Was he just testing me or was he attracted to me? Would it happen again? I definitely wanted it to happen again. I took a hesitant step towards him, unsure of what to say.

"Dmitri will take you back to your office and give you instructions for the rest of the night," Adze said, leaning back in his chair and extending my belt towards me. "You've done very well today and I know you're still adjusting. If you need to stop working early to catch up on sleep, you are welcome to do so."

"Oh, um, thank you," I said, taking the belt and threading it around my waist. He said nothing else and I went to the door. As I reached out to the doorknob, still confused, he said my name. I turned back to him.

"I'm pleased that you're living here now," he said, and I blushed deeply. Then he waved his hand to dismiss me, though not with any malice. It seemed like a gesture he made a lot, as if it were instinct when he wanted someone to leave. Not an insult, but not especially warm. Still, he was pleased I was here. That was enough for now.

CHAPTER TEN: DENIED

I did end work early, heading to my room around three. Most nights I would work from nine until four or five, depending on how much work I had, Dmitri told me. He also told me that once I had sorted out the work backlog, I wouldn't be doing work that entire time. I was in charge of correspondence and would interpret as it came in. I now had access to the house email account, or at least a portion of it, and spent the night sorting out a vast amount of email. Dmitri assured me that none of it was pressing and I could take as long as I needed. I could leave when I needed for a week as I adapted, but after that I needed to be on call for most of the night.

My body still tingled and as I headed to my room, I glanced towards Adze's office. I couldn't figure out what had happened and what it meant. Did he actually want me? And how was I supposed to deal with it? I couldn't tell anyone; I knew that much. I wondered if it counted as workplace harassment. Probably. But was it harassment if I wanted it? I knew it still was, because there was a power imbalance and I wasn't really capable of consenting when he controlled my job. If someone else were in my position, I would tell them that they were being manipulated and taken advantage of. But somehow it didn't seem to apply to me.

So I couldn't say anything or talk to anyone as I took a last look at Adze's office and went through the kitchen. Margaret offered me a snack and I demurred, instead heading straight to my room. Many of my things had been put away, I saw with surprise. My computer was already set up and the boxes were arranged for easiest unpacking. I put some of my clothes away and got my bathroom stuff out. It was such a strange time to go to bed but I wanted to sleep for a really long time. This would be my first time sleeping here in my pajamas, I realized. I was grateful the bed was already made but I added my own pillows, which were a little firmer. I snuggled into the bed and drifted off into a deep sleep.

I was a little disappointed when I woke up and hadn't dreamed about Adze, but my body still had a pleasant ache. I didn't need dreams when I had him in real life. The curtains were closed, as Margaret had recommended, and I stood and opened them to see a beautiful, sunny day. It was three in the afternoon. That meant I had slept nearly twelve hours, far more than I slept even when I was being lazy. I had needed it, because my schedule was so off, but it was still surprising.

The kitchen was empty but there was a note on the fridge letting me know there were leftovers available. After a late lunch, I decided to walk around and explore the grounds. As I left, I noticed the steps to the basement where Adze was no doubt sleeping. If he did sleep. I was still unclear on that. I watched plenty of movies and shows with vampires but none were actually played by vampires, since vampires didn't show up on film. There were no vampire writers, either, at least that I knew of, so most of what was portrayed in the shows was false. In some movies, vampires slept during the day, but in my favorite romcom, vampires didn't need to sleep, they just couldn't be in sunlight. Was Adze awake right now, trapped in the basement away from the sun? Or was he sleeping in a coffin as was always shown in movies? Neither option sounded especially good and I shivered as I went into the sunlight for an afternoon of exploring.

I returned as the sun was setting and met Dianne and Margaret heading to the main house. We chatted and Margaret gave me a wonderful breakfast before I changed into more formal clothes and went to my office. I was starting to know how to do my job: there were several letters on the desk and I did those first, then started going through the emails. Three emails came in as I worked and I did those immediately, as requested. I tried to figure out who they were from and how House Elviore was getting them, because they clearly weren't intended for Adze. I had assumed people asked House Elviore to translate their mail, but I wasn't so sure anymore. After all, I had seen two letters that I knew he wasn't supposed to have, and these emails seemed to be sent to me exactly as they were sent to the intended recipient. I wasn't getting cc'd on them. I was just getting them.

I tried not to worry about it and keep working, and soon the night was almost over. It was almost four and I wasn't tired yet, but I didn't want to push it. I'd spent my midnight lunch hour chatting with Margaret in the kitchen. I would finish up this email, then call it a day. As I finished typing, I glanced up and jumped. Adze was there, in the doorway, watching me. I hadn't seen him all night and I blushed as I looked at his glowing eyes. He was expressionless, as always, and I tried to figure out why he was here and what he thought of me.

"Finish and follow me," he said.

I quickly typed the last few comments, being careful not to make any mistakes despite my distraction, and then followed him to his office. He shut the door and my heart hitched. We were alone. Was this work, or pleasure? He went to his desk and sat down, turning to the computer and gesturing for me to approach. I stood next to him nervously, looking at him until he gestured to the screen. I blinked in surprise. It wasn't any operating system I'd ever seen and it took a minute to even figure out what I was looking at. It looked like everything I had forwarded to Dmitri today. Adze would of course have access to it, but why was he showing it to me?

"You're extremely fast, and effective," Adze said, and I smiled cautiously. "This amount of work would take most humans at least a week."

I stared at the screen in surprise. It wasn't hard to translate, for the most part, and it was just a matter of doing the work and not slacking off. With thoughts of Adze to inspire me, I had no inclination to slack off. Thoughts of him were occasionally distracting, but generally I wanted to please him so I was working harder than I might otherwise work.

"Are you having any problems? Do you have any other questions yet?"

"Everything's great," I said, but my mind was filled with questions about him and what had happened. I knew he probably meant questions about the job, but all I could think about was his hands on my body, his cock inside me. I shied away from him as a rush of arousal flooded over me.

"Um, about yesterday," I started hesitantly.

He turned to me and reached up to caress my cheek and run his hand through my hair. I was temporarily stunned by the touch, by the sweetness of the gesture as his dark eyes pinned me.

"Yes?" he asked.

I didn't know how to continue, what I even wanted to ask. His hand against my cheek was too enticing and the words wouldn't form. What did I want to ask? If he wanted me. But I couldn't say it. I was afraid to ask.

He wrapped his hand around the back of my neck and pulled me towards him, and downward. His other hand went to his waist and I gasped as I realized what he wanted me to do. He wanted me on my knees, pleasuring him. I let him pull me to my knees as he unzipped his pants and exposed himself. I sighed in pleasure at the sight of his hardening member. He was incredibly beautiful, and larger than I would have imagined. No wonder my body still ached. I looked up at him, wondering what this would mean to him. Did this mean anything or did he just want my mouth? Did he care about me? Looking back down at his cock, I realized I didn't care enough to refuse this. I wanted him and I would take him no matter how, no matter what it meant to him.

Guided by his hand still in my hair, I leaned towards him and braced my hands against his thighs as I let my tongue lap against him. I'd sucked cock before, but this was completely different and he tasted different, too, like moonlight piercing through the clouds. I continued to slick him up with my tongue, savoring the sweet and strange flavor, using my hands to caress him. He was completely hard now and I slid him into my throat. His hand tightened in my hair and he pulled me forward faster than I was ready for and I pushed back slightly as his cock filled my throat unexpectedly. He let me withdraw and I gasped for breath, but now I knew what he wanted and I was determined to give it to him. I was on him again in a moment, not hesitating this time, letting him fill me farther than anyone else had before. He thrust against me and used his hand to guide me and I let him, enjoying every sensation.

I was pretty hard myself and as his rhythm quickened I wondered if I would be allowed to come this time. I wanted it so badly and I could feel moisture around my hard cock. I was dripping and I didn't want my pants ruined so I started to unzip myself. His other hand grabbed my wrist and planted it firmly on his thigh. He was sliding in and out of my mouth quickly and I focused on that instead of trying to undo myself. His message was clear; it was not allowed.

With a sigh, he exploded into my mouth and I lavished his cock with my tongue, encouraging him as my mouth filled and I swallowed and swallowed again. His cum tasted sweet, unlike any I'd ever tasted. It was still musky and tangy, but it was nothing like I'd tasted before and I wanted more of it. I lapped up every bit of it before he pulled my head back. His eyes were glowing and I wondered if now it was my turn. I was ready to go and wanted it so badly.

He let go of my head and turned in his chair slightly, breaking the intimacy between us, and gestured towards the bathroom. He was going to leave me like this. Again.

"No," I said, then flinched as he grabbed my hair again. But he simply caressed me, then ran a finger along my cheek to my lips. I leaned into the touch. This was what I needed.

"Go clean yourself up," he said.

I opened my eyes in shock, and some anger. I got to my feet and obeyed, and pushed my rage aside long enough to imagine him inside me, to savor the taste of him, and release my lust. But my orgasm was tainted by my anger and I didn't enjoy it nearly as much as I should. I rinsed out my mouth, though I would have liked to keep tasting him longer. Did he care about me? It was becoming apparent that he didn't. Maybe he was just using me. What should I do?

There were no mirrors for me to check my appearance. Vampires didn't reflect in mirrors so it made sense that there weren't any, but I wanted to make sure I looked presentable. What should I say to him? How should I react? I needed to do or say something so he knew this was unacceptable. I would have sex with him, sure – and I hoped that part continued – but the rest could not continue. He had to value me and want my pleasure as much as I wanted his. I nodded and steeled myself, then heard someone talking in the other room. Was someone else there?

My cheeks flooded with embarrassment at the thought of Dmitri realizing what Adze and I were doing. What would he think? What would any of them think? I waited but the voice continued. It was only one voice, I realized, and it was Adze's. I opened the door a crack. He was on the phone and glanced at me, gesturing me to come out. I obeyed. He covered the phone with his hand.

"You're dismissed for the night," he said. "Get some rest."

Then he returned to his call, which I realized in surprise was in a different language, one I'd never heard before. He was ignoring me. I considered staying and demanding that he deal with me, but I might lose my job if I did that. I wanted this job. I wanted him. I just didn't want him like this.

CHAPTER ELEVEN:
PARK ASSAULT

I stormed out to the grounds and looked around. I wanted to get away. Not just somewhere on the grounds but away. I needed space to think. It was a couple hours before Margaret served dinner, so maybe I could drive into town and walk around. I went to my car. It was in the farthest garage and I sat in the driver's seat and turned the music up, then looked at my phone. There was a park near the center of Redmond that had several walking paths indicated on it. I would go there, walk around and cool off, and try to figure out how I would handle this situation. It would take thirty minutes to get there but it was worth it. I could always message Margaret if I was going to be late.

Traffic was bad but I got a parking spot less than a block from the park entrance. As I got out, I realized this was my first time in a vampire city and I wondered if there were anything I needed to watch out for. Vampires couldn't bite me, but they had mentioned that I might be targeted. I would be careful. The entrance to the park was brightly lit and reassured me. I hadn't thought about the time, but it was still pitch black out. The park, though, had lighting every few feet along the paths and large lamps that spread a halo of golden warmth in large, intersecting circles that covered the grassy areas. Even the trees had lights on them, or many of them did. It was designed for night, but that made sense since this was a nocturnal town.

I went to a path with a small sign indicating a one-mile

loop. Good enough. I just needed to walk. As I set out on the brightly lit path through the trees, I tucked my hands in my pockets and tried to keep an eye on my surroundings while I descended into my thoughts.

What did my relationship with Adze mean? Did he care about me at all or was he just using my body? I desperately wanted him to care about me but everything he did seemed to indicate that I was nothing more than a pretty body to him. A valuable pretty body, I amended, since he was using my talents for my job as well. But that was it. And I wanted to be more.

"Hey," a voice said, and I jolted from my thoughts to see two men approaching with sneers. They were larger than me and I tensed. This wasn't good.

"What's a pretty human like you doing all alone out here?" the larger man asked.

I blinked and examined him closer. He was human. Definitely human. So why was he referring to me as human as if that were different? Or was this park usually frequented by vampires so my presence was unusual?

"Who's your house?" the second man asked.

I backed away. I was still near the start of the trail and the large open area of the park. If I ran and got there, I could get to the crowded street, or at least within view of it. They wouldn't rob me in public, would they?

The larger man was suddenly at my side, folding my collar down to see my tattoo, and I gasped. How had he moved that fast? He wasn't a vampire; I was sure.

"Elviore," he said in surprise. "What's House Elviore doing here?"

The second man edged away from me, but the larger man leered. "Well, you're awfully pretty for Elviore."

"We should go," the second man said. "This has to be a trap."

"There's no one else here," the larger man said, keeping his eyes locked on me. I felt frozen in place. He was still right next to me, his hand on my neck. He grabbed my throat and

I panicked. Was he going to kill me? But his hand loosened and he trailed his fingers up my neck to my cheek. There was a lustful light in his eyes. To my surprise, I felt a responding surge of lust rush through my body. He laughed as he eyed the bulge in my pants.

"They're not within range," he said. "We have at least twenty minutes."

"He's bait," the second man insisted. "Maybe they're just waiting."

"Do you sense a vampire nearby?"

The second man was silent and I gulped. I forced down my arousal and prepared to run. The second man might not hurt me, but he wasn't going to help me, and the larger man's intentions towards me were all too clear. I was not going to get raped. The larger man caressed my cheek and I moved, ducking out of his grasp and running towards the main park. I got three leaping steps before the larger man knocked into me from behind and I fell forward, landing hard on my hands and knees. I gasped in pain and he grabbed me, flipping me onto my back.

"What's an ancient house doing with a resistant human?" the larger man asked, sounding angry. "You'll obey me."

I gasped as my body flooded with lust once again. I fought the feeling again. He had to be a vampire but he wasn't. He was somehow using a glamour on me, and I was fighting it, but not enough. He straddled me and I couldn't move. I was frozen in place and as his thighs brushed against me, I moaned. I needed his touch. I writhed against him, wanting more of him, and he chuckled as he unbuttoned the top of my shirt.

He leaned forward to kiss me and then he shuddered. His body flew sideways off me and I flinched, seeing a female vampire standing over me. I looked at the man's body, now on the ground next to me, and saw blood running from the back of his head. Had she killed him? Was she going to kill me? I was terrified but my body was still aroused, still needed relief. She stared at me curiously, then pinned her gaze on the other man.

"Don't make me chase you," she hissed, and the man dropped to his knees.

"Please, Mistress, it was a mistake," he said. "I didn't do anything to him. I wouldn't cross your house."

My arousal wasn't quieting but the words still registered. She was in my house. There was nothing that marked her as such but I could feel a link between us. She wasn't going to kill me; she was protecting me. She might protect me, but my body was still completely out of my control. Would she help me? Could she? I needed that man. I wasn't sure if she had killed him. It looked like he was still breathing but he was definitely unconscious, and I didn't know how bad the injury was. I was still frozen from the foreign lust, my body aching for someone to touch and caress and penetrate me. She came to my side and placed her hand against my tattoo.

A flush of cool strength ran through me and all of my lust evaporated. My body was completely under my control again, my mind clear, and I flushed in embarrassment over how desperate I had been just a moment ago. She helped me to my feet before placing me behind her and facing the second man, who was still on his knees and paper-white with fear.

"If he had not been in my house, you would have attacked him," the vampire said calmly. "That is a crime. Since you weren't attacking this time, I won't punish you. But I will let all of the ancient houses know your face and if any humans are attacked, you will be hunted down. Your friend, too."

That meant the other man would survive. I was relieved I hadn't just witnessed a murder, but a flash of anger overtook me as I looked at the still body on the ground. What had he done to me to make me want him so badly? No one had the right to touch me like that, and I shouldn't have felt that way about anyone. Anyone other than Adze, that was. The vampire eyed the man's body, then stared at the second man again.

"You'll get him help. If he dies tonight, you will also die. And if either of you ever commit a crime, both of you will be blamed. Watch him and watch yourself."

"I'll help him, but can we go out with you?" the man asked, sounding desperate.

"No," the vampire said. "Deal with the blood on your own."

I wondered what that meant, because the man seemed frightened by her words. She took my arm and led me forcefully back on the path to the grassy area. I stopped when we reached the large area, but she kept dragging me and she was bringing me away from my car. I stumbled to a halt and she stared at me as if in surprise.

"Um, my car is over there," I said, then fell silent under her icy gaze.

She was very beautiful, but also very cold. She had waves of ebony hair and a hawkish nose, and lovely brown eyes, but her face was as expressionless as Adze's. It must be a vampire trait. I had no idea what she was thinking as she studied me for a moment, then took my arm and led me the way she had been going.

"We'll talk when we reach my car," she said.

We walked through the park and it was larger than I had imagined. We walked for nearly five minutes in complete silence until I heard the sound of traffic and soon we were at what must have been the opposite entrance to the park. There was a limousine parked right at the entrance with two people – humans – standing by it. Both were women and had long dark hair like the vampire's, though they were human. Of course, I had been certain the men who had attacked me were human too, and I still wasn't sure about them. Maybe these weren't human. But they had tattoos, I realized, identical to mine. I didn't feel connected to them the way I felt with the vampire, but I knew they were in my house.

"Where are you parked?" the vampire said abruptly and I glanced around.

"Um, a different entrance, about a block away from the park," I said. "I don't know the street name."

Her lips tightened. "Do Adze's servants know your car?"

"Margaret's driven in it," I said.

"Then she'll retrieve it. Get in."

She gestured towards the limo and one of the women opened the door for me. I stared at it a moment before getting in. I had never been in a limo before. The seat was quite comfortable and there was another row of seats across from me, facing me. Where was I supposed to sit? I looked towards the door and the woman gestured for me to sit on the opposite side. I scooted over and she got in and sat next to me. Then the vampire got in across from us and the other woman closed the door. She must be the driver.

"Um, where are we going?" I asked nervously.

"You're needed," she said. "We just received word. Why did you leave your house?"

"Am I not allowed to leave?"

I had gotten the impression that I could spend my hours after work however I wanted, though I knew Margaret would be disappointed if I didn't eat her cooking.

"You should tell the other servants when you leave," the vampire said. "You're too new and too human to be out on your own. If I hadn't happened to be taking this route, we wouldn't have found you for hours. You could have been killed."

I gulped. I hadn't realized I was putting myself in danger leaving like that. The memory of that strange lust had lessened but I was ashamed I had reacted that way, especially since she had seen it. She hadn't said anything, but she must have known how desperate I felt. My body had made its desires known even with my clothes on. She had to know.

"How did you find me?" I asked nervously, not able to meet her eyes.

"Your mark," she said, gesturing to my neck. "I suppose no one has explained it to you yet. If you're in danger, it instantly sends out a signal to anyone in our house within a limited range. It continues traveling beyond that range but at a slow pace. It fades beyond five miles. I felt you just as we drove out of range and had to turn around to confirm it. You were incredibly lucky."

"Thank you," I said, not knowing what else to say. She sighed.

"Are you feeling better now? Is there any trace of his glamour?"

I shook my head. It had been a glamour then, but he wasn't a vampire. I was sure of it. What did it mean? Could humans learn to use glamours? Was I safe around anyone?

"I'm fine," I said, keeping my eyes down as another wave of shame swept over me.

"Do you even know who I am?"

"A vampire from House Elviore," I said slowly, because I didn't know.

The human next to me shook her head in exasperation but didn't say anything. The vampire extended her hand.

"I'm Lilith. The head of House Elviore."

I shook her hand and tried not to let my hand tremble in hers. I had assumed that vampires within a house were equal, or at the least that Adze was head of his house. I couldn't see him following anyone's orders, even a vampire as imposing as Lilith. Did she have the power to fire me even if Adze wanted to keep me? Would she fire me now that she knew how weak I was?

"I'm Kairos," I said, and she smiled. Slightly, but it was a smile. So vampires could smile.

"I know," she said. "I know all about you, and that's why I'm so worried about what might have happened to you. But you're safe now, and you'll get to where you need to be a lot faster. I think we're here, in fact."

"Where are we?"

"House Elviore meets here," she said. "Adze is waiting for you. He already knows you're safe."

The car stopped and I wondered what Adze would think. He would be relieved, I was sure. I was valuable, after all. But would he care about what had almost happened to me? Would he be happy that I was safe, or would he judge me for reacting the way that I had? Would he be as ashamed of me as I was of myself?

"An allied house is with us as well," she warned. "Try not to be intimidated."

I nodded weakly, not sure what she meant as the door opened and the driver helped Lilith out. Adze was called Master Adze; did Lilith have a title I was supposed to use? Mistress? That didn't seem right, even though it made sense. That was what the man at the park had called her. She seemed more like a Queen. Maybe Lady. I would have to find out from a human and just avoid using her name until I figured out how to address her.

The woman next to me gestured for me to get out next and I crawled to the door and stepped out. I looked around and was surprised to see a large cathedral. It was still pitch black but as with the rest of the city, it was well-lit. There was an iron wrought fence circling the cathedral and I could see a graveyard to one side. It was very large and quite beautiful, but I remembered the letter I had read that referenced a religious building. Was it referring to this one? It was Sunday, I realized with a start. The full moon. The second letter. This couldn't be related, could it?

I felt a chill along my tattoo and turned to the entrance of the cathedral to see Adze rush out with a look of concern on his normal emotionless face. He dashed to my side and swept me into a hug, wrapping his arms around me and kissing the top of my head. I shut my eyes and leaned into the embrace for a moment. Did he know what had happened and was reassuring me, or did he not know? Did he just think I was attacked? He knew I was safe, but did he know what I was safe from? I leaned into him but I was too embarrassed to stay there for long and gently pushed against him.

Adze let go of me and ran a hand across my face. Lilith didn't seem surprised by the intimacy. Maybe vampires always touched humans like this. Or maybe she knew the real reason for Adze's concern, and for the jealousy I could see in his eyes.

He had to know, with a look like that, but I couldn't tell what he thought about it. He touched my tattoo and I felt another wave of cool strength, though there was nothing to flush away this time.

"You're safe?" he demanded, and I nodded. "What were you thinking leaving like that?"

I shivered under his wrath and hoped it was jealousy and fear driving him, not anger at me. Lilith pulled him back a step and gestured to the building.

"They're waiting, aren't they?"

"Yes," Adze said, then reached to tousle my hair. "Let's go in."

CHAPTER TWELVE: CATHEDRAL PLOT

For someone who had never been around vampires before, and whose experience with Adze and Lilith was extremely limited, it was a shock to walk into the cathedral and have over a dozen vampires all stare at me. I flinched and Adze pulled me forward. I felt like an insect about to be pinned to a bug collection. It was all I could do to stay at Adze's side and try not to look too overwhelmed.

"You have a resistant human?" one of them asked.

He wasn't in my house. I could feel the other four who were in my house but they were mingled with the strange vampires and I was too frightened to look at them more closely. The feeling of being pinned increased and suddenly I couldn't breathe. But I couldn't move to clutch my throat or indicate in any way that my body was now completely frozen, too frozen to even gasp in air. My mind spun slowly, completely out of touch with my body, and I wondered if I were going to die.

"Back off," Adze said. "He's resistant, not immune."

The sensation of being pinned lessened and I gasped in relief. I edged behind Adze, not wanting to be near the vampires. Lilith's servants hadn't followed us in, I realized. They probably knew enough not to be around this many vampires. I wondered how the vampires knew I was resistant. The sensations I had felt had to be their glamours and I didn't think I could have reacted more strongly than I did. Would a non-resistant human have fainted from the force of their gazes? Possibly.

"Why do you have a resistant human?" the same vampire demanded, but another vampire cut him off.

"We'll ask later. This is the right human?"

"Yes," Adze said, and pulled me out of his shadow. I trembled as the vampires considered me, and then the vampire who had asked if I was the right one, who seemed to be in charge of the vampires who weren't in my house, gestured for me to go to his side. I looked at Adze, wondering if I was supposed to obey. Adze took my arm and walked with me to the other vampire's side.

"Analyze this," the vampire said, and gestured to a table along the wall where I saw several pieces of paper. "Don't touch it."

With Adze still at my side, I went to the table. It was a letter, but it had been badly burned and carefully pieced back together. About half of it was destroyed, including the beginning and most of the end. Only the middle was legible.

"We don't need to know how you know what it says, Kairos," Adze said. "We only need to know what it actually says."

I nodded and cautiously pulled out of his grasp to study the letter. I scanned it, struggling to read in a few places, but as I read a chill ran down my spine. It was orders again, and it was about this place. It was about tonight. I glanced at my watch and shivered. It had already started.

"What does it say?" Adze asked softly.

"What if I'm wrong?" I asked fearfully. "What if we're hurt?"

"You won't be wrong," he said calmly. "And you won't be hurt. We just need you to confirm what this says."

He gestured toward the letter and I took a deep breath.

"Um, there are two of them. They're bringing something here. Multiple somethings. Maybe explosive somethings," I added, wondering if there were bombs nearby, if we were all going to be destroyed. Adze touched my shoulder and I realized I had shivered again. I kept going.

"They're bringing them someplace in the basement, maybe, but maybe also the graveyard," I said. It was hard to understand everything without any knowledge of the building but I knew if I messed this up, we might be in real danger. "Is there a graveyard in the basement?"

"The crypt," one of the vampires said.

"That fits," I said slowly. "One is coming through the east. There's a grate along the wall that's loose. The other one, um, isn't clear. Near a bell. They started an hour ago. They should be done soon. Like, really soon. Within the next ten minutes. I don't know what happens when they're done. It's destroyed."

The other vampire gestured to his vampires, who split into four groups. Two of the groups left in different directions. The third group headed to a set of stairs leading into a basement, probably towards the crypt. The fourth group circled us protectively, surrounding all of the vampires in House Elviore.

"We'll stay here and see what's actually happening," the vampire said, then eyed me. "I see why you turned down my offer."

The pieces clicked together at that comment. This was the vampire that Rory represented, the one who had wanted to fill my job and help House Elviore. Well, it did seem like he was helping, so he had gotten his wish. But why did they need help? Adze took my arm and led me away from the letter to the center of the room. I looked at the other vampires in my house cautiously. All of them were utterly impassive. Two were men, one tall and pale, with blonde hair down to his shoulders, and the other was nearly as dark as Adze though his eyes were an eerie green. The other two were women. One was Asian, with gorgeous almond eyes and straight, ebony hair to her waist. The other had olive skin and black hair with strong features. She reminded me of my Italian relatives. Definitely Mediterranean, and definitely beautiful. All of them were beautiful and though I was probably prejudiced, they were far more beautiful than the other vampires surrounding us. They were studying me, but I didn't feel pinned as I had when I first entered.

Less than a minute passed when two vampires returned and pulled the leader aside. He nodded and sent them away again, then turned to Adze and Lilith.

"It is the crypt. They've brought in dozens already. If blame for this fell on your house, you would not have survived."

"You'll speak on our behalf, then?" Lilith asked.

"You were the only one absent," he said. "What delayed you?"

"I was getting this human," she said. "He wasn't at the house."

"Where was he?" the vampire asked, staring at me.

"At the park," she said. "Getting attacked by two unaffiliated dhampir."

I blinked. I had never heard that term before. It must be a type of vampire and that was how they had used a glamour on me, but since they weren't vampires, they had seemed like humans to me. Was it really possible that a whole subsection of vampires existed and I'd never heard of them? I knew almost nothing about vampires, but surely I would have heard a rumor or seen it in a movie or something.

The vampires from the other house glared at me and I shrank back. Adze took my arm again as if to reassure me.

"What happened?" the leader asked me. For a moment I was too nervous to talk, but then Adze squeezed my arm.

"Tell him the truth," Adze said. "He needs to know."

"I, um, wanted to walk around, so I went to the park in town," I began, and all of the vampires looked at me as if I were crazy. Adze sighed.

"Kairos has never been in a vampire city," Adze said. "You know parks are used differently in human cities."

I glanced at him, wondering what vampire parks were used for. Was it common to get attacked in a park here? Adze squeezed my arm again as if telling me to continue.

"I was walking, and two guys came up behind me. One of them attacked me. I tried to run away but he grabbed me and I couldn't move. Then, um, she showed up and knocked him off me," I said, wishing I knew how to address Lilith. I knew without question that if I said her name without any honorific, I would be insulting her and possibly the entire house. "She threatened the other guy and brought me here."

"Only one of them attacked you? Why?"

"Um, he said I was bait or something," I said. "I don't know."

"You did end up being bait," the leader said with a slight smile. "Lilith, I assume you dealt with them?"

"They'll survive, and their faces are known to the ancients," she said. "I'd be happy to give you sketches."

"Thank you."

Another vampire entered. "We've caught them," he said. "One is stunned. The other died before we could stop her. They're unaffiliated vampires and the survivor is in withdrawal."

"So they could have caused the deaths on their own," the leader said, then turned to Lilith. "How should we report this?"

"Blame them," she said. "We're not ready to move yet and if you name the real culprit, they'll know we're tapping them. But keep the case open. When we move, we'll include this."

"I hate having so many open cases," the vampire warned.

"They will be closed soon," Lilith assured him. "But not yet."

The vampire nodded and gestured to his vampires. "We'll escort you to your homes and keep an eye on you until daybreak. We need your alibis to be flawless. I'll need those sketches and I'll need to bring the two dhampir in to confirm your story," he added. "Where were you?"

She gave several street names and suggested several places that must have been hideouts nearby. I looked around. Whatever was happening was seemingly over, but were we safe? I was more than confused. One vampire had been caught, but the other had been killed? Or had she died from something else? I didn't understand what deaths they were talking about, or what they meant by the real culprit. But I froze as the leader approached me and cupped my face in his hand, tilting my head up to meet his cold blue eyes. I could feel Adze tense, but he said nothing.

"If you're ever in danger, come to my house for protection," he said. "We'll get you home safely."

"Thank you," I whispered, not knowing what else to say. "Um, what house are you?"

Again that slight smile, and I could tell the other vampires were amused as well. I couldn't help the fact that I knew nothing about vampires. If he wanted me to go to him for help, I needed to know who he was.

"House Tennison," he said. "The premier vampire hunters in Redmond."

My eyes widened and he flashed a smile before he let go of me. He was a vampire hunter. He was a good ally, then. But frightening. This was a vampire who was allowed to kill other vampires, so he could potentially kill Adze. That must be what this was about. House Elviore had been framed for something so that vampire hunters would be allowed to kill them, but because Adze had requested their help instead, it hadn't worked. Who was responsible for it, though? And what exactly had been done?

"Um, what were the things they were bringing in?" I asked, wondering if they would answer my question or not. The leader seemed to consider and looked at Adze, who nodded.

"Bodies," he said.

I shivered again. Maybe I should have expected that. But...

"How were they explosive?"

"The letter used that word?" he asked. "I didn't see it."

"It was partially burned but was the only word that made sense."

The vampire studied me again. "If House Elviore were accused of killing that many humans, it would indeed be explosive news," he said. "Does that fit with what you understood?"

"Yes," I said, and relaxed just slightly. We weren't going to blow up. The danger really had passed.

The vampire looked at Adze. "He's an unusual choice for you. You should take better care of him," he said, and I felt Adze stiffen behind me. "He's too valuable to be wandering alone."

"I don't keep slaves," Adze said coldly. "And rest assured, he will no longer be wandering in dangerous areas."

"Of course," the leader said. "I apologize. It is your house, after all."

He went to Lilith and started speaking to her. She nodded to Adze and then focused on the leader. Adze, who was still holding my arm, pulled me towards the exit. Two vampires from House Tennison followed as we went outside. In a moment a limo pulled up and to my surprise, Dmitri got out. He eyed me curiously and bowed to the vampires, then opened the door. The other vampires got in first and then Adze got in and pulled me into the seat next to him. I could tell he didn't want the other vampires there, but he wasn't going to say anything. He had to stay in sight of the vampire hunters or else he would be accused of participating in whatever had happened.

Perhaps it was a blessing in disguise, because I knew he wanted to yell at me for leaving like that and walking straight into danger. Now that all of the various dangers seemed to have passed, though, I started to wonder why he was so angry. Was he angry that I had put myself in danger because I was valuable to his house? That I had disobeyed to the point where someone in another house could scold him in public like that? Or was he genuinely worried about me and the danger I had unknowingly put myself in? Or, and I didn't like to think of this, was he angry that I had let myself fall prey to that man, that I had wanted him and been desperate for a complete stranger? There was jealousy in his eyes as he looked at me, after all, and even though I hadn't said anything about how the man had attacked me, I knew that Adze at least knew. I hoped no one else knew. I wasn't sure what to make of Adze's anger, but at least he was as focused on me as I always was on him. Maybe I could turn that to my advantage. Once we were in private, we could sort things out and I wondered when that would be.

CHAPTER THIRTEEN: LATER

"We'll talk later."

That was what Adze had said before retreating into the basement with the other two vampires, leaving me confused and uncertain. What did he mean by later? After the vampires left? Before work tonight? After work? Never? Probably not never, I decided. He was too angry to ignore this.

Dmitri led me into the kitchen where a large meal was laid out. Margaret smiled at me brightly.

"You're back! I just returned with your car," she said. "Why did you go downtown? I was so worried when we heard you'd left with no word. You should let Dianne or Dmitri know before you leave."

They didn't know I had been attacked, I realized. The attacker had knocked me down; I glanced at my outfit and realized the scuff marks on my knees were barely visible. I looked fine. Of course they wouldn't know anything had happened to me.

"Master was quite concerned when he needed you and you weren't here," Dmitri added.

"I didn't know I needed to be here after work ended," I said.

"As long as we know where you are, it's not a problem to leave," Dmitri said. "But sometimes things come up at odd hours and you'll be needed. You'll be paid overtime, of course."

Given the amount I was getting paid, that really didn't matter, but I appreciated it all the same. As we ate Margaret's lasagna feast, I felt worse and worse about leaving without saying anything. I had worried them and I shouldn't have. I had worried Adze. They were right to worry, too, because I had gone somewhere I shouldn't and if I had asked Dmitri, he would have warned me not to go to the park. I had put myself into that position and could still feel the shame of losing control of my body like that.

After dinner, I went to my room and got ready for bed, then started up my computer. I knew if I tried to sleep right now, all I would think about was the feel of that man against my body and how much I had needed him. Plus, I should know more about vampires and about this city if I wanted to stay safe. But as I searched, there was very little information available on the practical aspects of living in a vampire city. I looked up House Tennison and aside from listing them as vampire hunters with eighteen vampires, there was nothing. Curious, I looked up the house my teacher had mentioned, House Salvite. They were also vampire hunters, I was surprised to see, and far larger. There were thirty-one confirmed vampires in the house, though it seemed the house size fluctuated more than most houses.

Redmond was the capital city of the vampires, I learned, and by far the largest. The other vampire cities were scattered around the world with populations in the thousands and rarely over a hundred vampires per city. Redmond had a population of four hundred thousand, but only a thousand vampires. I wondered if dhampir were counted among those and looked up the term. To my surprise, I found it. It was a real thing, though it was listed as a myth with no basis in reality. According to the site, it was unrelated to real vampires, as many vampire myths were. A dhampir was a vampire-human hybrid, usually born to a human female and sired by a vampire male. But the vampires tonight had definitely used that term. Were there actually hybrids hidden in vampire cities?

The possibilities stunned me. Were they vampires, or human? What limitations did they have? They could use glamours, obviously, but were they immortal? Could they be in the sun? How did no one know they existed? How many of the supposed four hundred thousand humans were actually dhampir? And why would a vampire possibly want a child with a human?

But if there were hybrids, and vampires did have children with humans, then maybe they loved those humans. If that were the case, then maybe Adze could love me. It wasn't much hope, but it was a little and that was enough for me. Assuming he didn't hate me after tonight. My heart clenched. He was so angry. Was he angry at me, or at what had happened? Did he blame me for not fighting harder?

As I scanned through the various vampire cities, the math started to add up for me. There were less than six thousand vampires in the world. Possibly far less. Yet they were an extremely influential force in the world and had fought the Species War to a draw. Some people even claimed they had really won the war, since now all humans were required to give pay a blood tax twice a year. I was due to go in this month, I realized. I would ask Dmitri if there were a station nearby. It was a painless process that only took a few hours and all employers were required to give paid time off to do it. It was strictly enforced and if you didn't go during your assigned months, a warrant was placed for your arrest. I had forgotten once in high school and been scooped up by the police only three days into the following month. Since I apologized and let them take me to the station immediately, they didn't charge me with anything, but I knew if you resisted, you were thrown in jail until you agreed to get your blood drawn.

It was several hours before I realized I needed to sleep. I had been awake for an incredibly long time, but it was light out now and I had my window open, so I felt awake. A little groggy, but awake. My mind was blurred enough that I could probably fall asleep but I worried about nightmares. Still, I needed to get on a night schedule so I shut the windows, drew the light-blocking shades, and the room plunged into darkness. I felt my way to the bed and collapsed.

Once more, a pressure leaned against me and I realized

someone was kissing me in my dreams. I panicked. It was the man again, the dhampir, and there was no one to stop him this time. Then I heard my name in a whispered voice and the tension left my body. It was Adze. He was here, in my dream, and he was holding me gently. This time I would stay asleep, I vowed. I would enjoy the feel of my vampire. I'd had sex with him now, in the real world, so maybe my dreams would go farther. Adze plundered my mouth as his hands traced down my body, then stroked my length as they never had in real life. I was hardening rapidly and I pressed against him, eager for more. This was right. I was allowed to lust after him. He drew one hand against my waist, tracing along my bare skin with a teasing slowness as he inched back towards my ass.

My eyes were closed, I realized. Maybe I would stay asleep if I couldn't see him. He slid his hand to my ass and squeezed, and I moaned softly. The world seemed to shift slightly. I was waking up. I tried to cling to him, cling to this, but suddenly I was in my bed, desperate for more.

It was getting dark and I moaned, fisting my hand in my groin. I was on fire with the memory of Adze. There was a glitter of light and I saw a firefly fluttering to the wall. Surely it hadn't been in here since the last time I had seen it. I tried to regain control of myself and went to open the window, but when I looked back, the firefly had moved and I couldn't see it anywhere. I left the window open and lay back in bed. I had a few hours before work and I wanted to sink back into Adze's embrace, and I let my hand move on my body the way Adze never allowed. As I climaxed, I thought of his face and the longing for him intensified my pleasure but left me feeling drained. Would he ever care about me, or just keep using me? Would I let him keep using me if that were the case? I wasn't sure. But the memory of the dhampir was almost gone and I was relieved. The thought of Adze had flushed it away just as the touch of Lilith's hand had flushed away that strange lust.

I got ready for the day – the night – quickly and by the time I was out of the shower and dressed, I heard Margaret cooking.

After saying good morning, and being reminded it was night, I ate the pancakes she had made for me. I hoped I didn't get fat here, since she seemed determined to give me plenty of food and not very healthy food either. I would have to get an exercise routine. Maybe I could jog around the grounds before work. That would be nice, and perhaps I would see more fireflies. I returned and shut my window before heading towards the garden.

Dmitri called my name just as I was about to go outside and I stopped, worried.

"I can go out here, can't I?" I asked.

"Yes," he said. "But Master would like to see you. Will you come with me?"

"Oh," I said, my breath hitching. So it was later. "Yeah, of course."

Dmitri led me to the stairs to the basement, oddly. He looked annoyed as he gestured down the stairs.

"It's still too light for his comfort, but he wants to talk to you. Be careful. Open the door at the end of the hall. Don't snoop. Humans are not normally allowed here."

I nodded, curious about Adze's private area. A vampire's lair, and I was invited in. I went down the stairs and darkness enveloped me. I stopped and looked around for a light, but there was none. I took a few steps forward and there was a soft glow from the walls, where I noticed small sconces. I couldn't tell how they were lit, but I appreciated the little bit of light they provided. There was a single hall with two doors on each side and I had to hold back my curiosity as I walked past them to the door at the end. I wanted to get invited back here, so I couldn't satisfy my curiosity. Yet.

I knocked when I reached the door, not knowing what I was supposed to do. The door opened and Adze stood there in the darkness. His eyes glowed in the soft lights like a firefly sparking to life. His eyes always seemed to glow, but here in the darkness, they shone with a strange light. He gestured for me to enter, studying me with those beautiful eyes. I entered and looked around. It was an office much like the one upstairs except the walls faded into shadow. There were four sconces, one on each wall, but the corners of the room were completely black. He had a similar desk and chair, and a similar computer, but there was no other furniture in the room. The floor and walls were stone and everything seemed very cold, though appropriate for a vampire.

A hand on my shoulder and Adze pulled me backwards against me, my back pressing against his front. My breath caught and I tensed at the intimacy of the position. His arm slid around my waist and held me in place.

"Why did you run from me yesterday?"

His voice was silken against my ear, but there was a hint of anger. I had no idea how to answer. How could I explain what I wanted? Especially when he was holding me like this and all I could think about was his body pressed against mine.

"Did he touch you?"

"What?" I was breathless and for a moment I didn't know who he meant. Then I remembered the man who had attacked me. Of course that's who he meant. That was the cause of his anger. He really was angry that I had been aroused by that man and my shoulders slumped in shame. "He didn't really touch me, but..."

"But he used a seduction glamour on you, didn't he," Adze said, and it wasn't a question.

"I guess so," I said. "I don't know what it was."

"How did he touch you?"

"He knocked me to the ground. Then he got over me, but then Lilith – um, the vampire," I stopped, not knowing what to call her.

"Mistress Lilith," Adze corrected.

"Yeah. Mistress Lilith hit him or something and he fell off me. But even so, I still felt- I couldn't- She touched my neck and I felt better."

He held me closer. "She cleared your mind of the glamour. So he didn't do anything to you? I won't judge you if he did."

"He didn't," I said. "She stopped it."

Adze sighed. "I'm sorry, Kairos. You should have been better protected. I should have had Dmitri watching to stop you from leaving on your own."

"It's my fault," I said, ashamed of the lust I had felt once again. But Adze wasn't blaming me for it. He wasn't even commenting on it, though he knew I had felt it. "I didn't know vampire cities were different."

"You shouldn't have left," Adze said. "Why did you leave?"

I was silent, thinking of him and the way he pushed me away once he was satisfied, ignoring my needs. He had to be using me but as he held me like this, maybe I didn't mind being used.

"Is it because of this?" he asked, pulling me close against him and wrapping his other arm around my chest so he was cradling me. "I had thought you enjoyed this. If you want me to stop, I will."

"No," I said quickly. "You don't need to stop. I just, um, want a little more."

"More?" he asked, his voice husky as he pressed against me. I could feel his cock against my ass through our pants and I shifted back, longing to feel him.

"I want you to touch me, too," I said softly.

CHAPTER FOURTEEN: EXPLOSIVE ENCOUNTER

There was a moment of silence and I wondered if I'd gone too far, been too bold about what I wanted. Then one of his hands slid forward along my inner thigh. He stopped about an inch from my cock and I trembled. I could feel a growing rigidity at the thought of his hand so close to me, not quite touching me.

"Touch you? Like this?" he asked, and stroked his fingers inward to brush against me very lightly. His fingers trailed from the base of my cock to the tip. I moaned and started to press forward against him, but his other hand kept me in place. He stroked again in the opposite direction, tracing my cock through my pants down my length and then brushing against my balls. "Or like that?"

"Yes," I said, arching against him as he stroked me again, and again, until I couldn't bear it. I needed him against my skin, I needed him inside of me.

"Your pants will be ruined," Adze observed, and started unbuttoning me. "Let's get them off."

My pants slid around my ankles, then my boxers. I stepped out of them and at his command, I pulled off my shirt as well until I was completely naked. He took my clothes and set them on the desk, returned behind me, and then – finally – he touched me. I shuddered against him at the unexpected pleasure.

"He couldn't make you feel this, could he," Adze murmured, and I flushed. I didn't want to think about the attack with Adze stroking me like this, but it was true: nothing that man had done came close to this. I had been overwhelmed with lust at the time, but now I realized how minor it was. As one of Adze's hand played with my cock and another pinched my nipple, I moaned and leaned back against him. I had wanted that man, but it was nothing compared to how I wanted Adze.

"More," I whispered. I was teetering on an orgasm already and desperately needed his touch.

Adze's hand flicked me forcefully and I cried out in surprise as I exploded. I was gasping for breath and felt him slick up his fingers with my cum, then he leaned me forward and slid his fingers along my ass.

"Do you want me, or do you just want this?" he asked softly, then slid two fingers into me.

"You," I moaned. "Only you. More of you."

I was thoroughly slicked up and his hand returned to my cock as I felt his penis pressing against me. I spread my legs and leaned forward, bracing myself with my hands on my thighs as he eased into me. I wanted more. I gasped and moaned as he rushed into me, his hand stroking and coaxing my cock. He bent me further forward and began thrusting into me, using the hand on my cock to slam me back on him as I cried out at the unexpected pleasure. It was incredible as he burst into me and I felt weak as my knees trembled. This was too much. There was no way I was going to last as his hand stroked me firmly, yanking me backwards onto his cock. This felt too good.

Dizzy with desire and lust, I moaned softly and felt my pleasure bubble up. I had just come, I tried telling myself. I couldn't be ready again so quickly, but the feel of Adze against me was irresistible. He thrust into me hard as his hand squeezed against me and it was too much.

"I'm gonna- Stop, I'm gonna-"

Adze increased his pace and my head spun as my body exploded a second time. I went limp against him, but he didn't slow for a moment, instead slicking his fingers up once again and sliding along my cock, which – for some reason – felt like I still needed more.

"You're mine," Adze hissed as he started withdrawing more fully between each thrust, still using his hand on my cock to hold me in place as I moaned. I squirmed against him but he was too strong, and I didn't really want him to stop. I wanted this to last forever, but I was exhausted and didn't know how long I could stand like this. I leaned forward, pressing against my thighs, gasping and shuddering as he kept going. It seemed to last forever, but soon I felt a trembling at the base of my cock and I knew I was going to come again. Would he keep going afterwards? I was so exhausted and the pleasure was so all-consuming. His hand began stroking me at a faster pace and I whined and struggled against him, but he was too strong. His pace increased and just as I gasped and cum spewed from my cock yet again, I felt him come deep inside me and the thrusting slowed, then stopped.

I was gasping for breath, my head nearly between my legs I was bent over so far, completely spent. He slowly pulled out and his slick hand moved from my cock to my chest as he drew me up to lean back against him. My heart was still racing and I couldn't catch my breath. He kissed my neck, just over my tattoo, and again seemed to hover there. This time I didn't imagine him biting me. That would be too much at this point. He kissed me as his hand stroked my chest. He could probably feel my pounding heart and he was getting my whole body sticky, but I didn't care. I just wanted to lean against him like this, cradled like this, my head spinning in a pleasure only he could give. Nothing in my life had prepared me for this kind of pleasure and I couldn't seem to come down.

"Is that what you wanted?" he asked, his breath tickling my ear. I shivered. I was still hard, I realized. He was holding me so intimately and even though I didn't want more, I knew I wouldn't refuse.

"Yes," I whispered.

Adze kissed my neck again and his hand traced down my

chest to my belly.

"What a mess you've made," Adze said. "See why I don't do this in my office?"

I blushed deeply as I looked down. There was indeed a mess from me, and I myself was a mess. Part of it was because of him, but most of it was me. Was that actually the reason he had avoided me upstairs? Because he wanted to avoid the mess? I hoped he invited me back down here more often, if that were the case.

Adze released me and went to his desk, taking out a towel and tossing it to me. I started to clean myself when he stopped me and pointed at the floor where the evidence of my pleasure had splattered against the stone.

"Clean yourself later," he said. "This should be done first."

I obeyed, kneeling to clean it up as he sat at the desk and wiped his own hand off on another towel. It was oddly arousing being on my knees like this, cleaning up after such an explosive encounter. When all the evidence was gone, I stood up awkwardly. It was cold and I hadn't noticed before. He was staring at me with those glowing eyes, and then he gestured to the door.

"There's a shower in the first door to the right. Don't go anywhere else. Come back here to dress."

I obeyed and felt shy going into the hall naked. The darkness helped. Even if Dmitri looked down here for some reason, he was unlikely to see me. I slipped into the room he indicated and looked around in surprise. It was a little brighter than the other room, though still quite dark, and it seemed like the entire room was a shower, with a shower head along one wall and a hose attachment hooked up to it. There was a grate in the center of the slanted floor for the water, but there were also strange hooks along the wall. Not hooks, really. They were circles of metal embedded in the wall around shoulder-height and some hanging down from the ceiling. I had no clue what they were for. I showered quickly and shivered as the water was freezing and I couldn't seem to figure out how to change the temperature.

There were no towels, I realized as I shut the water off. Adze had towels in his office, but was I supposed to walk back there dripping wet? I tried to brush off as much water as possible but it seemed like I had no options. I slid the door open and peeked out. Almost pitch black. I snuck back to where I hoped Adze was waiting with towels. He was at his desk and as I came in and quickly shut the door behind me, he eyed me. A very faint smile appeared on his impassive lips and my heart throbbed. He was smiling. I didn't know what I was doing, but I needed to keep doing it.

"Come here," he said. I approached, hoping I wouldn't do anything to disappoint him. I was leaving a trail of wet footprints, I realized. I had shaken as much water out of my hair as possible but it was still dripping down along my body. It was quite cold in here.

Adze got out a towel but didn't toss it to me. Instead, he just watched me as I shifted awkwardly. That smile was still there as his eyes ran up and down my body and I crossed my arms across my chest, a little embarrassed to be so exposed. Somehow, being sopping wet made me feel more vulnerable than if I had just been naked. Finally, he stood up and came to my side, then wrapped the towel around my shoulders. He started patting me dry and I nearly melted into him. He was drying me off. It was such a sweet, sexy gesture and when he finished with my body, he tousled the towel against my hair to dry it. I was aroused, I realized, and as he dried my hair, one of his hands slid down my chest to rest just above my hard cock.

"You like this?" he asked.

"Yes," I said softly.

"Good," he said, leaning forward to kiss my forehead. "Your clothes are on the desk. Get dressed quickly. We're needed upstairs."

CHAPTER FIFTEEN: BLOOD TAX

Work passed in a blur. I was exhausted and just wanted to sleep, and during my lunch hour, I even napped a little after scarfing some food. Margaret was quite sympathetic and encouraged me to end early, and when I returned to work, she made a point of going with me and telling Dmitri not to let me work too long.

I was working a little slower than on previous nights, partially because I was so tired, but partially because I was distracted. As I sat there, I could still feel Adze inside me, still feel wave after wave of pleasure, still see that slight smile on his face. I didn't know what I had done to make him smile and that bothered me. I had to be extra careful while translating not to let my lurid thoughts come across in my interpretations. I still finished a lot, but not nearly as much as the night before. I was just considering leaving when there was a knock on the door. I looked up hopefully, though of course Adze didn't knock, he just showed up. I hadn't seen him since we had returned upstairs and I was hoping to talk to him again before I went to sleep.

It was Dmitri and I stifled my disappointment. He came to my side and rested a hand on my shoulder, looking at the screen and the email I was on. I was about half-done with it. There were so many emails to get through, but at least they went a lot faster than letters.

"Finish this, and then go to bed," Dmitri said. "You've done a lot tonight."

"Thanks," I said. He didn't move and I looked at him. He was watching me consideringly.

"You know, Kairos, if Master ever tells you to do something and you don't want to, you don't have to," Dmitri said seriously. "He won't fire you."

I blushed, wondering if he knew what had happened between us or if there were some other reason for this out-of-the-blue advice. Dmitri studied me a moment longer, then sighed and looked away.

"The Master often wants things he shouldn't, and you need to be able to refuse him. I can tell you won't, not yet, but you always can."

"Why are you telling me this?" I asked nervously, because another thought sprang to mind. He might not know about what Adze and I had done, and he was still warning me. Were there other things to be worried about? I thought of all the stories I heard about working for vampires and the risks, how vampires often fed on their servants until there was nothing left of the servant except a dry husk. Adze had paused over my neck several times. He hadn't bitten yet, but would he? Was he just waiting? Would I be able to refuse him if he wanted my blood? I didn't really think I would refuse, and maybe that's what Dmitri was warning about.

"Master isn't around humans like you much," Dmitri explained. "But he's fascinated by humans. He's already trusting you quite a bit and if he wanted something from you, I expect you would feel... pressured to give it to him. You can say no."

I shivered. Maybe Adze would feed on me. But I frowned.

"Isn't he around you and Dianne and Margaret all the time? Aren't you human?"

My mind flashed to the myth of dhampir and my eyes widened. "You have to be human," I said a little desperately, thinking of the men who had attacked me and used their glamour against me. No one here was anything like that. They hadn't attacked or manipulated me at all.

"Master told me you were attacked," Dmitri said, and he brushed back my hair. "We're not like them, but we're not human."

I shivered and withdrew from him. "Dianne and Margaret too? Are you... dhampir?"

"Yes," he said. "Almost everyone in Redmond has vampire blood. It's extremely rare to see someone like you who is pure human."

"So is your father a vampire? Who is he?" I asked, but Dmitri shook his head.

"Most dhampir are generations past their vampire heritage. We still have some powers but only a little vampire blood. I'm one eighth vampire, which is pretty strong. Dianne is actually a fourth, she's very strong, but Margaret is a hybrid, which is most common, and just means she has some vampire blood from multiple family lines but not enough to qualify for any privileges. It's rare for dhampir to know who their vampire ancestor was. Vampires don't keep track after the first generation. Too many of us."

"Privileges? Does that mean powers?"

"No," Dmitri said, glancing away. "None of this information is really for humans to hear. Humans who live in vampire cities often find out about it, as you did, if a dhampir reveals themselves to that human. But we prefer to keep the details of our society a secret."

"I'd never even heard of dhampir," I said. "And it didn't show up as a real thing when I looked it up."

"Well, as I've said before, it's extremely rare that a human would be hired for your position, in an ancient house, and there are some dangers in that. Nothing you can't handle, and nothing that should put you at risk, but just remember that you don't have to do everything Master requests."

"I'll remember," I promised, though I knew I would find it almost impossible to refuse anything Adze wanted from me. I enjoyed what he wanted too much. I couldn't tell if Dmitri knew what Adze had done to me or if this were a blanket warning, and I didn't want to press again and risk him finding out if he didn't already know, so I didn't say anything else. Dmitri looked at the computer again, at the email I was nearly finished with.

"Master won't see you today. He's not at the house. When you're done, you can just leave. Take a nap, then have some dinner, and sleep as long as you can today."

"I will," I said. Dmitri stood and left. I quickly finished the email and sent it to him, then stretched and felt a tingle along my limbs from the remembered pleasure of Adze's touch. I was quite sore from what we had done and I had never enjoyed being sore before. I checked with Margaret and told her to wake me for dinner, then went to my room and sank into a deep sleep.

The next day and night went smoothly, but I didn't see Adze at all. Dmitri informed me that he was out of the house again. My pace returned to normal without the distraction of sex and with the knowledge that Adze wasn't going to show up at any time. Even though the emails had seemed endless, I was actually quite close to finishing them. One or two more days. But as I went to sleep after an almost-full day of work, I wondered what Adze was doing. Was he avoiding me? He had smiled at me; had I done something since then to disappoint him? As the sun began setting on another day and I went to breakfast, my heart was heavy. I missed him and I wasn't sure what I had done to make him ignore me. I didn't want to be ignored again.

Dmitri and Dianne ate with me, which didn't always happen, and both seemed in good moods. Margaret was out for her weekly trip to the big store across town. The fruits and vegetables we ate were purchased every day from a nearby vendor, but the bulk goods came from across town. Although Dmitri and Dianne were both quite reserved, they were far more friendly now than they had been at first. I was part of the house now. They accepted me. But did Adze?

"You'll be getting your first paycheck today," Dmitri said.

"Are you going to spend it?"

"No," I said. "I'll just put everything in savings."

Then I paused. "Wait, I get my paycheck today? What day is it?"

"First of the month," Dmitri said. "Would you prefer a different schedule?"

"First of the month?" I repeated, my mind flashing to everything I had to finish before the month was done. "Um, I may need to leave today. Is there a blood station nearby?"

Dmitri and Dianne looked puzzled. "Of course there's one, but why would you need to leave?"

"I can go during the day," I said. "I forgot my month. I put it off and then got the job and didn't realize the month was already over. I really don't want to get arrested again. I heard they're not as easy on you the second time."

"Oh, the blood tax," Dianne said, sounding amused. "You've been arrested for that before?"

I blushed. "I forgot once. I know you're supposed to do it at the beginning of the month but I always put it off. I'm sorry. I won't take long."

"You won't be going," Dianne said. "You no longer have to pay. No one who works for a vampire house has to give blood."

I stared at her in surprise. "Are you sure?"

She glanced at Dmitri. "I'm not, actually. I've never heard of a pure human like you working for a vampire house like ours. Will he have to pay?"

"The law is that anyone who belongs to a vampire house is exempt," Dmitri said slowly, tapping a finger against his lips and deep in thought. "But it's also the law that all pure humans are required to do it. I'll check with Adze. They might make a new law just for you," he added with a smile. "Because regardless of the law, he won't allow it. You won't be giving blood."

I considered. Even if I didn't give blood at the vampire blood station, I should still give blood. It wasn't safe to give too frequently, but I hadn't given in over a month. If I didn't need it for the tax, I should give my blood to the humans.

"Is there a human donation place nearby, then?"

"Donating what?"

"Blood."

"Humans don't need blood," Dianne pointed out.

I was used to that response, since almost no human considered the needs of their fellow humans. I wouldn't even know about it except my dad had nearly lost his life and only a blood transfusion had saved him. Blood was hard to get and a lot of people died because there wasn't enough. I had a rare blood type, too, so everyone was always grateful when I donated.

They seemed surprised to learn the human uses of blood, as most people were, and since they were clueless about it, I suspected I might have to go to a human city to donate. It didn't seem like a vampire city would have anything to help humans like that. But I asked again, just to check, and Dianne shook her head.

"You won't be giving any more blood, Kairos. It's very generous and it's good of you to help humans like that, but no one in a vampire house gives blood. Once you're marked," and she gestured to my tattoo, "Your blood is different. It would hurt any human you gave it to and it's almost worthless to vampires outside of our house."

I pressed my palm against my tattoo. I hadn't realized it changed anything for me, but it seemed to have done a lot. It let vampires from my house know when I was in danger, it prevented other vampires from feeding on me, and it seemed to have changed the very blood in my veins. I felt like I should have gotten a warning of some sort before Adze had done it to me.

"What about when I leave?" I asked. "Will it go back to normal?"

"Are you thinking about leaving?" Dmitri asked, exchanging a worried look with Dianne.

"Not now, but in a year or two. When I've saved up enough.

What happens then?"

"You could consider staying longer," Dianne suggested with a smile. "We'll do what we can to make you happy here."

I looked at her, and at Dmitri. "I, um, I don't know yet. I just started. Everything's still so strange here. But if I do leave, what happens?"

"Master will remove our house's mark, and you'll return to normal," Dmitri said. "There are no long-term physical consequences of working for vampires."

I was relieved, but Dianne's offer made me consider. Would I want to stay longer? I couldn't ever imagine wanting to leave Adze's side, but I had planned on being a professor my entire life. Even before I knew what I wanted to teach, I wanted to teach. Both of my parents were professors and we had all assumed I would be one, too. What would they think if I didn't get a PhD? I had only told them about this job in the vaguest of terms since I didn't want them to worry. I only talked to them once or twice a week and I realized it had been a while, but I didn't plan on telling them much. I had a job and was saving up for school. That was all they wanted to know. But did I want to go back to school?

"Is this the only job here?" I asked. "I mean, are there promotions or anything?"

"Would you want to do something different?"

"The work's fine, I like it, but aren't you supposed to always be getting new jobs and advancing and stuff?"

That was what I knew about life outside of academia. For professors, you had to start as a lowly lecturer, get experience and publications, and then compete for the incredibly rare tenure-track jobs scattered across the country. Once you had that, you had to slave away and publish like mad to actually get tenure, but then you had a relatively secure job with good pay. From what I knew of other industries, it was a rat race with everyone desperate to advance however they could, taking as many jobs as possible and trying to get ahead. It had never interested me, but I knew that's what you were supposed to do with your life.

"Your salary is always open for negotiation, and there are benefits that could be added in time," Dmitri said. "But jobs in vampire houses tend to be very stable. My job is mostly the same as when I started almost ten years ago, but more responsibilities have been added."

I considered. That actually sounded quite good, if it were a stable job. And I already had the job, so I wouldn't have to search for it and work myself to death trying to get it. Maybe I would consider staying longer than a year.

"I don't know what I'd spend my money on if I'm not saving for school," I said. "That's the only reason I wanted a job in the first place."

"You can still save it," Dianne said. "Maybe in time you'll find something you want."

She glanced at her watch and I glanced at mine, too, and realized it was almost nine. I needed to change into fancier clothes. I had taken a jog around the grounds after waking up and planned on making that my routine. Once I had my sleep schedule under control, I hoped to take another jog before going to bed, too, but for now, one walk a day was probably good. I stood up and stretched, then took my plate to the sink and rinsed it off.

"I'll be ready in a few minutes," I said. "Is Adze here today?"

"Master Adze," Dmitri said firmly, and I blushed.

"Sorry. It's weird calling my boss that."

He shook his head but was smiling, so I knew he wasn't mad. "Don't call him that to his face. He expects obedience. And yes, he is here today. I'm sure he'll be in to see you at some point. Some mail came in during the day, but you know what order to do things by now, don't you?"

I agreed cheerfully and we split, me heading to my room to change and them to their jobs. Adze would see me today. My heart was singing.

CHAPTER SIXTEEN: MASTER

I was almost finished with the backlog of emails. I was getting more new messages than yesterday, and Dmitri had brought me two small batches of physical letters throughout the night. I worked quickly, but after each email and each letter I looked up, hoping to see Adze watching me. As I worked, I wondered if I would be happy doing this for the rest of my life. It was certainly interesting and challenging work, and I knew that if I stayed, I would definitely learn all about the house's secrets. I knew a few of them now, but there were still so many unknowns. Luckily, none of the messages I read indicated anything dangerous or imminent and I felt like I could relax. We were safe, for now, and I was honored that I had helped secure that safety.

The emails and the letters were still orders about vampire deaths and I wondered how it was possible that so many vampires were dying. It seemed like at least one vampire was killed per week. Based on what I read, there seemed to be patterns: a vampire would lose control – it was usually referred to as "withdrawal," which was also the term that had been used at the cathedral – and humans would be killed. The vampire hunters would track down and kill the vampire, but it seemed like there were patterns in which vampires went into withdrawal and where the humans were killed. I wondered what they were in withdrawal from, since there was no reason a vampire couldn't get blood. Every human on the planet gave blood twice a year and there were billions of people compared to thousands of vampires. Did they really need that much blood?

I couldn't figure it out and the messages were little help, but I was starting to see patterns in the attacks as I worked. They tended to be grouped by location, with one or more happening in the northern district, then the east, then north again, then south, then west. They were scattered and the timing between them was random, with some having weeks between them and some mere hours, but the locational pattern was the same. I suspected that the pattern was about to shift to the south and wondered if I should tell Dmitri or Adze, or if this were something they already knew. Cautiously, I sent a message to Dmitri letting him know I'd noticed a pattern and wondering if he was interested. After a moment, he responded that he would talk to me soon.

I finished another few emails and looked up, as I had been doing after every email, and saw nothing. I turned back to my computer and heard a footstep. I looked up again and saw nothing, then I realized Adze was standing next to me. I flushed. How long had he been here? Why hadn't I noticed him? I had only been looking in the center of the room. I hadn't thought to look anywhere else. Adze reached out and stroked my head as I stared at him, stunned that he was here.

Memories of our last encounter flooded through me and I could feel my cheeks turning red as my heart pounded loudly and I tried to keep breathing steadily.

"You've been waiting for me?" Adze asked.

"Yeah," I whispered. "Dmitri said you'd be in to see me today."

"Dmitri said you'd found something. Tell me."

He withdrew his hand from my cheek and leaned next to me, looking at my computer. Hesitantly, nervous because he was so close, I showed him what I had found and explained why I thought the south was about to be hit next. He listened carefully, nodding occasionally, and when I was done, he clasped my shoulder and stared into my eyes. I felt like I was melting.

"Thank you, Kairos," he said. I loved hearing him say my

name. "This will help us a lot, and save lives. This job suits you."

His hand moved from my shoulder back to my face as he stroked my cheek with the back of his hand, drawing his fingers across my cheekbone. I drew in a sharp breath, my thoughts scattering in the pleasure of his touch.

"It's almost time for you to finish," Adze said. "When you're done, come to my office."

"Sure," I said, brightening. His office wasn't nearly as good as his private room in the basement, but either place meant me and him alone and I wanted to feel his body against mine. I missed him.

Adze ran a finger along my cheekbone and traced the edge of my lower lip as I trembled and tried to fight a wave of arousal. Then he turned and left. I got back to work immediately and tried not to rush. I was working until 4:30 today, as Dmitri had recommended, and would leave then regardless of how quickly I worked. I didn't want to rush any conclusions and mess up my interpretations, because I didn't want to disappoint Adze. These messages were important and I needed him to value me.

I finished and let Dmitri know that I was leaving for the day. He told me to wait a minute before leaving, as was usual, then paused.

"Did Master talk to you about what you found already?" he asked.

"Yes," I said. "Should I wait for you to come and explain it to you, too?"

"No, he'll inform me later. But Kairos, remember what I said," he said. "You can refuse him. And remember to address him properly."

"Thanks, Dmitri," I said, though I knew I wouldn't be refusing Adze. I could at least call him Master. It was such a suggestive name to call someone and I wondered that everyone else was able to say it without any problems. It was one of the reasons I was pretty sure Adze didn't sleep with anyone else in the house, though I had briefly worried about it. If they had ever seen or felt Adze the way I had, they would never be able to call him Master without blushing.

Adze called for me to come in when I knocked but as I shyly entered, I realized he was on the phone. He gestured for me to wait and I cautiously went to the chair I had sat in last time as he spoke in that strange language. From his tone of voice, he was annoyed and trying to wrap up the conversation and after a few minutes, he said what had to be goodbye and hung up, then turned to me.

"Did I give you permission to sit down?" he asked.

I remembered how Rory had stood in front of him and realized that he probably expected humans to wait for him in the middle of the room, not make themselves comfortable. He wasn't angry, nor did he sound annoyed anymore. His voice was quite warm, now. But I couldn't read any emotion in his face and stood quickly.

"Come here," he said, extending his hand. I placed my hand in his and he yanked me forward onto his lap. Flustered, it took me a moment to realize that I was straddling him and my increasing arousal was completely exposed. He turned me on as no one else ever had. Everything he did was sexy.

He locked his hands behind my waist and stared at me with his glowing, dark eyes. I wanted to kiss him but since he didn't look like he wanted to kiss me, I didn't. I did shift against him, because my hips were far enough back that I couldn't feel him and I wanted him pressed against my groin. He let me scoot closer until I could feel him and I relaxed against him, my cock finally resting on his body. He was hard too, I realized with pleasure. He liked this as much as I did. But he wasn't smiling. I needed to make him smile again, because it was the most beautiful thing in the world.

"You're doing very well in your job," Adze said softly. "Do you have more questions for me?"

I should ask about my job, I knew. That was why he was offering. But with him this close to me, all I could think about was our time together. Still, he valued me for my work ethic as well as my body, so I needed to focus. I had started to figure out the patterns, but I did have a lot of questions.

"Why was someone trying to hurt House Elviore?"

"There is another house committing crimes, and we're researching them on behalf of the vampire hunters. They only recently found out how close we are to exposing them and they're taking drastic measures," Adze said. "You saved our house. We're very grateful to you."

I preened at the praise, but he wasn't smiling. He was just stating facts. I was a little chilled that there was another house determined to hurt my house, but it was a secondary concern right now. I wondered if he'd allow another question, because aside from work concerns, I did want to ask about us.

"Um, about last time," I started, and he didn't stop me. "Did you enjoy me... Master?"

I blushed as I said the word, wondering if it were appropriate, but my worries evaporated when the corners of his lips lifted in what had to be a smile. He was smiling at me again. I was doing something right but I still didn't know what, exactly.

"That's the first time you've called me that," he said, then leaned forward so his lips brushed my ear. "I like it."

My heart was pounding. I would call him Master as much as possible, I vowed, but he hadn't actually answered my question. It seemed like the answer was yes, though. I shivered as I felt something warm against my earlobe, then he sucked it. Hard. I fought a moan at the sudden pleasure, my hands wrapping around his neck as I leaned into him. His lips worked down my neck and as usual, paused over my tattoo. I remembered what Dmitri had said, and what I had worried about, but none of that mattered. I wanted to keep pleasing him in any way that I could.

"Are you going to bite me?" I asked softly.

He kissed my tattoo and stared into my eyes, our faces nearly touching, we were so close.

"You sound like you want me to," he said.

"Do you want to... Master?"

Again that smile. I was delighted to have found such an easy way to make him smile. Now that I had seen that slight smile, though, I wanted more. I wanted a real smile.

"Blood from a willing human is a rare thing," he said, leaning to kiss my cheek. "You shouldn't offer it so easily."

I couldn't tell if that meant he did or didn't want to bite me, but it did seem like he wasn't going to regardless of what he wanted.

"Dmitri tells me you were thinking of giving away your blood," he continued. "Your blood belongs to me now. You belong to me."

I remembered the blood tax and Dmitri and Dianne basically forbidding me from donating blood. It would be strange not having to report in, but what he said was true. My blood was his now. And so was I.

I curled forward to his chest, resting my head on his shoulder. My cock was pressed against his and I sighed in pleasure at being held like this. I wanted more, but at the moment, his arms around me and his body against mine were enough. He started stroking my back.

"Did you enjoy it, last time?" he asked.

"Yes... Master," I said, still stumbling over the word but needing to please him by saying it.

"All of it?"

I hesitated, wondering what he meant. Had it seemed like I enjoyed some of it less than the rest?

"Yes," I said. "All of it."

"Good," he said, stroking his hand up my back to tousle my hair. I loved when he did that. "Come downstairs at noon. Everyone else will be asleep. Come to the same room you were in before. Nowhere else. Understand?"

My heart pounded in my chest and my mouth went dry at the thought of repeating what had happened. I couldn't speak, so I nodded. He pushed me back slightly, that smile still on his lips. It was only barely a smile, though. What did I need to do to get more? He leaned forward and kissed my lips gently.

"Then you're dismissed for the night."

I felt like I was in a daze as I stood up. I was still hard, still aroused, but he gestured for me to leave through the main door and I obeyed without thinking. Once in the hall, I clutched my pants. I needed to cool down so I could walk around without everyone knowing I was turned on. I would be absolutely humiliated if anyone saw me like this. I heard footsteps and slid into the shadows, trying to be as unobtrusive as possible as Dmitri approached and opened the door to Adze's office, taking a step inside.

"You wanted something?" Dmitri asked, and I flushed as I hid. Had Adze summoned him, knowing I was right here and knowing what state I was in? Somehow, the threat of getting caught was making me harder and I carefully snuck past the open door as Dmitri faced Adze. I could feel Adze's eyes on me and knew he saw me as I darted past. Maybe that was why he had asked Dmitri into his office, because otherwise Dmitri would have seen me. I raced to the nearby bathroom, locked the door, and let out a sigh. Then I smiled. I would be seeing Adze again and I couldn't wait.

CHAPTER SEVENTEEN: DARKNESS

I was up at eleven and took a shower, trying to kill time until noon. I wanted to be early, since he seemed to like me being early, but not too early. I was aiming for five minutes early. That was enough to definitely be early, but not enough to annoy him if he wasn't expecting me. I dressed carefully. I wanted to look good, but there was a good chance I wasn't going to be in the clothes long, so I needed pants and a shirt that came off easily. I blushed as I selected my outfit. Ease of undress had never been one of my considerations before. And finally, a quarter to noon, I left my room and made sure no one was up and around. It was quiet and I went to the top of the stairs and glanced at my watch. I had ten minutes. Maybe I would just go now instead of waiting any longer. He wouldn't be too annoyed, I didn't think.

I crept down the stairs, one hand on the wall because it was so dark. As I reached the bottom, I waited for my eyes to adjust to the dim lights as they had last time I was here. They didn't. I waited a little longer, then, one hand still on the wall, felt my way forward. I couldn't be late, after all. I felt the two doors as I passed them, then the door in front of me. I knocked. I still couldn't see and it was quite disorienting. I felt the door in front of me open and a hand took my arm and led me forward. I heard the door shut behind me. It was completely black.

"Um, are there any lights?" I asked. Adze had let go of my arm and I now had no clue where he was, or where I was in relation to anything else in the room.

"I can see you just fine," Adze said, and there was a hint of amusement in his voice. "I won't let you trip on anything. Take a few steps forward."

I hesitantly put one foot forward, feeling along the ground, then took another slow step, and another. I stopped. It was strange knowing that he could see everything perfectly while I couldn't see a thing. I felt at a distinct disadvantage and I wondered if he often used this technique to disorient humans who were so reliant on sight and sunlight.

"You don't need to be frightened," he said gently. "I won't let anything happen to you. Do you trust me?"

"Yes," I said, trying to relax in the darkness.

"Good," he said. "Then strip."

I blinked in surprise. He wanted me to strip... in the pitch black? But he could see. So it wasn't really pitch black, not for him. I cautiously untucked my shirt and pulled it over my head. I couldn't even see the fabric less than an inch from my eyes, it was so dark. I'd never been in such absolute darkness in my life and it was starting to be terrifying. I stopped once my shirt was off, letting it dangle from my hand.

"You can drop it," Adze said. He was in the same place, it sounded like. In front of me. But it was so dark.

"Um, can there be a little light?"

I heard him shifting and tensed. He touched my shoulder, then took the shirt from my hand. I heard it drop to the floor. I trembled. He was right next to me and I couldn't see him. I flinched as his hand caressed my cheek.

"Are you frightened?" he asked, and I nodded. "Don't be. I'm here."

He embraced me and I sank into him gratefully, but no mention was made of turning on any lights. Was he really going to leave me in the dark when he knew it scared me? He had left me without release, I considered, even though I hadn't believed he would. So he probably would keep the absolute darkness. He wanted it, therefore that was what happened. I shut my eyes as he cradled me. Shutting my eyes helped. I could pretend I couldn't see because of that, not because of the darkness around me. It helped me feel a little more in control.

"Humans are so beautiful when they're afraid," he said, his breath whispering past my cheek. I opened my eyes to look at him but it was all darkness. He was right next to me and I saw nothing.

"Before we made peace with the humans, we would hunt them," Adze continued. "On moonless nights, we would hunt them in the darkness and watch their terror. Their eyes, with pupils so beautifully dilated, their quick breathing, their rapid heartbeats."

He tightened his arms around me and I inhaled sharply as his hand stroked my inner thigh and I started to respond.

"Their arousal," he whispered. "So beautiful. And when we caught them..."

He kissed my tattoo and I shivered. He was talking about hunting humans and drinking their blood, yet I was turned on.

"You would not mind being caught, I think," Adze murmured. "Of course, I would not catch you the same way I caught them. Catching you would be quite enjoyable. For both of us. What do you think? Should I hunt you?"

I shivered again. "I'd rather you just caught me," I said.

There was a huff of breath against my neck. Was that laughter? Had I made him laugh? He had to be smiling. I ached to see that smile, but the ebony darkness was all-encompassing. He kissed my cheek.

"Then why don't I catch you, and see how you feel?"

His hand stroked along my thigh again and I moaned softly. I wondered what he meant, but I knew I wanted it, whatever it was. Was he finally going to bite me? He could. I would let him. I just wanted him.

His hand went to my arm as he stepped back from me.

"Come with me," he said. "I won't let you trip."

He tugged me and I hesitantly took a step. He pulled faster and I started walking, the darkness oppressive as he hurried me faster than I liked. He paused me and I heard a door open, and then a few more steps forward before another pause as he must have shut the door. We had to be in one of the other rooms and I wondered what was in here. It couldn't be the shower room; the floor was stone but not as smooth as it had been there. I was led forward again, slower this time, and he seemed to be guiding me around things as he put both hands on me to assist me.

"There's a bed in front of you," he finally said. "Reach forward to feel it, then get up on it."

I obeyed and felt in front of me, bending over slightly until I felt silk. Cautiously, I felt my way forward and then climbed onto the bed. It was higher than usual but easy enough to climb on to. I was careful, checking to make sure the bed didn't end abruptly, and I had no way to judge how far onto the bed I was or when he wanted me to stop. But after a few moments he commanded me to stop and I did, still on my hands and knees and wondering if I should lay down or stay like this. I wondered what I looked like, and if he were smiling right now. I wanted to see that smile. How was this kind of darkness even possible?

I flinched as his hands caressed my hips, then slid forward to unbutton and unzip my pants. I shifted to help him pull them off, then he slid my underpants off as well. I shivered. It was cold here, but I was so turned on I felt like I was on fire. I stayed on my hands and knees because he hadn't told me otherwise, and his hands slid from my ankles up my legs, then along my hips to my sides. I twitched as he ran his fingers along my ribs and it tickled me. He continued slowly stroking up my body, over my shoulders and then down my arms. He was over me, I realized, crouching on the bed over me. Then the bed shifted and his hands left me for a moment. I heard something clinking, then his hands were on my wrists again.

"If I've caught you, I need some way to keep you in place," Adze said in a soft voice.

Something cold wrapped around my wrist and he pulled my hands forward. There was a snap and I realized he had

121

handcuffed me. I tried to pull back, but my wrists were tied together at the top of the bed. I shivered. I had never been bound before and it was rather thrilling.

Adze's hands ran back down my body to my hips. He pulled at the creases of my hips and I scooted back, though I couldn't go far with my hands bound. He caressed my ass and I shut my eyes against the darkness, enjoying his warm hand against my sensitive skin. His hand vanished and I heard a whoosh of air, then something smacked against my ass. Hard. I cried out in surprise and pain and Adze's hand returned, caressing me again. Had he spanked me?

"Do you want me to stop?" he asked. He had. But even though my ass was stinging in pain, I realized I was quite turned on. Was I the type of person who liked getting tied up and spanked? Maybe I was. I had to be, or this situation wouldn't be getting me so hot. Was there anything wrong with that, if Adze wanted it? I licked my lips.

"I want what you want," I whispered.

"No," Adze said, to my surprise. "You need to answer for yourself. Do you want me to stop?"

Was he really going to make me say it? Admit what kind of person I was? Admit what turned me on? I flushed. I knew I was bright red and wondered if Adze could see it. It was so dark in here but instead of being terrifying, it was beginning to feel arousing. I felt helpless in his hands, helpless in the darkness. And I liked it.

"Don't stop," I said.

I heard him lean forward and then he kissed my back. He leaned up and I heard the rush of air again, and then I cried out as he spanked me again. This time, he didn't pause before smacking me again. I moaned softly as he continued, and sank until my head was against the bed. I kept trying to grab on to something for support as the stinging pain continued, but there was nothing to hold. I whimpered and suddenly, it stopped. Then I felt his hands on my hips again. He was breathing heavily, I realized. Was he turned on as well?

His fingers slid down my crack to my opening and I winced as my skin stung, but the pain was almost refreshing against the backdrop of my pleasure. Adze slid one finger inside me, then two, and I tried to relax against him and not squirm. I wanted more. I wanted him. I didn't like having to wait like this and my cock was starting to drip with my need. How was I possibly this turned on? Then his fingers teasingly slid out and I felt what I really wanted against me.

He entered me slowly and I struggled to hurry him, but he kept gripping my hips so I couldn't back up. Not that I could move very far; my arms were completely extended and I couldn't move more. By the time he was fully inside me, I was panting and sweating and desperate for more. He paused deep inside me, leaning over me until I could feel his chest against my back. His breath tickled my ear.

"What do you want?" he asked.

"You," I gasped. "Please, more."

He leaned back and withdrew quickly, then thrust into me. I moaned and arched my back into the motion as he began penetrating me at a pace that finally satiated my need. I clenched my hands into fists, struggling to brace myself as he pounded into me. The skin on my ass stung and as he thrust into me, I gasped and moaned and twisted under him as my cock felt like it would explode. But I held back, because I knew he wouldn't want me to come until he was ready. But it was getting harder and harder and I was getting so desperate.

"Please," I whispered.

"Please what?" he asked between breaths.

"Please let me come," I pleaded.

His hand slid to my cock and his pace increased. He stroked my length and I twitched under him, barely able to hold back. This was driving me insane and there was no way I could control myself with him touching me like this.

"You have permission," he said softly.

Then his hand clenched around my cock and he jerked hard, and everything seemed to explode. I cried out again and felt a surge of pleasure and pain and ecstasy seizing my belly as I came. He was still inside me, still moving in me, and I felt a smaller explosion within me as he came, but my body was still singing with pleasure until I finally caught my breath and gasped in air, desperate for some sort of control as my body hummed with satisfied desire. Air flowed back into my lungs as my body relaxed. I was exhausted and collapsed into the bed, turning my head as I breathed heavily and lay there, completely limp.

Adze tapped my ass and I flinched, but it was a playful tap, not a spank. I heard him moving and then the metal around my wrists was removed.

"Good boy," Adze murmured. "Get up now."

I achingly scooted off the bed at his command. He took my hands and led me through the room. He opened the door and shut it again once we were out, then steered me to a different door. The floor was slick and I guessed it was the shower. Something glimmered slightly and I blinked in surprise. I could almost make out the wall in front of me. There was light. Vague light, but it was no longer pitch black.

"Stay here as your eyes adjust, then shower, dress, and return to your room. Get some sleep," Adze commanded. "I'll see you at work tonight."

"Yes," I said, because I didn't know what else to say. Was that it? I found myself longing for more even though my body was spent. I could just make out Adze leaving and then the door shut and I was alone. I realized the light was slowly getting brighter, so slowly that it wasn't painful. I would have been blinded had the light returned too quickly and I was grateful for Adze's thoughtfulness. When I could see well enough, I noticed that there was a towel on a small stool across from the shower head. He was indeed thoughtful. Then I turned the freezing water on and tried to cool the residual lust that lingered despite my exhaustion. Adze was incredible, but I wondered if I was biting off more than I could chew. I had already given him permission to spank me; would he ask for more? Would he eventually drink my blood? I wouldn't mind, I decided. Whatever he wanted, I would give it. Anything for him.

CHAPTER EIGHTEEN: FRAUGHT MESSAGES

I barely got any sleep after returning to my room. My mind kept repeating what had happened and how wonderful it felt, but how terrifying, too. Was I getting in over my head? I had never done anything like this before, but I had definitely enjoyed having my hands bound like that, and having him spank me like that was quite arousing. But how much farther would he take it? Was I okay with this? Well, I would worry about it later. I finally shut my eyes and sank into sleep.

The pressure against my body was almost familiar by now. I was dreaming and I knew it would be Adze if I opened my eyes. But I didn't want to open my eyes, because I didn't want to wake up. His hands caressed my body, sliding along the smooth skin of my back, tracing delicately along my chest and across my nipples. I arched my back and gasped. This felt so good. I could feel his breath against my cheek and ear. He was so close to me and I desperately wanted him, the same way I wanted him when I was awake. But I wanted this sweet side to him as well. There was no pain or loss of control here and I wasn't sure which I liked more. But I would do anything to extend this and as I felt my body begin to reenter my awareness, I fought it.

"Still so much energy," he whispered. "How do you want this dream to end?"

"With you," I said, then opened my eyes and looked around. I had said that out loud into the emptiness of my room and I blushed. Had anyone heard that? How loudly had I said it?

No one probably heard it. Dmitri's room was nearby, but I had never heard anything and I assumed the house was well-built and relatively sound-proof. I got up and pulled the light-blocking shades to one side. It was getting dark. Probably close to four or five. A good time to get up and take a jog. As I reached for my sweatpants, I noticed a glow from the wall near the window. Another firefly. I stretched my hand towards it.

"Come here," I said softly. "I'll put you outside."

Another glowing burst, and then the firefly leapt into the air. Instead of going to my hand or to the window, however, it went into the shadows. It didn't glow again. What was up with the fireflies here? It had to be confused, but why not go to the window? I pushed it aside and turned the lights on. The firefly could find its way outside on its own. But as I left the room, I did open the window in case the insect found its way out.

The house was silent as I trekked through the halls to reach the outside. Dmitri seemed to get up at six, and I assumed Margaret and Dianne were on similar schedules over at the house they lived in. I would probably adapt to that schedule soon, but I wasn't quite synced yet. I set off across the grounds to the path I had found earlier that wound around two gardens under the shade of the trees. It was quite beautiful and I wondered if this was where the fireflies came from. It was probably a beautiful run right when the sun had set and the fireflies glittered around the newly darkened sky. That would happen in a few hours, I considered. I might be able to get out and run then, but it would be quite close to the start of work. Better not risk it. Maybe when I was more established at my job, I could start a little late and take some time admiring the grounds at sunset.

My phone buzzed in my pocket and I paused, taking it out. It was a message from Dr. Grayson, asking if I knew who my house was yet. I froze. Didn't he know who my house was? Margaret said he had followed me, or had me followed, after I left from his final. Was I not supposed to know that? And what was I supposed to say? That I still didn't know? I couldn't say that. Was I allowed to tell him my house, though? I didn't know, but Dmitri would probably know. I didn't need to respond immediately, even though I normally would. Dr. Grayson would know I was on a night schedule now and most people on that schedule wouldn't be awake yet.

The manor was still quiet and I paused in front of Dmitri's door. Should I knock? Should I get his help now, or wait until he woke up on his own and ask him then? Should I go to Adze, I wondered, but that didn't seem like a good idea. The basement was pretty clearly off limits unless I was specifically invited, and even then, I wasn't allowed everywhere. I didn't know where he would be and if it were dark, I wouldn't even be able to search for him. Not a good idea. But I needed some sort of guidance.

With a deep breath, I knocked on the door. I tried to be as polite and quiet as possible, but I did want to wake him up. I glanced at my phone. It was five thirty. He might already be up, and it wasn't an unreasonable time to wake him. I hoped.

After a moment, I heard movement, and I waited a couple more minutes until the door opened a little. Dmitri seemed surprised to see me. He somehow looked almost as polished as he did when working. How did anyone look that put together right when they woke up? But he was in pajamas, not his usual uniform, and that did make him look a little more casual.

"What is it, Kairos?" he asked, sounding slightly irritated. I gulped. I hoped this was appropriate.

"My professor contacted me," I said. "The one you guys were worried about, who had me followed."

Dmitri drew in a sharp breath. "What did he say? What did you say?"

He opened the door more fully and I showed him the message on my phone. I blushed, as the messages above were my apologies on being late for a meeting earlier in the semester. But he didn't comment on the previous messages. He was focused on the single question at the end.

"You haven't responded?" he asked.

"I didn't know what to say," I admitted. "I thought you might know how to handle it. I'm sorry I woke you up, but I usually respond to messages immediately and I didn't want to seem suspicious because I'm taking so long to answer."

"It's fine," he said. "Give me a minute to dress and think. Wait in the kitchen. And don't respond, or even start to."

"Okay," I said. It wouldn't do to let Dr. Grayson think I'd received the message already and was planning my response, so I wouldn't be entering anything until I knew for sure what to say. I went to the kitchen and turned on the lights. Dmitri came out far sooner than I expected, already in uniform and looking impeccable as always. I wondered if he had always been like that, or if it were something he'd picked up working for vampires. I hoped I someday learned to look that good.

"I spoke to Master," he said, and I blinked. But of course Dmitri would have some way of contacting Adze during the day. I should have expected that. "You can tell him the name of our house, but don't tell him anything about Master Adze specifically. I need to see how he responds."

I nodded, then looked at my phone. How would I phrase this? How would I react to this question if I didn't know something was wrong?

Hi. I'm working for House Elviore, I wrote. *They're an ancient house, but they seem fine so far.*

Dmitri was watching as I typed and I showed it to him. He nodded. It was more information than he had specified, but it was what I would normally say. I tended to be quite wordy and formal in my texts with professors. He would be suspicious with anything less.

There was a short pause and I could see that he was typing. Then his message flashed up.

Are you liking the job? What do you do?

I looked at Dmitri.

"Our house handles blood for the city of Redmond," he said. "Tell him you help divide the blood into portions for the vampires throughout the city."

"Is that true?" I asked, mind whirling. Did vampires really receive portions of blood like that? I supposed it made sense. The blood tax was collected and stored somewhere, and then individual vampires could draw from it. Dmitri nodded and gestured to my phone impatiently. This was not the time to learn more.

I help divide blood between vampires, I wrote. *Elviore is in charge of that. It's pretty interesting, so I like the job.*

There was another pause, longer this time, and then I could tell he started typing. It was a little unnerving having Dmitri watch the conversation, and even more unnerving that I couldn't have a normal conversation with my professor, but I'd rather have help than put Adze in danger.

If you want to change jobs, let me know, Dr. Grayson wrote. Then a pause. *There are jobs available that would use your degree more. You might find them more interesting.*

"Do I ask about that?" I asked, looking at Dmitri.

"Would you normally?"

"Yeah."

"Then do it. But be careful."

I nodded.

What kind of jobs? I'm pretty happy here but always looking to the future.

"Good," Dmitri murmured, and I felt relieved. This was quite a tense conversation.

Translating messages, Dr. Grayson wrote, and my brow crinkled. Translating messages? That was exactly what I did here. I looked at Dmitri, who was still looking at the phone. Dr. Grayson was writing more, I could tell.

The house I work with is always looking for people like you to translate messages, he continued. *When you're ready to work somewhere else, let me know.*

Dmitri didn't say anything or recommend any responses.

Thanks, I wrote. *I will.*

Don't tell your master that I contacted you, Dr. Grayson said, rather unexpectedly. *It's not polite to try to poach good workers, but I think you'd do better elsewhere.*

I looked at Dmitri.

"I don't want to lie."

"I'll be the one to tell Master Adze, not you," he said. "You won't be lying."

I won't. I've got to get ready for the day. Talk to you later.

I hoped that wasn't too rude but I wanted this conversation over and it wasn't uncharacteristic for me to end a conversation like that.

Stay safe, Kairos.

Dmitri and I waited several long moments, but that seemed to be it and I was a little chilled. Cautiously, I let out a breath. It was perfectly normal to leave a conversation like that. No further response was needed from either of us, though his last message was a little unnerving.

"Take a screenshot of that conversation and send it to me," Dmitri said.

"But-"

"You never said anything about sharing this with me," he pointed out. "I need a record of this."

I obeyed, my hands trembling as I looked at that last message. Was it just a wish for safety, or was it a warning? He had warned me about ancient houses before. Did he really think I was in danger? *Was* I in danger? I sent the screenshots to Dmitri and then closed out of the message.

"Good job, Kairos," Dmitri said.

"But why was he asking that? Why does he think I'm in danger? Who does he want me to work for?"

Dmitri paused. "Master might be the better person to explain," he said slowly. "It's a complicated situation. I'll let him know that you're ready for some answers."

"But I wasn't ready before?" I asked, a little angry. Had they been hiding things from me?

"It's complicated," Dmitri said. "But you'll learn more tonight when you start work. Can you wait that long?"

"I guess," I said, since it didn't seem like I had any options.

Dmitri nodded.

"What are you doing up so early? That message didn't wake you, did it?"

"No, I was out jogging."

"You had your phone on you?"

"Of course."

"Good," he said. "Don't go anywhere without it. If something happens to you, if you trip while running or something, you need a way to get in touch with us."

I shivered. Even though he had specified tripping, I had a feeling he had other dangers in mind. How much danger was I in here? The first time I had realized that I might be in danger, the thought of Adze was enough to erase my worry. Was that still true? I thought about Adze leaning over me, the feel of his hand smacking against my skin. Yes, it was still true. I would go through any danger to stay at his side. But I couldn't help but hope this talk of safety from Dmitri and Dr. Grayson was exaggerated.

CHAPTER NINETEEN: EMPLOYMENT HISTORY

There were twelve envelopes on my desk when I entered and I was a little surprised. That was quite a lot for one day. I sat down and checked the house email. I had nearly been done, but the inbox was full once again. Where was all of this coming from?

"The rest of House Elviore is sending their messages to you now," a voice said, and I looked up in shock to see Adze in the middle of the room. My heart leapt and my mouth went dry. He was looking at me expressionlessly but his eyes glowed warmly. Was he pleased to see me? He approached and gestured to the letters.

"These need to be finished before midnight. Can you handle that?"

"Yeah, of course," I said. "No problem."

"I understand your professor contacted you," he said. "Dmitri showed me the conversation. You handled it perfectly."

"Thanks," I said, feeling a little proud.

Adze leaned back against the desk, facing me. I was uncomfortably aware that my head was close to the same level as his cock, but I was pretty sure he wouldn't ask me to do anything here or now. I looked up at him and saw a hint of amusement in his eyes, as if he knew what I had been thinking. But for once, I wanted actual answers, answers about my job and my safety, not just about our relationship.

"When I first received your application, I was inclined

to reject it out of hand," he said. "It was clear you had no experience with vampires, and knowing about our society and Redmond is important in proper translations. But I knew the name of one of your references, Dr. Grayson. So I had Dmitri check you out. I did not expect what he found."

Had he not expected me to have good references? Who would list a reference who wouldn't say wonderful things about them? I was a little worried that he had dismissed my application so quickly, but I had the job now. Something had made him reconsider me, and it must have been Dr. Grayson's recommendation.

"Dmitri must have accidentally used a key word that indicated we were House Salvite," Adze continued. "Because when he asked about you, Grayson said, 'this is the one.'"

"The one?" I repeated, confused. Adze nodded.

"Dmitri was equally puzzled and Grayson must have realized he wasn't from House Salvite, because he proceeded to give you the worst recommendation Dmitri had ever heard."

"He gave me a bad recommendation?" I exclaimed. "Why would he do that?"

"Because you were supposed to work for House Salvite and no one else," Adze said calmly. "And that is precisely why I hired you. When I saw you in person, I knew you had no idea what had happened or who you were supposed to be working for. House Salvite grooms its future employees carefully so they can't give anything away until they're safely employed. I caught you in time, before they could get to you."

"House Salvite?" I repeated. "They're the ones Dr. Grayson wanted me to work for. They're vampire hunters, right? You make it sound like working for them is a problem."

"It is a problem," Adze said. "Or it is if you prefer to follow the law. You do respect the law, don't you, Kairos?"

"Of course," I said, puzzled. Then I remembered what he had said after the cathedral. Another house was breaking the law, and House Elviore was looking into it. Was House Salvite the one breaking the law? Were they the ones trying to frame

Elviore? Were they the ones behind that strange attack on the cathedral? I glanced at the letters, eyes widening. The letters were either from or for House Salvite. There was no question about it. And the emails I intercepted were from or for them as well. I was translating their mail.

"House Salvite uses a complex code in their messages that's very difficult to break," Adze said, glancing back at the letters as well. "Those who specialize in human culture can sometimes break it, but it takes time. Only those trained in it can read and translate it easily. You were intended for House Salvite, so Grayson naturally taught you the code you would be using there."

"Then... that's why Dmitri was surprised I got so far? That's why you said it would take most people much longer? I'm doing something that other people can't do?"

Adze nodded, and I tried to think. I had taken private lessons from Dr. Grayson at a few points, gotten his help studying different subjects. He had taught me things in addition to what my classes taught me, but I had thought he was just giving me advanced work that no one else was ready for. I thought it was preparation for grad school, not a special code.

"But he was helping me get ready for grad school," I said slowly, not really understanding how everything was fitting together even though the puzzle was nearly complete.

"They don't usually recruit until a student is finished with school," Adze said. "It might seem suspicious if you intended on going to grad school and then changed your mind after undergrad. They want to avoid suspicion above all else."

"Why didn't you want them to know I'm translating for you? Do they know you're spying on them?"

"They might suspect it after the cathedral," he said. "But as long as they don't know you're easily translating things, then they'll assume that we're limited by access and translation. They have no idea how much access we have to their communication."

He gestured to the letters and the computer with the emails. "It's taken decades, but we can finally see everything they send. We just haven't been able to translate it quickly enough to avoid suspicion."

"And now you have me," I said slowly. He nodded. I looked around. So that was why I was hired. I was practically designed for this job. But I felt almost guilty that I was working here instead of House Salvite, since that was where Dr. Grayson wanted me. Still, I didn't want to be with a house that broke the law. And thinking back to the letters and emails, it did seem like they were breaking the law quite a bit. The messages were about vampire deaths and human deaths. Was House Salvite behind those deaths? I licked my lips nervously.

"We'll keep you safe," Adze said. "And as long as they think you're doing clerical work and not translating, they won't target you."

"But if they figure it out, they might?" I asked nervously, my fears about this job crowding back.

"They might."

I took a deep breath and looked at Adze again. I wanted him more than I was afraid of the danger. I wanted to keep this job. I wanted to keep him.

He reached out and caressed my cheek before running a hand through my hair. I leaned into the caress and couldn't help the spark that flickered deep in my belly, a slow fire that burst to life with his touch. He was so beautiful, looking at me with those ebony eyes that gleamed in the harsh light of the office. I would do quite a lot to keep looking into those eyes.

"Focus on work today," Adze said, stroking my hair one last time. "Dmitri will show you how to handle the new emails. There will be a different protocol. Work until midnight, and then I'll come and get you."

My heart stuttered. "Come get me?" I whispered, my mind whirling with what had happened during the day in his lair, and how good I had felt afterwards. Was he really going to do that to me in the middle of a workday?

"Lilith has requested your presence," Adze said, and there was clear amusement in his voice. I looked up to see a hint of a smile. I suddenly remembered that I should be calling him Master to get him to smile. I had completely forgotten.

"Will you go with me, Master?"

That slight smile got a bit more pronounced. My heart thrilled.

"I wouldn't leave you alone," he said. "But you need to have these letters finished first, and the newest emails, if possible."

"I will," I promised.

"Good boy," Adze murmured, then stroked my head one more time and left.

I took a deep breath and smiled. I would get to spend time with Adze today. And with Lilith, and that was a less desirable thought. She was quite intimidating. My smile slipped further as I thought of Dr. Grayson. At least I hadn't had to lie to him. I hated lying to people. And at least now I understood more of what was going on. I glanced at the letters. Should I start, or wait for Dmitri? There was a gentle knock at the door and I was glad I didn't have to decide, because Dmitri was already here.

He showed me how to organize now that I controlled the entire House. Each message had to be forwarded to the staff of the individual vampires in the House, but it was easy to tell which message came from which staff member. Dmitri told me that if I was ever in doubt as to who to send it to, to send it to him and he would sort it out.

After he left and I put gloves on to start examining the letters, I wondered what exactly about the translations I was doing was difficult. What was I doing that other people couldn't? Everything seemed so straightforward and clear, but I had spent a lot of time with Dr. Grayson learning to translate and interpret human writing. I hadn't realized he was teaching me anything unusual and I wondered how many students like me there were. Was it common for House Salvite to teach people these things? Groomed. I shuddered. That was how Adze had phrased it. I had been groomed by House Salvite, groomed to participate in crimes. I was so glad I was working for Adze.

By the third letter, I noticed something new. These were letters from today, I could tell, and all of them referenced an icon. They never said what that meant, but the word appeared in every letter. I remembered this from a couple of messages yesterday, but it hadn't stood out. I wouldn't have noticed it if I were reading these separately, but it was too much of a coincidence seeing them all together. The next few letters confirmed it, but I couldn't tell what the icon was. There were questions about the icon, as if they didn't exactly know what it was, either. I carefully noted it in the individual files and on my pad of paper where I took notes. I considered telling Dmitri immediately, but I was curious if it continued into the emails so I put it aside for the moment. It didn't seem urgent.

Three new emails came in as I worked on the letters and I turned to them first. I wasn't sure if I was surprised or not that an icon was mentioned in the first email I examined. There was definitely something going on. I called Dmitri.

He answered right away.

"I've noticed something new in the letters, and the email," I said, and briefly explained the mentions of the icon.

"Are you done with the letters then?" he asked, not responding immediately to the icon.

"I just finished."

"I'll be in to collect them."

He hung up and I stared at the phone. Was the icon not important? And was I supposed to tell him when I finished the letters? I didn't remember him telling me that. But I supposed if the letters were illicitly acquired, it was smart to get them to their locations as quickly as possible. Only a couple of minutes passed as I finished translating the first email. He came in and gestured for me to finish before he spoke.

"You've noticed this in the emails, too? Which emails?"

"I've only done one," I said. "It's the most recent, that just came in while I was working. It's from, um, Lilith's house."

"Mistress Lilith," he corrected, but he gestured for me to open the email and came around to view my screen easier.

I pointed to the word.

"It doesn't stand out on its own, but it's been in every letter and now this email, too," I explained. "I don't know what it means. There seem to be all kinds of questions about it. I don't think they know what it means. Do you?"

"I have an idea," he said grimly. "I'll take the letters and contact Master Adze. I'm asking Dianne to come in and wait with you while I talk to him. If your professor contacts you, don't tell him anything without her consent. Understand?"

I nodded, confused, as he first called Dianne and then put on gloves and collected the envelopes into a velvet bag. Dianne came in and smiled at me, but it wasn't very reassuring. Dmitri left with a warning glance at me and I shrunk into my seat. Had I noticed something I wasn't supposed to notice? Was I in trouble?

"You should keep working," Dianne said.

"Um, why do I need you here? I mean, I'm glad you're here, but why are you here?"

"In case your professor contacts you," she said.

"Why would he? I just talked to him a few hours ago."

"If he does, it means they're worried that you're working here," she said. "If he doesn't, it means he bought your lie."

"I didn't lie," I said a little angrily. "I just didn't tell the truth."

"I apologize," she said, and her face softened a little. "I didn't mean to imply that you would lie. You said what you needed to say, and I appreciate that. I just hope your professor bought it."

I nodded, and wondered if he would contact me or not. I put my phone on the desk just in case, and got back to work on the emails, all of which mentioned the icon. Did the icon have something to do with me? Was I the icon? Were they asking each other what to do about me? My hand hesitated over the keyboard and I looked at Dianne.

"Um, I think I'm the icon they're talking about," I said cautiously. Dmitri had briefly filled her in on what I had noticed. She nodded.

"It does seem likely. We'll see what happens next."

CHAPTER TWENTY: ALLOTMENT

My phone sat on my desk, silent. I had actually gotten a message already and nearly had a heart attack, but it was just Janae wishing me a good night and asking if I could get together soon. I checked with Dianne to make sure I could answer, and told her I was at work and would contact her later. She wished me luck and I tried to calm my heart and go back to work. My professor wouldn't contact me. They didn't suspect me. They just had questions about me, questions that were evident in the new emails that popped into the inbox even as I worked. I had just calmed back down when there was a knock on the door and Dmitri came in with Adze at his side.

Even though I wanted Adze to come to my side and reassure me, I was a little glad he didn't. I didn't want our relationship exposed. Dianne excused herself, since she probably had all sorts of things she was supposed to be doing rather than babysitting me, and I showed Dmitri and Adze the mentions of the icon in the latest emails I had translated.

"They're all asking what to do about it," I said. "I'm pretty sure it's me they're talking about."

"Any signs that they've come to a decision?" Adze asked calmly. So he guessed the same thing. Had they all come to that conclusion and just not told me? Maybe they hadn't wanted me to panic, or they thought knowing I was the icon would impact my translations. Or maybe I should have realized it earlier and they assumed I knew. I was the one in charge of translating, after all. I blushed that I hadn't immediately realized the letters and emails were about me.

"No, it seems like they're trying to gather information before figuring out what to do. No one seems to know anything."

There was a bing as another email popped up. Adze leaned forward to examine the email and nodded.

"Translate this email. This is from the vampire associated with your professor."

I nodded, trembling slightly. This was an important email, then. I followed the protocol they had set up for me, even though that meant a slight delay before I got to the message itself. I couldn't tell who the email was meant for, and I wouldn't have known who it was from, so I tried not to let my knowledge tint my translation and interpretation with fear. I finally got to the message and frowned, then read it again, taking notes in my pad. I glanced at my notes and the email, translating the words that I knew meant something else when humans used them. Then I paused. There were a set of words that I automatically switched out, because Dr. Grayson had taught me that humans always used these words to hide their meaning. Was that the code he had taught me to break? I looked up, wondering if I should say something, but Adze gestured to the screen. This wasn't the time.

As I translated, I began to relax. I scanned the email again, typing in the results as I went through each line, and because Dmitri and Adze were reading as I typed, they began to relax as well. House Salvite had reached a conclusion. The icon was irrelevant, and could be ignored for now. There was a promise of future action, but nothing imminent.

"That's it," I said as I finished. I knew they had read it and wondered if they wanted me to summarize the findings. "Um, who do I send it to? You, Dmitri?"

"Yes," he said. "Send it to Mistress Lilith as well."

I obeyed, and Adze placed his hand on my shoulder. I hid a shiver of pleasure at the touch and my heart hitched unexpectedly. I felt guilty being touched like this in front of

Dmitri, even though there was nothing intimate about a touch like this at all. Guilty, and a little turned on. But I buried it. While it was exciting thinking about being intimate in front of a stranger, this was not the time. Not that Dmitri was really a stranger, I considered. I would probably feel more comfortable around a stranger. It was because I knew Dmitri that I felt awkward like this.

"Good job, Kairos," Adze said, and I beamed. "Do you feel safer now?"

"Yeah, for now," I said. "I'm glad I read that."

"There should be quite a few responses over the next ten minutes, but Lilith wants you at her house," Adze said. "We won't keep her waiting."

"Of course not," I said, and the two men headed to the door. When I didn't immediately stand and join them, Adze made a small gesture for me to come and I obeyed, straightening my jacket and hoping I looked presentable. She had seen me get attacked, and I definitely looked more presentable than I had then, but I wanted to make a good second impression because I had messed up my first.

Dmitri helped us into the limo before getting in the front to drive and I trembled beside Adze, who casually laid his hand on my thigh. He wasn't doing anything, but as we started to drive, my breath started coming in quicker. I wanted him to do something. How could he just touch me like that, so casually, as if unaware what it was doing to me? Then I noticed how carefully he was watching me. He was very aware of what he was doing, then.

He must have noticed my attention because his hand slid higher on my thigh and my breath hitched. The gentle rub of his skin through my slacks was irresistible and I shifted. I was getting turned on.

"Um, how long does it take to get there?" I asked softly, wondering if we would have time to do anything. Dmitri was driving but he wouldn't notice if we were quiet. We couldn't do much, but I wanted him to keep touching me.

"Five minutes," he said, and his hand trailed higher until he was almost making contact with my groin. Five minutes wasn't much time. Why was he teasing me like this when there was no way we'd have enough time to do anything? Did he just like teasing me? He began stroking his thumb across my thigh as if smoothing out a wrinkle in my slacks. I let out a sigh and shifted, trying to rearrange myself so his hand came into contact with me. He adjusted as well, still stroking me. There was a twinkle in his eye and I moaned softly.

"Master," I whispered, not knowing what to say. I wanted him to touch me, to caress me, even if we were only in the car for a few minutes and there was no way this could end well. I was so turned on and it was beginning to be apparent as he kept stroking his thumb so close to me.

Adze's lips curved slightly and I ached for him even more, licking my lips as I imagined kissing him while he was smiling like this, the press of his lips against mine, the press of his flesh against him, but all he would allow me was this simple stroke of his thumb. I inched closer again and again he maintained the same position.

"Please," I said softly, desperately.

Adze leaned towards me, his hand smoothing over to the outside of my thigh as he wrapped his other hand around my shoulders. I leaned into him and tilted my chin up for a kiss, and wasn't disappointed. His lips met mine and I melted into him. But I shifted closer, because I wanted more. The feel of him was like lightning and I desperately wanted more. I wanted all of him and my breath hitched in our kiss as I clutched his arms.

He pushed me away gently, untangling from me and pushing me back into my seat, no longer in physical contact.

"We're almost there," he said calmly.

I took a deep breath. My mind felt scattered and my body was on fire. How could he do this to me? How could he tease me like this? This wasn't fair. But there was a hint of a smile as he watched me try to calm my body down and I knew he enjoyed seeing me like this. He liked seeing me out of control even as he controlled me. Was I okay with this? Could I handle a relationship like this? I didn't have much choice. I was still desperate for him. If this is what he wanted, then I would do it.

I took a few more deep breaths and by the time the car came to a stop, my body had cooled off and I felt presentable. Dmitri opened the door and Adze got out first. I looked around as I stepped out. We were at an estate similar to Adze's, but while Adze's felt fairly modern, this place looked like a haunted manor out of a scary movie. There were gargoyles on the roof and an iron-wrought fence that circled the lawn like skeleton fingers trapping everyone inside. I shivered.

A servant was there to greet us and I recognized the woman from my previous encounter with Lilith. She eyed me curiously, without the disdain of our first meeting. Then, I was a foolish human who got himself attacked. Now, I was a valuable member of the House. I wondered how much she knew about me and if she knew why I was so valuable. She greeted Adze formally and led us up the shadowed steps through a foreboding door into a large antechamber filled with dark wood and crimson velvet accents. Was the whole thing supposed to look like a scene from a movie, or was this genuinely what vampires liked and the movies copied from them? I wasn't sure, but I was grateful Adze's mansion didn't look like this. I wouldn't feel comfortable in an atmosphere like this, and I wouldn't want to invite Janae over. She would like Adze's, though, and be extremely impressed. I would have to get back to her about a visit before I went to sleep, I remembered. But not during the work day.

Once we were inside, Adze led me down a hallway into an office similar to his, but with the same overly vampirish décor. Lilith stood as we entered. The servant trailing along bowed to her and I wondered if I was supposed to bow as well. Her eyebrow arched and I looked at Adze, uncertain. Adze gestured for me to bow and I did hastily, though probably not correctly. I didn't feel pinned the way I had in front of all of the other vampires, but I was aware of the fact that there were now two vampires surrounding me. I wasn't sure how I could feel it, but it was like a pressure on my mind, a weight that tingled against my senses without actually dragging me down into paralysis. They probably could paralyze me the way the group of vampires had done last time, but neither Adze nor Lilith were interested in overwhelming me. I hoped.

"Welcome, Kairos," Lilith said.

"Thanks, um, Mistress Lilith," I said, catching myself in time and adding the title. I did not want to forget with her, because she was the head of House Elviore. She had even more authority than Adze and I shouldn't forget it.

"Thank you for coming," she said. "Adze has kept me informed of recent events. Since you may need to know more details about the business of House Elviore, my servant will walk you through basic blood allotments. This is Denise."

The servant stepped forward and smiled. "Please come with me."

I glanced at Adze again and he gestured at me to follow, so I obeyed. The two vampires remained in the room as Denise led me through another hallway into a large room with several computers at stations in the center of the room. There were three other servants here and they looked up as I entered.

"This is Kairos," Denise said. "We're teaching him what to do."

She introduced the two men as Kyle and Daniel, and the other woman as Candace. She had been the driver last I time I met with people from Lilith's house and I could tell she recognized me. I smiled cautiously and Denise brought me to the empty station that must be hers. There were three monitors showing all sorts of spreadsheets and it looked completely overwhelming. She sat down and pulled up a new window on the primary monitor.

"I know this is a lot to absorb, but it gets easier once you know what you're looking at. I heard you don't know anything about vampires. Do you know anything about the blood tax?"

"Just that you have to pay it twice a year," I said uneasily. She grinned and the others looked amused. I wondered if they had to pay, or if they were dhampir. Almost certainly dhampir. Dianne and Dmitri made it sound highly unusual that a pure human would work for an ancient house.

"I'll start with the basics, then," she said, and pointed to a list of letters. "Each person's blood is assessed and given several letters indicating the quality. See here?"

I leaned forward and studied the acronyms. They were fairly detailed and had to do with things like blood type, oxygen levels, platelet counts, and flavor. I shivered. Did someone taste all of the blood? How else would they get flavor? And I was a little surprised that the blood stayed isolated. I had assumed it was all dumped together and divvied up from there. It was probably good they were teaching me this if they expected me to be able to pretend to know how to do this.

"Every vampire has preferences, and also a complicated ranking system," she continued, pulling up several other windows. "It's our job to match the supply to the demand."

I looked at the complicated spreadsheets on the three monitors, then looked at the other computers. They all had basically the same types of information. This looked far more complicated than I had imagined.

"There can't be that many vampires in Redmond, can there?" I asked.

"We get new blood input every day from around the world," she explained. "Blood is only good for a short period of time, but Redmond gets first claim on all of it. There are some vampires here who get the highest quality blood no matter when it comes in, and there are some who only qualify for what's left over. It's a complicated system, I know. Here, sit down."

I obediently sat and she started walking me through the columns and going through the basics. Under her guidance, I sorted through the list of local vampires who were due to receive their monthly blood allotment, then went through the list of available blood and matched them. She had to correct and guide me quite a bit, but at least now I knew the process. She had me do another match on my own and watched. I had to ask for quite a bit of help understanding the acronyms and rankings, but I got through the process on my own.

"Good job," she said.

"Do all of you do this every day?" I asked, impressed. It was hard work and even if there weren't a lot of vampires to deal with, it was still complicated. And this was only one city. Redmond got first claim on everything, but there were other cities working with the exact same dataset and it was easy to lose blood to a faster worker in another city. The vampire she had given me to do on my own had perfectly matched a set of blood but by the time I entered it, the blood had already been claimed. It didn't matter, because he wasn't a high priority vampire, but I was impressed at how fast-paced the job was.

"Blood stats are released at nine every evening," she said. "We get the priorities taken care of before midnight and then Daniel and Candace shift to other matters while Kyle and I sort out the details. We're always looking for help on this, though, for that immediate rush. I know you have your own job but if you ever do want to help, you're welcome to."

"My job's kind of the same," I said cautiously. "It's pretty busy right at the start of the day."

"That's too bad," she said. "We really need to hire someone else, but Mistress Lilith just told us we can't hire anyone for quite a while now that you're here."

I flushed. They couldn't hire someone new because House Salvite had to think that they just had hired someone new: me. I felt bad that my presence was making them all work harder and denying them the opportunity to make a much-needed hire, but it wasn't my call. If Lilith and Adze thought this was best, then it was their decision to make.

"So you have a basic feel for it?" she asked, and I agreed. "I'm giving you a list of the acronyms to learn. Apparently you need to memorize them."

I agreed to that as well and wondered what exactly they'd been told about me and why I needed to know how to do this job even though I wasn't doing it. Then she grinned.

"You pay the blood tax, right?"

"Um, not this year," I said. "I guess you don't if you work for a vampire house."

"But you have?"

"Yes," I said.

"Want to see what kind of blood you have?"

I blinked, startled. "What?"

The others were grinning, too.

"We've never met someone who's paid the tax," Daniel said. "I'm curious to see how the blood types line up with the people. And aren't you curious to know how much your blood is in demand?"

"Not really," I said slowly. Did I want to know what vampires thought of my blood? My mind went immediately to Adze, and the way he lingered over my neck. I wanted him to taste me. And I wanted to taste good to him. "How would you even know?"

"These are tracked by government ID," she explained. "Some humans have consistently good blood and vampires request them specifically, even though the vampires themselves aren't allowed to know who the people are. But if they like the allotment they get, they can request the same human twice a year."

I rubbed my wrist, very aware of the blood pounding through my veins. What if Adze requested my blood? What if he had already drunk it without knowing? Now I was curious, but I didn't want them to know.

"So it's by ID number?" I asked. "How do you look it up?"

"One of us would have to do it for you," she said. "You need special access. Want me to?"

I was tempted. Sorely tempted. I wanted to know if I had good blood to offer Adze. But what if I didn't? What if my blood was categorized as useable, but nothing more? Or what if the taste was off? I probably had good oxygen and platelet levels, I figured, but that was only part of the equation. What if I didn't live up to Adze's standards?

"Maybe later," I said, not wanting to rule it out in the future but not wanting to find out right now. She laughed.

"I'm sure you have good blood," she assured me. "But let one of us know anytime and we'll look it up for you. Do you have any questions?"

"No," I said. "Thank you for teaching me this."

"Not a problem," she said. "Hopefully when your job isn't needed as much, you can come help us. We used to have someone at Master Adze's house doing this job, but not for several weeks."

"They quit?"

"Got poached," she said. "Even though House Elviore is in charge of the blood for the city, every House has someone in charge of pleading for their preferred allotment, so there's always demand for this skill set."

"Do you plan on staying?" I asked curiously.

"All four of us have been here for at least five years, and aren't going anywhere," she said. "It's only the satellite workers at the other vampire's mansions who come and go. I heard you'll be staying a while," she added. "That's good. Master Adze needs more full-time help. If you need anything to help you get settled into the House, just let us know. We'll be happy to assist."

"Thank you," I said, and wondered again how much they knew. And was I going to be staying for a long time? At least a year. But Dianne had mentioned staying longer, and I couldn't ignore that idea. It would be nice to have a permanent, steady job. Especially one with a handsome boss. But could I handle the relationship long-term? I wasn't even sure if I could handle it short-term. I would have to see, but I was with House Elviore for at least a year no matter what. After that, it was up to how much I wanted to stay with Adze.

CHAPTER TWENTY-ONE: REFUSED OFFER

Lilith and Adze were sitting and chatting in a different language when Denise brought me back to them. Adze stood and put his hand on my shoulder as he passed me.

"Lilith will speak to you," he said. "I'll be at the car when you're done."

Denise led him out and I shifted uncomfortably as Lilith gestured me closer. I wondered if I were allowed to sit down or if she, like Adze, preferred humans to stand. Since she didn't motion towards any seats, it looked like I would be standing. Well, that was okay. I should probably get used to it, since it seemed like a vampire preference. I wished smiling were a vampire preference, I thought in annoyance. I couldn't read her at all. I had no idea if I was in trouble or if she just wanted to make sure I understood everything. I shifted again, still uncomfortable.

"If anyone asks about your job, you'll tell them that you help us divide blood," Lilith said. "Anyone. You will tell no one the truth outside of our House."

"But people in the House can know?" I asked uncertainly, thinking of Denise and the others. They obviously knew I wasn't doing the job. If each vampire in the House had their own servants, would I lie to them? And what about my family? My friends? I would have to lie to Janae and my mom, I realized with a sinking heart. Maybe I could just brush off their questions and say I didn't like talking about the job. Then

I would be lying less.

"My servants know, as do Adze's," she said. "All of the Elviore vampires know. They may choose to tell one or two of their most trusted servants, but even within the house, do not talk about your real job unless you know for sure that person already knows. Did you say anything to Denise?"

"No," I said. "I wasn't sure if she was supposed to know."

"Good. If you're ever in doubt, hide the truth. Has Adze explained why? Do you need more information?"

"He explained it, mostly," I said, wondering if she was offering to answer any questions I had. Adze often answered my questions. It didn't seem like anyone was hiding things from me; there was just a lot I didn't know.

"If you feel you need more information and Adze isn't providing it, please let me know," she said, then narrowed her eyes. "And if you feel Adze is providing too much, you must also let me know."

"What do you mean?" I asked. One of her eyebrows raised and I felt my cheeks flush in embarrassment. She was talking about my relationship with Adze. How much did she know? She hadn't been surprised by his show of intimacy at the cathedral, but what did she really know? I edged back a step.

"We ancient vampires view humans as curiosities, and often our interest gets snagged," she said. "If his interest in you becomes too great, you must let me know. I would see that you are moved to another household within House Elviore. Adze would not hold it against you, nor would any of us. But you are too valuable to lose over his lack of control."

I flushed further. Adze had lost control over me? But what did it mean that I was a curiosity? I was embarrassed further at the reminder that this wasn't just any vampire but an ancient, one who viewed my entire species as a curiosity. She had fought in the war, I remembered. Had she been head of Elviore then, or had she taken someone's place? I didn't know, and either seemed likely. She was staring at me with that expressionless face and I didn't know how to react or what to say. Really, what could I say? If my relationship with Adze became something I couldn't handle, what would I do? Would I just quit, or would I want to stay with my job and go to another part of Elviore? Maybe I wouldn't want to have anything to do with vampires ever again. They needed me, though. And if House Salvite had been grooming me, then they would try to get me to work for them if I ever quit, wouldn't they? It was a complicated situation that I wished I weren't in, but it was only a problem if I couldn't handle Adze. If I wanted to be with him, then none of this was an issue.

"I want to stay where I am," I said cautiously, not entirely sure how I was supposed to respond. A flicker of a smile lit her lips. Good. I had done something right.

"Remember that you have options," she said. "Though I am pleased you are adapting well to life in a vampire city. It's easy to forget how different life is for humans. If you feel we aren't providing something, Adze's servants will take care of it for you."

"Everyone's been super helpful," I said. "Thank you so much."

Her smile briefly became genuine. I wondered if Adze would ever smile at me like that. She held out her hand and I took it, a little confused because she didn't seem to want to shake it. She chuckled.

"You're supposed to kiss it," she said in an indulgent voice. "It's unusual to be around a resistant human."

I bent over and kissed her hand, feeling like a prince in a movie. I wondered if a non-resistant human would have known what to do, if maybe she had been using a glamour to try to dictate my actions. How strong were glamours? And more importantly, how strong did they have to be before I felt them? I remembered the dhampir who attacked me. His glamour had completely undone me; how many vampires and dhampir were capable of that? Could Dmitri disable me like that if he wanted? I shivered and she tightened her grip on me.

"What is it?" she asked softly.

"Am I in danger being a resistant human?" I asked softly, not entirely sure how to phrase what was bothering me.

"Traditionally, ancient houses do not tolerate resistant humans," she said, releasing my hand. "In the war, we killed them. No human should be able to resist us, and we don't want those genes getting passed on. No vampire in our house will hurt you, but vampires who realize you're resistant might try to test you, or challenge you, to see if they're strong enough to get past your resistance."

"Like what happened at the park?"

"He was an exceptionally strong dhampir," she said. "And you didn't recognize what was happening. No other dhampir should have the strength to overpower you like that again. And if any vampires attempt to harass you, just show them which house you're from. They'll stop. We don't allow anyone to interfere with our servants."

I rubbed the tattoo on my neck, thinking of how frozen I had felt when the vampires from Elviore and Tennison had all looked at me. They had all probably sensed I was resistant and been trying to test me. And Adze had told them to stop, and they had. Vampires would respect my house. They wouldn't attack me like the dhampir; they would obey, like Tennison. I hoped.

"Thanks," I said, and she smiled again.

"Your safety is very important to us. But Adze is waiting for you, and you still have most of the night to work. I don't want to keep you."

"Thank you very much, Mistress Lilith," I said, far more formally because I remembered again that this was an ancient, and I wasn't being properly respectful. She seemed amused and dismissed me the same way Adze had once, with a wave of her hand. Probably a vampire habit. I bowed, hoping that was appropriate, then headed the direction Adze had gone. Daniel was waiting outside and showed me to the car, reminding me to let him know if I needed anything. Everyone here was incredibly friendly, I decided as Adze and Dmitri came into view. Was it just that I was valuable and they wanted to keep me? Or were they like this all the time? I would hate to think they were just flattering me, but it was a little fun getting this much attention because I was good at my job.

I got in as Dmitri held open the door and Adze slid beside me in the seat. Dmitri started the car and he took my hand.

"Will you be staying with me?" he asked.

I was a little startled. Was I supposed to leave? Did he think that Lilith had offered to let me move to another household immediately? I certainly didn't want that.

"Of course," I said.

"But you understand that if you ever feel like this is too much, you have permission to go to another household?"

He put his hand on my thigh and my heart leapt in my chest.

"I- I understand," I managed.

He leaned forward and kissed my cheek. "I won't hold it against you."

I shut my eyes. This was too much. How could I even think of leaving someone like this? I tilted my head towards him but he didn't kiss me. He tapped his finger on my lips and I opened my eyes.

"You have work to do when you return," he said. "And you need to get onto a night schedule fully."

"What does that mean?"

He tapped my lips again. "It means that you need to focus on your work and your schedule for the next few days."

"What if I'd rather see you?" I asked without thinking, then blushed. He knew I wanted him, but I'd never actually said it before. Not like that. "I mean, I'll obviously do my job, and I want to get on a good schedule, but I'll be able to see you, too, right?"

"I'm sure we'll have work matters to discuss."

"That isn't what I mean," I said rather boldly. Was he backing off because Lilith had warned him not to scare me? It was odd to think of someone having that kind of control over him, to make him stay away from me when he didn't want to. He was the one in control; was she really more powerful than him? Or did he just value my ability to translate over my body? That was a little flattering, I supposed, but I wanted him to want me every bit as much as I wanted him.

He placed his fingers on my lips again but kept them there. Letting my boldness lead, I opened my mouth and caressed his fingers with my tongue, then drew him into my mouth. He tasted like moonlight. How could everything about him taste so good? Would I taste good to him? My mind flashed to the acronyms and categories of blood and I wondered what my blood was like, and what preferences he had. Were we a match? Or was I fooling myself? I wrapped my tongue around his index finger as he shoved slightly further into my mouth, stretching his fingers to stroke my tongue. This felt good. Everything with him felt good. I wanted more. But he withdrew his fingers and tapped my lips one more time before removing his hand entirely.

"We'll be home soon. I'd like you to get through as many emails as you can, but don't rush your translations."

"I'll do my best," I promised. For him, I would do anything.

CHAPTER TWENTY-TWO: FUTURE PLANS

"What are the other vampire households like in House Elviore, Margaret?" I asked as she served breakfast to me. Dianne and Dmitri had been finishing when I got up and had left to begin their work. Although they were technically on the same schedule as me, I had learned that they generally started whenever they were ready, which was often before nine. Since no one was pushing me to do the same, I figured they didn't mind that I didn't start until almost exactly nine o'clock. Based on what I had learned at Lilith's house, that was when most work in the city began. And I still wasn't quite on a good schedule. Today I had slept in later than usual and had to skip my run, but I had gotten one in last night. This morning, rather. It was still extremely strange thinking of the day as the time when people slept, because the morning was now the end of the day and the evening was the start.

"They're all fairly similar," she said.

"Who works there?"

"Someone is in charge of the grounds, like Dianne, there's usually someone who takes care of basic things like cooking, like me, and a personal assistant to the house's vampire, like Dmitri. Sometimes they have two people like that. Each house has a specialty and at least one person dedicated to that, like you. And then there are more temporary staff."

"Like the others who help with blood allotment?"

"Yes, most households have someone dedicated to that task, and someone dedicated to communications. But those skills are in fairly high demand so they don't usually stay long."

I wondered if I was putting anyone out of a job now that all of the house's communications were coming through me. Possibly. And I also wondered about the previous people in my job. They were translating messages from House Salvite, but they left. Were they sworn to secrecy? Or did they not realize who the messages were from? Adze had indicated that House Salvite didn't know they were under surveillance, but if they ever talked to someone who had my job, they had to know. Didn't they? If they suspected Elviore, as it seemed they did, then surely they would question people with my job, and if each of the six vampire households had someone like me and if those people left regularly, then there had to be quite a few people who knew what was going on. How did they maintain secrecy?

"What specialties do the other houses have?"

"We're in charge of communications, obviously," she said. "And Mistress Lilith is in charge of the blood allotment. Hers is the primary house of Elviore, but you probably knew that."

She didn't continue.

"What about the other four?"

Margaret smiled. "I'm sure you'll find out eventually."

"So I can know some of your secrets, but not all of them?" I asked in annoyance, and she laughed.

"You've barely been here a week, and you expect to learn everything?"

"I suppose that's fair," I said. "And I still don't know how long I'm staying."

"You're still thinking of leaving at the end of the year?"

"I don't know," I said, thinking of Adze. "I don't really want to. How long have you worked here?"

"Three years," she said. "And I still don't know what two of the houses do. We know what we need to know, and nothing else. But I took this job knowing it would be my job until I retire. You were intended to be a temporary hire while we found someone permanent. I'm glad you're the one we're keeping, though," she added. "And I hope you stay longer."

"I do want to," I said slowly. "I don't know how my parents would react, though. I told them I took a job with a vampire to help raise money to go to grad school. They want me to get a PhD. I don't think they'd accept me if I didn't."

"It's your life, and I'm sure once they see you're happy, they'll be happy for you," she said.

"Maybe," I said, wondering what my dad's reaction would be. He often bragged to his friends about how smart I was, and how I was going to take after him as a professor. He had all sorts of connections to several universities and had told me on several occasions that he would help me land a tenure-track job once I was ready. I wasn't sure he could actually help, as his connections were in Geography and I wanted a job in Human Culture, but I knew he was delighted at the prospect of helping even if didn't make a difference. He just liked bragging about me, and wanted to brag about me being a professor of a prestigious university. There was no way he would accept me going into the private sector and leaving academics.

My mom would be a little easier, I considered. She would value my happiness, as Margaret said. If I convinced her I was truly happier here, she would eventually accept it. But she bragged just as much, and also wanted to say I was a professor somewhere. It seemed like their whole identities were based on my future career choice. They would be devastated if I left academics. Was I willing to disappoint them to follow my heart and remain here?

My phone buzzed and I tensed, as did Margaret. It was a message from Janae asking if I was off work yet. I had forgotten to get back to her when I finished in the morning. I let her know my schedule and glanced at Margaret.

"Is it okay if my friend visits in the morning after work? Do I need to ask Ad- Master Adze?"

"You'll need to ask, but I'm sure it's fine," she said. "One of the ones I met?"

"Janae," I said. "She really wants to see this place."

"The place or your boss?" Margaret asked with a grin. "I'm not sure you'll be able to introduce her to Master if she comes too late."

I blushed, remembering how Janae had mentioned Adze's hotness in front of Margaret. I was a little embarrassed that Margaret knew I was attracted to Adze and I hoped she didn't know there was more going on between us than a crush. Eventually she would find out. It was almost inevitable. I would say something, or do something, and everyone here would realize the real relationship between me and Adze. But what was that relationship? It wasn't defined at all. He was interested in me and enjoyed me, but was there anything more?

Work went smoothly. Adze came in after midnight, after I came back from lunch, and spoke to me briefly about my translations, mostly confirming that there were no more mentions of me in the letters and emails. There weren't. It seemed they were satisfied with the decision to ignore me for now and I was relieved. As he started to leave, I cautiously reached out to take his hand. He seemed surprised and turned back to me.

"Something else?" he asked in a smoky voice.

"I had a question about the morning."

"We should wait a few days," Adze started, but I blushed and shook my head. I did want to go to his lair again, but for once I wasn't overwhelmed by lust.

"I have a friend who wants to visit. Margaret said I should ask you."

"Oh," he said. "Do they know what you do?"

"Last time I saw her, I didn't know what I would be doing, so I can easily tell her I'm doing blood allotments. We probably won't talk about it much, though. I want to show her around and see how she's doing."

"A female friend?" he said, and relaxed slightly. I realized he must have been worried that I would invite over someone I had feelings for, or had been in a relationship with. Did that mean he was jealous? He was possessive, but I wouldn't have expected jealousy. He had to know that I wouldn't invite someone like that over. I didn't even have someone like that. But then I remembered Scott and his flirtation at the end. If I invited him over, he would probably try something that would cause jealousy. Well, I had already decided to only see Scott in a group setting, and I would just have to make sure it was nowhere near Adze.

"She's my best friend," I said.

"After work today? Or another morning?"

"I'll see if she can do today, but she might already be asleep and not able to make it early enough. Does it matter which day?"

"It matters. I'll assume it's this morning. If it isn't, tell Dmitri when you do expect her."

I wondered why it mattered. I still wasn't allowed to leave this room on my own. I had to call Dmitri and let him know, and always had to wait a minute or two. What other secrets were going on that I wasn't supposed to know about?

"Thank you," I said, not knowing what else to say.

Adze reached out and stroked my head and the lust I had managed to avoid soared to life. I inhaled sharply and leaned into the caress, tilting my head so that he was stroking my cheek. I wanted to catch his fingers in my mouth the way I had before, but he drew away before I could and I was disappointed. He wanted it, I could tell. But he wouldn't do it because Lilith didn't want him to alienate me. It wouldn't, though. Adze was the only reason I was here, and the closer I got to him, the more I wanted to stay.

"If she comes before seven, I would like to meet her," he said. "Dmitri will arrange for that."

"She might not get here that early, but I'd like it if she met you," I said shyly. I would have to make sure she got here that early, though I knew she would resist. Adze reached out and briefly stroked my hair again before leaving the room. I immediately got out my phone and texted Janae, hoping she was still awake. Of course, if she was still awake, that meant she wouldn't get much sleep before coming over. I left my phone on the desk as I returned to emails, hoping she would respond. In just a few minutes, my phone buzzed.

You have terrible hours

I chuckled. So she was up, or I had woken her up. Either way, I proposed meeting in the morning at six, which shouldn't be ridiculously early and would get her here in time to meet Adze. There was a long silence, then she asked for the address. Another long pause and I realized she was nearly an hour away even without traffic. If she came at six, she'd have to leave at five and get up even earlier.

Fine. But I'm not going to have time for breakfast. Any chance I can eat when I get there?

Sure, I wrote, pleased. I knew Margaret would enjoy cooking for another person and wondered if she knew how to make Belgian waffles, Janae's favorite breakfast. That would make up for the inconvenience of getting up so early. We normally ate dinner-type foods in the morning, since it was dinner for us, but there was no way Janae would want dinner that early. I didn't think Margaret would mind.

A few more messages confirming everything, then I shut off my phone and returned my full attention to the emails. I felt a little guilty texting when I was supposed to be working, but I was still getting everything done. It seemed like there was a never-ending supply of emails to translate, and new physical messages as well, even though I finished those first. Still, if I was translating every single email that House Salvite was sending, it made sense that I was getting this many. Most were fairly simple and didn't seem to have a deeper meaning, but every few emails I could tell they were using the code I had realized I was breaking, and I always flagged those messages. Now that I recognized how I was translating, it was easier to tell which emails were important but I tried to remain alert even if the emails seemed perfectly normal. Just because they weren't using a code didn't mean they were innocent. And I did not want to let something slip through and disappoint Adze.

So I worked hard the rest of the day and at five, I stretched and told Dmitri I was done for the day. He had me wait a few minutes, as usual, and then I headed to the kitchen to put in my meal request to Margaret and get ready for Janae's visit in a couple of hours. She would be leaving about now, I thought, glancing at the clock. I hoped her drive went well, and couldn't help but smile. It felt like years had passed since I'd seen her. So much had happened. I couldn't tell her most of it, but it would be good to see her and see if her life had changed as dramatically as mine had.

CHAPTER TWENTY-THREE: AN EARLY VISIT

"I am never going to forgive you for making me get up so early," Janae moaned as I hugged her tightly. She was looking around curiously, though, with quite a bit of awe. The estate was pretty impressive. She had pulled up at front and Dmitri came to the door as well to greet her and offer to take her car around back. She seemed stunned to see him and I knew she had never seen anyone who so perfectly embodied the idea of a servant before. But she handed him the keys and I brought her inside.

"This place is insane," she said, looking around. "Do you really live here? No wonder you were so quick to abandon us."

"I didn't abandon you," I said. "I got a job."

"And then didn't text me for over a week," she pointed out, which was true. I'd been sending her the occasional message after work, but nothing like our chats when I was still a student. Then Dianne and Margaret came in and I introduced the formidable woman. Margaret said hi and Janae recognized her and seemed far less intimidated. Maybe she just needed to see something familiar here besides me. I looked around and wondered if Adze would appear. I wanted her to meet him but I had no idea what his hours were.

"Master Adze will be here after we eat," Margaret said, as if in answer to my unspoken question.

"Food? Oh good, I'm starving," Janae said. "Thanks so much, Margaret."

We went to the kitchen, where Margaret had gone far

beyond what I had requested and made an entire breakfast buffet. I assumed Dianne and Dmitri would be joining us, since there was so much food, but Dianne excused herself and Dmitri hadn't returned, so it was just me, Janae, and Margaret who sat down to eat. Janae was extremely impressed and complimented every single thing she tried, and I realized that I rarely complimented the food so I tried to join in. I made a mental note to thank Margaret more. I was sometimes good about that, but she really was doing a lot and I needed to appreciate it more.

Janae was full of news and I happily let her take over the conversation. After she had eaten her fill, she leaned forward conspiratorially.

"Lee and Angie are about to break up," she said. "It's not official, but I talked to Angie about it."

"What?" I said, shocked. "But why?"

"She says they just fight too much. You know how they are. Now that they have stable jobs, she wants a stable relationship and doesn't think she'll ever get it from him. She wants more commitment."

"It's not like he cheats on her," I pointed out. "They just get into squabbles about minor things. She really wants to break up with him?"

"She says if he doesn't prove he's serious by the end of the month, she's dumping him."

"Does she even realize what that does to us?" I asked in annoyance. "Who are we supposed to side with?"

"Well, she apparently wants to remain friends with him, and with us, and when I asked her about it, she said it wouldn't even be a problem because we would just be friends with both of them, same as always."

"That's not really how it works," I said, and Janae shrugged.

"I don't know. I guess I kind of see her side of things, but I feel bad for Lee. He doesn't even know it's coming, and she told me in confidence so I feel like I can't warn him."

"Maybe I can contact him and ask him about it," I said

slowly. "He needs some kind of warning. He's super serious about her. Maybe he'd do something if he knew."

"That would be nice," Janae said. "It feels like you've dropped off the map these past few weeks. You barely talk to me and don't talk to anyone else. Scott is a little freaked out that you just stopped talking to us."

I blushed. "It isn't on purpose. These hours are just so weird, I never know when to contact you guys, and then I'm always so busy I don't think of it during the few hours it would make sense to chat."

"You can leave us messages, you know," she said. "I don't know what the others do, but I turn off notifications at night. You can text me all you want and I'll just get it in the morning. Then I'll respond to you, and you can get it when you get up."

"You got my text last night," I said, and she laughed.

"Well, I have your number exempted just in case. But I can turn that off."

"I could do that," I considered. "I have lunch around midnight."

"You know I'm always up that late," Janae scolded. "Why aren't you calling me?"

"I guess I'm just so focused on work," I said.

"So what do you do here? You've never really told me."

I hesitated. I hated lying to her, but I was aware of Margaret eyeing me. I didn't want to lie, but I had to. Not only was my job at stake, I had to keep up the secret to prevent House Salvite from finding out that Elviore was tracking them and potentially stopping their crimes. I had already saved House Elviore once, and that wouldn't have happened if Salvite knew I was involved.

"It's pretty complicated," I said. "You know the blood tax? Well, I help divide it and assign it to different vampires in Redmond."

"That's weird," she said. "That's really a job? I thought you said they wanted someone with a degree in Human Culture. How does that relate?"

166

I glanced at Margaret. I hadn't expected this question, and didn't know the answer. Was it okay to say I didn't know? Would I know, if I actually had this job? Margaret smiled and leaned forward.

"He's training to become our main contact with the humans in charge of the process," she said. "People with that kind of expertise are needed to translate between the needs of the humans and those of the vampires."

"Oh," Janae said. "Wouldn't you already have someone doing that job? Seems pretty important."

"He's leaving at the end of the month," Margaret said, and I was impressed at how easily she lied. Did she lie like this a lot? I hoped not.

"So you have a really important job?" she asked me, and I nodded. "But you're still planning on going back to school, right?"

I hesitated again. "Well, I-"

"Kairos," she said, sounding shocked. "Your parents would kill you if you didn't get a PhD. That's been your dream since you were a kid. You always talk about it."

"I like working here," I said. "Maybe eventually I'll get a PhD, but for right now, I want to stay here."

"You like working here or you like your boss?" she asked skeptically. I blushed, and she sighed. "Whatever. If you like the job, you should keep it. But you have to keep in touch better. You don't get to vanish just because you got a job you like."

"I'll be better about talking to you," I promised. "I didn't realize how long it's been since I've talked to you guys."

Dmitri entered the kitchen and we looked up at him.

"Master Adze will see you now," he said, and I leapt to my feet eagerly. Janae's curiosity seemed to return full force as we followed him to Adze's office. I could tell Janae was still extremely impressed by the manor as we walked up the formal stairs and then Dmitri opened the doors to the office. We came in, and then Janae paused beside me, staring at Adze in shock

167

and admiration. I wondered if I had looked the same way when I first saw him.

"You must be Janae," Adze said, coming from behind the desk to stand in front of us.

"I, uh, yes," Janae said. Her eyes traveled up and down his body before fixing on his dark, glowing eyes. He was truly beautiful, I thought as Adze studied her. I wondered if he were using a glamour to stun her like this. Maybe he couldn't even control it.

"I'm glad Kairos has friends willing to come so far to visit him."

"Oh, it's not far at all," she said, breathless. "I don't mind."

"You are welcome to visit again, if you wish," Adze said, and I smiled, pleased. "It's a pleasure to meet you."

"I'm the one who's pleased," Janae said, then her cheeks tinted deep pink. "I mean, the pleasure's all mine. I mean, I like meeting you."

Her cheeks tinged into crimson and Adze nodded as if he wasn't surprised she was tongue-tied. He glanced at Dmitri and made a gesture, and then Dmitri herded us out. Janae looked back as the door closed, and as soon as we were out of the vampire's presence, she let out a sigh. She didn't speak as we returned downstairs and I took her to the back to show her my room. She didn't say a word until Dmitri left and we were in private, and then she exhaled loudly.

"I've never met a vampire before," she said slowly. "I had no idea they would be... like that. Do you feel that, every time you're around him?"

"What do you mean, feel that?"

"That... impressed," she said. "You're right, he is super hot. I see why you're staying here, why you'd give up on grad school to stay close to him."

Adze must have been using a glamour, I decided. It might have been unconscious, but I didn't think Janae would be acting like this unless he had been doing something to her. Or maybe it really was because I was resistant, so his presence didn't impact me as much. Repeated contact with him probably helped as well. I had been pretty stunned the first time I met him, after all.

Janae seemed to come back to herself and looked around.

"This is smaller than I thought it would be," she said. "And where's all your stuff?"

"A lot of it is in storage, but a lot is in the rest of the manor," I said. "And this is just my bedroom. I use a lot of the other rooms to relax. There's a pretty cool library, and they set aside another room for the tv that's like a private theater it's so nice."

"I'm glad you're not working the whole time. You're such a workaholic I was worried you'd never relax."

"Well, I don't do much outside of work, but I'm also not on a good schedule yet," I admitted. "I'm still having trouble getting up when the sun is setting and sleeping during the day. But I've been taking walks around the estate. It's really pretty. Want to see?"

"Sure," she said, and I led her out on the path I had found. It was the shortest path, because I knew she didn't especially like walking, but she seemed entranced by the gardens and when we walked by the pool, she whistled.

"This place is like a resort," she said.

"There's tennis courts, too," I said, feeling proud for some reason, as if I had anything to do with how the grounds looked or what was here. But I had managed to get a job at this exclusive place, so maybe I had the right to be proud. We walked and she kept complimenting things, stopping a few times to see the species of flower because they were all neatly labeled. I'd never noticed the labels before; in all honesty, I wasn't especially curious what the plants were, but Janae had minored in biology and apparently the garden had some rare plants. She was extremely impressed but when we began the loop back, she glanced at me with a crease between her brows.

"Hey, did something happen between you and Scott?"

"No," I said quickly, thinking of Scott's advances before we left. But nothing had happened. "Why?"

"He's really worried that you're not talking to him," she said. "It's like he feels guilty about something and thinks you cut him off because of it. He's worried you're not talking to all of us because of something he did. He hasn't really said it, but it's pretty clear. So did he do something?"

"Well," I said, considering. It was safe enough to tell her. I told her everything. "Right before I left, he kinda… made a move on me."

"What?" she asked, sounding scandalized. "He wouldn't. Right before you left? What did he possibly think would happen?"

"I dunno, something quick," I said, thinking of the way Scott had grabbed me. What had he expected from that? He knew I was leaving, but he had still wanted something from me. Had he honestly expected me to drop everything and have sex with him right there? Or had he wanted to get me to admit my feelings for him and then continue the relationship long distance? Neither especially made sense, but I had a feeling he didn't really know what he wanted either, and just knew he had to do something before he lost his chance.

"Is that why you're avoiding us?"

"No, it's not," I said firmly. "This job just takes all of my time. And the hours are weird. Once I get used to things, I'll chat with you guys more. No, I'll chat with you guys more starting tomorrow, even though I'm not used to things."

"Have you talked to your parents at all since you started?"

I winced. I hadn't. Janae groaned.

"Kairos, they're definitely overworking you. You always call your mom. She's probably panicking."

"I'll call her before I go to bed," I promised.

"You're really getting lost in this job," she said. "Now I see why you're staying, but is it really best for you? I mean, you're giving up your lifelong dream and abandoning your friends and family. Is that really what you want? Is he really worth all that?"

I didn't know what to say. We walked in silence and I

turned her question over and over again in my mind. Was this really what I wanted? Was I giving up too much? I thought of Adze looming over me in the darkness, the feel of him against my skin, the absolute helplessness of it all and the way that turned me on even more. Was I giving up too much just to experience that? Surely I could find someone to dominate me like that somewhere else where I wouldn't have to give up on everything and everyone I valued before working here. But I didn't want anyone else. I wanted Adze.

"I like working here," I said finally. "I promised them I'd be here a year, and then I'll re-evaluate. If I think it's not worth it, I'll leave. Maybe you won't be worried about me at the end of a year. Once I get things balanced, it'll be better."

"Maybe," she said. "If I'm still worried about you in a year, will you take my concerns seriously?"

"You're my best friend, Janae," I said, smiling at her. "I always take your concerns seriously."

"I hope so," she said, then turned to the large rose bushes we were passing. "Is this a rose garden?"

"I think so," I said. "I'm pretty sure it's marked on the map. I should have brought the map with us."

"This is absolutely gorgeous," she said with a sigh of contentment. "They're really spoiling you. I really do see why you like this place."

I smiled, pleased. Maybe she really wouldn't be worried in a year. But I wondered. I had isolated myself and buried myself in work. What was I getting in return? My job challenged me, and I felt like I was using all of my skills and that was quite satisfying, and I was in love with Adze and everything we did together, but was that enough? It was like my whole life had been replaced when I started working here. All of my hopes and dreams had dramatically shifted and I hadn't even realized it. I wondered what my mom would say. I would definitely have to call her before bed. I glanced at the time. It was just after seven. Janae would stay another hour or two, I hoped, and then it would be a reasonable time to call her. She always slept in on the weekends and I had learned not to call too early, but it should be perfect. I just hoped Janae hadn't talked me out of my job by the time she left. But I thought of Adze, and my promise to stay at least a year. No, I was locked in this job for now, and at the moment, I was completely satisfied by that decision.

CHAPTER TWENTY-FOUR: PERSUASION

"Kairos," my mom said eagerly as she picked up. "I saw it was you and almost didn't believe it. What have you been doing that you're too busy to call your own mom?"

"Sorry, mom," I said. "I got a new job and I've just been so busy with it. I didn't realize so much time had passed."

"So you're living closer to your job? I can't believe you didn't ask me for help moving in. You know I love to organize your new places."

"It's not really like that," I said, and took a deep breath. "I'm working for a vampire house, and staying with them."

Silence. Then I heard her clearing her voice.

"A vampire house? You're living in a vampire house? Do you have any idea how dangerous that is? Why didn't you tell me what kind of jobs you were looking for? You know better than to do something this stupid. You need to quit immediately."

"It's not a dangerous job, mom," I said. "Plenty of other humans live here. There's just one vampire, and he's nice."

I flushed. Nice was not the word I would use to describe Adze, but it was what she needed to hear.

"He doesn't feed on you?" she asked skeptically. "You know it's illegal for them to feed on people, don't you? If he tries it-"

"He won't, mom," I said. I almost wished he would do it, as I longed for him to feed on me and he seemed to want it as well, but he wouldn't do it. It was illegal, after all, and above all else he followed the law. "It's a good job. I'll just be here a year or so and then reassess the situation. I should have enough money by then to go to grad school."

More silence. "An entire year? That's too much time. If you need help finding a job, I'm sure your father would love to help. He can find something at the university where he works. If you're worried about money, you can move back in with us."

"I have a good job already," I said. "And I have a good place to live."

"You may have a job, but it isn't a good job. What do you do? Transport?"

"No," I said, though it was a fair question. Most jobs with vampires involved moving goods and other physical labor. Those were the jobs I had specifically avoided. I wasn't interested in that sort of job. I wanted to tell her what I was supposed to tell her but I suddenly realized she might not accept that job. Working with blood, while a good excuse and a legitimate and highly sought after job here, would not be what she wanted to hear about. If she didn't like the idea of me with vampires, mentioning blood might be too much.

"I just do paperwork," I said. "Probably the same as any secretary job."

"I'm sure we can find you something closer to home, with a professor nearby," she said, and I sighed.

"Mom. I have this job. I told them I'd be here a year. I'm not going to quit."

Yet another silence. "Have you told your father about this?"

"Not yet," I said. "I mean, I told him I have a job. I told you, too. But I wasn't exactly sure what I'd be doing when I started and I didn't want you to worry."

"I've been worried because you haven't been calling," she said. "And now I know I had reason to worry. I've heard that jobs with vampires pay well but you know it's because they're so dangerous. There's no need to put yourself in danger just to save up faster."

"Look, the job's mine, I've already started work and I've

been trained, and I'm staying here a year," I said. "Is dad there? I can talk to him right now if you want."

"No," she said, taking a deep breath. "If this is really what you want right now, then I'll talk to him first. Give him some warning. But you'll be ready for grad school next fall? You'll have to start looking for universities soon. I'm sure he wants to help with that."

I shut my eyes. Did I want to go to grad school? I didn't, not really, but I didn't know how to tell her that. I didn't know how to tell my dad that. They would be crushed. Would it be easier to pretend that I was interested and look for universities, then change my mind at the last minute? Or maybe I could say I wanted to work another year first, and keep delaying until I finally had the courage to tell them. And maybe I would be ready for grad school eventually. I had no idea. I had barely started working at this job and who knew what I'd want in a year or two.

"I'll get in contact with him," I said. "I know how important it is to him."

"Good," she said. "Well, I'll let him know about your job. Do you really need to live there? Where are you? In Redmond? You could move back home and commute."

"There's no way that's a commute," I pointed out. My undergrad was well over an hour away and my home was three hours further. And I worked every day, so it wasn't like I could come home on weekends. I could probably take a day off to visit them every once in a while. I had vacation days. But there was no way I would move anywhere else. I wasn't even sure that was an option. I remembered Adze's response when I had been surprised that I would be living in the house. He had made it seem like commuting wasn't an option and I was pretty sure living here was part of my contract. I needed to be on call at all times and that wasn't possible anywhere else.

"I'm on the outskirts of Redmond," I said. "It's beautiful."

"I don't like thinking of you so isolated," she said.

"Janae just visited me," I said. "I'm still in touch with

everyone."

"But not with me?"

I winced. "I kind of forgot about every else, too, but you know how good Janae is about keeping in touch. I'm going to be more careful in the future. I'll be calling a lot more."

"I want you to call every day," she said. "I'm worried about you."

"I can't call every day, but I'll call as much as I can," I said. "I'm on a night schedule so it's hard to find times that are good to call."

"A night schedule," she said softly. "You really are working for them, aren't you?"

"Business is done at night," I said. "The whole city's like that. It's not dangerous, just a weird adjustment. I'm happy."

"If you say so," she said skeptically.

I tried to wrap up the conversation after that and after a few more protestations that I was doing fine and not in danger, she finally let me go. I took a deep breath and stared at the phone. She was going to talk to my dad and I trusted that that was the best solution. I did not want to face his disappointment. And dealing with his worries on top of my mom's would be unbearable. But he would probably call me at some point. I hoped my mom mentioned that I was on a night schedule so he didn't call when I was sleeping, but I would turn the ring on while I slept today. Normally I turned it off when I slept, but today I wanted to talk to him if necessary. I couldn't miss this call or he might order me to come home, or at least insist on coming here and meeting the vampire I worked for. I didn't want that happening. Hopefully he would call at a good time. Even if he called this evening while I worked, I would take it. It was too important to miss.

With that taken care of, I sent a text to my other friends just letting them know I was fine and busy at my job, and would get in contact with them later. Then I headed to my room and gratefully sank into a deep sleep. When I woke up, it was starting to get dark outside and my father hadn't called.

Good. I felt refreshed and looked at the clock. Seven thirty. Just enough time for a run and a shower before work. My alarm was set to go off at eight and I turned it off, then got dressed and headed out. I glanced at the map. My usual loop went all along the edge of the grounds and passed several gardens but I hadn't paid attention to them before. This time, I would stop and look at them, since Janae had indicated that the flowers here were rare.

I started slow, and soon reached the first garden. I jogged in place for a minute as I admired the cornflower blue flowers. They had little tiny flowers and leaves and I stopped to lean down and examine them closer. I heard something behind me and straightened with a start, looking around. Nothing. I was at the outskirts of the grounds and eyed the woods nearby. The grounds weren't completely fenced in and this was one of the areas without a fence. I remembered the dhampir attacking me and shivered. I got out my phone and went to my messages with Dmitri.

Are any workers out by the Thistle Garden?

I was glad I remembered the name of the garden and hoped it was just nearby workers. I didn't know their hours but hadn't ever noticed them before. I hadn't been running this route long, though. Maybe they were only out once a week.

Head back to the house, Dmitri responded after a long moment. *The shortest route.*

I shivered again. Did that mean I was in danger? It certainly indicated that there weren't workers nearby. But maybe I had been imagining the noise. I looked around. Nothing. It was quite dark now, though the path was extremely well-lit. Dark enough for vampires to be out, I realized, and heard another sound.

I turned and saw three shapes emerge from the trees. I edged back. They were vampires, I could tell. I could feel a chill from them and suspected they were trying to use a glamour. I didn't recognize them, so they weren't from House Elviore. I turned and started running back the way I had come and heard them following.

Their footsteps grew closer and I pushed myself faster. Then, without warning, a shape sprang up in front of me and I crashed into the figure, who grabbed me and flung me to the ground. I lay there, shocked and out of breath, stunned from crashing into them. I got to my knees and looked up at them. Six vampires surrounded me now. They were beautiful, as all vampires were, but there was something different about them. Their eyes were faintly bloodshot and their clothes were ragged. They looked nothing like the vampires I had seen so far.

"A human," one of them said, staring at me intently. "Just like they said."

"Fresh," another murmured. "I can smell his sweet blood."

Panic set in. They were going to feed on me. I was a human and they were going to feed on me. My mind flashed to my mom's warnings, to Janae's warnings. I might not be in danger from Adze, but there were other vampires. I jumped to my feet and bolted away from them, hearing exclamations of shock and dismay. They must have thought I was stunned by a glamour. Was that all of them? That had to be. I wouldn't run into more. But I could hear them following and as with before, they were gaining on me. I felt something brush against my arm. They were reaching for me. They were close and I pushed myself harder, already gasping for breath. Where was the house? Would they follow me all the way there? Who were these vampires?

A dark shape in front of me again but this time I had enough time to dodge it and to my surprise, it let me past. Then I heard the vampires chasing me stop. Abruptly.

"Master," one murmured, and I paused to look back.

The shape was Adze and he was now standing between me and the vampires. My heart raced and I gasped for breath. Adze looked back at me.

"Get to the house now," he said. "I'll handle this."

CHAPTER TWENTY-FIVE: SECOND THOUGHTS

Adze looked deadly serious as he told me to get back into the house. He stood between me and the other vampires and my heart raced at what would have happened if he hadn't shown up. I wondered if he were about to kill these vampires. But no, he wasn't a vampire hunter. He wasn't allowed to kill another vampire. I didn't pause, though. I started running towards the house. I went much slower than when I had been escaping them, sticking to a pace I could maintain. I was out of breath and running like this wasn't helping, but I wanted to get to safety. Adze had stopped them, but what if there were more? What had been wrong with them? Why had they looked like that? Every other vampire I had seen was extremely polished and formal, but they had looked almost like beggars.

Dmitri was waiting at the edge of the path and grabbed me, hurrying me back to the house. Once I was inside, I took several long breaths and tried to recover. He clutched my arm and patted my back.

"What happened?" he asked. "Where's Master Adze?"

"There were vampires," I managed. "They chased me. Adze stopped them and told me to come back."

His eyes narrowed and I realized I should have said Master Adze, but he didn't comment. He probably knew I was too shaken to follow proper protocol.

"Vampires," he said angrily, and I realized he wasn't mad about my protocol breach. He was mad about what I had said. "How dare they come to our house."

Margaret rushed in the room and swept me into a hug.

"You're safe now," she said reassuringly. "Master Adze will take care of things."

I took another deep breath. My heart was starting to return to a normal rhythm. Margaret and Dmitri gave me some space, then Margaret gestured to the entrance.

"Come inside," she said. "You were pretty far away. I'm sure you're tired."

"Thank you for contacting me," Dmitri said seriously as we went further into the building and Margaret brought me to the kitchen to sit down. "We wouldn't have known anything was wrong for hours if you hadn't."

I shivered. That was probably what the vampires had been expecting. They had ambushed me far from the house with the intent that no one would know I was missing. Margaret would have noticed I wasn't there for breakfast but might have assumed I was just sleeping late. No one would have gotten worried until a little before nine when it became clear I wasn't there. What would have happened? Would the vampires have killed me, or just fed on me? There had been a desperation in their eyes and I suspected they would kill me. If I hadn't thought to message Dmitri, I would be dead right now.

"There was something wrong with them," I said, my heart slowing from its quick pace. "The vampires. They didn't look like any other vampires I've ever seen."

"What did they look like?"

"I don't know," I said, thinking back to the differences. "Disheveled. Hungry."

I shivered again. I was truly chilled by what had almost happened. Dmitri and Margaret looked at each other. Did they know what was wrong with the vampires? They had to, with a look like that. Would they tell me, though, or was this one of the many things I wasn't allowed to know yet? This impacted my very survival, though. Surely they had to tell me.

Dmitri cleared his throat. "They were in withdrawal," he said slowly. "I'm sure of it. They wouldn't dare come here otherwise."

"I've heard that before," I said, thinking of the cathedral. The vampires who had been caught were in withdrawal, according to House Tennison. "What does that mean?"

"You know how drugs work in humans," he said. "How addiction works."

I nodded. One of my childhood friends had started doing drugs. At first it had been simple, just to get a high and have some fun. I had considered trying it, as he always had a good time, but had decided against it. Good thing, too, because I had watched as a desire for fun turned into a need for it, then a desperation. He would do anything for a fix and he had pushed me away and turned into an addict. There was nothing I could do to help anymore and I had watched him slip away into someone I no longer knew.

"So vampires have drugs too?" I asked, thinking about the wide assortment of legal and illegal drugs. My friend had started on legal drugs, prescribed by his doctor, then started abusing them and eventually turned to other drugs as well.

"Human drugs don't work on them, and most vampires have no desire for them," Dmitri said. "Feeding on blood is pleasurable enough. But there is one drug that can be mixed with blood. It's highly addictive and enhances hunger and a desire for blood."

"That's why they attacked me?" I asked, thinking of their words. "They said someone had said I would be there. Can they track humans?"

Dmitri blinked in surprise. "They knew you would be there?"

"I think so," I said.

"Master Adze will find out if they were sent," Margaret said, then put a cup of coffee in front of me. "Drink this. You look like you're still in shock."

I obediently drank the coffee. I did feel in shock. Nothing was really making sense and I ought to be a lot more frightened than I was. Adze had said it was possible I would be targeted because of my job, but after the messages from House

Salvite had quieted, I hadn't noticed anything about me. Was this an attack from them? My eyes widened.

"I saw this," I said, my mind rushing back to the email yesterday morning I had translated. "In an email. I didn't think it was anything."

"You think it's House Salvite?" Dmitri said darkly. "I hope not, for their sake. Are you going to be able to work today?"

"Of course," I said, startled. Why wouldn't I be able to work? I had caught my breath and felt better.

"Go get dressed, get some food, and then show me that email," Dmitri said, and I stood up and headed to my room. My hands were trembling, I realized. I wasn't fully back to normal.

I still had forty minutes until work started so I got in the shower. I needed to wash the sweat and fear off and as the steaming water crashed against my skin, I realized why Dmitri had asked me about working. Should I keep working? He wasn't just asking about today. He was asking in general. Did I still want to work here if I was attacked like that?

This was exactly what my mom had warned me about, I realized. Janae had warned me, too. Working for vampires was dangerous. Even if Adze didn't hurt me, there were plenty of others who would. My house was essentially at war with another house and I was being targeted as a result. Why would I possibly keep this job? Sure, it paid well, but as my mom had pointed out, I could easily get another job and move back in with her. Scott would love to have me as a roommate. He had been willing to let me crash with him for a while and even though I didn't especially want a relationship with him, I could handle it. I didn't have a lot of experience and my degree wasn't that useful but my dad could probably find me a job helping some professor or another and I could slowly save enough for grad school. I would have to work through grad school but I had planned on that anyway. I couldn't keep putting myself in danger like this, though. Something needed to change.

I dressed quickly and went to the kitchen. Margaret was

just laying out a bowl of biscuits next to an egg casserole. I would miss this if I stopped working here, I thought wistfully. It was great getting good food without having to work for it. Or even pay for it, really. I would miss Margaret, too.

"Are you feeling okay?" she asked.

"Yeah," I said, and sat down. She helped me get a plate and I ate in silence. She looked rather nervous, though I wasn't sure why.

"Do you want to talk about anything?" she asked, smiling anxiously and sitting across from me. "What did your friend think of the house? She seemed to like it here."

"She said it was too dangerous," I said. "I talked to my mom this morning and she said the same thing. I guess they were right."

Margaret's smile seemed strained. "You won't be in danger once we sort things out," she said. "It's not any more dangerous working here than anywhere else."

"I've been attacked twice now," I pointed out. "I don't think they would have killed me the first time but they would have killed me tonight. That wouldn't happen anywhere else."

Her smile wavered and her eyes were serious.

"Are you thinking of leaving?"

"I don't know," I said. Did I want to leave? Always before when I had thought about it, Adze was enough to make me stay. I didn't want to lose him, so I ignored the danger. But was he really enough to stay somewhere where my life was in danger? I needed to talk to him, I decided. I needed to talk to him about my job and my safety and our relationship. There was nothing formal between us, after all, and he had pulled back since talking to Lilith. I didn't want a normal working relationship with him. I wanted to be in his lair with the darkness around me. If I couldn't have that, what was the purpose of staying?

Dmitri entered as I slowly finished my food and I glanced at my watch. I had about fifteen minutes until work started. Margaret returned to the kitchen after exchanging a serious look with Dmitri.

"When you're finished, Master Adze would like to talk to you," he said. My hand trembled and suddenly I felt full. I set down my fork beside the half-eaten casserole and folded my napkin beside my plate. "You can finish," Dmitri said, but I shook my head.

"I'd like to talk to him," I said.

Without another word, Dmitri led me to Adze's office. Adze was at his desk when we entered and the sight of him was deeply reassuring. His perfect face and beautiful body were why I was staying here and I needed to see him and hold him to remember that. Adze stood up and came to the front of the desk, his dark, glowing eyes fixed on me. He waved a hand to Dmitri.

"Thank you, Dmitri," he said. "We'll need some privacy."

Dmitri bowed and shut the door as he left. It was just me and Adze and I had no idea what to say. Should I tell him I wanted to quit? Did I want to quit? I didn't want to be in danger anymore. Was he really worth all this?

CHAPTER TWENTY-SIX: REASON TO STAY

The office was silent as Adze looked at me from the front of his desk. We were alone now, and I wasn't sure what would happen. He approached me carefully and stopped right in front of me, reaching up to caress my cheek. His eyes were hypnotic and I wondered if he were using a glamour on me. There were so many dangers here, I considered. I was resistant and the vampires I met would want to test themselves against me, so I wasn't really safe around anyone except Elviore vampires. I needed to leave this whole world behind and get somewhere as far from vampires as possible.

"I'm sure you're upset," Adze said. "We need to talk about what happened."

"Dmitri told me they were in withdrawal," I said.

"Vampires in withdrawal are dangerous," Adze said seriously. "They'll feed on anyone, even dhampir. But it's an extremely rare condition."

"They were looking for me," I said. "And I remember reading something about it in the emails yesterday. I was being targeted."

"Yes, you were," he said, and I was a little surprised he didn't deny it. "But it won't end if you quit."

I hadn't mentioned quitting but it was probably obvious I was considering it. But quitting would end everything and remove me from danger. My dad would help me get a new job, a safe job, and I could live with Scott or my parents, and when I earned enough, I could go to grad school and get my PhD.

Exactly as I had planned my entire life. This brief episode with vampires would be forgotten.

"I would get a different job, far from Redmond," I said. "I wouldn't have anything to do with vampires."

"House Salvite selected you," Adze said. "If you quit, they'll recruit you. If you refuse, your life will once again be in danger. They don't want someone like you working for anyone besides them."

"Why would they care?" I asked with a shiver. "Don't they only care if I'm helping you?"

"I don't think they know how much you're helping me," he said. "They're just trying to eliminate potential threats and unless you're working for them, you are a threat."

"How is that any better?"

"They're not focused on you," Adze said. "The attack today shouldn't have happened. The grounds should have been better protected. You should have been better protected. It won't happen again. They're leaving it to vampires in withdrawal, so they aren't serious about killing you."

"They're not serious?" I asked in shock. "If I hadn't told Dmitri where I was, I'd be dead!"

"I know," Adze said, and looked down for a moment. His face was so expressionless but I saw anger in his features. "That should not have happened. I will never let you be in danger like that again."

He ran a hand through my hair. It felt so good. "I'll keep you safe, Kairos," he said. "No one will dare hurt you while you belong to me."

"Do I?" I asked. He looked puzzled and I took a breath. "Do I belong to you?"

"Of course," he said, stroking my hair and running his hand down my cheek to linger on the mark on my neck. "This is proof enough of that. You belong to House Elviore, and to me specifically."

"That's not what I mean," I said.

He drew in a slow breath. "Kairos, relationships between

humans and vampires are not lightly entered into."

"You've never hesitated with me before," I pointed out, and he sighed.

"I didn't expect you to be this serious about me."

"Are you serious about me?"

Adze studied me, then the faintest hint of a smile crossed his lips and my heart leapt.

"I never enter into a relationship if I'm not serious," he said. "But I didn't anticipate your reaction. Humans always find ways to surprise me."

"How did you think I would react?" I asked, wondering what I was doing that was so different than most.

"I thought you would choose another house within Elviore," he said. "I didn't think you would want to stay with me."

"The whole reason I'm with Elviore is you," I said, and that smile grew a little more pronounced. "And if I do stay, you'll be the only reason."

His hand slid to my waist, then snuggled back to pull me into an embrace.

"Let's give you a good reason to stay, then," he murmured, and my breath hitched. Right now? Here? We had done it in his office before and I was all for it, but it was so much better in his lair. If he took me right here, right now, and then left me without release as he always did here, I wasn't sure I could take it. I pushed away and he released me.

"Not now," I said. "Not here. I- I have work to do."

"You're a good employee," Adze said with a trace of amusement. "Very well. I'll expect you in the basement at ten tomorrow morning. Is that better?"

"Yes," I said breathlessly, all thoughts of quitting vanishing from my mind. I needed to stay, because I needed to be with Adze again. What would we do together? I shivered at the thought and for the first time all evening, it wasn't a shiver of fear. I just had to get through a day of work, and then we would be together.

Adze smiled and leaned forward to kiss me briefly, then pushed me away.

"Show Dmitri the email you remember and try to have the physical mail finished before midnight."

"Of course," I said, and he waved his hand to dismiss me as he returned to the other side of the desk and sat down. I smiled at him cautiously, then headed back to my office where Dmitri was waiting. He looked uncertain for once as I sat down.

"I'm supposed to show you the email I saw," I said, quickly sorting through the system to pull up the email in question. I pointed to the code words I hadn't recognized until too late. "There," I said. "I thought it was referring to somewhere outside of Redmond. I guess this is outside of the city a little," I considered. "But it doesn't read like a physical attack, just that something is going to be attempted."

That was in my interpretation but because I hadn't considered it especially relevant, I hadn't flagged it as dangerous. I was flagging every message that used code, but the ones that seemed to indicate imminent plans or deaths were given a far higher priority.

"If you saw this code being used again, would you recognize it?" Dmitri asked. That was the important question, I knew. If I were targeted again, would I recognize it in time? I studied the code being used.

"Now that I know that this type of reference to outside Redmond means here, I should notice anytime this house is brought up specifically," I said. "But it's not the kind of direct plan I would really notice. All of their emails seem to mention vague plans like this."

"But you'll notice if anything has to do with this house?"

I nodded, and he looked relieved. He glanced at me.

"Are you planning on staying?"

"For the moment," I said slowly, thinking of tonight when I would see Adze again. Would he give me a good enough reason to stay? When I saw him, there was no question of me staying.

Of course I wanted to be at his side. But now that he was in a different room and I was staring at an email ordering me killed, I felt very different. It was dangerous here. I couldn't pretend it wasn't. The attack in the park had been due to carelessness on my part, so I hadn't really thought of myself as being in danger. As long as I was careful and learned how to navigate a city of vampires, I thought I would be safe. But I wasn't safe. There was another house targeting me specifically and I wasn't entirely sure what to do about it. Would they really track me down if I left? I didn't want to work for them. I didn't want to work for any vampires if I didn't work for Adze. If I couldn't have him, then I wanted to be as far from this life as possible and even though I couldn't imagine House Salvite hunting me down if I went somewhere else, I also hadn't thought they would try to kill me. Anything was possible. At least here I had Adze.

"Let me know if you see anything else," Dmitri said. "Flag anything that looks even slightly suspicious. I don't care if you flag every single message. We'll sort through everything and make sure this doesn't happen again."

I nodded, wondering who "we" was. I didn't think he meant him and Dianne. Maybe him and Adze, but it seemed like Adze did other things during the night. Maybe there was someone at another household who worked with Dmitri on things like this. I still barely knew anything about House Elviore, despite what Margaret had shared. Dmitri left and I got to work on the physical mail first, sorting through the envelopes carefully and being careful not to let the paper touch anything except my gloves. Since even the desk had fingerprints on it, I had to be very careful with everything as I snapped pictures of each piece of mail and entered my translations.

They were planning something, that much was clear, but I couldn't tell what. Something was happening and many of the messages referred to a plan, but gave no specifics. I uneasily marked each message that referred to the mysterious plan and wondered if Dmitri and whoever else looked over my translations would understand what was happening. It didn't have to do with me, I was pretty sure. I finished before lunch and Dmitri took the letters away as I went to snack with Margaret. She was overly friendly and seemed a little nervous and I assured her I wasn't leaving yet. She laughed, sounding relieved.

"Oh good," she said. "I like you a lot. I wouldn't want you to leave like that."

"I don't know how long I'm staying," I pointed out.

"But at least you're not running out," she said. "You shouldn't be in danger here. We'll protect you better from now on. You'll see."

"Has anyone ever tried to kill you?" I asked curiously, wondering if this were something common to working with vampires. After all, I had been attacked twice, not just once, and it was well-known that working with vampires was dangerous.

"Never," she said. "Once, when I was growing up, a vampire in withdrawal cornered me on the way home from school, but there were police nearby who stopped him. I was really scared, though."

"How often do vampires go into withdrawal?"

"Not often," she said, then glanced at the door. "I probably shouldn't be talking about it. It's a vampire thing, not really for humans to know about."

"I work here, and I was attacked," I said. "Don't you think I deserve to know?"

"Well," she said slowly. "Withdrawal seems to happen in waves. No one can really track down how the blood is tainted with the drug or how it's dispersed, since blood is divided with such a rigid system."

"Wouldn't they just add the drug to whatever blood they receive?" I asked.

"Sometimes," she said. "But sometimes it seems like the blood is tainted when it leaves the facility."

"Wait, so a vampire could receive drugged blood and not

even realize it?" I asked in shock.

"Yes, and it's addictive enough that one dose is often enough," she said. "House Elviore tracks when that happens and is trying to pinpoint who is behind it."

"Is Adze at risk, then?" I asked. "I mean, Master Adze? If anyone can be drugged, why wouldn't they try to get House Elviore addicted?"

"Ancients are immune to it, luckily," Margaret said with a smile. "It only effects new vampires. So our house is safe. You won't ever have to worry about one of our vampires targeting you."

I hadn't even considered that, and it was good it was out of the question. I didn't want to have to worry about the vampires within Elviore attacking me because they were in withdrawal. I remembered how disheveled the vampires had looked when they were in withdrawal and remembered my friend who had become an addict, and how bedraggled he always looked. No one should become so desperate for a drug that they lost all ability to care for themselves or do anything other than seek the next high.

I glanced at the clock and realized my lunch hour was almost up, and thanked Margaret for the wonderful meal before heading back into my office to focus on the emails for the day. The job required a lot of mental strain and while usually it was rewarding being able to translate so much, today that strain was doubled by the stress of not knowing what was being planned and having to pay attention to threats to my own life. Maybe I didn't want this job after all, I considered as I sorted through the emails. I would have to see what Adze offered.

CHAPTER TWENTY-SEVEN: BOUND

The basement was dark but not pitch black as I went to the door at the end of the hall. I eyed the other doors as I went, wondering what was behind them. I had been in two of the rooms, but I had only seen one of them where I had showered. One of the rooms had a bed at least, and probably more, but I had no clue what the other rooms were for. Probably related to work, not play. Or to survival. I still wasn't sure if vampires slept or not.

I knocked at the furthest door and heard a reply, so I opened the door. It was pitch black but this time I tried not to be frightened as I slid inside. I left the door open so there would be a sliver of light.

"Close the door and come closer, Kairos," Adze said. I shivered but obeyed, shutting the door quietly but firmly and plunging everything into night. It was hard to imagine that it was sunny outside, the sun firmly on its trek across the sky. Down here, everything was inky darkness suited for a vampire like Adze.

I took a few cautious steps towards him before coming to a stop, unwilling to go further without being able to see. I knew he wouldn't let me trip on anything but I felt so vulnerable in the darkness. I heard movement and flinched as something touched my shoulder. Adze stroked up to my shoulder and wrapped something stiff and cool around my neck. I heard a click as he shut it around me and my breath caught. Was that a collar? It had to be. It fit snugly around me. I could breathe easily but felt bound by him, to his will. It was a delicious feeling.

"So you need a reason to stay with me," Adze murmured. "You shouldn't even be thinking of leaving."

I drew in a slow breath as he rested his hands on my shoulders. All thoughts of why I wanted to leave fled into the darkness and all I could think about was him, here, next to me. How had I even considered leaving Adze?

"Come with me," Adze said. I could feel him grabbing the front of my collar and leading me towards the door. There was no light when he opened it and he pulled me quickly down the hall into the same room as last time. I shivered in anticipation. He led me to the right of the door and then stopped, tugging at my collar as if indicating to me that I should stay still.

"Undress," he said.

Last time it had been frightening undressing in the darkness but this time I felt oddly empowered as I pulled my shirt over my head, making sure it didn't catch on the collar, shuffling off my shoes and socks, and then pulling off my pants and boxers. I stood in the cool air of the vampire's lair completely exposed and I felt safe, because Adze was here. I would always be safe while he was here.

"Turn around," he commanded, and I obeyed. He pulled my arms behind me and crossed them so that my left wrist was next to my right elbow. Something silky smooth was tied around my wrist, then my elbow, and when I flexed I realized I could no longer move. He pulled my other wrist to my elbow and tied that as well, then began lacing the silky rope down my forearms until I was completely pinned. I had never been tied up like this before and I wasn't entirely sure how I felt about it. I was helpless, but it was Adze. I trusted him.

"Get on your knees," he breathed, and I pulled at the bonds tying me before realizing I wouldn't be able to use my hands and arms to lower myself. I felt awkward getting to my knees like this but managed it, and felt him run his hand through my hair as if in reward. Then his hand slipped to my chin and pulled my face upwards and I opened my mouth, knowing what he wanted. The collar pressed against my throat gently in the new position. I could feel his heat right next to my lips and extended my tongue to make contact with his silky smooth, warm skin.

His hand clenched in my hair as I caressed him with my tongue, slicking him up. I had forgotten how large he was. I had gotten him down my throat once, so I would be able to do it again, but I was a little intimidated by the size of him as I wrapped my lips around his tip and leaned into him, pulling against the bonds because I wanted to use my hands as well but couldn't. His hand tightened and he thrust forward gently, entering me more fully but not completely. Almost like he was teasing me. He began thrusting gently as I worked my tongue around him, getting a little deeper each time before withdrawing and letting me stroke him. Soon his pace picked up and he was deep in my throat in a pattern that was leaving me dizzy with pleasure and desperate for breath, but he didn't slow down. My hands clenched in fists. I was completely hard, and completely helpless as the collar around my neck seemed to tighten every time he thrust. Normally I would be able to push back on him slightly to give myself time to breath but he was in control and he wasn't slowing down, and I couldn't possible say anything because he was no longer withdrawing completely. I gagged as he thrust into me completely and he withdrew a little further and slowed down as I struggled to gasp for breath, but then he was inside me again. We continued like that for a long time as my body buzzed with the unexpected pleasure of having him in control of my breathing, and then he pulled completely out and I inhaled deeply as I licked my lips. I had never been so aroused in my life but for once, I wasn't on the brink of coming.

"Stand up," he said softly. It was difficult without being able to use my hands for balance but I again managed to obey his commands and get to my feet. As soon as I was up, he grabbed the collar around my neck and pulled me forward.

Something firm but soft hit my knees and thighs and he pushed me forward. Without my hands to balance myself, I fell right into what had to be the bed. I cried out as the soft material laced against my cock, and couldn't help but grind against it. Adze pulled my hips up to stop me and wrapped his hand around me.

"Not yet," he said. That was at least promising, since it implied that I would eventually get to come.

He spread my cheeks and I felt something cool drip against my opening, then his fingers swirled around me before pressing inside. Two of his fingers were deep inside me in an instant and I shifted uncomfortably as he pressed against my insides. Then he must have brushed against my prostate because fire sparked deep within me and I cried out, my cock jerking against his other hand. He stroked me again right there, deliberately, then began pressing against the spot in a quick tattoo that had my heart and cock throbbing as I pressed my face into the silky sheets and moaned helplessly. I struggled to move my arms but they were bound and there was nothing I could do except lie here and take the pleasure, and hope he let me come soon.

Suddenly he added a third finger and I whimpered as I felt myself stretching. But surely this was just as wide as when he entered me himself. It shouldn't feel so much different but it did for some reason, and he kept striking that spot. Then he added a fourth finger and I winced. This time it was starting to hurt. He didn't push as deep and I cried out as the pain suddenly spiked.

"Stop," I managed. He pulled his fingers out and chuckled.

"Looks like you're not ready for that yet," he said. "But soon I'll be able to fist you and you'll be desperate for it."

I shivered at the thought of his entire fist inside of me, but couldn't deny that the thought turned me on. Still, I was relieved he wasn't going to do it right now. Instead, I felt something that wasn't a finger press against me and sighed in pleasured anticipation at the thought of his cock finally entering me. He slammed into me and I cried out in surprise as he rapidly entered me until I could tell he was fully inside me. He had never been so quick and it burned, but felt good.

He thrust deeply, withdrawing almost completely before fully plunging into me, and he gave me no chance to adapt as he quickened his pace. I kept moaning with each thrust, and then he began stroking his hand along my cock and I cried out again at the doubled pleasure. I pulled against the rope binding my arms as the collar pressed against my throat and felt completely helpless in a new and unexpectedly pleasurable way. My body was his to control, and he was controlling it skillfully. Finally, I couldn't stand it anymore.

"Please, Master," I managed to whimper. "Please let me come."

"Not yet," he said, and I squirmed under him. There was no way I could hold on much longer. His hand on my cock began long, firm strokes and I moaned and thrashed against the cock stabbing into me. I couldn't hold on. But I did, because I couldn't displease him.

"Please," I whispered.

One of his hands was busy on my cock and while the other hand had been on my hips helping keep me in place for the deep thrusts, it now reached up to tousle my hair.

"Yes, you may come," Adze said just as he jerked against my cock hard and plunged all the way into me.

I let out a soft scream and exploded into a million pieces, nearly blacking out with the pleasure as fire raced through my entire body before concentrating on my cock and the pleasure bursting from it. It seemed to last forever, but it began to fade. Soon I had control of my breathing again, the collar pressing against me, and soon my body returned to my awareness. He pulled out and I wondered if he were smiling.

He pulled me back to my feet and I wobbled slightly, my knees weak and my hands and arms still bound behind my back. The rope tugged and then loosened, and in moments my wrists were free, then my forearms, then I could swing my arms to my sides. The collar stayed on, though, as he tugged it and I knew he wanted to lead me forward. He brought me out of that room and from the feel of the floor, into the shower room. Then he took the collar off.

"Wait until you can see, then clean yourself up," Adze said. "Your clothes are here, so get dressed and then return upstairs. I'll see you at work tonight."

"Thank you," I murmured, though I wasn't entirely sure what I was thanking him for. Everything, I supposed. Then I heard the door close and I was aware of a dim light around me. Slowly, over the course of several minutes, the light grew brighter. When I was just able to make out the room around me, I turned on the shower. Icy cold water, just like last time, and again I didn't see a way to change it. I didn't mind much, though. I needed it because my body was still hot from what had happened. When I felt clean enough, I noticed several towels lying on a low bench next to my clothes. I dried off, dressed, and headed back upstairs, knowing that my dreams were going to be wonderful today.

CHAPTER TWENTY-EIGHT: FRIENDSHIP

I got up early that evening and considered going on a jog. Should I risk it? I knew the grounds were probably safer now than they ever had been after the attack, but I was wary, so I jogged in a circle around the house itself without going anywhere else. It only took about twenty minutes and I was amazed at how enormous the house was. As I showered and got dressed, I glanced at the time. 6:23pm. I wouldn't start work until nine, so I had quite a lot of time to kill. I thought about Lee, and Angie's silent ultimatum, and this was a perfect time to call. I dialed the number and waited while it rang. When it picked up, Lee sounded delighted.

"Kairos!" he exclaimed. "Here I thought you had died! Janae said you were fine, but I didn't believe it."

"Hi Lee, I'm sorry about dropping out of touch for so long," I said. "I just wanted to chat."

"Hey, I wanted to tell you something," he said in a conspiratorial half-whisper. "You can't tell anyone, okay? I got a ring."

"A ring?" I was puzzled. Lee wasn't the type to wear jewelry but he sounded excited about this.

"You know," he said. "For Angie."

"Isn't her birthday in six weeks?" I asked, wondering why he would buy a present for her so early. Maybe it was a really cool ring.

Lee laughed. "Idiot. I'm proposing to her."

"What?" I was stunned. "Does she know?"

"Of course not," he said. "I mean, we've been talking about getting more serious. Fighting about it, really," he admitted. "I'm pretty sure she'll say yes. But I'm waiting until her birthday."

Six weeks, I thought. But according to Janae, Angie was going to break up with him in four unless he proved he was serious. Proposing would definitely prove that, but he couldn't wait that long.

"I think you should propose now," I said. "You know, when you're still excited about it."

"Trust me, I'm going to be this excited then, too," Lee said.

"Yeah, but can you keep a secret that long?"

"I'm really good at secrets, you know that," he said, and I had to agree that was true. He was still keeping a few of my secrets. We were high school friends and he was the first person I came out to. He had kept that a secret for years, at my request, and when I finally told people, he managed not to make a big deal about the fact that he'd known for so long. Yes, he was good at hiding things, but this was one time where that might backfire.

"I don't know about her birthday," I said, trying to think of reasons to pressure him to propose sooner. "You'll want to celebrate, and it might take away from her special day."

"It'll just make it more special, don't you think?" he asked. "I mean, this is the present she's always wanted."

"She'll want to celebrate your proposal anniversary," I pointed out, because I knew it was true. "She won't want to share that with her birthday every year."

"I hadn't thought of that," he said consideringly. "I know she wouldn't mind this year, but you're right, it might be a problem in the future. Maybe I'll do the first day of summer. That would be pretty special."

That would be cutting it close, I knew. I didn't know how exact Angie was going to be, or even when exactly she had told Janae. There was a chance she wouldn't wait that long, too. She might give up after two weeks, not a month.

"You really should propose now," I said. "Especially if you're fighting about it. This would prove you're serious, and sometimes it helps to do things right after an argument rather than waiting. You don't want her to give up on you, after all."

I said the last in a light, kidding voice, though I was deadly serious. She was going to give up if he didn't act quickly but I didn't want to come out and say it.

"Kairos, do you know something?" he asked, and I gulped. Apparently that wasn't subtle enough. "Did she say something? I didn't think you were even talking to her lately. What did she say?"

Should I tell him? It was breaking Janae's confidence but he did deserve to know, and I didn't want to lie to him.

"She wants you to prove you're serious," I said. "She's tired of waiting. That's all I know."

Technically I knew more, but this was close enough that I didn't feel like I was lying. He sighed.

"I should have known. She's so impatient. All right. But I want to make a big show of it. Any chance you have time off this weekend? I'd love for you to be there."

I considered. I was on call every night, but I could take a few hours in the morning or evening and go home. I wanted to be there and see everyone. Was it safe, though? Last time I went home they had sent Margaret with me. Would she be willing to come again? And would she be enough? Last time I hadn't really been in danger. They were worried House Salvite would talk to me, maybe attempt to kidnap me, but I wasn't in physical danger. This time I was. If I left the house, would I be targeted? And if they followed me and saw who my friends were, would they be targeted as well? I didn't want to risk it, I decided slowly. I might be overreacting but the fear of the attack was still sharp and I didn't want to put my friends in harm's way if I could avoid it.

"It's really hard to get away," I said. "I'm on call every day even though I don't officially work on the weekends. And I'm still adapting to a night schedule, so going during the day would really throw me off."

"Are you really happy with a job like that?" he asked skeptically. "One where you can't take time off to see your friends?"

"In the future I'll probably be able to," I said, wondering if that were true. "It's just the schedule and I'm still learning the job so they call me in whenever anything comes up so I can learn to handle it. It's temporary."

"I dunno, you've been there a while now," he said. "You're still learning?"

"It's really complicated."

He sighed. "Well, if you can't come, you can't come."

"Are you sure she wants it in public?" I asked. "Maybe she would prefer you asking in private. I know she loves everyone, but maybe this should be your special thing."

"That's true," he said slowly. "I hadn't thought of that. I wanted to make a big deal out of it but maybe she would prefer something quiet. She's funny like that, wanting to spend so much time with everyone but liking quiet things too. That's a good point, Kairos."

I smiled. That would make me feel less guilty as well.

"So what exactly is your job?" he asked. "I talked to Janae but she didn't really have any details."

I gave a description, trying to be as vague as possible even though he had some pointed questions. Luckily, I knew enough to answer him, though I hedged on quite a few answers. I shifted the subject as soon as possible and soon we were chatting about his new summer job working for a local charity. He had volunteered for them several times in the past and when they had a spot open up in marketing, he had quickly applied. It wasn't his major but he knew a lot about social media and that was their main requirement.

It was nice talking to him. Janae's visit had reminded me how much I missed my friends and this was a balm. I would call Angie tomorrow, I decided. Maybe Lee would have proposed to her by then. I would have to act surprised. I didn't want her to know I'd talked Lee into it. And maybe after that I would get in touch with Scott. I was a little hesitant about that because I knew he would want to visit, but maybe it wouldn't be so bad. Maybe he would have gotten over his feelings for me. According to Janae, he felt bad about what he had done, so maybe it was safe. Yes, I would call him, too. Maybe I would make a call every evening when I got up. That would be a good addition to my schedule and since evening jogs were temporarily out of reach since I was too afraid to go out, it would fill my time nicely.

We chatted for nearly an hour before he had to go get dinner with Angie. He sounded excited and I encouraged him as much as possible. I was pretty sure he was going to propose tonight, but not positive. He might lose his nerve since he didn't have a lot of time to prepare. Lee was not a spontaneous person, and might want to take a day or two to lay everything out. He had told me once that he liked planning all of his conversations in advance so that he was never surprised, so it was likely he would hold off proposing until he figured out how to handle any and all of her possible reactions. Or maybe he would just go for it, though it would be uncharacteristic.

We said goodnight and I headed out for breakfast in a good mood. Margaret was pleased by that and we chatted as well. She didn't bring up what had happened or even asked if I was staying. It was probably obvious from my mood that I had no intention of leaving. And I didn't. I had wondered if Adze was enough to make me stay and after feeling him dominate me after work, I had my answer. I wanted to stay. I didn't want to give him up, not when he made my body and heart sing. I wasn't entirely sure what I meant to him and that bothered me a little, but he seemed serious. He had said he didn't enter relationships lightly and his actions proved that there was a relationship, so I was important to him in some way and that was enough.

Dmitri came in about fifteen minutes before work started and eyed me talking to Margaret. I had finished eating already and was dressed, so I was really just killing time until work started. I blushed under his gaze. He started work before nine, so maybe I was supposed to start sooner too. He gestured for me to follow and I said good night to Margaret and obeyed. Once we were in the hall outside the kitchen, he pulled me to a stop.

"House Tennison is here," he said in a low voice. "You'll need to tell them what happened. They seem to be here for other reasons, too. They showed up not knowing you were attacked, but refuse to say what prompted the visit. They want to talk to you alone. Don't tell them your job, don't tell them anything about our house, but answer their questions as honestly as you can. I don't think they'll press you hard but I also don't know what they want."

A chill ran through me. I would have to describe what happened?

"Can I say the vampires were in withdrawal or is that secret, too?"

"You can tell them that," he said. "And you can tell them Adze stopped them. I don't think there's anything about the attack itself you have to hide."

I nodded, but wondered what about the house I was supposed to hide. I barely knew anything about it, after all. Maybe it was just a blanket statement, since I knew House Elviore liked to keep everything about them secret. I wondered how much Dmitri knew about the house. He had to know more than Margaret, didn't he? But I wouldn't ask, and I wouldn't share with Tennison. I took a deep breath and mentally prepared myself to be surrounded by vampires again. When I was ready, Dmitri led me to the entrance hall. A single vampire stood there in a heavy cloak and I was relieved. At least I wouldn't have a swarm of vampires staring me down. It was the vampire who had spoken to me last time I met House Tennison. He was probably the head of their house. He smiled at me and I felt a flash of surprise to see any expression on that vampiric face. Maybe newer vampires were more open with their emotions than the ancients. That had to be it. Dmitri bowed to him and I hastily followed suit.

"Kairos," the vampire said. "I would like to speak with you in private."

CHAPTER TWENTY-NINE: PURE BLOOD

I followed the leader of House Tennison into a small antechamber. Dmitri nodded to me before leaving and shutting the doors behind him. I suspected he would be right outside and wondered where Adze was. Then I turned my attention to the vampire in front of me and felt stunned for a moment by those blue eyes. They seemed to penetrate my very soul and I inched backwards nervously. His lips curled in a slight smile.

"I'm not used to dealing with resistant humans," he said, and I realized he had tried to use a glamour on me. Was he trying to make me do something or just testing me? "I suppose I'll just have to rely on you telling the truth. You will tell the truth, won't you, Kairos?"

"Of course," I said. So he had been trying to use a glamour to make sure I would be honest? I supposed that wasn't especially threatening. If he wanted to ask me questions, he would want me to be honest.

"First, tell me what happened to you," he said. "You seem to attract attention."

It was true, I thought as I described the attack. I did attract attention, and not the kind I wanted. He listened dispassionately as I talked about going for a jog and noticing movement, then the vampires who had surrounded me and chased me. His eyes narrowed when I said Adze had rescued me, though I did remember to say Master Adze. I ended the story when I reached the house. He didn't need to know more.

Maybe that was what Dmitri hadn't wanted me to talk about, after all.

"You shouldn't be vulnerable like this," he said when I was finished. "I'll have to speak to Adze about your security."

"It isn't his fault," I said quickly.

"First, you were wandering in a park, alone," the vampire said. "Then, you were wandering the grounds, alone. The first shouldn't have happened at all and if he knew you preferred going out alone, he should have done a better job protecting you."

"He's protecting me now," I said.

"After the fact," he said, shaking his head. "But it is his house. Still, I don't want a human injured, and you're more valuable than most."

He sighed. "That isn't why I'm here, however."

He was wearing a heavy cloak and he reached inside and withdrew a syringe. I flinched. Why did he have that?

"I need to test your blood," he said. "Will you let me?"

"Why? Master Adze said I'm not supposed to give blood anymore."

His lips curled in another slight smile. "You no longer have to pay the blood tax, but that's not why I'm asking. I'll only take a few drops."

I felt dizzy for a moment and met his eyes, then realized he was probably trying to use another glamour on me to make me agree. I shivered and stepped backwards and the sensation ceased.

"I apologize," the vampire said. "It's habit. Will you allow me?"

I was supposed to obey him and do what he wanted, I remembered. So I took a deep breath and stepped forward, extending my arm. He seemed to know exactly what to do as he had me sit down and tied above my elbow. I hated when they did that, though I was sure it was necessary to draw blood. He must have done this before because I barely felt when the needle entered, it was so smooth. He drew a vial, then had me press a small wad of cotton over the spot.

"Um, why do you need my blood?" I asked cautiously.

"I just need to test it," he said, and withdrew a small electronic pad with cloth over part of it. He poured a little of the blood on it and waited. After about a minute, there was a low-pitched beep and two of the lights turned green.

"Good," he said. Then he grinned at me, took the rest of the vial and tipped it into his mouth. I flinched, not expecting that. I had never seen a vampire drink blood before and this was my blood, probably still warm from my body. I felt uneasy as he licked his lips. "You have delicious blood," he said. "A pure human."

I flushed, unsure how to treat that compliment. I had been worried about the taste of my blood, since I wanted Adze to like it, but I didn't like that he had drunk it in front of me like that. I shifted slightly, still seated in the chair, and wished he weren't looking at me like that. I belonged to House Elviore; was he even allowed to drink my blood? He wouldn't have been able to drink it from me directly, I was pretty sure. The mark on my neck would have stopped him. But I had volunteered to let him draw my blood. And hadn't Dmitri or Dianne said my blood would be useless to other vampires? Or was it just that it would hurt humans? My mind whirled and I couldn't remember, but clearly my blood tasted good to him.

"Thank you, Kairos," he said, gesturing for me to get up. I obeyed, eager to be out of the room with the vampire who had drunk my blood. Surely he wasn't allowed to do that. Only Adze had the right to drink my blood, I thought a little angrily. He hadn't, and I didn't think he would, but he was the only one I ever wanted drinking my blood. I supposed other vampires had drunk it over the years, but not anymore. I was his, and didn't like that this vampire had stolen blood from me. Why did he need to test it, anyway?

There was a knock at the door before it opened and Adze came in, his dark eyes glowing. He held out his hand and I immediately went to his side. He touched my arm. I was no longer holding the cotton to it as the bleeding had stopped, but there was a faint mark from where I had gotten the blood drawn.

"Was this really necessary, Darius?" Adze asked, looking at the other vampire. This was the first time I'd heard his name, I realized. It suited him.

"Unfortunately, yes," he said. "I'm testing everyone in House Elviore before making my recommendation."

"You know we don't drink blood from our servants," Adze said.

"It had to get in your supply somehow," he said. "A servant with tainted blood is the most obvious way."

Tainted blood? He had thought my blood was tainted? I was offended but not entirely sure why. What would it be tainted with, though? My mind went to the drug and I shivered. It couldn't be that, could it? Was the drug naturally occurring in some people and that was how it was distributed? I was relieved my blood was clean.

"We need to discuss his safety," Darius added, and Adze's eyes narrowed.

"I have taken appropriate steps," he said coldly.

"He should have a guard with him at all times," Darius said. "We can't afford to lose him and he's clearly a target."

"He's not a slave," Adze said, then glanced at me. "And I've already made sure he won't be alone anytime he leaves the house."

Was that true? I hadn't noticed anyone on my jog around the house, but maybe there had been people watching and I just didn't see them. I didn't think Adze would lie about this, after all. Maybe there had been people keeping an eye on me.

"I'm glad you were there to protect him," Darius said. "What did you do with the vampires?"

"I knocked them out and questioned them. It was as I suspected, as I'm sure you suspect. They knew he would be there, but there was no direct link to our target. They're very careful."

"And very determined," Darius said. "They're targeting your entire house, not just him. Your other servants need protection as well. I'm talking to all of House Elviore about this. I'm going to station two of my people to each of your houses."

"That's a little excessive," Adze said. "You have other duties. Your House isn't large enough to support such a thing for long."

"At least until we figure out who's tainting your House's blood," he said. "After that, we'll reassess."

Adze nodded, then glanced at me. I had no idea what I was supposed to be doing. I was following most of what they were saying even if they weren't speaking directly, and I didn't know if I was supposed to pretend that I didn't understand. It seemed like the vampires who had attacked me were sent by House Salvite, though not directly, and something was tainting House Elviore's blood. But why? Weren't ancient vampires immune to the drug? And how did they know the blood was tainted in the first place?

"Thank you for your assistance," Adze said. "I feel it's too much, but I appreciate it all the same, and I'm sure all of my servants do as well."

"Thank you for giving me open access to them," Darius said. "Your cooperation will be noted, and will help you if this goes to court."

Adze nodded. "I'll have Dmitri show you to the others," he said, then took my arm and pulled me out of the room. Dmitri entered just as we passed through the doorway and I heard him politely offering to show the other vampire to where Dianne and Margaret were waiting, no doubt to have their blood drawn as well. Adze brought me to his office and placed me in front of his desk before sitting down and staring at me.

"Did he do anything other than draw your blood?"

"He asked me about the attack," I said. "Dmitri said it was all right to talk about it so I did."

"Good," Adze said. "It's important to cooperate with him.

Anything else?"

I thought about Darius drinking my blood and wondered if that was part of him drawing the blood or if I should bring it up. I didn't want it happen again, so maybe I should mention it.

"Um, after he drew my blood," I said, then hesitated. Adze gestured for me to continue. "Uh, he, uh, drank it," I finished weakly.

Adze hissed. "He drank your blood?"

"Yeah," I said. Adze looked furious.

"How dare he," he said in a low voice. "He may be an allied House, but drinking blood from a servant of another House is strictly forbidden. And then he dares lecture me about your safety?"

I shrank back slightly. I had never seen him angry like this before and it was fearsome. I could feel his rage pouring off him and suspected it was a glamour, but even though I was resistant, I wasn't immune and this was driving terror through my heart. Adze noticed my furtive shrinking and blinked. The haze of anger seemed to withdraw.

"I apologize, Kairos," he said. "He should not have done that to you."

"I thought vampires from other Houses couldn't drink my blood anymore," I said rather tentatively, and he sighed.

"The vampires of House Tennison are descended from House Elviore, so they can technically feed on our servants. I didn't think he'd dare. I suppose if he didn't drink it from you directly, he wasn't breaking the law, but..." He sighed again. "He shouldn't have done that."

That was a little reassuring, though not much. "How many other Houses are descended from you like that?" I asked.

"Only one other, and you're unlikely to encounter them," Adze said. "They're located in Europe."

I nodded. I wasn't worried about House Elviore anymore, and it seemed House Tennison was the only other threat. And really, as long as I never volunteered my blood again, it wouldn't happen again.

"Um, is House Salvite trying to frame your House again?" I asked, wondering how much he would share.

"It seems that way," Adze said. "Have you noticed anything in the communication?"

"They're planning something, but I can't tell what."

"Any talk of something they've already done, or are currently doing?"

"Yes," I said slowly. "I don't tend to flag the messages about things that have already happened unless they involve deaths, but there has been a lot of talk about something that happened."

How had I not noticed that? I had noticed, to some degree, that many of the letters and emails included references to a recent event, but I had assumed the event they were talking about was the cathedral attack. But they wouldn't still be talking about that, would they? No, they were talking about something else and I had missed it.

"I'm sorry," I said. "I didn't see it. I can go back and find the references."

"Continue your work as usual," Adze said. "If you have time, you can go back, but your other work is more important and it's not worth working overtime. You can't be expected to pick up on everything."

I agreed, but still felt guilty. I had let him down. I had let the House get attacked, though this wasn't a direct attack.

"How did they know the blood was tainted?" I asked. "Do they test all blood like that?"

"No," he said. "It would be too time-consuming and expensive to test blood with every allotment. Instead, each House submits to blood tests twice a year. I suppose you have your blood tax, and we have our test to prove that we're worthy of getting that blood. Elviore just tested two days ago and every single one of us was flagged for the drug. It hardly matters, as we're immune to it, but it is unusual. And suspicious."

"But if you're immune, why do they test you?" I asked. "And why does it matter if your blood has the drug in it?"

"Everyone is tested, regardless of age," Adze said. "It's only fair. And while it doesn't matter in terms of addiction, it could be used to argue that our House is involved in the drug trade. It's nothing to worry about yet," he added. "But look out for that in the messages."

"I will," I promised.

"Then start your work. Will you come to my chamber again tomorrow?"

My heart skipped a beat. "Do you want me?"

"Noon, same room," he said.

"I'll be there... Master."

His lips curved into a hint of a smile and my heart beat louder. He wanted me again, and I would give him anything he wanted.

CHAPTER THIRTY: SURVEILLANCE

Two vampires from House Tennison arrived around midnight and one joined me in my office after lunch along with Dmitri to hear what I had found so far. He introduced himself as Alessandro but didn't say anything else. My schedule had been altered slightly because now I had to let Dmitri know any pressing matters I found after lunch and before I finished for the day, since I was finding so much. I hesitated before entering, since it would be obvious that I wasn't doing work with blood allotment, but the vampire just smirked.

"I know what your job is," he said. Dmitri didn't look pleased by that but didn't object, and I cautiously began laying out all of the patterns I had noticed. I wasn't sure how much to say with another vampire here so I tried to be circumspect, but Dmitri questioned me thoroughly and I ended up giving him all of my information. I just hoped Adze didn't mind. The vampire, who had taken a seat across the room, just stared at me as I reported to Dmitri and I felt uncomfortable even though I didn't think he was using a glamour on me. Then Dmitri left, instructing me to keep working, and the vampire remained. It took nearly thirty minutes to get into my rhythm, but soon it was almost as if he weren't there.

It was unnerving being followed by a vampire, because when I left to use the restroom and stretch for a little bit, he came with me. At least he let me into the bathroom alone. I knew it was for my protection but as Adze had said, it was a little excessive. I wasn't in any danger in the house, after all.

When I was finished for the day and was waiting for Dmitri, the vampire shifted and spoke for the first time since those few words at the beginning.

"Why don't you work for House Salvite?" he asked.

"They never offered me a job," I said cautiously, unsure what the correct answer was. Was I allowed to talk about this or was it considered some of the House secrets? Well, I wouldn't give too much information but it wasn't really a secret how I started working here.

"I find that hard to believe," he said, narrowing his eyes.

"This was just supposed to be a temporary job," I said. "Until I saved enough for grad school."

"But it's not temporary anymore?"

"I don't know," I said, because I still didn't know. I was happy here for now, and wanted to stay forever, but my friends and parents were pressuring me to leave after a year and I might give in to that. But the vampire looked satisfied and then Dmitri came in and quizzed me on everything. According to the emails, something was happening right now and it made me nervous. Some plan of theirs was coming to fruition but I couldn't tell what, except that it had the potential to bring down their enemies. I suspected it was the fact that House Elviore had been found with tainted blood and shared that suspicion, since I found several references to blood and to the number six, which I associated with Elviore. Dmitri seemed to share my suspicions but warned me not to tell anyone else. I glanced at Alessandro, wondering if he was supposed to know, but there was no helping it, I supposed.

I headed to the room where the TV was set up to catch up on the news, since Lee had referenced a few current events and I had realized how out of touch I was getting. Alessandro came with me and lounged nearby. I wondered what he would do during the day. Surely he couldn't stay much longer. I flipped around for a bit, looking for my usual news channels, but only found channels specific to Redmond. I hesitated on one, which seemed more like scandal stories than actual news. It was talking about House Elviore and while it wasn't giving specifics, it was implying that the House was involved in the drug trade. I glanced at Alessandro.

"Do other people know about this?"

"I'm sure House Salvite let the press know as soon as it happened," he said calmly. "Nothing will be formal until a trial, if it gets that far."

"If you know they're behind all of this, why don't you charge them?"

The vampire smiled slightly. "Our House wonders the same thing, but Elviore wants an airtight case. No loose ends. They're very thorough."

He glanced at his watch. "What else do you do before you go to sleep?"

"Um, have dinner, then... well, I'd usually jog around the grounds, but I don't especially want to do that right now," I said, feeling shy to be admitting my fears.

"There will be one of our servants assigned to you during the day," he said, and I inwardly sighed. So I wouldn't get any time to myself. "For now, I'll say good day. I'll see you this evening."

"Thank you," I said, because he was doing me a favor by watching me. He flashed a grin.

"You're very valuable, you know," he said. "It's no problem."

He stood and left as I blushed, unused to the compliment. All of the vampires seemed to think I was valuable and I supposed I was, since I could translate the messages from House Salvite. After a few minutes, a human servant came in and I was surprised to recognize him. Rory, who had come here to request that their House fill my job. He showed very little recognition and I remembered that Adze had used a glamour on him so that he wouldn't notice me. I greeted him cautiously and tried to act like I didn't know him, either. We had seen each other at the cathedral, I supposed, so it was fine to show some recognition.

I hesitantly asked him if he knew the channel for my

preferred news and he gave it. I watched the news just for twenty minutes, but it was enough to catch up on the latest scandals in government. The President was attempting to push back on some of the policies the vampires had put into place after the Species War, though he was mostly unsuccessful. Still, it was an unprecedented effort and I wondered what the vampires thought about it. That was why Lee had mentioned it to me: now that I worked for vampires, I was invested in them remaining in power.

Rory had dinner with me and there were two other servants from Tennison who joined us as well. Margaret seemed delighted to be cooking for so many people but Dmitri and Dianne, when they joined us, looked less pleased. They probably didn't like having strangers getting into their business. I attempted to make small talk and succeeded to some degree, but the other servants weren't especially chatty. I couldn't tell if they resented being assigned here or were just quiet people, but they probably didn't like being stationed in a strange House any more than Dmitri and Dianne liked having them here.

Rory was given a room down the hall from me and he informed me that if I left my room for anything more than the bathroom, I was to wake him no matter the time. I agreed, but knew I wouldn't be waking him at noon when I went to see Adze. I slept for a couple of hours until my alarm went off, then quickly dressed in clothes that were easy to take off and snuck to the basement. And froze. I could see movement at the bottom of the steps, but it was so dark I couldn't make out what it was. Hesitantly, I went down into the darkness, but luckily it wasn't pitch black. As I stepped off the final step, I felt a chill and whirled to my right to see Alessandro looking at me in amusement.

"Are you supposed to be here?" he asked.

I was tongue-tied and felt pressure against my senses. He was trying to use a glamour to make me answer.

"Yes," I finally said, not knowing what else to say. Then

the door at the end of the hall opened and Adze emerged. He gestured for me to come to his side and I cautiously slid past Alessandro to reach him.

"He's allowed to be here now," Adze said. I suddenly noticed another vampire emerging from one of the rooms. I hadn't seen her since she had shown up at midnight and I wondered if she was tailing Adze the same way Alessandro tailed me.

"Is that wise?" asked the new vampire.

"He wants it," Adze said, and I blushed. They had to know why I was here. Would we be able to do anything with other vampires down here? If Adze tried to make it absolutely dark, I wouldn't be able to perform, I already knew. I would be afraid these other vampires would sneak in when I couldn't see.

"But you're not feeding on him?" she asked.

"House Elviore does not feed on its servants," Adze said firmly, and I was a little disappointed. Part of me wanted him to feed on me, even though the thought frightened me, too.

The other vampires shrugged and returned to one of the rooms where they must be sleeping. Or staying. I still wasn't sure if vampires slept, but at the very least they would probably stay there. Despite that, I knew I wouldn't be comfortable leaving Adze's office down here, and I didn't want absolute darkness. He led me into his office and embraced me.

"Are they a problem?" he asked.

"Sort of," I said, not wanting to disappoint him but wanting to warn him what I wasn't willing to do with them around.

"Perhaps it's best to wait, then," he said. "They'll be here a week, maybe less."

"If we stayed in here, I wouldn't mind as long as there's light," I offered, and his lips curved in the faintest hint of a smile. I longed to see a real smile on him. Maybe, with the lights on, I would.

"Then let's stay in here," he said, and my heart started pounding. He kissed me, and I was enveloped in lust.

CHAPTER THIRTY-ONE: INTERRUPTED

Adze kissed me thoroughly as I wrapped my arms around him and let him take over. I didn't shut my eyes, though, because I was still a little on edge. He pushed me backwards until I felt the desk against my ass and he lifted me so that I was sitting on it. He continued to kiss me, then pinned my arms behind my back. Then the phone rang.

He said something in another language that had to be a curse, then pecked a kiss on my cheek and went to the phone, answering it in that other language with a hint of anger. His tone changed quickly, however, to one of urgency, and he hung up after just a moment. He turned to me and sighed.

"Lilith needs to see you immediately," he said. "They're starting to send messages by day."

"Okay," I said uncertainly. "Um, what does that mean?"

"Dmitri will take you and Rory to her house. It's a physical letter and needs to be translated immediately so that no one notices it missing. I apologize," he added, reaching out to stroke my head. "It'll likely be too late when you get back. You do need sleep. But come again tomorrow at noon and nothing will interrupt us."

I nodded, speechless as he kissed me again and I felt weak. I did not want to leave, but maybe it was for the best. I was nervous about the other vampires, after all. So I stood up and he straightened my shirt slightly, then led me out. Alessandro was waiting and eyed me.

"I spoke to Lilith," he said. "If I could go with you, I would.

Rory will take good care of you. I don't think anyone will expect you to be traveling during the day, so you should be safe."

"Thank you," I said, uncertain what else to say. He sounded genuinely remorseful that he couldn't go with me but I didn't expect it. He was a vampire, after all. While it was possible to be in the sunlight, it was prohibitively expensive and they wouldn't waste something like that on such a simple thing. And since it was the day, it was extremely unlikely I would be attacked by vampires, just dhampir, and with Dmitri and Rory I felt safe. They could handle any dhampir.

I went back upstairs and found Dmitri waiting at the top of the stairs. He didn't look pleased to see me there and I wondered if he had known where I went in the middle of the day. Apparently not, and he didn't like it. I remembered his warning about Adze asking too much and blushed to think that Dmitri at least now knew what my relationship with the vampire was. But he didn't say anything, just examined me and told me I was dressed suitably for the visit. I was glad; even though I had picked these clothes to come off easily, they were still formal enough to visit another vampire's house. I just hoped it wasn't too obvious why I had chosen these particular clothes. The fewer people who knew about my daylight trysts to Adze's lair, the better.

But when Rory showed up a few minutes and glared at me, I realized that of course he would guess where I had been since I hadn't woken him up. He seemed angry about that and as soon as we were in the back of the car with Dmitri driving, he spoke.

"You should have let me know you were awake, even if I didn't follow you," he said. "In the future, just check in with me. I realize you were with the vampires so you were safe, but you needed to be watched on the way there and back."

"I'm sorry," I said, not knowing what else to say. Was I really supposed to tell him that? That implied that he would be waiting for me the whole time so he could watch me as I went back, and I definitely didn't want that. He sighed.

"I suppose it's not the biggest problem since you stayed in the house, but let me know in the future. If anything happens to you during the day, it's on me."

"I'll be more careful," I promised, not wanting to get him in trouble. "I'm sorry."

He just shook his head. It didn't take long to get there and I happened to glance outside as we drove. Everything was a blur and I squinted, trying to make sense of it. There should have been traffic but instead it was just a blur, and then we were there.

"What happened?" I asked, and Rory's lips twitched in a smile. At least he wasn't angry anymore.

"Dhampir who serve ancient houses are allowed to skip over the traffic," he said. "If anyone else tries it, they would get in trouble, but ancient houses get a lot of exceptions."

I was startled as Dmitri opened the door and I got out. I remembered how quickly Margaret had gotten me back and forth from the house while I dozed. She must have been waiting for me to fall asleep so I wouldn't notice what she was doing, since I hadn't known she was dhampir at the time and she probably didn't want me to figure that out. And I remembered how quickly we had traveled from the park to Lilith's house. I hadn't been making it up, then; we actually were traveling faster than the traffic would normally allow.

Dmitri led me to the house and one of the servants who had taught me to work the blood allotment greeted me warmly. She brought me in and we exchanged pleasantries, but it wasn't long before we came to a set of stairs identical to Adze's. I gulped, thinking of what happened when I entered his lair. But I knew the same wouldn't happen here. The servant gestured.

"Go down the hall to the door straight ahead," she said. "Don't go anywhere else."

Those were the instructions I had received the first time I entered the basement at Adze's and I wondered if her other rooms were anything like his. But I obeyed as the others remained upstairs. Did they think it unusual that I was allowed down here? Did they realize I had been in Adze's rooms like this? I blushed and hoped not. It was dark downstairs but with just enough light to see. I eyed the other doors curiously but went to the appropriate door, the door that led to Adze's office in his lair. I knocked, uncertain if I should open the door, and heard a muffled voice inviting me in. I opened the door. It was luckily light enough to see and I went in front of Lilith's desk, where she sat staring at me emotionlessly. There was a letter on the desk in front of her.

As soon as I was before her, she gestured to it. She was wearing gloves, I noticed, and handed me a pair. I pulled them on, the plastic tugging at my skin even though they were the right size. All gloves were just a little tight.

"I need you to analyze this quickly," she said. "They can't know we have it."

I picked it up and weighed the letter, then took the letter out of the envelope.

"Do you want me to do everything first or as I notice it?" I asked.

"As you notice it, and I don't care how you know what you know," she said. I nodded.

"There's a mismatch in envelop and letter, though that's fairly normal in the letters they don't want caught."

I studied the letter and felt a chill, as I often did when reading the more dangerous of the letters.

"They're about to do something. The number eighteen keeps showing up," I added. "Do you know what that means? I'm not sure I can tell you more without knowing that."

"House Tennison has eighteen vampires," she said with a slight twist to her lips. She wasn't pleased with this. I studied the letter further.

"The word tapped is implied. House Tennison is tapped? I think that means their mail or their phones or something, but they're definitely being monitored."

221

She hissed. "How dare they," she said in a low voice. She was definitely not pleased. I had seen Adze this angry before, but it was rare. Normally the vampires showed no emotion at all. The ancients, at least. The newer vampires seemed far more likely to smile and otherwise show emotion.

"Well, I mean, we're tapping them," I pointed out, and she shook her head.

"Ancient houses are given great leeway, and House Elviore in particular," she said. "A newer House like them shouldn't dare do it. I'll have to let Darius know immediately. You're sure about this?"

"Well, assuming eighteen is House Tennison, then it's certain they're being tapped," I said. "I guess that could mean something else, but I don't think so."

She nodded and gestured for me to replace the letter in the envelop.

"They're starting to send letters during the day, and there won't be time to send them to your house to translate," she said. "I may summon you here again around this time. I apologize, as I know you need your sleep, but you weren't sleeping anyway, were you?"

I blushed deeply and looked down. She sighed.

"If he pressures you in any way, you must tell me."

"He's not," I said, but didn't want to elaborate.

"Does House Tennison know?"

I reluctantly nodded, thinking of the two vampires who had seen me downstairs and their faint amusement at my presence there.

"I suppose there's nothing to be done," she said. "As long as he doesn't feed on you, it isn't a problem, and he wouldn't dare. Don't offer yourself," she added. "I know humans often do in relationships like this, but you can't tempt him. It would be deadly to our House if he fed on you."

"I won't," I promised. There was some part of me that wanted him to feed on me but there was enough fear in the thought that I could easily resist it. Maybe in time it would become harder to resist, but for now, there was no risk of me offering myself. I wondered what would happen once House Tennison stopped watching Adze as closely. Would I offer myself then? There was little chance of being found out if the vampires weren't watching his every move. But I wouldn't, because Lilith had ordered me not to. I wouldn't disobey the leader of my House.

"Thank you for your time, Kairos," she said. "Dmitri will take you back now. Stay safe."

"Thank you, Mistress Lilith," I said, pleased that I remembered to call her by her proper name. She looked amused and gestured for me to leave. I obeyed and Dmitri and Rory were waiting at the top of the stairs with Lilith's servant. To my surprise, they didn't ask what I had been doing. Dmitri just confirmed that there was nothing else I needed to do, then led me to the car. The servant waved goodbye in a friendly manner and I briefly wished she were following me around instead of Rory. But she was probably under watch, too. I wondered if there were other vampires in Lilith's lair just as there were in Adze's and I hadn't seen them. Probably. If Elviore were accused of having tainted blood then all of them would be under watch, not just Adze. I was grateful I hadn't seen them, since strange vampires put me on edge. Maybe they knew that and they had stayed hidden because of it. Whatever the reason, I was grateful.

Soon we were back home and I glanced at my watch. There was technically still time to go see Adze but he wouldn't be expecting me, so I wouldn't go. I thought of what Lilith had said about possibly needing me other times during the day and hoped she didn't. I was technically on call at all times for this job, but I wanted to spend the time with Adze, not translating messages. Well, I would just have to see, and hope.

CHAPTER THIRTY-TWO: TENSE GAME

By the time the weekend arrived a few days later, I was used to having surveillance. The only thing that threw me off was seeing the vampire's amusement when I came down to see Adze every day at noon. After that first day, though, they didn't question me or say a word, just let me by. Adze and I stayed in his office and while things were a little more tame than they had been, I was content. I still hadn't started my routine of jogging around the grounds before and after work, though this was probably the safest time since I had people with me at all times, but I was keeping active. Now I faced a dilemma, though. During the week, my nights were filled with work, but on the weekend, I had been spending a lot of time outside. Now I didn't especially want that, but I wasn't sure what else to do to fill the time. I didn't want to laze around all night. I was fully on a night schedule now so it would be strange to do anything during the day. But there was just something about the night that unnerved me. I didn't want to go out when vampires could potentially ambush me. I knew I was safe, knew it was an irrational fear, but I couldn't help it.

I got up on Saturday and dressed in casual clothes, wondering if I would see Adze. I didn't usually on the weekends. He seemed to work every day and I was glad I didn't have to be on that schedule. I supposed the rest of the staff worked everyday, too. Work never ended for Dmitri and Dianne, and Margaret cooked every meal so she didn't get a break, either. Were they ever jealous of me? And did they ever get breaks? Margaret did take time off when she went to the other side of town to shop. She usually took the entire day off and it couldn't all be spent shopping. So she got a day off every week. But the others?

As soon as I left my room, Rory was right next to me, waiting for me to use the bathroom and requesting that I wait in the hall for him to finish. Ever since I had snuck downstairs that first time, there was no way to escape him. I had to check in with him every night but at least he didn't try to follow me to the stairs. He just insisted I tell him when I left and returned. It was the only other part of the surveillance I wasn't entirely comfortable with. Margaret was waiting with an enormous breakfast. She loved having extra people here and the others had warmed up a little, though Dianne and Dmitri still seemed irritated being tailed. The woman staying with Margaret was quite friendly and the two laughed as they served us. It was probably fun getting to stay in the kitchen and cook all day and I wondered if that was her job at her house or if this were a treat for her.

Rory sat beside me as Margaret doled out portions of the egg casserole. It was one of my favorite meals of hers, with strips of bacon layered in and chunks of ham throughout. I had requested she start adding peppers and she had, and at my further request she started making it with jalapeños just for me. With company, though, she was serving the milder version. I didn't mind.

"Do you have any plans for tonight?" Margaret asked me. Rory glanced at me as well. He usually watched me until I went to work at nine, so he had an hour or so left until Alessandro took over. What did he do during the night? I hadn't ever wondered before. Maybe he returned to his house and did work there. After all, it wasn't much work watching me during the day and he got nearly as much sleep as I did. It wouldn't be unusual for him to work at night the same as me. The others from House Tennison followed Dmitri, Dianne, and Margaret around at night, but because I was vulnerable, I had a vampire assigned to me. I was valuable, too, and I knew that was a big reason they watched me.

"I don't know yet," I said. "I'm not sure what to do."

I didn't relish the thought of lounging around with a vampire watching me. I didn't like the thought of a vampire following me on my day off. But I didn't have a choice.

"You play tennis, right?" Margaret asked, and I nodded. I had even coaxed Dmitri into a game last weekend and he was surprisingly good. I had played on the team in high school and while I was a little rusty, I was better than most. "Vampires tend to enjoy activities like that."

I hadn't even considered doing something with Alessandro. I had just assumed I would do something and he would watch, just like at work.

"That might be fun," I said hesitantly. I would ask Alessandro. I worried that he might be far better than me, since he was a vampire, but he probably didn't play a lot. Maybe I would stand a chance.

We finished eating and I went to the library to read the day's paper. Normally I only had time to scan the headlines before work and I did it while eating, but I had plenty of time today. Ever since Lee had scolded me for losing touch with the world, I had been trying to keep up. Two newspapers were delivered, one that I had requested and was the most trusted human newspaper in the country, and one from Redmond that discussed local matters. Dmitri read the one from Redmond every day. I suspected it was part of his job to stay informed. I usually skimmed it, as most of it involved places and people I was unfamiliar with. Lately, though, there had been scandalous rumors about House Elviore and I was always careful to read those articles. There wasn't anything certain and House Elviore was denying the rumors categorically, but they still remained.

I was still reading when Alessandro entered the library and gestured for Rory to leave. Rory was reading the human newspaper while I was scanning through Redmond's and set it down without a word, bowing to the vampire before heading out. I hesitated, wondering if I should be doing something else now that he was here. But Alessandro sat where Rory had been sitting and picked up the National Times. Cautiously, I returned to the Redmond paper.

When I had finished, I glanced over at Alessandro, who was reading with an amused expression on his face. It was odd how much more expressive he was. It was still hard to read him, but he wasn't nearly as impassive as Adze or Lilith. I suspected it had to do with them being ancients. How did a vampire become ancient, after all? Was it solely determined by age? Was there a cutoff and after a certain point a vampire gained ancient status? But there seemed to be other things associated with being an ancient. Adze had said that the drug didn't affect ancient vampires, which implied an actual, biological difference. But what was it?

Alessandro clearly noticed that I had finished but didn't look up immediately, probably finishing the article he was reading. Then he looked up with the hint of a smile.

"It's odd what you humans concern yourselves with," he said. I blushed, feeling embarrassed because he was including me in that category – I was human, after all – and he was condescending to some degree. "Your president is making quite a few mistakes."

He must be reading the article outlining the president's latest plans to avoid the blood tax. I couldn't believe someone was actually challenging the vampires and hoped the president wouldn't spark a conflict. There was a lot of concern about that, and protests had broken out in several cities in an effort to stop what people saw as his war-mongering.

"What happens if he's successful?" I asked. "Everyone's saying it'll be another war."

"There won't be a war," Alessandro said dismissively. "And it won't happen. If this continues for much longer, a vampire from House Elviore will be sent to deal with it."

I gulped. So my house would be confronting the president? How much power did my house have, and what would the vampire do to the president? Would they kill him?

"Nonviolently," Alessandro added, again with a hint of amusement. "Elviore doesn't kill. Anymore."

"But they did?" I wasn't entirely sure I wanted the answer.

"Elviore is the premiere house in our society because they led and won the Species War," Alessandro said. "All of them have killed plenty of humans in their time. Most of us are descended from them, some directly, some indirectly. We all owe them. Which is why rumors like those," he gestured to the paper I held, "are so insulting."

I had known that Elviore led the war, but it was odd to hear it said like that. The Species War had been fought so long ago and even though I knew vampires were immortal, it was a hard thing to get my head around.

"Those rumors will be laid to rest soon enough, though," Alessandro said. "Our house is presenting evidence to the court this weekend and the matter will be settled. By Monday, you won't need me here to observe you."

I let out a sigh of relief. Even though I had gotten used to the surveillance, I didn't like it.

"What do you have to do to prove it?"

"Confirm that none of House Elviore are showing signs of addiction or withdrawal," he said with a shrug. "It only takes a week to be sure."

"I thought the drug didn't effect ancients," I said, puzzled, and he smiled.

"It doesn't," he said. "But the court wanted to make sure. Why else would the drug be in their systems if they weren't using it?" He set the paper down and stood up. "I heard from the others that you were finally interested in going out on the grounds."

I laid my paper on the end table and stood as well. "I mean, if you don't mind," I said. "Margaret said you might play tennis with me."

I felt extremely bold proposing that, and nervous, too. I had never demanded anything from a vampire and while this wasn't exactly a demand, I was imposing on him without knowing if it was appropriate.

"That would be acceptable," he said, and I let out a sigh of relief. I looked at what he was wearing and blinked. Every other day he had been in extremely formal clothes, the same type of clothes Adze wore. I had assumed every vampire dressed like that because I had never seen one in anything else. Even at the cathedral, all of the vampires had been dressed formally. Tonight, though, he was in a more relaxed outfit. Definitely still imposing, but he would be able to play tennis in it. Had he known I would ask? Had he dressed specifically for this? Or did vampires always wear more casual clothes on the weekend? I suspected Adze always dressed up but maybe other vampires didn't.

I was dressed to be active as well and we headed out. Normally I would have let Dianne know that I was heading out to the grounds but with Alessandro at my side, I assumed I didn't have to. We passed Rory on the way and the vampire nodded at him, which seemed a good enough signal that I was going out. Besides, Dianne had been at breakfast and knew I was planning on this. I sighed as we headed out to the grounds and I finally got a chance to be outside and surrounded by nature. I had been afraid to come out here with only Rory to watch me but I felt safe with a vampire at my side. Tomorrow would be like this as well, and then, if he were right, I would be by myself again.

It took several minutes to walk to the tennis court, as it was on the other side of the garden and I paused a few times to admire the plants. Some plants closed their buds at night but these were all chosen for the darkness and looked beautiful. There was enough artificial light that even the flowers that went to sleep might be fooled into staying open. When we arrived, there were two tennis rackets and a basket of balls waiting. Dianne must have had the yard staff leave them out since she knew we were headed this way, because I had walked by the courts before and never seen anything out.

Alessandro picked up one of the rackets and hefted it, then handed it to me. He picked up the other one and seemed satisfied. I wouldn't dare question his choice and luckily I didn't have to because the racket he handed me felt perfect. It was well-balanced and I could tell I wouldn't have any problems adapting to it.

"Do you need to warm up?" the vampire asked. That was probably a good idea so I agreed. We hit balls over the net for a while and I couldn't help but notice how good he was. He practiced his serve and I wondered if I would be able to hit it. Possibly, if I were lucky. I'd watched professional tennis players and he looked just as good. When I felt as warmed up as I was going to get, I suggested a match cautiously. He smiled and went to the other side of the court.

I served first and he easily returned the ball, though without the same intensity that he had had during our warmup. Was he going easy on me? As we continued, I decided he had to be and when he served, it wasn't the same blisteringly fast serve I had seen earlier. I started to sweat before long and realized that he wasn't going easy on me exactly. He was matching me, and just a little bit better to give me a challenge. He was good enough to be able to control his responses like that and I was beyond impressed. At the end of our game, I was exhausted. He won, naturally, and after a break to drink water and unwind a little, I challenged him again. He accepted and soon we were locked in another game, with me just a little bit behind. I made points on him and every time, I felt a thrill of pride and exhilaration, even though I knew he wasn't playing at his full ability. Still, it felt good. He won again, but I had done well.

After our second game, I was truly exhausted and we walked around a little before heading back to the house for a shower. I planned on relaxing the rest of the night, maybe reading, maybe watching a movie, but I felt less intimidated by the vampire at my side. Maybe this weekend wouldn't be as bad as I had worried.

CHAPTER THIRTY-THREE: SURPRISING ANSWERS

Sunday passed smoothly. As the night drew to a close and Alessandro and I were in the study reading, I glanced over at him. He immediately looked up at me. How closely was he paying attention to me? It was a little unnerving.

"Are you going to be here tomorrow night?" I asked.

"I don't know," he said. "The courts will clear House Elviore at the close of work today." He glanced at his watch. "They may already be cleared."

"Then why would you stay?" I said, a little pleased that my house wasn't under suspicion anymore.

"You know that our house is being tapped," he said, and I nodded uneasily. "We've given the impression that we're leaving after tonight. If Salvite is going to attack you, this would be an ideal time for it. They won't be expecting me to stay."

I swallowed hard, fears rising back in my mind. I had felt safe these past two nights and had even gone on my usual evening jog when I got up this morning, even though it was Rory accompanying me and not Alessandro. I was planning on another run before bed. It felt good to be outside after being hidden inside since the attack. Was I going to be attacked as soon as that protection was gone?

Alessandro's lips curled in a hint of a smile. "I doubt they'll attack you, and Adze has his own protection as well. You'll be safe. But better not to take chances. Besides, if they try anything, I'll be able to catch them in the act."

"You sound like you want them to try something," I said, not liking the way he said that last part.

"It would make things easier," Alessandro admitted. "If we could catch them in the middle of a crime, we could press charges immediately instead of waiting. But I wouldn't question Elviore and they insist on waiting."

"You are questioning them, though," I pointed out. Alessandro's smile widened.

"Elviore and Tennison have a complicated history," he said. "I wouldn't challenge them. None of us would. But perhaps I would question their methods."

"What history do you have?" I asked, suddenly curious. I knew almost nothing about vampire society despite living here for weeks. There just wasn't a lot to find out because they were so secretive. The dhampir knew more, but they weren't any more talkative than the vampires. In fact, Alessandro was the most talkative vampire I'd ever met. He was volunteering more in this one conversation than I had learned in almost all my time here.

"I assume you learned about the Species War," Alessandro said, and I tried to hide a flutter of anticipation. He was actually answering my question. I nodded. "House Elviore led the vampires. They were an ancient house even before the war and all of the other vampires obeyed them. And on the human side, there were a number of generals who led the fighting. Do you know what happened to them?"

I considered. All I really knew about the war was that the humans lost. Well, it was technically a draw but the vampires had come out on top.

"I don't know," I said, hoping that was acceptable. Did they teach students more about the war in a vampire city? Probably. In human cities, though, we only learned the outlines.

"I was one of those generals," Alessandro said, and I drew in a sharp breath.

"For the humans?"

"Yes," he said, and smiled humorlessly. "House Elviore ambushed us. I was one of the first. They caught us and turned us into vampires. Slowly, one by one, all eighteen of our highest ranking people. Once we were vampires, we had no choice but to switch sides. The humans wouldn't accept us. And without anyone to lead the war effort, the humans gave up."

"Wasn't it officially a draw?" I asked. "I mean, I know the vampires essentially won but I learned no one won the war."

"We gave the humans their dignity," he said. "They can call it what they want. We know the truth."

I stared at him for a long moment, questions welling up inside me. So he had fought in the war just like Adze, but for the other side. And he had been turned into a vampire against his will by House Elviore.

"Why don't you hate Elviore?" I asked, still trying to process everything.

"We do, to some extent," Alessandro said. "That's why the courts trust us to be impartial. We have as much reason to hate them as revere them. But it's in a vampire's nature to respect the ones who turned them. Our houses have always been close."

"How do you become a vampire?" I asked. "I know it happened a lot in the war, but I've never heard of it happening since then. Why not?"

"Thinking of becoming a vampire?" he said in amusement. I blushed and shook my head. "Good," he continued. "Because no matter how interested Adze is in you, he'll never turn you."

"But how does it happen?"

"You don't need to know," he said, and I inwardly sighed. Another thing I wasn't supposed to know. Well, I had already learned quite a bit from this conversation. I didn't need to know everything. There were myths about a vampire's bite turning people but I knew that wasn't true. There were always horror stories in the gossip pages about vampires feeding on people and none of them ever turned. It probably had to be deliberate, and very difficult.

"Which vampire from Elviore turned you?" I asked, then regretted the question when he stared at me. Maybe that wasn't a good thing to ask, since he clearly hadn't wanted to be turned.

"Which do you think?"

"I don't know all of them," I admitted, and the vampire's lips curled in another smile.

"There's a reason I was assigned to Adze," he said. "We're all with the vampires who turned us. The courts wouldn't trust anyone else."

I drew in a sharp breath. Adze had turned him into a vampire? I couldn't imagine Adze kidnapping a general from an opposing army and forcing him to become a vampire. I had been willing to believe it when Alessandro had spoken of the house overall doing it, but Adze? There was more to him than I could ever truly understand. Would I ever get to know him better? I desperately wanted to learn everything about him, but maybe there were things I would prefer not to know. I thought of the pleasure he took in seeing me helpless and blind. He must have hunted Alessandro the way he had once offered to hunt me. Only he would have been hunting to kill, or at least capture and turn, not hunting to please as he was with me. I shivered.

"I may see you tonight," Alessandro said, rising and setting his book back on the shelf. "Stay safe. You're more valuable than you know. Adze is risking a lot being with you."

I nodded, unsure what else to say, and he left. A few moments later Rory came in and smiled at me.

"You'll have your freedom back soon," he said. "The courts just announced that House Elviore is cleared of any suspicion."

"Are they curious why Elviore had the drug?"

"Our house is handling the investigation," Rory said with a shrug. "As far as the courts are concerned, the matter is closed. That's all that matters."

I agreed, though I wondered. Elviore had been cleared, but

wasn't anyone curious why the entire house had been found with drugged blood when the drug didn't have any impact on them? It seemed obvious that someone was framing them but maybe it wasn't. I had a lot of additional information about the situation, after all.

"Margaret said dinner will be in an hour," Rory said, then picked up a book of his own. "Do you need to do anything first?"

"No, I'll just read," I said. "Do you mind?"

"Not at all," he said.

I returned to my book, a fantasy I had read before about dragons and a sword-wielding princess who was in the process of defeating the evil King. It wasn't the best book I had ever read but it was fun and a good way to relax. I frequently read it when I was stressed and even though I was currently relaxed, I had been on edge with the attack and the vampires constantly tailing me. Lee always read literary books but I always went to the fantasy section and I was glad I had packed my own books because Adze only had histories and other dry reading. Margaret had commented on my book selection and asked if she could read a few and I had happily agreed. Once she had a chance to finish one, we could chat about it. Occasionally Janae and I talked about books but she preferred mysteries. I hadn't found anyone with the same literary tastes as me and I hoped Margaret would like the books I had brought.

Nearly twenty minutes passed in silence before my phone buzzed in my pocket. I pulled it out and was aware of Rory setting his book down instantly.

"Who is it?" he asked. I remembered how my professor had contacted me once and knew he was worried, but this was nothing to worry about.

"It's my friend, Janae," I said. "Do you mind if I take it?"

He relaxed. "Go ahead. I'll have to stay in the room."

"Thanks," I said, and slid my thumb against the screen. "Hi, Janae."

"I was hoping you'd be there," she said, sounding thrilled. "This is a good time, right? I just don't understand your schedule. Are you at the beginning or end of your day?"

"The end," I said. "I'm having dinner soon. You must be up early."

"Work starts in an hour," she said. "I thought I'd try to get a call in. Your mom called me."

"She what?"

"Yeah, she's worried about you."

"Why would she call you? I didn't even know she had your number."

"Remember when we went to the lake together? I gave it to her then."

That was a couple of years ago. Janae and I had gone with my mom and dad to a nearby lake to celebrate me getting into college. I still had a boyfriend at that point, though he hadn't gone with us. He had been busy. He had always been busy. He never had time for me and it was one reason we had broken up, the not the main one. I tried to push that out of my head. This wasn't the time to obsess over all the little things in that relationship that should have been red flags and weren't. I had successfully forgotten about him and besides, I had Adze now. Though I supposed there were red flags in our relationship too. But the red flags between me and Adze were so glaringly obvious that they almost didn't matter. Our relationship was limited, would always be limited. I enjoyed him and he enjoyed me, but it would never be anything serious. It couldn't. He was a vampire, and I was a human. I thought about what I had asked Alessandro about being turned, but even Adze offered to make me a vampire, I would refuse. The idea of immortality frightened me. I didn't want to die, but I also didn't want to live forever.

"Anyway, she wants me to visit you again. I told her what a great place it was and how you seemed happy, but she's worried."

"I'll ask if you can come," he said. "It wouldn't be until next weekend and you'll have to come in the morning or evening. I can rearrange but not that much."

"Morning is probably better," she said. "That's after work for you, right? Why not Saturday morning? What time do you finish?"

"I'm done at five. Dinner is usually around six, and I'm sure you're invited. When can you come?"

"If I leave here at four, I should get there around five and miss most of the traffic," she said. "I don't mind getting up that early just this once. If I get there too early could you leave early? Or I suppose I could just talk to Margaret. She seems nice enough."

"I'll ask," I said. "I might be able to leave a little early. Kind of depends what kind of work I have that day."

I was aware of Rory looking at me sharply but I wasn't about to volunteer my job. Doing work for blood allotment varied day by day, just like translating letters. It wasn't unusual that I wouldn't know exactly what I'd be doing.

"Great," she said. "Then I'll see you next week."

"I still have to ask for permission," I said.

"You'll get it, I'm sure," she said. "Seems like you and your boss have a good relationship."

I could hear a note of amusement in her voice. She knew I was attracted to him, but she had no idea that attraction had turned into something more and I didn't want her to know about it. She was already hesitant about me working here and if she thought I was sleeping with my boss, she would want me to leave immediately. I had to avoid that.

We wrapped up the call and I returned the phone to my pocket.

"Your friend is coming over?" Rory asked, sounding skeptical.

"Yeah, she's been here before." I wondered why he sounded like that.

"But you'll clear it with your master?"

"Of course," I said. "It's his choice if she comes."

"Be careful," he said. "Two humans are a tempting target. Stay with others from the house at all times."

I shivered. It hadn't even occurred to me that Janae would be in danger. Should I tell her Adze wasn't allowing it? I couldn't tell her there might be danger or she would insist I quit. But if she thought Adze was refusing to let me see friends, then she might also want me to leave. No, she would come visit and I would just be careful. I wondered if Rory would want to come back to protect me. No. He barely tolerated following me and certainly wouldn't volunteer for more. Maybe Margaret would stay with us. That seemed like a good solution. And surely we wouldn't be attacked. Alessandro was staying an extra night just in case, it seemed, but there was no reason for Salvite to attack me. They still thought I was doing work with blood allotment. Every once in a while I saw a reference to me but it was always met with assurance that I was harmless. If they were going to attack me, I was pretty sure I would notice it. Not positive, but pretty sure.

"I'll be careful," I promised. He nodded and returned to his chair, picking up his book again as if unaware how much his words had thrown me off. Was Janae going to be in danger? Should I call her back and cancel? Pretend to have extra work or something? I didn't have any options, though. She would come visit and we would just have to be careful.

CHAPTER THIRTY-FOUR: FRIENDLY VISIT

The week passed in a blur. The messages from House Salvite continued to be vaguely threatening, and I continued to go to Adze's lair every day at noon. Twice more Lilith had summoned me and I ached every time she did, because Adze was ruthless about stopping no matter what we were in the middle of doing. We were back in the absolute darkness and he had started tying me up, which thrilled me. I couldn't believe how good it felt to have him controlling me so completely. My mind occasionally went to Alessandro and the other people Adze must have done something like this to, for much darker reasons, but then the pleasure would spike and I would be his again. Nothing had ever felt better.

He had reluctantly given permission for Janae to visit, hesitating for the same reasons Rory had. I assured him that we would stay close to the house at all times and Margaret had agreed to accompany us. I wouldn't let anything happen to Janae, but I also couldn't tell her not to come now that I'd agreed.

Work on Friday went slowly. I was nervous and more alert than usual for messages, since Janae was coming over and I couldn't afford to miss anything if they were going to strike. About quarter to five, I received a call from Margaret informing me that Janae had arrived. I gulped, and called Dmitri.

"Hi Dmitri," I said when he answered. He always answered so promptly. "Um, I wondered if I could possibly finish a little early today. My friend just got here."

"Of course," he said, and I let out a sigh of relief. I had asked him during our lunch debriefing and he obviously knew she was coming today, but he hadn't confirmed whether or not he would actually let me leave. "I'll be there shortly."

I finished another email while I waited for him, then gave him my report. Nothing much going on. They were still tapping House Tennison and they were trying to figure out their next move against House Elviore. Many of them were furious that their attempt with the drugged blood had failed and there were questions of repeating it the next time Elviore gave blood to be tested. Repeated tainted results might get more action. But there wasn't anything active, certainly nothing happening tonight. Oh, there were other things happening. They were about to shift to the east again in terms of their killings and Dmitri was very interested to hear that. I still wasn't able to pinpoint exactly who they were going after each time, just the general location, but Dmitri assured me that Elviore usually knew the types of people who were targeted. He assured me that I had already saved several lives and the thought pleased me. I had never expected to have a job where I got to literally save lives. Then again, I had never expected a job where I was in physical danger. There were downsides to everything.

Once I had finished filling Dmitri in on the details of the emails I had finished since lunch, I headed towards the living areas. I needed to change into more casual clothes before hanging out with Janae but would have to go through the kitchen where she was waiting on the way.

"Kairos!" I was just entering the kitchen when she spotted me and swept me into a hug. "Ooh, you look good!"

I flushed and she took a step back to examine me.

"Wow, you really dress up for work," she said. "I don't think I've ever seen you look like this!"

"Of course I dress up for work," I said with a smile. "Especially here."

"I guess that's true," she said. "I'm surprised you have that many nice clothes. Maybe we should go shopping for you."

"Maybe some other time," I demurred. I didn't have a lot of nice clothes and repeated the same outfits on a fairly regular basis, but I had no desire to leave the house to go shopping. I didn't like the thought of being alone and vulnerable in a vampire city, even if I went during the day when the vampires were sleeping. Margaret had actually gotten me a couple of shirts when she went out, since I wore such a standard size and almost anything looked good. I probably did need a shopping trip to get work-appropriate clothing. I barely spent the vast amounts of money I was earning and that would be a good way to start spending it. I sometimes felt almost guilty that I didn't have to spend money on anything, but it was nice not having to worry about it. It was almost like being an undergrad again, not worrying about rent because I had a dorm, not worrying about food because I had a meal pass. Of course, I was still paying for those things, but only on an annual basis, not on the day to day basis that made up adult life. This time, I wasn't paying at all except through the work that I did.

"Let me change, and then we can hang out," I said, and she agreed. I changed quickly into jeans and a short-sleeved shirt appropriate for the weather. It was pleasantly cool at night, and right now, but it would get hotter as the sun came up and started shining directly on the house and grounds. Normally I slept through the heat of the day and I wondered what it would be like in winter when temperatures at night plummeted below freezing.

I went to the bathroom and freshened up a little before returning to the kitchen, where Margaret was finishing cooking. She was making French toast. I had recommended a breakfast meal for Janae, since she would probably find it weird to be eating dinner so early in the morning and I didn't mind. Janae was chatting with her and I joined them, sitting at the table next to Janae. I knew that Margaret would be cooking dinner for everyone else in about an hour, our normal mealtime. She was a sweetheart to go out of her way to cater to me and Janae. If I did go shopping, I would have to get her something.

"So what have you been up to?" I asked, and Janae launched into an account of her new job as we ate our breakfast. She was enjoying the job, luckily, and thought she could get a promotion pretty soon if she kept working hard. It wasn't a long term job, unfortunately, but jobs rarely were. I was grateful my own job was so secure. If I did decide to go to grad school, I would hopefully end up with a stable tenure-track job. I really needed stability in my life. I hated that sense of never knowing what was coming next, of having to live on the edge because you could be fired at any time. At my previous job, I had been passed over for promotion time and time again but I hadn't wanted to leave. It was a minimum-wage job and I just did it to have experience so it wasn't vital that I advance, but it still stung. I loved my job here because I felt valued. There may not be any promotions available, but I was doing work I enjoyed and people appreciated it.

She asked about me and I gave her a vague answer, hoping she didn't pry. She didn't. It seemed like she was only asking because my mom had told her to, because soon she got to the part she clearly really wanted to talk about.

"Lee proposed to Angie," she said. "Privately."

"Angie said yes, right?" What if my advice had been wrong?

"Of course," Janae said with a grin. "That was exactly what she was hoping for. You talked to him, didn't you? I know you did. He's the type of guy to wait for a huge, splashy proposal and she would have hated that."

"Yeah, I did talk to him," I said, pleased everything had worked out but a little hurt neither Lee nor Angie had told me about it. "Why didn't you tell me?"

"You're always so busy."

"You could have texted."

She sighed. "I'm sorry. You just live so far away and it was so clear you had said something that I didn't think to tell you. Besides, I wanted to surprise you today."

"Well, thank you," I said. "It is a surprise, though I was certainly hoping that would be her response. I can't imagine if he had gone with his plan, or if she had said no."

"I know," Janae said with an exasperated shake of her head. "They don't appreciate the precarious position they put the rest of us in."

"So this is changing the subject, but what do you want to do while you're here? I was hoping we could stay inside this time."

I tensed, hoping she didn't realize how much depended on her answer. Would she find my request suspicious? Would she insist on going outside? I didn't mind going out for a little, since Margaret could come with us, but Margaret did have to cook for everyone else at a certain point. She was willing to stay with us the whole time, and no one else would complain – there was plenty of food in the kitchen even without her cooking – but I wanted to interrupt people as little as possible. I didn't want Dmitri or Dianne to suffer because my friend was here. I might never be able to invite her back.

"Sure," she said, and I was relieved. "What do you usually do when you're not working?"

"A lot of reading, I watch TV sometimes, or movies."

"You're such a homebody," she observed in amusement. "I hope you do get out sometimes."

"Yes, I do," I said with a laugh. "You know I do."

She knew my habits and knew that I usually went for a jog in the morning and at night. That was less true the past week or so since the attack, but I had always had that habit. It was true, though, that most of the rest of my time was spent indoors.

After we finished, we headed to the library. I hadn't really shown her the house last time, just the grounds, and she was thoroughly impressed. She wouldn't get to meet Adze this time but didn't seem to expect it. Good. Not that he wouldn't meet her, but there was no need. They had met. He approved of her and she of him, and that was all that needed to happen. There was no reason they should have a relationship. I suspected Adze didn't have many human acquaintances other than servants, and probably only servants within Elviore. When Rory had come to ask for the job, he hadn't seemed warm. In fact, he had clearly only been tolerating the request because Tennison was an allied house. He had probably hated having so many strangers here when they were under surveillance. I felt a flash of guilt over the surveillance, even though it wasn't my fault. I could have caught it before it happened, though, and felt bad. I kept wondering what else I was missing. I could understand the messages, but didn't always understand their significance.

Janae and I chatted and it was nice having a friend to talk to. Margaret was great, but we didn't have the same shared history. It was nice having inside jokes and memories together. I was really isolated here, I realized as we talked. Dmitri and Dianne were distant and I didn't see anyone else on a regular basis. Well, other than Adze, but somehow he was in a category of his own. I didn't socialize with him, exactly. I spent time with him, adored him, craved him, but he wasn't a friend. He was always in charge of me, my master. We would never have an equal relationship and I didn't particularly want one. I was happy with how things were, though Lilith's words about not letting him drink my blood flashed through my mind while I knelt in front of him, bound and helpless. I wanted his fangs in me.

Janae stayed a few hours and left about thirty minutes before midnight. I knew Dmitri and Dianne were already asleep, though prepared to get up in case of emergency. Margaret would have been asleep as well but she stayed up to keep watch on us. As I waved at Janae, I wondered if she would be safe on the way home. Would she be targeted because she had visited me? I shivered. I had thought the danger was here on the grounds but what if it followed her home? I thought back to the letters and emails but couldn't recall anything that would indicate they were tracking this house or the people who came and went. They might notice her but if they thought I was harmless, and they did, then they would probably assume Janae was harmless as well.

As soon as Janae had left the property, I glanced at my watch. Margaret said goodnight in a sleepy voice and I considered my options. Adze wasn't really expecting me today. Since we didn't know how long Janae would stay, he had said I didn't need to come. But I wanted to see him. Would he be upset if I went down to his lair? There was only one way to see, I decided, and headed down the stairs.

CHAPTER THIRTY-FIVE: BOLD DEMAND

The light dimmed as I crept down the stairs. Everyone else was asleep. Good. I didn't want anyone knowing about this. Dmitri knew I came down here, but I didn't think he had told anyone. He hadn't ever commented on me coming down here at noon and I didn't know what he thought about it. He had warned me about Adze asking for too much but I wanted this. Did Dmitri approve or did he think Adze was pressuring me? It didn't matter. I was here of my own free will. I glanced at the doors to each side of me as I went to his office door. I had been in two of these rooms. One was a bathroom where I had washed off a couple of times. There didn't seem to be hot water but I didn't mind. The other room was where he took me to play. I had no idea what it looked like because it was pitch black when he brought me there. There was a bed, but I didn't know anything else except that he had all sorts of things to tie me up with. What would it be like to see? What other things did he have in there that he just hadn't used on me yet?

I had no clue what was in the other two rooms but at least one was a place for other vampires, since Alessandro and the female vampire had stayed here. Maybe both other rooms were for other vampires. Or maybe one was Adze's room. I still hadn't figured out if vampires slept or not. Lilith and Adze were awake into the afternoon but that didn't mean they didn't sleep at all. And maybe there was a difference between ancient vampires and the newer ones. Maybe new vampires slept and Adze didn't. I wasn't sure and as I slunk to his office door and knocked, I suspected I would never know. Even though Alessandro had told me a lot more than I had expected about vampires and his relationship to Adze, I still knew next to nothing about them.

"Come in," I heard, and opened the door. It was pitch black. I took a deep breath and took a few steps in, the faint light from the hall showing a shadow that I knew was Adze. Then I obediently closed the door behind me. Night fell over me like a cloak and I gulped. I had been in darkness like this so many times this past week but I still felt a flutter of terror every time.

"Um, I hope it's okay that I'm here," I said hesitantly. Really, though, if he didn't want me here, he wouldn't have let me in.

"Your friend has left, then?"

"Yeah."

I heard movement and tensed, then his hand caressed my cheek. It was so absolutely unnerving not being able to see anything. He moved so quietly, too, and I was pretty sure the only reason I heard him moving at all was because he wanted me to hear. He didn't want to completely terrify me. But if he were hunting me as he must have once hunted Alessandro... I would be absolutely helpless. I couldn't imagine fighting a war against creatures like Adze who controlled the night so absolutely. They had weaknesses, like sunlight and holy water, and they avoided garlic, but they were so incredibly powerful it hardly mattered. How had humans even stood up enough to bring the war to a draw? Or had the vampires not wanted to win? They needed humans to feed on, after all. Perhaps the vampires had fought enough to put humans in our place and then let us claim some measure of victory so we would agree to be fed on.

"Did you enjoy seeing her?"

I could feel his breath against the back of my neck and shivered. He kept stroking my cheek. He was right behind me and I inhaled sharply as his other hand wrapped around my waist and pulled me backwards into him.

"Yeah," I whispered, my mind skittering into the pleasure

of his touch. Why was he still talking about Janae when we were together like this? All I wanted was him. He held my head still and kissed my cheek.

"Good," he said softly. He took my hand and withdrew from my side. "Come with me."

I heard the door open and then he was leading me into the other room. I went as quickly as I dared. I knew he wouldn't let me trip but I might stumble over my own feet. I took shuffling steps as he urged me faster into the other room, and then I heard the door shut and my heart skipped a beat.

"Strip," he ordered in a soft voice. The first few times he had said this, I had been shy and embarrassed by the darkness. I still wasn't entirely comfortable but I didn't have any hesitations as I pulled off my clothes and let them drop to the ground. I wondered if he enjoyed seeing me strip like this or if there were anything I could do to make him enjoy it more. I had no experience stripping in front of people, especially when I couldn't see anything, and it was simply a process of undressing, not like the sexy strip-teases I always saw in movies. I had no clue how to do that. Maybe I should practice on my own time, I considered. If I felt confident doing it when I could see, maybe I would feel confident enough down here in the darkness. But I didn't like the thought of stripping like that in my room upstairs. My life up there felt almost completely disconnected from what happened down here. Sure, Adze teased me upstairs and we had had sex in his office, but even that was limited to being with him. Something about doing this on my own, without him involved, felt way too naughty to even contemplate.

"You're blushing," he observed, and my cheeks heated up further. It was so bizarre that he could see me clearly when I couldn't see a thing. His hand touched my arm and I flinched. "Do you enjoy this, Kairos?"

"Yes," I whispered, fighting the impulse to cover myself. He led me forward until we reached the bed. It brushed against my legs but he didn't tell me to get on. I shivered. Sometimes he didn't. I flinched again as something soft brushed against my wrists and then he was pulling my arms behind my back. He bent my arms and bound my wrists to my elbows, then began tying the rope against my chest, down my torso, and finally between my legs. The rope brushed against me teasingly, just tight enough to put pressure on me but not enough that I would panic at being bound like this. He went carefully, his hands delicate against me as they threaded the rope across my body. I wondered what I looked like tied up like this. The rope seemed to be everywhere and I let out a sigh as Adze looped the soft rope between my legs and let his hand stroke against my length. I was getting hard and at his touch, I got harder. He stroked me several times and I stifled a moan, and then his other hand was on my shoulders pressing down. I obeyed, unsure what he wanted, until I was on my knees.

I heard him move in front of me and realized what he wanted me to do with a start. He was going to sit on the bed and I was going to please him. He wrapped his hand around my neck and pulled me forward. I shut my eyes, not that it mattered, and opened my mouth and extended my tongue. He stopped me before I reached him.

"You're looking forward to this, aren't you?" he asked, and I could hear a hint of amusement in his voice. Was he smiling? I opened my eyes but it was too dark to see if his lips were curled. It sounded like he was smiling. Would I ever get to see him really smile? Had anyone ever seen him really smile? Maybe he always hid in the darkness like this when he let his emotions show. "You love getting on your knees, don't you?"

I shivered. "Yes, master," I said, and he patted my head.

"Good," he said, and his hand returned to the back of my neck to pull me forward. I felt the warmth of his cock just before I felt him against my tongue. He tasted like moonlight and I immediately coaxed my tongue across his head before leaning forward more to reach more of him. He allowed it.

My knees were far enough back that I was leaning forward to reach him and I felt off balance. I shuffled my knees forward but he tightened his grip on the back of my neck and told me not to move in a sharp voice. I obeyed. I would just have to trust him, as I always did. He liked seeing me vulnerable and off balance. I liked it too.

I leaned forward precariously as I slid my tongue against him, tasting him, slicking him up, waiting for him to command more. I kept pulling my arms forward, instinctively trying to balance myself, and the rope kept getting tighter each time I did. As my arms moved, the rope along my entire body shifted, the rope tingling against my chest and nipples and between my legs and soon I was hot and wanting more. I moaned against him and then his hand tightened and he yanked me forward. I opened my mouth and he slid inside smoothly. He pushed until I gagged and I blushed. I shouldn't have gagged. He pulled out slightly, then began pulsing into me deep enough to slide down my throat but not enough to make me gag again. It felt wonderful to be fucked like this and I let him control my body and my mouth, focusing on adding to his pleasure in whatever way I could.

He withdrew after several minutes of pounding my throat and I returned to massaging him with my tongue, and then he entered me again. We alternated like that for a long time. It felt like forever and I never wanted it to end. He gave me exactly the right amount of time to recover but soon my tongue started to get sore and I knew this was going to get uncomfortable before long. Right when I started to feel exhaustion in my jaw, he pulled me off completely. I licked my lips. My mouth and chin were slick but I couldn't wipe them off with my hands bound behind my back. He pulled me up and I staggered to my feet, the motion tugging along the ropes as I moaned and my cock jerked with need. I was desperate for something, anything, to touch me.

"Please," I whispered. He liked it when I begged but he didn't usually do anything to help me. He turned me and pushed me back. My legs hit the bed and he shoved me hard. I fell backwards, my legs leaving the ground. He immediately grabbed them and pulled them up, one on each side of him. I relaxed and shifted on the bed, trying to get my arms comfortable behind my back. He bent my legs and pressed them against my chest, one hand tweaking my nipples before sliding to my cock.

"You want this?" he asked softly.

"Yes," I whispered. "Yes, please, master, take me."

"So desperate," he murmured, and I could hear pleasure in his voice. He was still holding my legs with one hand, but his other hand that had been on my cock left my body and I shivered. He wasn't going to leave me like this, was he? He had before. I remembered when he had taken me in his office, how he had refused to help me at all. He had allowed me to come on my own once he was done with me but he hadn't done anything to help. Was he going to leave me like that again? Use me and then leave me starving? I shivered harder.

"Please," I said. "Please touch me."

Abruptly his hand was on my ass and I gasped at the sudden pleasure of his touch. He wasn't going to ignore me. I could feel him pressing against me and then, without warning, he was pushing inside of me. It burned with pleasure and I cried out as he slid inside me quickly, then began a ruthless rhythm and had me moaning in no time. The rope tightened against me as the thrusts pulled them in the same rhythm and I struggled to stay in a comfortable position. I was gasping for breath before long as he stroked deep inside of me. It was impossible that he should be able to reach so deep but he could, and soon I felt pleasure stirring in my loins that I knew couldn't wait.

"Master, please let me come," I moaned. If he didn't want it, I would have to fight to control myself.

"So soon?" He was definitely amused. "Not yet."

He pulled almost completely out, then slammed into me, then began long strokes as he nearly left my body between each thrust. I gasped each time he pulsed into me, arching my back and squirming against the rope that teased my entire body and made my sensitive skin nearly as aroused as my cock. Every part of me wanted to explode but I couldn't. I bit my lip as Adze's pace quickened and he pulled my legs apart further to reach deeper into me. I tasted blood and heard an indrawn breath from the vampire. Did he smell the blood? Did it turn him on? I had barely bitten my lip but I stopped sucking at it and opened my lips, hoping the scent aroused him. Indeed, he began thrusting faster and soon he jerked into me and I felt something explode. But he hadn't given me permission, so I cried out and did everything in my power to hold back as I felt him orgasm. He pulled out slowly and I whimpered. I had obeyed him. Surely he wouldn't leave me right now.

He pulled me forward and I scrambled to get on my feet. Then he was behind me and wrapped his arms around my waist. I drew in a breath and tried to adjust myself so his hands would come closer to my cock. I was about to explode. His lips closed over my neck and I moaned in pleasure as he began stroking my nipples and tweaking them. My cock jerked as his tongue caressed my skin.

"Please bite me," I said, then gasped. Had I really said that?

CHAPTER THIRTY-SIX: BLEEDING

Adze started in surprise at my words, his tongue leaving my skin immediately.

"I'm sorry," I said quickly. "Don't stop. Please don't stop."

My body was on fire and I was desperate for him to continue touching me even as I longed to feel his fangs inside me.

"Don't say things you don't mean," Adze said in a smoky voice. Did he want to bite me right now?

His tongue returned as his hands crawled across my bound body. Why had I said that? Yet somehow the thought of his teeth penetrating me right now filled me with a lust unlike any I had ever known. My body was on the brink but I knew if he bit me, it would be better than anything else. It would be true ecstasy.

"I want you," I said. "I want you to bite me." Again his tongue left my body and I moaned. "Please keep going. Don't stop. I want you to bite me."

"Kairos," Adze said breathlessly. "Stop saying that."

"But I want it," I said, pressing back against him and arching my neck back so he would have better access. "I want it more than anything. Please bite me."

"I can't," Adze said in a strangled voice. "I can't."

"Please," I whispered. "I know you want to. I know you want my blood."

"That isn't the issue," Adze said, but I could feel his breath against my skin. He was close. So close.

"I want this," I said. Every fiber of my body ached with the need for him to feed on me. What would it be like when his fangs punctured my skin? What would it feel like to have him draw my blood out? My cock twitched and I nearly came just at the thought. I needed him. "Don't leave me like this," I whispered. "Please bite me."

His tongue caressed my skin again.

"You mean this?" he asked softly. "You can still refuse."

"I mean it," I said, and his lips returned to my throat, right over where I knew my tattoo was. Then he tilted my head to the other side and licked my throat there. I arched my head in the other direction so he would know my invitation stood. My body throbbed with pleasure and I felt something sharp pressing against me. I inhaled in anticipation, my entire body tensing. The sharp pricks withdrew.

"Please," I said, not knowing what else I could say to persuade him. The pricks returned to my skin. Two pricks just barely touching my skin. Then the pressure increased.

His fangs pierced my skin abruptly and I gasped. It was extremely painful but only for a moment, and then I felt him inside me just as he was when he fucked me. Deep inside of me where he belonged. My body hummed and I felt a sucking sensation as if I were being drawn into his fangs. He was drinking my blood and I thrilled to be able to pleasure him like this. I shut my eyes and relaxed my head back even as the rest of my body went into overdrive. His hands moved to my cock and I tensed as he touched me, then began stroking me. I whimpered as his strong hands began touching me, arousing me even though I was almost beyond the point of arousal. I was ready to come in moments as the sucking sensation turned into a star of pleasure on my neck, then he jerked his hand and I gasped as my body exploded. My head fell backwards, my neck completely exposed as I felt him draw deeply as if feeding from my pleasure. As my cock exploded outwards, my mind pulsed inwards in a spiral of pleasure that ended in his fangs inside my body. A wave swept over me, then another, of pure bliss. They crashed through my senses and left me limp and weak. I felt him withdraw and kiss my neck, then I went limp against him.

I felt dizzy as he laid me on the bed. My whole body throbbed in a very pleasant way and I felt happy in a way I never had before. I had fed him. Completely. Body, soul, and blood. I belonged to him now. He was truly my master.

Adze began untying me, his hands lingering on my skin as if wanting more from me. But I was spent. There was no way I could do anything else. My eyes were shut and I almost felt too weak to open them. I took a deep breath and my veins throbbed. How much blood had he taken? He wouldn't put me in danger, but how much was safe to take? The blood tax sometimes left me dizzy but this was a stronger sensation.

"Rest," he said, placing his hand on my forehead. "I'm sorry."

"I wanted it," I mumbled, though sleep was encroaching rapidly. "You don't have to be sorry."

"But I am," he said, and I caught a hint of some other emotion in his voice. Fear? "I shouldn't have done that. I may lose you because of it."

I wanted to reassure him, but sleep was already washing through me and I couldn't manage anything more than a murmur. Then my mind went as black as the room around me and thoughts scattered into oblivion.

Everything zoomed into focus after a while and I realized I was lying in a bed. I could see, though just barely. The light was enough that I could see the room around me. It was elaborately decorated but seemed to be an ordinary room with a bed, dresser, and several plush armchairs around a small table. It was empty. I got to my feet and a wave of dizziness swept over me. I clutched the rich quilt until the feeling passed, then stroked the fabric under my hands. This was a different bed. This must not be the room where Adze took me. But where was I?

"You're awake?"

I jumped and whirled to see Adze leaning against the wall to one side. His face was expressionless, as usual, but his lips were softer than usual. Did he want to smile at me? I hoped so.

"Where is this?"

"A guest room," Adze said. So that meant the other two rooms were for guests, and that implied that vampires slept. Why else would there be beds like this unless vampires slept in them? Had a vampire slept in this bed? I shivered. The world felt a little uneven but I regained my sense of balance quickly. "How do you feel?"

"A little dizzy," I admitted, and he pushed himself off the wall and came to my side. He pressed his hand against my forehead and I was reminded of how my mom used to do the same to check if I had a fever. Whenever I felt bad as a kid, I would beg her to touch me like this, wanting to hear that I had a fever and wouldn't have to go to school, but I never did. Sometimes I wondered if it were accurate at all but it seemed like what all moms did to check for fever so it had to have some value. Why was Adze doing it, though? To see if I had a fever? But why would I have a fever from blood loss?

"You'll feel better this evening," he said. "You just need rest."

"What time is it?"

"Around three," he said, and I blinked in surprise. Three? I had slept for longer than I had realized. "You'll have to return upstairs now but you'll be safe. Perhaps it wouldn't be a good idea to go on your evening jog today."

"I won't," I said, then looked at him shyly. A rush of emotions swept over me and I couldn't figure out what to say to express everything I was feeling. "Um, thank you," I finally said in a soft voice. "I really wanted that."

"You've cost me a lot," Adze said. "It won't happen again."

"I'm sorry," I said, a little puzzled. What had it cost him? Had he not wanted to drink my blood? No, if he hadn't wanted to, he wouldn't have done it. But why couldn't it happen again?

Surely now that we'd done it once, we could do it again. Or had he not liked the taste of my blood? That had to be it. He hadn't enjoyed it and didn't want to repeat it. It had been better than anything I ever could have imagined but he hadn't liked it. My eyes grew warm and I realized I was on the brink of tears. Adze stroked my cheek.

"What's wrong?"

"You didn't like me?" My voice caught at the question.

"What?" Adze stared at me in bewilderment, then his lips curved into a gorgeous smile. "No, that's not it at all. Did you really think that? You're delicious, Kairos, far better than I had imagined. But we can't repeat it. Vampires in ancient houses don't feed on their servants. I shouldn't have done it to you at all but it's too late now. We'll just have to avoid doing it again."

"Even if I want it?"

His smile faded. "Even then. You can't beg me like that again, Kairos. This cannot happen again. Can you promise me that? Otherwise I can't let you down here again."

I drew in a sharp breath. He was going to cut me off? He was willing to never see me again just to prevent himself from feeding on me? I couldn't allow that. I needed him. I could live without being fed on. It was incredible but I didn't have to repeat it. I would just cherish the memory for the rest of my life.

"I won't," I promised. "I won't ask you again. Please don't push me away."

Adze caressed my cheek and that hint of a smile grew stronger. "Good. I don't want to have to push you away. Are you ready to return upstairs? Go straight to bed."

"Yes, master," I said, and that smile increased. I loved seeing him smile. He brought me to the hallway where the light was brighter and recommended I go upstairs slowly so my eyes could adjust, as he always recommended. I agreed and he retreated to his office. If the two rooms I didn't know about were both bedrooms like the one I had just been in, and if both of them were guest rooms, then where did he sleep?

Maybe they weren't both guest rooms. Or maybe he slept in the room where he brought me when we had sex. I licked my lips at the thought of everything we had done. I had told him I would go straight to bed but I really needed a shower first. That wouldn't be disobeying, I didn't think. I was still going to bed, just not immediately. He shouldn't mind.

As I stripped for the shower, I went to the mirror and studied my neck where he had bitten me. There were two red indentations. They weren't bleeding at all and had almost completely healed but I would have to wear a shirt with a collar today. I usually did to work but not on the weekend. Still, I needed it because today it would actually serve a purpose. I stroked the marks, feeling the faint dent in my skin, and shivered at the memory of how good it had felt. And I could never feel it again. He had been deadly serious about that. If I begged him like that again, he would never be with me. He would cut me off. And I couldn't let that happen. He was everything to me.

Seeing Janae had brought back some of my worries about the job since I had been so worried about her safety but after being bitten like that, I knew nothing could ever part me from this job. Even if I never felt that again, and it seemed I wouldn't, I wanted to be with Adze. No matter how much danger I was in, I would stay here. As I let the cool water sluice off my sticky body, I tried to reclaim the feeling of being bitten and my hand stroked along my length. Somehow, in spite of how exhausted I felt, I was eager for more and started hardening immediately. It didn't take long until the memory of Adze's fangs inside me had me crashing into an orgasm.

I took a deep breath and quickly cleaned up. I shouldn't be masturbating in the shower that I shared with Dmitri. That was incredibly rude. When everything was as clean as I could get it, including my own body, I returned to my room and sank into my bed. Would I even see Adze today? Would I be welcome tomorrow at noon? I wasn't sure. It felt like everything had changed and I just hoped I could still be with him.

CHAPTER THIRTY-SEVEN: DISCOVERED

I awoke to a knock on my door and sat up groggily. Had I slept in? But it was a weekend. I called out that I was getting up and noticed a flash of light near the window. A firefly. I had seen them several times and this wasn't the first time one had been in my room but for once, my window was completely shut and had been all day. How had it gotten in? I went to the window and opened it. The firefly shone briefly but stayed on the wall. I shrugged and got into jeans and one of my collared shirts. I could just stay inside and hope no one commented that I was dressed a little nicer than usual. Maybe I would say seeing Janae had made me want to look a little nicer on the weekends since she had been impressed by my appearance in work clothes. After I dressed, I looked for the firefly to shoo it outside and didn't see it. It must already be outside. And if it wasn't, then it might be able to get out however it had gotten in. I shut the window and opened the door.

I heard a bustle of voices from the kitchen but the bathroom was more pressing. Soon enough, I was emerging into the kitchen. I stared. Margaret, Dmitri, and Dianne were there, but so were three other servants. They weren't from House Tennison. They didn't look familiar at all, and all of them had grim looks on their faces. Margaret immediately came to my side.

"Are you okay, Kairos?" she asked.

"Yes," I said, completely bewildered. "What's going on?"

"We heard what happened," she said. "Are you sure you're okay?"

"Why wouldn't I be? What happened?"

Dmitri scowled and pulled me to the table. "You should get something to eat while you can. You'll spend the day at Mistress Lilith's."

"But why?"

"We know that Master Adze fed on you," Dmitri said, staring at me evenly. I gulped. How did he know? "I don't know what the circumstances were, but vampires aren't allowed to feed on their servants. Especially not in an ancient house. Especially not Elviore."

I licked my lips. No wonder they all looked at me so strangely.

"He didn't hurt me," I offered, not wanting to explain what had really happened between us. "I don't have any problems with it."

"That doesn't matter," Dmitri said. "You should eat. Margaret."

Margaret obediently got me a plate of pancakes and eggs and bacon. She sat next to me as I ate. I felt incredibly uncomfortable with everyone all staring at me. This was worse than being under surveillance. At least then the other servants were watching all of us. Now everyone was entirely focused on me. I felt caught out in a way I never had before. They knew. They all knew. How could they possibly know? I hadn't told anyone. My hand went to my neck but the marks were completely covered. They couldn't have seen. And they must have known long before I got up for all of these people to be here. Had Adze told people? He must have, but why? Why would he possibly share something that should have remained between me and him? I felt violated. This should have been private and it wasn't.

As soon as I finished, everyone herded me to a limo outside. It looked like the same limo I had ridden in when Lilith had saved me in the park. None of the servants here looked familiar though. Margaret said goodbye in a sad voice and I wondered what was going to happen as I got in the car. Dmitri and two of the other servants got in. Normally Dmitri drove and I was a little surprised he wasn't, but I didn't question it. I was sure there was a reason that I didn't need to know about. I was aware of the traffic flashing by and it was less than ten minutes before we were pulling up to Lilith's estate. The others got out first and then I got out and gulped. I still didn't fully understand what was happening.

I recognized Lilith's servants as I entered the house, and they looked just as somber as the others. There were quite a few people inside. I didn't see anyone who worked on the blood allotment but they were probably hard at work. I suspected they didn't get the weekends off, since blood would need to be rationed every single day, not just during the week. They probably staggered their weekends throughout the week to give them a break, but it was still a work day.

Dmitri and one of Lilith's servants led me upstairs and down a hall. They opened a door and gestured for me to enter. My breath caught as I stared inside. There were five vampires, all staring at me. Lilith was there, and I recognized the other four from the cathedral. This was all of House Elviore except Adze. Why were all of them here? I entered cautiously. I could feel them pressing against me and knew they were using some sort of glamour on me, but I didn't feel like I couldn't breathe and as long as I was somewhat in control, I would survive. The door shut behind me and I took a deep breath and tried to relax.

"Tell me what happened," Lilith commanded. I was completely surrounded by them and felt the pressure rising with the question. What could I possibly say? "We know your relationship with Adze," Lilith continued. "You shouldn't hide anything."

"How did you find out?" I managed, trembling slightly from the force of their gazes.

"What happened?"

I shivered and for a moment, my body locked. I couldn't move. Lilith gestured sharply and the feeling retreated.

I shuddered and took a step back. Every other time I had been surrounded by vampires, Adze had been with me. I felt abandoned and helpless to be in this situation alone. But there was nothing I could do about it.

"We were, um, together," I said cautiously. I did not want to go into details. "I asked him to bite me."

Lilith's eyes narrowed. "I told you not to ask that. Why did you disobey me?"

"I'm sorry," I said, realizing she had indeed warned me against exactly what I had done. "I just... forgot."

"So you asked him," Lilith said, sounding displeased. "What then?"

"He stopped," I said, again not wanting to get into details. "I, um, begged him to bite me. He kept refusing but I didn't want him to stop."

One of the other female vampires shook her head and I blushed, knowing I had made a mistake in begging him. It was humiliating to have to talk about it. But one of the male vampires looked almost amused and turned to Lilith.

"If that's really what happened," he started, but Lilith shook her head sharply.

"We're not done. Kairos, what happened next?"

"I kept begging," I said, blushing deeply now. "I know I shouldn't have done it. I'm sorry. But then he... he bit me. I wanted it. I don't regret it."

"And afterwards? Did he say anything to you afterwards?"

I hung my head. "He said if I begged like that again, he would stop seeing me completely. I won't ever do it again."

"Did he say anything else?"

"No," I said. "Well, just to sleep."

"Did he use a glamour on you at any point?"

"No," I said, puzzled. "He never does. I want to be with him."

"Are you sure?"

"I think so," I said, feeling very uncertain. "I mean, I think I can tell when vampires are using glamours like you're doing right now. But maybe I can't. I don't know."

"You can feel us using glamours?"

I nodded, because the pressure was still all around me. Lilith sighed.

"Thank you, Kairos. Would you like to be transferred to another house within Elviore? Any of us would be happy to take you."

"Why would I leave?" I asked, feeling a flutter of panic. Were they going to force me apart from Adze because of what had happened?

"Adze may be expelled from our house," Lilith said in a flat voice. I gasped.

"What? Why?"

"Our house does not feed on our servants," Lilith said. "He knew what might happen when he bit you, and he knew we would feel it immediately. He knew what he was risking."

I remembered what Adze had said about this costing him and my stomach churned. Was I going to be the cause of him being thrown out of House Elviore? When he had fought in the war with them? When he belonged to them? That couldn't be right.

"You can't do that," I said, and the vampires seemed shocked that I was challenging her. "I mean, um, you shouldn't. He didn't do anything. I did. I forced him to do it."

"Humans do not force vampires to do anything," said the female vampire with long dark hair.

"Still," said the sharply handsome male who had looked amused before. "If a pure human was flinging himself at me, I would be hard-pressed to refuse. Especially if it were clear his intentions were honest."

Lilith shook her head. "This is exactly why I warned you, Kairos," she said. "Your mistake may cost our house dearly. You're too valuable to be compromised like this."

The other female vampire sighed. "He is, but there's nothing we can do now. I don't think expelling Adze will make a difference. They'll argue he's compromised no matter what we do."

"No one knows yet," said the other male vampire, who had a thoughtful expression. "We can easily prevent them from finding out."

Lilith shook her head slowly, then pinned me with a glare. I froze, feeling like a rabbit who had just seen a wolf approaching. I felt the pressure of a glamour and for a moment, I couldn't breathe.

"You will tell no one, Kairos, and you will look for any hint of this in the messages you translate."

I felt like I was choking and couldn't say anything. Surprise flitted across her face and then the restrictions loosened. I gasped for breath.

"I apologize," she said. "But you must obey."

"I will," I said. "I won't tell anyone, and I'll look for anything."

She sighed. "That will be all, Kairos. I'd prefer if you remain here the rest of the day."

"Thanks," I said, unsure what else to say. Lilith gestured to the door. I bowed to her, glanced at everyone else, and turned. As I left, I heard Lilith sigh again. "Selene, go get Adze."

That sounded a little promising, I thought as I returned to Dmitri and the door was shut behind me again. I had survived and it seemed like they would forgive Adze as well. I still wasn't sure how they had known so quickly. The tattoo on my neck could alert any vampire in my house to any danger I was in, so perhaps it allowed them to know other things, too. But he hadn't bitten the tattoo. He had bitten the other side of my neck. I rubbed my neck and then dropped my hand when I saw Dmitri's eyes narrow. I hadn't meant for him to notice the movement. Dmitri led me downstairs and one of the other servants smiled at me wanly.

"You certainly know how to stir things up," she said. "Mistress Lilith said you would be staying here tonight. Is there anything you want to do?"

"Um, not really," I said. "I usually just hang out on the weekends."

"Perhaps you could observe," said a familiar voice, and I turned to see Denise, the woman who had shown me how to do blood allotments. She smiled at me. "Might as well see what we do during the rush hour."

"All right," I said, and she led me into the room I had been in last time. Kyle and Daniel were there, but not Candace. She probably had the weekend off. It seemed like Denise wasn't working, either, since she led me to their consoles rather than hers.

"Mind if we watch?" she asked Kyle. He flashed us a smile. "Just don't interrupt."

He was fast. I was extremely impressed as he went through the steps they had taught me. I recognized everything he was doing but he did it so effortlessly. He barely even seemed to read the information before he was matching things up and dealing out the blood to the various vampires. I glanced at Denise as we worked, wondering if she knew why I was here. It seemed like everyone else did. She looked over at me and our eyes met. She smiled and returned her attention to Kyle's monitor. I wasn't sure what that meant. If she did know, she wasn't angry about it, or sad, or upset in any way. Maybe she didn't know. I just had to get through today and hope no one else found out. I wasn't sure what would happen if House Salvite found out that Adze had drunk my blood but I suspected it was bad. I would keep the secret, and I knew everyone else would, too, but how many people already knew?

CHAPTER THIRTY-EIGHT: WEEKEND AWAY

I spent an unhappy weekend at Lilith's house. I ended up sleeping there that day, in one of their guest rooms in their second house, since at Lilith's house the women slept in the main manor and the men slept in the little house a few minutes walk away. After the first couple of hours everyone else left, including, I assumed, the other vampires. I didn't see any vampires the entire weekend. Denise mostly stayed with me and Daniel was the one to show me my room. Dmitri had stayed for a couple of hours but left when everyone else did with a warning look at me. I was assured this was temporary, just for the weekend, and had to believe it. If I didn't get to return to my home, I wasn't sure what I would do. If they tried to make me switch houses, I would just quit. I didn't want anything to do with vampires if I couldn't be with Adze.

Finally, Sunday night ended and Monday morning began. Would they let me go home to sleep in my own bed, or would they force me here another night and drive me to work in the evening? I had worn my same outfit two nights in a row, not having anything else, and didn't want to wear it to work. They had kindly given me pajamas to wear during the day but I wanted my own things. I didn't like how they had essentially kidnapped me and brought me here without even letting me pack. They had to have known I would be staying overnight. Why hadn't they given me an extra five minutes to pack the essentials? I was even having to borrow a toothbrush and the taste of the toothpaste was foreign. I missed home.

I had never consciously thought of Adze's house as home

before but now, being away from it, I realized I did think of it that way. It was my home and I missed it. I also missed the people. Dmitri and Dianne weren't the friendliest but they had warmed up to me and enjoyed talking to me. Margaret was a good friend. And now, because of my actions, I was forced away from them. Why had I begged Adze like that? I had been so desperate. No matter what the vampires had said about humans not forcing vampires, I knew I had made it almost impossible for him to refuse. Maybe he could have. Maybe. But I had done everything in my power to make him bite me and now everything was a mess. I really wouldn't do it again. Adze had warned me against repeating it, Lilith had warned me with the weight of the rest of the house behind her, and while no one here was warning me exactly, I knew one of the reasons they were forcing me to stay here was a warning. If I disobeyed, if he ever bit me again, I would lose Adze. I would be brought to another house, possibly even this house, and lose the home I loved.

Not that the people weren't nice, I thought as I sat down to dinner with Kyle and Denise. They had been working today and I had tagged along to watch them, not having anything else to do. Candace was nearby. She had let me practice some of the lesser deals on her console, correcting me frequently and occasionally taking over when my slow pace threatened to lose one of the vampires their ideal blood. But for the most part I had done it on my own and felt quite proud of myself. Denise had assured me that I was being paid overtime for my work with them even though I wasn't helping much. I didn't really need the overtime since I was paid so much already but I appreciated the gesture. Dianne was in charge of my wages and she had offered to provide documentation of all of my hours but last month I had demurred. I trusted her. It was enough to know that she was keeping careful records. If I were really curious, she told me I could check anytime to see what I was getting paid when I worked after hours, as when I went to Lilith's to read the time sensitive letters.

The dinner was delicious, as it had been the night before. Hiring a dedicated cook really made a difference. Living alone in my apartment before coming to work here meant I scraped together whatever food I could find and when I had lived with my ex before that, we had both been too exhausted from the rest of our lives to spend a lot of time cooking. But the man here, Sam, was a great cook, as was Margaret. It was a thoughtful gesture on the vampires' part to have a cook for all of the human servants since vampires didn't eat. They could have easily left their servants to fend for themselves but they catered to their human servants, offering them sky-high wages and all possible comforts.

As soon as dinner was underway and I had mostly finished my roast chicken with lemon and herbs and a side of potatoes, I looked around. The woman who seemed to have Dmitri's position, Hera, was here. I had met her every time I had come here. She resembled Lilith in a lot of ways with her long dark hair and strikingly beautiful face, though no one could really compare to a vampire in terms of beauty. Still, she was quite pretty for a human. If I were interested in women, I would find her quite attractive, but while I could appreciate her appearance, my heart was too caught up in Adze. All of the servants were attractive, I realized. They were at my house as well. Maybe the vampires selected their servants based on looks and not just abilities. They could be as picky as they wanted, after all, because so many people wanted the jobs.

Hera had come in late and was just starting to eat, but she was the one I wanted to talk to. She was Lilith's personal assistant and she would know when I was allowed to go home. I waited for her to finish impatiently, staying at the table long after the others wandered away. In fact, soon it was just me and her, though Denise and Kyle chatted nearby with Candace and Sam. Hera finally set her fork down and met my eyes with a smile.

"You clearly want to talk to me," she said. "What about?"

"When can I go home?" I asked, deciding to get straight to

the point. "I've already spent two nights here and I start work this evening."

"You could spend another day here," she offered, and I shook my head. "Very well. I'll bring you back to your house this morning. Do you plan on making the same mistake?"

I blushed. "No," I said, embarrassed that she, like everyone else, knew that Adze had bitten me. They all seemed to know that I had invited it, too. I wasn't sure how they knew but maybe the fact that I didn't have any resentment over it gave me away. I clearly hadn't minded it and Adze wouldn't have done it on his own, so it must have been obvious I had invited it.

"Good," she said with a nod, and stood up. I got to my feet as well. "I have a few things to do and then I'll take you to your home. Be ready in about thirty minutes."

"Thank you," I said, and she left the room. I went over to Denise and the others, unsure what else to do. It wasn't like I had anything to pack, or anything to do for half an hour. I was just waiting at this point.

"Thanks for your help these past two nights, Kairos," Denise said.

"I'm not sure I actually did anything," I said, and she and Kyle laughed. Candace grinned.

"Just having another body in the room helps," Candace said. "You took care of a lot of minor details so we could focus on the important vampires and I didn't have to do it myself."

"I'm glad I could help, then." I was, too. I had felt useless but maybe I had actually done something worthwhile. It was true that I had completed quite a few allotments on my own. Even though Candace had supervised, I had been doing most of the work. It wasn't just figuring out which blood should go to which vampire, after all; there was a lot of typing and inputting information that was quite boring and that was what I had spared her from doing.

We chatted until Hera returned and I said goodbye to all of them. I tried not to sound too eager, since they were good people and I had enjoyed spending time with them, but I wanted to get home. One of the other servants accompanied me in the limo as Hera sped past the traffic and then Adze's welcoming house appeared before us. I let out a breath I wasn't even aware of holding as the sight melted the tension in my chest. I was finally home.

Margaret was at the door with a hug for me and Dmitri and Dianne were behind her, smiling at me. Even Dmitri looked pleased to see me and gave me a stiff, formal hug. Dianne left it at the smile but I wasn't as close with her as I was with the others. A hug from her would have been out of place.

"I'm so glad you're back," Margaret said, beaming. "Have you already eaten? There are some leftovers if you're hungry."

"I already had dinner," I said, not wanting to disappoint her but genuinely not hungry. "Maybe I could have a snack later," I offered, and she agreed happily.

"Make sure to get enough sleep before work," Dianne said. "I'm sure you've been under stress."

"I will," I said obediently.

In my mind, though, I was just starting to realize that in a couple of hours it would be noon. Could I possibly sneak down to see Adze? Dmitri must have seen my gaze flicker in the direction of the basement stairs because he cleared his throat.

"I'm sure Adze will be pleased to hear that you've returned when work starts tonight," he said. "It may be a few days before he's in to see you. A precaution."

My cheeks heated but luckily the others didn't seem to be judging me. So I had to avoid Adze for a while. The message was clear. Adze hadn't been expelled from Elviore but seeing him too soon might change the vampires' decision in that matter. I didn't want him in any more trouble on my account, so I wouldn't go to his lair until he specifically invited me. Could I really wait days to see him again, though? I didn't want to, but if my choice was waiting a few days or never seeing him again, I could be as patient as required.

Margaret bustled about the kitchen happily as I went to all

of my favorite places in the house and spent an hour or two in my beloved bedroom among all of my own things. I returned for a snack, as promised, and she filled me in on everything that had happened the two nights I was gone. Not much, as nothing really happened, but it was clear that everyone had missed me. I was a little pleased by that. They wanted me here. They might be angry at my actions, or worried, as Margaret was, but they still enjoyed my presence. I was happy I was home again and as the sun ascended in the sky, I went to my room in a good mood.

CHAPTER THIRTY-NINE: UNDER WATCH

A pressure on my lips. A kiss. I drifted towards awareness and felt the body pressing me down in the bed, pressing against my groin in particular, shifting as if trying to arouse me. It worked. I tried to open my eyes and felt completely paralyzed. But somehow I knew it was Adze. I was so used to being blind with him that I knew his body even with my eyes shut. He was caressing me, his hands sliding along my chest to my nipples, his tongue entering my mouth to caress me there, everything a caress as I felt myself harden against him. I wanted him. But I wasn't allowed to have him right now, was I? In fact, I shouldn't even be seeing him right now. How was he here right now? Where was I? The sense of his body faded slightly and I tried to open my eyes to see him. I tried to lift an arm to embrace him but my body wouldn't budge. I tried to jerk myself into movement and gasped as my body suddenly crashed into my consciousness and I sat up in my empty room. A firefly glowed on the wall, then went to the windowsill and glowed again.

A dream. It had been a dream. When I had first come here, I had dreamt like that. Sexual fantasies of Adze that faded as soon as I regained consciousness. But as soon as I actually had Adze in the real world, those dreams had pretty much stopped. Why was I having them again?

I got up and let the firefly out, then paused as I watched it fly away into the dusky sky. The sun had already set but there was still just enough light in the air to be appealing to a firefly and I could see dozens of them nearby. Every time I had a dream like that, there had been a firefly in my room. I had often seen fireflies in my room, even though I had no idea how they got in here. Why?

It was a little earlier than I usually got up but I was wide awake now so I went to the bathroom and got dressed. The marks on my neck had faded and everyone here already knew about it so I pulled on a t-shirt to wear until I changed again for work. I went to my computer and searched for fireflies, finding only pictures and scientific information. I considered, then entered fireflies and vampires and started scouring the results. One caught my eye and I blinked when I realized it had drawn my attention because Adze was in the title. I opened it and started reading. Adze was an African vampire. That wasn't especially surprising, since vampires often took on the names of vampire myths and he was black, so he might have chosen an African name. But adze were closely linked to fireflies. I couldn't tell if they turned into fireflies or if they controlled them, but it made perfect sense why there would be a firefly in my room every time I dreamed like that. It was Adze. Was he actually here? Or did he just plant himself in my dreams through the firefly? I wasn't sure. I glanced out the window. It was unlikely Adze himself would risk becoming a bug so easily smashed. He had to just control them. Did he control all of them? On many of my evening jogs I had seen fireflies and thought nothing of it but I remembered what he had said about me being protected. Was he protecting me through the fireflies? Could he see me, and see if I got into trouble? I smiled.

I had started having those dreams before we slept together, before I had any clue he felt the same. If he really were giving me those dreams, then that meant he was attracted from the first. For some reason that thought pleased me. He had liked me far earlier than I had imagined. I shut my browser and stretched. The fireflies outside might make it safe enough for an evening jog but I was still wary of going outside on my own. I didn't even know if Adze did control the fireflies.

There was a chance it was just a fluke that fireflies seemed to always be in my room. No, that wasn't a fluke. It was Adze watching me, seducing me, and the dream tonight meant that he still wanted me even if he had to keep his distance. I hoped I dreamt like that every day until I could finally see him, and I vowed to stay asleep longer next time. This time I had wanted to move but next time, I would remain frozen. I was often bound and helpless with him so it wouldn't be the first time I was paralyzed as he caressed me. Next time would be different.

I could hear Dmitri getting up as I wandered into the dark kitchen and flipped on the lights. Dianne and Margaret would arrive in about an hour, I knew. Back when I was on a good schedule of running each evening, this was when I would get up, but I had started sleeping in after being too scared to run. I went to the back door to retrieve the various newspapers we received and returned to the kitchen. Sometimes Dmitri was the first one out here and got the newspapers, and sometimes Dianne brought them in when she and Margaret arrived. I skimmed through the Redmond paper for any news of my house. Nothing. Good. I shivered at the thought of what would happen if word got out that Adze had fed on me. Not only would Redmond explode, if I were named, then my friends and family might find out. I would definitely need to keep this a secret.

Soon the others were up and it was a morning like any other. Work went smoothly. I was alert to any changes in the content of the letters and emails but it all seemed to be the same as usual. Good. I wasn't sure what I was looking for exactly but I was pretty sure something would change in tone or content if they learned that Adze had violated protocol and bitten me. I wasn't sure how exactly that compromised him but it would certainly ruin his reputation. Or maybe Lilith had meant that it would compromise me. I wasn't sure, but nothing seemed different. They had indeed shifted to the east and would be staying there for some time, I could tell, and Dmitri was pleased when I reported that. Apparently Elviore had the east under control and as the day advanced I noticed a spike in frustration. Elviore had stopped one of their plans, I could tell, and Dmitri was happy about that when I reported it at the end of the day.

Adze didn't show up or send any messages, and I didn't ask. I didn't want to get him in any more trouble. Dmitri offered to jog with me that evening, as he had a couple of times before, and then it was time for bed again. I left my window slightly open to make it easier for a firefly to get in, not that they'd ever had any trouble before. Sure enough, in my dreams I felt Adze leaning over me. Despite my best intentions, though, as he touched me, my body got hotter and hotter until I burst into awareness on the brink of an orgasm. Gasping, I finished it myself. I had wanted to stay with Adze longer but it was enough for now.

The next few days passed in the same pattern. Work went smoothly with nothing changing except an increasing frustration. My days went smoothly and I dreamed of Adze every day, waking filled with longing and arousal, knowing he was thinking of me. On the fourth night, though, I noticed something new in the letters. Something was being planned. I couldn't tell what, and it didn't seem immediate. Something was being watched. I immediately called Dmitri in and explained the situation.

"You have no idea what is being watched?" he asked, scanning the email I was showing him. The message had shown up in several emails and one letter. "Is it being tapped, like Tennison, or watched?"

"Watched," I said. "I don't know the difference but there is one. And I'm not sure what it's referring to. But they're waiting, and something big will happen when they're ready."

"Does it involve you in any way?"

"They've always referred to me as an icon before," I said. "I haven't seen that in anything the past few days. That is a little unusual," I realized. "Normally someone brings me up every couple of days, but they haven't."

"Would they have changed your reference name?"

"Maybe," I said, a chill running down my spine. "Um, I think I'll be staying in the house for a few days."

"That's a good idea," he said, and studied the email again. "What code words are they using? How can you tell they're watching something?"

I pointed out the phrases I had been taught meant watching. I was again surprised that I had never realized I was being taught a code. The language itself had nothing to do with watching but my professor had taught me that when humans used those words, it meant they were watching something. Why hadn't I ever questioned it? No human I knew had used language like that but he was my professor; I accepted his word without question. Dmitri nodded grimly.

"I'll tell Adze. You should stay in the house. This might be worth having House Tennison return for a while. You need a vampire with you to ensure your safety."

I gulped. "It might not involve me," I said, and he nodded.

"It might not, but we're not taking any chances."

"All right." I did want to be safe.

"Let me know if you see anything else, or figure anything out," he said, and patted my shoulder. "Thank you for telling me immediately."

I returned to work as he left, probably to report immediately to Adze. A familiar sense of dread started to work its way down my spine as I continued translating. I flagged every message that used the new language, and there were an increasing amount. Whatever they were planning, they were excited about it. They were getting ready, and they were watching for something in particular to happen. When it happened, they were going to act. Only I couldn't tell what they were watching for, or what they were watching, and it was increasingly frustrating me. Were they watching me? I didn't think they were watching Elviore or Tennison since they weren't referring to any numbers, and they weren't referring to the cathedral since there weren't any religious references. The language was flowery, but what did that mean? Were they watching for flowers or were the specific flowery words they were using refer to something else? Either would be in keeping with how they hid their messages. There were several references to roses but was that literal or did it represent a person? I kept Dmitri updated throughout the night and when he came to debrief me that morning, I told him everything I possibly could and laid out all of my limited ideas on what they meant. He was deep in thought.

"How immediate is the threat?"

"They're waiting for something, whatever they're watching for, but as soon as they see it, it seems like they're ready to act," I said.

"And rose is the only keyword you're getting?"

"They're talking about several types of flowers but that's the one that stands out," I said. "But I have no idea what the flowers refer to. They might be actual flowers for all I know."

Dmitri nodded and seemed just as puzzled as I was.

"You're free for the morning," he said. "Stay up for a few hours. We may need you again and Adze may want to speak to you about this. Only about this," he emphasized. I blushed and nodded, but my heart leapt. I would finally get to see Adze? The circumstances weren't the best, but I deeply missed him. Dreaming about him wasn't nearly enough.

I headed back to the living area and changed into more casual clothes. The marks on my neck were completely gone now and I didn't have to worry about wearing collared shirts anymore, though I still did when working. Margaret was getting dinner ready when I went back out – beef stroganoff, one of my favorites – and I decided to chat with her. She never minded and never seemed distracted, even though she frequently turned to me and ignored everything else while we talked. Yet somehow, everything got done on time and nothing was ever overcooked. She had an excellent sense of timing and I was always impressed. Dmitri and Dianne were more somber than usual at dinner and I suspected it was because of what I had seen in the emails. When we finished and had brought our plates into the kitchen, Dmitri looked at me.

"Master Adze would like to speak to you," he said. "He'll be waiting in the front lobby."

"Thank you for telling me," I said, and winced at the warning in his eyes. "And, um, I won't do anything."

Dmitri nodded and I considered changing into more formal clothes. I rarely saw him dressed like this. Well, actually, he did see me like this a lot, I realized. This was what I typically wore when I went to his lair every day at noon. Just because I couldn't see myself didn't mean he couldn't see me. So I wouldn't dress up. It wasn't work hours anyway, so he probably didn't expect me to still be in work clothes. I went to the lobby and my heart throbbed at the sight of him. He was dressed in a formal black suit, as always, and looked exceptionally handsome. How had I forgotten how handsome he was? His lips curved in the hint of a smile at the sight of me and my heart skipped a beat, then returned to its throbbing pulse. I wanted him so badly. He gestured to the door.

"Let's walk," he said, and I glanced to the door nervously.

"Is that a good idea?"

"If you were alone, no, it wouldn't be a good idea," he said. "But you'll be with me. I want to talk to you outside of the house. You'll be safe with me."

I nodded and he took my hand. My knees went weak for a moment before I braced myself. He had never shown affection for me before in public. No one was around, but it was still public. The others could still potentially see. I suddenly realized why he wanted to be outside. He wanted complete privacy for whatever he wanted to say and nowhere in the house was completely safe. Even if we went to his office, we might be interrupted. I wasn't sure what he wanted to say to me but I took his hand and went beside him as he led me out of the house into the grounds. We would just have to avoid any rose gardens.

CHAPTER FORTY: DEADLY APOLOGY

The stars were sparkling and the horizon was just starting to get lighter. The sun would be up soon so we couldn't stay out here long. Maybe thirty minutes. We went to a grassy area far from any of the gardens and I was glad. He knew about the flowers so of course he was avoiding them. I was reassured. We weren't taking any chances. I felt a little vulnerable but I was with him. He could easily protect me.

"Kairos, I wanted to apologize," he said, taking my hand. "I shouldn't have done that to you."

"But I wanted it," I said, surprised by the apology. "You know that. You didn't do it against my will. You don't need to apologize."

"You're my servant," he said. "You're human. A pure human. I'm an ancient vampire. You have no ability to resist me."

"I'm resistant," I pointed out, and his lips curved.

"You are," he said. "But this is not an equal relationship."

"I know," I said. "I don't want it to be. I don't mind that you control me."

He reached out and stroked my hair. I shivered with pleasure. I loved it when he touched me like this. What I had said was true. I wanted him to control me. Nothing brought me greater pleasure. Then he narrowed his eyes and looked towards the nearby garden. I looked as well, wondering what had drawn his attention.

The air cracked and Adze flung me to the ground. A gun?

Another crack and blood splattered across my side. Adze hissed in pain and flinched away from me. He held his arm, which had been shot. A dozen shadows approached from the garden and Adze straightened and faced them. As they came closer, the ragged appearance of the vampires gave them away immediately. They were in withdrawal. But none of them had guns. Who had been shooting? Were there more of them out of sight? Adze loomed over the vampires and they flinched, but kept coming.

"Don't you dare come closer," Adze growled. Again they flinched.

"Attack him," another voice said with malicious delight, and four vampires appeared at the back of the dozen vampires in withdrawal. These four were not in withdrawal and were in pristine clothing. Two had guns and the one who had spoken aimed it at Adze with a smirk. He fired and Adze dropped to the ground to avoid it.

The vampires in withdrawal rushed forward and one grabbed me. I jerked away and started running towards the house but other shapes loomed in front of me. I stumbled to a halt and backed away. Guns rang out behind me and the vampires were coming closer. Another one lunged at me and grabbed my arm. She yanked me close and her fangs glistened in the harsh light of the lampposts. For a moment, I froze as the vampire must have used a glamour on me, but I couldn't afford to freeze. She was going to drink my blood and kill me. Only Adze had the right to drink my blood. I punched her, not really knowing how but throwing my whole weight behind the blow. I wished I had taken self-defense in college. She collapsed to the ground and I looked for some sort of escape. The four vampires were focused on Adze and keeping him pinned. The other vampires were coming after me and I needed to get away. But could I leave Adze? He was a vampire, an ancient, but he was avoiding those bullets and that meant they could potentially kill him. I remembered from history that vampires could survive being shot and he hadn't flinched at the first gunshot, but after the bullet had hit his arm, he was dodging.

Another vampire grabbed me and I broke away. If I wanted to survive, I had to abandon him and trust in his ability to survive. I scanned the area and noticed a place in the wall of vampires around me where there was a little path. I darted forward. The two vampires on either side of the opening quickly moved to block me and I barreled past them at full speed. One clawed at me and I cried out as her nails tore through my shirt into my skin. She dug into me and ripped out my flesh and I struggled to keep running as the ragged edges of her nails tore along my flesh. Blood seeped from the wound and suddenly all of the vampires stiffened. Even Adze. They all looked at me and I knew the scent of blood was triggering their instincts.

Adze took advantage of the pause to attack the four vampires and wrestle a gun from one of them. I took advantage of it to sprint away and hoped I wasn't making a mistake. I heard more gunshots behind me but the sound of advancing feet was a far more pressing matter. I was past the circle of them but they were hot on my tail and there were well over a dozen of them now. I pushed faster and the feet came closer. I heard a whisper of laughter, of anticipation. My arm burned and I tried not to think about what the vampires would do to me if they surrounded me. Drink my blood, yes, but would they also tear me limb from limb? My blood wouldn't be any good to them. Would they kill me when they realized my blood wouldn't satisfy them? My arm was on fire and I didn't dare look at it, knowing the sight of the damage would freeze me. Even as I ran, I kept feeling flickers of glamours from them and my heart would hitch, but I couldn't afford to stop. My breathing was completely ragged and I was gasping for breath as the glamours froze my lungs, but I had to keep going. I was halfway back to the house when a line of shadows loomed in front of me.

Vampires appeared before me and I flinched and stumbled

to a halt, falling to my knees. Immediately one of the vampires in front of me grabbed my arm and picked me up. The other vampires moved in front of me. The vampire holding me didn't attack and I looked up to recognize Alessandro. I nearly sobbed in relief. It was House Tennison. All of the vampires around me now must be Tennison and they surged forward over the other vampires who were starting to scatter in surprise. More gunshots and I realized they were killing the vampires. They were vampire hunters and allowed to kill other vampires. They probably didn't even need permission since the vampires were in withdrawal.

"Adze's in danger," I managed, pointing the way I had come with my uninjured arm. I noticed Darius next to me. His lips tightened and he dashed in that direction with six vampires surrounding him. Alessandro was still holding me. He finally released me and examined my arm carefully. He touched the edge of the torn flesh and I flinched. My entire arm throbbed and I was losing blood at an alarming rate. Alessandro's eyes were dilated and he licked his lips as he looked at the injury. Was he going to feed on me? I pulled back from him and he met my eyes. He was tempted by the blood but he wasn't consumed by it.

"What does this feel like?" he asked very seriously.

"What do you think?" I asked, my fear clouding my thinking. I shouldn't be angry at a vampire but I was still terrified and it was such a strange question. "It hurts."

"Does it feel like fire?"

My brow creased. "It feels like my skin just got ripped open," I said. "That burns."

His eyes narrowed and he took my other arm firmly. "You'll need to stay with me for now."

I looked in the direction of Adze. There were still the sound of gunshots.

"Is he safe? Those other four vampires had guns."

"What other four?"

"There were four who weren't in withdrawal," I explained.

282

"They shot him and I think it actually hurt him."

"I doubt it," Alessandro said, but he didn't sound too sure of himself. "Did you recognize the vampires?"

"No."

"I wonder if they would actually dare," he murmured, then tightened his grip and pulled me towards the house. "We need to get you to safety. Does your arm still burn?"

"Yeah," I said. The edges of the cut stung and my entire arm felt like it was on fire. I needed medical attention fast because I was starting to feel faint. Now that the shock had passed and I was safe, I felt dizzy and stumbled a little as he walked with me. He tightened his grip on me and I took a deep breath to recover. It was starting to get light out, I realized. All of the vampires would need to get inside soon. The fighting couldn't last. As we returned to the house, I saw Dmitri, Dianne, and Margaret waiting at the entrance. Margaret had tears in her eyes. Dianne vanished without a word and I wondered where she had gone. Alessandro escorted me in and brought me to Adze's office. I was a little surprised he was granted access, but Dmitri didn't question him. Dianne appeared with a first aid kit. Alessandro set me in the chair where I had once sat when Rory approached Adze about my job. Dianne immediately got to work, pouring a liquid that felt far more like fire than my arm already did. I cried out and tried to pull back but her grip was nearly as firm as Alessandro's had been. Her lips were set but her eyes were moist as if she were on the brink of tears herself.

She wrapped a bandage around my arm firmly. Blood immediately started soaking through and Alessandro licked his lips again. Would he be able to restrain himself? He seemed to be visibly holding himself back. Dianne finished with the bandage and felt my forehead the same way my mother had as a child. The same way Adze had after drinking my blood. My vision blurred for a moment and my entire body burned. I felt dizzy and couldn't stop gasping for breath, even though I could barely get enough air. My heart kept skittering erratically.

"He's in shock," Dianne announced.

Dmitri rushed in with a blanket and wrapped it around me. I was in shock? I didn't even know what that meant. I felt weak and couldn't stop trembling. All I could think about was Adze, trapped with those other four vampires. Had Darius gotten to him in time? Why had the bullets hurt him? Had I abandoned him to die? I was to blame for everything and tears warmed my eyes. He had nearly been expelled from his house because of me and now he might be dead because of me. An ancient vampire, killed because of me.

Alessandro knelt in front of me and gripped my injured arm, putting pressure on the wounds. He stared deep in my watery eyes.

"Does it still burn?"

"Why?" I managed. It did. My whole body burned, yet I somehow felt freezing cold at the same time. I was managing to take deeper breaths at least. I was starting to feel a little more under control.

"Because that vampire may have started the process of turning you into a vampire," Alessandro said very calmly. I gasped, my heart clenching in fear. Any control I had regained was lost. "You need to be under observation."

I started to reach for my torn arm but he stopped me. A tear slid down my cheek. I couldn't be a vampire. What would I tell my mom and dad? My friends? What would I do with myself? I couldn't be turned into a vampire by those monsters. My lips trembled and I stared at the bandage under Alessandro's hands where the vampire had torn through my clothes and dug deep into my flesh. It did burn, and I didn't want to believe this was happening.

CHAPTER FORTY-ONE: BURNING

"Where is he?"

Adze's voice. I nearly burst into tears. Alessandro had been putting pressure on my arm for nearly fifteen minutes as I struggled to get my body back under control. Dianne had brought me hot tea to sip and the burning sensation was starting to fade, though that didn't necessarily mean anything. We wouldn't know if I had started to turn for another day, according to Alessandro. But Adze was here now and I tried to get to my feet. Alessandro prevented me from rising easily and then Adze came through the door. He had bandages on his arm and side. He had been shot, then, and I winced at the thought that I had just left him there to die.

Adze came to my side and grabbed my chin, tilting my head up to look at him. He stroked his thumb along my cheek, then released me and looked at Alessandro.

"And?"

"He's showing the first signs, but we won't know for sure until a day has passed," Alessandro said. Adze shut his eyes and I could practically feel his rage boiling up. The other vampires in the room flinched. They probably could feel it, too. Darius was there and he came to Adze's side and examined me as well. At his gesture, Alessandro released my arm. Blood soaked through the bandage and Darius's nostrils flared. The other vampires looked suddenly intent and I felt pressure against my senses, my lungs seizing, and then Adze barked a sharp word and the pressure dulled. Carefully, Adze unwrapped the bandages. There were more nearby. At the sight of the injury, he and Darius looked furious. Adze touched the skin along the tear. I couldn't bring myself to look at my damaged arm. I would scar, that was for certain. Sections of my flesh had been ripped away. Would I be able to heal? The air was freezing against the injury and I was grateful when Adze carefully wrapped a new bandage around my arm. This time it didn't start bleeding immediately. Still, I felt dizzy.

"He needs blood," Adze said. "Call Lilith and tell her to find blood that matches his and bring it here right away."

Darius gestured and two of the other vampires left the room, one with his phone to his ear as he no doubt called Lilith. I was glad they knew to find blood that matched mine. Vampires were ideally suited to finding the right kind of blood. It was after hours, but her house controlled all of the blood in the city. There had to be some for me.

"Kairos, can you answer a few questions for Darius?"

"Sure," I managed. Alessandro, who had still been kneeling in front of me, got to his feet. Darius went to the desk and pulled the chair around so that he could sit facing me. Adze hovered over his shoulder, as did Alessandro, but I focused on Darius. My vision was a little blurred at the edges and it was easiest to just look at his face and not worry about anything else.

"Can you tell me what happened, Kairos?" Darius asked gently.

I hesitated and looked at Adze. What could I say about why we were out there? I couldn't tell anyone that Adze had fed on me. Lilith had made that clear. But I also didn't want to lie when it was clear Darius was trying to help me. I would just have to explain what had happened while leaving out the details and hope they didn't push.

"Adze wanted to talk to me outside," I said without elaborating. The other vampires stiffened and I quickly corrected myself. "Master Adze." Darius looked almost amused by my slip of the tongue. Was that enough? They already knew I was sleeping with Adze so hopefully the fact that we were talking outside wasn't too unusual. "We had barely said anything when he seemed to see something, and then there was a gunshot."

I went through everything that had happened, leaving out only my own emotions and fears. I did mention not wanting to abandon Adze and looked at him when I said it. He seemed to soften slightly.

"You did the right thing," he assured me, even though I could tell he wasn't supposed to talk while Darius was questioning me. Darius didn't comment, just asked me to continue and I did. When I had told him everything, I was trembling again. Reliving what had happened terrified me and I could still remember how helpless I had felt surrounded by vampires, knowing there was no way to escape them. And then that one chance to break through them that had ended with my arm getting shredded and possibly becoming a vampire. My voice shook as I finished and he looked sympathetic.

"Am I really going to be a vampire?" I asked softly, looking at Adze again. What would happen to our relationship if I were a vampire? Were we allowed to be with each other? It would no longer be an unequal relationship at least. Maybe it was more acceptable if both people were vampires.

"We don't know," Adze said. "The injury was severe enough and you showed the first symptoms, but we need more time before we know for sure."

"But what happens? If I am?"

"We'll take care of it," Adze said.

"Do you want to be a vampire?" Darius asked, and I shook my head emphatically.

"No."

"Why not? Many people want to become vampires."

"I want to be human," I said, not knowing any way to explain without insulting the vampires around me. I didn't want to have to drink blood, didn't want to risk getting addicted, didn't want to live forever. The vampires from House Tennison hadn't wanted it either but had been turned against their will. Had it happened like this? They were injured by Elviore and then, over the next couple of days, became vampires? Why hadn't the other humans killed them when they realized what was happening? I was pretty sure I was human enough to kill right now even if I did become a vampire. But it wasn't certain, I assured myself. There was no guarantee I'd become a vampire. There was still hope that I would remain human.

Darius stood up and rolled the chair back on the other side of the desk.

"We have to do something, Adze," he said seriously. "They attacked you directly. This can't stand."

Adze was silent, examining me. "We'll see what Lilith says."

"You have to act," Darius said, clearly impatient. "I don't care if you claim to need more time. Our house will stop supporting your efforts if you don't take action this time. This is beyond framing you."

"I agree with you," Adze said, meeting his gaze. He was still angry, I could tell, and he fingered the bandage on his side. "But Lilith makes the final decision."

"Is she coming?"

"She'll be here soon. We'll all be here soon."

I shivered. The entire house was gathering again, and again it was because of me. Would I have to be present? I was already a little on edge being around the five or so vampires here. I didn't want to be around any more of them. And what would Lilith decide? If they had attacked Adze, then they weren't fooling around anymore.

Darius turned to me again. "Adze told us you had found a warning in the messages. Do you know whether the target was you or him?"

"He's hardly in a state to think clearly," Adze began, but I furrowed my brow and thought hard. Did I know? The rose was the target, I now recognized. But which of us would be a rose?

"I don't know," I said. "The reference was a rose. I don't know who that would be."

"A rose," Darius mused. "Could be a vampire. Immortal, beautiful, and armed with thorns."

"Or a human," Alessandro suggested. "Pure, beautiful, and full of red blood."

I shuddered at the thought. Both of their interpretations might work, though. I was a little pleased he had thrown beautiful in for me as well as Adze. I might not rival a vampire, but at least they thought I was attractive. Then again, all of their servants were attractive. Maybe he wasn't talking about me specifically.

"Do either of those sound correct?" Darius asked me.

"They both do," I said. "I mean, either could work. I'm not sure."

Adze came to my side and caressed my head possessively. I was startled by the gesture. First holding my hand in the open earlier and now cradling my head in front of all these vampires. He was far more open about this relationship than he had been. Maybe it was just because everyone here likely already knew about our relationship. But what about earlier?

"He's still coming out of shock," Adze said. "We shouldn't pressure him too much."

"Doesn't stress make the process faster?" Darius said with an edge of anger in his voice. He must be referring to the process of becoming a vampire. Was that true?

"It does, but what if he isn't turning? Too much stress will harm him if he remains human."

"You really think he'll remain human?"

"He's resistant, and they didn't know what they were doing," Adze pointed out. "If anyone is going to remain human after this, he is."

That reassured me a little. My arm still burned slightly and I was dizzy, but if Adze thought I would remain human, then

I needed to have faith as well. Darius and Alessandro looked skeptical, however. They didn't believe Adze but I did. After all, Adze was an ancient who had turned at least two humans into vampires. Probably a lot more. If all of House Tennison were turned by House Elviore then all of the vampires in Elviore must have turned around three vampires each. And Adze had mentioned another house in Europe, so there must be even more. And who knew if Adze had turned more people than that. I doubted anyone in House Tennison had turned anyone before. If I was going to believe anyone here, it was Adze. But part of me hoped Lilith and the others would come and also reassure me that I would be fine. Maybe I did want to be in the room when they showed up.

Adze remained at my side, stroking my head, as Darius and Alessandro turned to the others and started talking quietly. I looked up at Adze's beautiful face, then at his injuries.

"What happened?" I asked. "I though guns didn't hurt vampires."

"They had holy water bullets," Adze said in a tight voice. "They were confiscated and destroyed after the war but they must have smuggled some out. I have no idea how they got them but it's another crime they'll be charged with, especially using them against an ancient."

"Will you recover?" I asked, horrified at the thought of Adze's beautiful body scarred because of me. So many things had happened because of me.

"It'll take time, but in a few years there won't even be a trace," he said. "They were glancing wounds. I know how to dodge holy water bullets, though I haven't had to do it in some time."

"I'm glad," I whispered, and clutched his leg next to me. I buried my head into his waist. He sighed, then unentangled himself from me and got the desk chair again, sitting in front of me and holding my hand. My uninjured hand, that was. My other arm stung too much for me to move my hand. Luckily, it was my left arm. It shouldn't disrupt my activities too much.

Assuming I went back to my ordinary life and didn't become a vampire, I thought grimly.

"It was House Salvite, wasn't it?" I didn't really need the confirmation but wanted to hear it anyway. Adze nodded.

"Their four house leaders were there in person to make sure it went well," he said in a bitter voice. "I'm sure I was the target. They wouldn't have had holy water bullets if I weren't."

"Did you tell them that?" I asked, gesturing to Darius with my chin.

"They wanted to hear what you thought, and they thought it unusual that Salvite would watch my house when I rarely leave at night. You, however, leave on a regular basis. They think you're the much more likely target."

"Last time they attacked me, you came to rescue me," I pointed out. "Maybe they were planning on you saving me again this time and that's why they had the bullets."

"That could be," he said thoughtfully. "But it still doesn't clarify whether they were trying to hold me off and kill you, or whether they were trying to lure me out and killing you was just a bonus."

Killing me was a bonus? I shivered. I was alternately freezing and burning up and I didn't know what that meant. My vision was still blurry and I was starting to get extremely tired. I leaned back and shut my eyes. Adze jerked my hand forward abruptly, startling me back to attention.

"Do not go to sleep, Kairos," he said. "If you're a vampire it won't matter, but if you're human, it could be deadly. You just need to wait until Lilith gets here with the blood. Then you can rest."

"All right," I murmured, but now that sleep had entered my mind, I could barely think of anything else. There was a commotion at the door and I felt pressure against my senses. More vampires. Then Adze stood up and a vampire I'd never met took his place. He was carrying several bags of blood and a lot of equipment. He studied the bandage before unwinding it slowly, then winced at the sight of the injury.

"A vampire did this?" he asked, and Adze nodded. "Is he showing symptoms?"

"So far," Adze said. "But take care of him anyway. It's not certain."

The vampire nodded and wrapped a fresh bandage around my arm. I wasn't bleeding anymore. Then I noticed Lilith and one other vampire from my house watching me intently. I felt a flash of relief that my house was here, protecting me. They might be angry at me because of what Adze and I had done, but they were here in our defense now. Would this be enough to push Lilith into action? Then I flinched as the vampire inserted the needle into my vein. I never especially liked getting my blood drawn and I had no idea what was involved in getting a blood transfusion, but I suspected I would like it less.

CHAPTER FORTY-TWO: DESTROYING EVIDENCE

I woke up with a start and looked around. I was lying down, but not in my bed, and from the pressure against my mind, there were vampires nearby. When had I fallen asleep? There was a low murmur of voices and I tried to get my bearings. I was in a cot. Not a bed. It seemed hastily constructed. I was still in Adze's office and as I looked around, I saw Elviore's vampires in close discussion with Darius, Alessandro, and four other Tennison vampires. Adze glanced over at me and his eyes widened.

"You're awake," he said, rising quickly and approaching me. He and the other vampires had been sitting around a table that must have been brought in and was covered in papers and computers. He knelt beside the cot and took my hand. "How do you feel?"

"What happened?"

"You blacked out," he said.

"Is that good or bad?"

"It's never good to black out," Adze said. "But it is a good sign that you won't become a vampire. Blood loss wouldn't cause us to black out."

Lilith and the rest of my house came to my side, as did Alessandro. He looked relieved. Lilith knelt beside me as well, her elegant gown creasing as she placed a hand on my shoulder.

"We have every confidence that you're still human, but we'll keep monitoring you to be sure."

I nearly sobbed in relief. My life would have been over if I had become a vampire. I had never been so glad to be a human before in my life. Adze's lips were curled in the smile I had gotten used to and he looked relieved as well. I wondered again what would have happened to our relationship if I became a vampire.

"We're going to need your cooperation, Kairos," Lilith continued. "We'll give you some time to recover, but we need to act quickly."

"You need me to translate something?"

"Yes, but that's not all," she said.

"That is pressing, though," Darius said from the table. "If he's able to stand, he needs to look at this immediately."

"Very well," Lilith said. "Are you strong enough to stand?"

I sat up cautiously. My head spun but I felt fairly stable. I swung my legs to the edge of the low cot and tried to push myself up. I couldn't. Adze took my arm and helped me up. Once standing, I felt a little more in control. I made it over to the table without any help and Adze had me sit in his chair. Darius turned the computer towards me.

"We need to know how they're reacting to this. There's been an explosion of emails but none of us can read them."

I scanned the email he showed me, my mind creaking to life.

"They're scared," I said. "They're exposed. They want something destroyed. Papers? Documents?"

I opened another email, my heart beating rapidly as it always did when reading about imminent threats.

"They're destroying evidence."

Darius drew in a sharp breath. "Where?"

"I think... is there a house with a gargoyle?"

"Yes," he said in a tight voice, then rose to his feet. "We'll go immediately. Ambrosia, get the court order. No delays. Go in person," he added to the petite vampire who must be Ambrosia. "Use the potion."

"Of course," she said. It had to be day, I realized. They were sending a vampire out in the sunshine with the potion that prevented it from doing harm. The potion was incredibly expensive, so this was clearly important and urgent. If House Salvite were destroying evidence, then they did indeed need to act quickly. I just hoped they could be fast enough.

"You have permission to jump traffic," Lilith said. "I'm granting it to all of you. Do your servants know how to do it?"

"Some don't," Darius said.

"Take mine, then," Adze said. "Dmitri and Margaret can easily leave right now."

I wondered why Dianne couldn't but knew this wasn't the time to ask. This was the time to act. All of the Tennison vampires except Alessandro hurried off. He remained and smiled at them apologetically.

"I'll need to keep an eye on you," he said. "Especially Kairos."

"Of course," Lilith said. "Kairos, keep translating. Keep us informed."

I obeyed. The emails were scattered and frequent and then, suddenly, one of the most prolific senders went silent. Then another. In less than twenty minutes, only a few emails were being sent, mostly inquiring in very clear language what was happening. They were barely hiding their meaning at all and just trying to figure out why everyone had gone silent. A few minutes of nothing, and Lilith leaned back in her chair. Adze was still standing behind me and he rubbed my back encouragingly.

"Looks like Tennison caught enough of them," she said.

"The others will flee, but we'll find them," Alessandro said. "We know where to look. You need to prepare your case. Salvite will press for it to go to court without delay."

"I would have preferred more time," she said, then sighed. "But it's too late now. They forced our hand."

"Maybe that was their intent," one of the other vampires said. "They knew we were on to them. Maybe they even knew we had his help." He gestured at me. "We don't know who the target was."

"Kairos," Adze said, touching my cheek as I looked up at him. "We're going to need your cooperation in this. Can you help us?"

"Help with what?"

"You'll need to testify against them."

I froze. "What?"

"We need you to give your side of the story. You're the one who translated their messages, so you'll need to explain it."

"I, uh, do I have to?" My mind whirled. Was there any way out of this? If people found out I had been translating messages, I would be in danger. And even if I weren't in danger, everyone would find out I had been lying. All of my family and friends. "Do I have to say anything else?"

"You'll have to explain how you were attacked," Adze said. "Both attacks, and the cathedral as well."

"I can't," I said. "I don't want my family finding out about any of that."

If my mom knew I was in danger, she would make me leave immediately. Janae would feel betrayed that I had lied to her and hidden the truth. All of my friends and family would hate me and I'd never be able to keep my job. I couldn't lose my job and my chance to see Adze.

"Everything that's happened will be in the open soon enough," Alessandro said in a grim voice. "The rest of us will be testifying as to what's happened. We need your perspective to verify the events."

Lilith leaned towards Alessandro. "Who is your counsel?"

"Alaric," he said. "Why? Would you prefer someone else?"

"He'll need to be filled on Kairos and Adze's... situation."

"Our house is aware of their relationship," Alessandro said. "It'll pose a problem, but we should be able to avoid any scandal."

Lilith's lips tightened. "That isn't the only problematic issue with them. I'll need to speak to Alaric as soon as possible. Where is he?"

"He's just outside," he said, then went to the door and called Alaric's name. A handsome vampire with blond curls came in and nodded to them respectfully. I wondered which vampire had turned him. He looked at me curiously. I had seen him before vaguely, in the mass of vampires I knew belonged to House Tennison, but he had never stood out.

Lilith eyed Alessandro. "You need to stay?"

"Yes."

"Then you'll keep this a secret until we figure out how to handle it." Alessandro nodded, looking curious, and Alaric took one of the empty seats at the table. Lilith sighed. "Adze fed on Kairos," she said without preamble.

Alaric and Alessandro gasped and stared at Adze in shock, then at me. I blushed, feeling the pressure of their glamours against my senses and wishing I could just sink into the ground. Lilith had said never to tell anyone. Why was she saying something now, and why hadn't she warned me she was doing it?

"You fed on him," Alessandro said, looking between us and appearing angry now. "You said you hadn't, that you wouldn't."

"Members of your house cannot violate laws like that," Alaric hissed.

"We judged the issue and took appropriate action," Lilith said evenly, as if challenging them to question her further. "It only happened once, it was an accident, and it won't happen again."

"Are you okay?" Alessandro asked me, and I blushed further.

"He invited it," Lilith said. Adze was keeping awfully quiet too, I realized, and glanced up at him. He seemed embarrassed, with a hint of anger. This probably wasn't a comfortable conversation for him, either. "And your head of house drank Kairos's blood as well. Not directly, but he also violated the rule."

"Darius wouldn't do that," Alaric said, but didn't sound

certain. "Did you invite that as well?"

"No," I said softly. I didn't want to get anyone in trouble but I had been completely unnerved when Darius had drunk my blood.

Alaric cursed softly and I was surprised. I had never heard a vampire curse before. He ruffled a hand through his elegant hair.

"This does complicate matters. Does anyone know?"

"Our house knows, and many of our servants," Lilith said. "They've all been sworn to secrecy."

"How many know about their intimate relationship?"

"Our house, but only two servants. And your house, it seems."

"We have to anticipate them finding out about all of it," he said. "Do you realize how much this could undermine your case? He's a key witness and if he's compromised, large portions of your case fall through."

"We're keenly aware of the consequences of Adze's mistake," Lilith said in a frosty voice. I flinched. I hadn't realized my desire to be bitten would have consequences in the case they were building. Did I regret doing it? Begging him like that? Somehow, despite everything, I didn't. I didn't regret begging him until he agreed. Even if he had been expelled and even if this case was destroyed, it was worth it.

"All right," Alaric said, tapping the table in a pattern and staring at me intently. "We'll figure this out. I can't tell you what to say but I can walk you through what they're likely to ask. You need to only answer questions. Don't volunteer any information. Can you do that?"

"I don't want to testify," I said hesitantly. They had called me a key witness, said all of this was going to come out anyway, but I was terrified at the thought of being in court have to tell the truth about all of this. "I don't want to see any vampires that aren't in my house or yours."

"I suppose you haven't had the best experiences with vampires," he said dryly. "Well, no one will hurt you."

"I don't like being around a lot of vampires."

"Understandable for a human, but no one will use glamours on you. They're forbidden in a court of law."

I looked at him, at Lilith, and glanced at Adze. They were all expressionless.

"Do I actually have a choice in this?" I asked, because it seemed I didn't. I was presenting fair objections and they were rejecting them. Would it matter what I said?

"We need to walk through your testimony," Alaric said, as if he knew that question meant I was giving up. I shivered. I was going to have to go to a court filled with strange vampires and discuss my private life, including all sorts of things I didn't want my family and friends to know. It didn't matter what I said, what objections I raised. They wouldn't let me leave without testifying. I didn't have any choice.

"Fine," I said quietly. "What do I have to say?"

CHAPTER FORTY-THREE: UNDER PRESSURE

The evening came too quickly. I slept in a lot later than usual, since I had been up much of the day in a highly stressful environment. Alaric had spoken to me for a long time, and to Adze as well, and I at least knew what was happening now. I felt scared and unprepared, but I knew the process. I got up and winced. My arm throbbed with pain. The vampire who had given me blood had seen me again and I realized he had given me a lot of pain medicine, but it was wearing off. I staggered to my feet and touched my arm tentatively. It stung and I could barely process anything else. I couldn't take a shower and risk my arm, and as I struggled to get dressed, I kept running into problems. My arm could move freely but it hurt to flex my hand or even move my fingers. I probably had serious muscle or even nerve damage. How had I not noticed this earlier? I returned to my bed and collapsed. I had gotten my pants on but there was no way I could get into my shirt and tears welled in my eyes. I was in pain and scared, and I didn't have any options.

A knock at the door. I didn't respond. Maybe they would just leave me alone.

The door opened a little and I saw the doctor peek in. When he saw me, he entered and shut the door after him.

"I didn't expect you to be awake already," he said, coming to my side and touching my arm. I hissed and pulled away. "Let me get you something for the pain."

He retrieved a syringe from his back and I flinched. He grabbed my shoulder to keep me from dodging him and inserted it into my shoulder firmly. It stung, though nowhere near as much as my arm. Still, any pain was unwelcome right now and the burning sensation seemed to sweep over me, sparking my fears of becoming a vampire. What if the continued burning meant I really was turning into a vampire? What if Lilith's reassurance was meaningless?

"Did that hurt?" he asked, and I nodded. He pressed a small cotton wad against the spot and narrowed his eyes. "It shouldn't. Does it still hurt?"

Suddenly I realized the pain was receding from my senses quickly. I flexed my left hand and was surprised to realize there was almost no pain, just a stiffness.

"It feels better," I said. "What is that?"

"Medicine known only to vampires," he said. "It's highly sought out among humans but we rarely share it."

"I barely feel anything now," I said, impressed that vampires had such effective pain medicine. Why did they have something like this? I didn't even realize vampires could be in pain. Well, I supposed the holy water bullets had hurt Adze. Maybe they had developed it in the war when they were in pain regularly. I was just glad it worked on humans. I hesitated. "I'm still human, right?"

"We'll need to wait until it's day again," he said slowly. "The ancients believe you'll remain human, but you're still showing signs of turning."

I shivered. That didn't sound promising. I trusted Lilith and Adze, but they weren't infallible.

"Do you need help dressing? You'll be having breakfast and then we'll head to the courthouse."

"Already?" I asked in dismay, though Alaric had warned me that House Salvite would press for an immediate trial to try to throw Elviore off.

"I'm not sure what order you'll be testifying in," he said. "You may have a chance to adapt before you're put on the stand. They know you're frightened."

I wanted to deny that I was frightened, but I couldn't,

because I was. I didn't want to be doing this. I took a deep breath.

"I don't need help," I said quietly. He patted my shoulder.

"Tell me if you're in any pain at any point today," he said. "Even if you're in the middle of testifying. Everyone will know you're injured and no one will object if you need more medication."

"They'll know I'm injured?" My voice rose sharply. My parents would know I had been hurt? "Will they know why? Will they know what... what might happen?"

"It's one of the charges against House Salvite," he explained. "Turning a human is a crime. They may not have done it directly, but the vampire who did it was acting under their orders."

"I don't want that charge included," I said. "Can it be left out? I don't want anyone to know."

"The charges have already been made," he said.

"My family is going to kill me," I said, cradling my head in my uninjured hand. "I'll have to return home. They won't let me stay here."

"I thought you were an adult." He sounded puzzled.

"I am," I said. "But they'll still insist. And my friends will hate me for hiding this from them. Isn't there any way to avoid this? You're ruining my life."

"House Salvite has ruined a lot of lives," the vampire said sharply. "They've been killing vampires for decades. You're helping bring them to justice."

"I suppose," I said, and sighed. There wasn't any point in fighting this. It was already out in the open. I just had to hope my relationship with Adze remained private. "I can get dressed on my own. Thanks for your help."

The vampire patted my shoulder again and left, shutting the door softly behind him. Getting dressed was much easier now that I could move my arm without pain. I wondered at the medicine. Clearly it did more than just numb pain, since I could move my hand far more easily than I had before. And

I didn't feel groggy at all. Most pain medicine made people a little dopey. They were completely out of it. I felt perfectly alert, and they wouldn't put me on the stand if they thought I couldn't think clearly. So what was this medicine?

As soon as I was dressed, I took another deep breath and went to the bathroom. I stared at the mirror for a long time, trying to see what the court would see. I was dressed in my finest outfit, as Alaric had recommended, though my left sleeve was puffed up because of the bandage underneath. I had been a little worried the fabric would rip going over the thick bandage but it hadn't, and now it neatly covered the white fabric circling my arm. My elbow was a little stiff from the bandage but I could still move my arm fairly well. I stared at my arm, trying to sense anything wrong, but aside from a faint burning sensation, I felt no pain. I shivered. The burning wasn't a good sensation to be having. And I had felt the medicine the doctor had given me even though he hadn't expected me to. Was I turning into a vampire? What would my family think when they realized the danger I'd been putting myself in? All of their fears were true, and I had ignored their concerns. I had ignored Janae, too, and she was going to be furious.

Another knock at the door and I reluctantly left the bathroom to see Dmitri. Had he been waiting? He didn't go in the bathroom after I left, though, just took my right arm and looked at me for a moment.

"Are you okay?" he asked. "I know this is a lot of pressure to put on you when you're already injured."

"I don't really have a choice, do I?" I asked, trying to sound flippant and failing.

"There's always a choice," he said. "The vampires won't offer it to you, but you can always stay silent on the stand and refuse to answer their questions."

"That might be worse than talking," I said, thinking about their reaction if I refused to participate. They would fire me. Adze would be disappointed in me. That above all else worried me. I wanted to make him proud. But by talking, by confirming everything that had been happening, I was also forfeiting my job. No one in my life would allow me to stay in this job knowing that I had been attacked multiple times and might become a vampire. What use was pleasing Adze if I lost him either way?

"Just remember you can refuse to answer," he said. "Do you think you can eat? You should, but I don't want to pressure you."

"I don't want to disappoint Margaret," I said.

"You don't have to please everyone," Dmitri said sharply, then sighed. "Let's go."

Breakfast was a somber affair. It was just me, Dmitri, Dianne, and Margaret. Just like every other morning, but completely different. I was caught up in my own thoughts and barely paid attention until I realized they were talking about the case. Dmitri and Dianne would be testifying as well. Margaret might be called to the stand, but it seemed unlikely and she seemed relieved. She kept shooting me sympathetic looks as I glumly ate the delicious food she had prepared. I didn't say much of anything. After today, this would probably never happen again. How long before my family and friends descended on me and forced me to leave?

Adze, Alessandro, and two other vampires from House Tennison were waiting in the lobby when Dmitri finally brought me out. It was a little after eight and court would begin promptly at nine. I gulped. This was actually happening. My life was falling down around me and there was nothing I could do. Then Adze reached out and embraced me, drawing me into a tight hug. I wrapped my arms around him and cuddled into him as he stroked my hair and murmured comforting words to me.

"It'll be all right, Kairos," he whispered. "This will be over soon."

Everything would be over soon, I thought bitterly. I remembered what Dmitri had said but as Adze cradled me in his arms, I knew I would be talking. I would give a complete, accurate account of everything they wanted because I didn't want to disappoint Adze. I might not be able to keep my job, but I at least wanted him to think fondly of me.

The limo ride was quick. Adze, Alessandro and I rode in one car, with me and Adze sitting together as he held my hand, while Dianne, Margaret and the other two vampires rode behind us. Margaret was coming because she wanted to support me. I appreciated the gesture. She was the only friend I had who wouldn't want me to quit my job.

We must have skipped traffic because in minutes, we were pulling into a reserved lot across the street from the courthouse. I stared up at it as Adze helped me from the car. It was an imposing building with thick columns stretching up three stories. There was a triangle above the columns with figures carved into it centered on the image of blind justice at the center. The entire building looked like marble: cold and uncaring. But I didn't drag my feet. I was committed to this. We entered a crowd of people to cross the street and Adze stayed right next to me, though he wasn't holding my hand. House Tennison surrounded us and the crowd around us kept their distance. Then we came to the steps and I realized most of the crowd around the building were reporters. And they were staring at us like wolves looking at their prey.

CHAPTER FORTY-FOUR: SECOND THOUGHTS

As soon as we finished crossing the street, we were swarmed by reporters. The vampires from House Tennison kept a strong circle around us but journalists were snapping pictures of us and shouting questions. To my surprise, a lot of the questions were aimed at me.

"How were you injured?" one reporter called, trying to jam her microphone between the vampires around me. "Is it true that House Salvite attacked you?"

"No comment," Adze said, pushing me away from her.

"Why does a pure human work for an ancient house?" another reporter asked me, and Adze took my uninjured arm and began leading me firmly up the steps.

"Why would a resistant human choose to work for Elviore?"

"Is it true this isn't the first attack?"

"How does this case relate to the reports that Elviore's been dealing in the drug trade?"

"No comment." This time it came from Alessandro, who looked angry at that last question. The press were preventing us from moving quickly but we were about halfway up the stairs, dodging reporters and ignoring their questions.

"Is it true that you've been having an affair with your master?"

I flinched and looked at the reporter who asked that, a large man with a sickly smile. He looked pleased to have caught my attention but Adze jerked me away and glared at the man.

"No comment."

"If it isn't true, why don't you issue a denial?" the man pressed, but Adze ignored him. So did I. The man kept pressing, kept following us, but then we reached the doors and Adze pushed me inside first. It was blessedly quiet inside and I took a deep breath, moving into the large lobby so everyone could enter behind me. They surrounded me again, and then we went to the gate leading into the main courthouse. There was a metal detector and I obediently took out my keys and phone, setting them in the little basket as I walked through the detector. To my surprise, one of the guards lifted the rope to one side to let Adze go through unscreened. As I waited for the rest of House Tennison to follow, I was shocked when each of them pulled out a gun before going through, and were handed their guns again on the other side. I had no idea they were armed. Were they always armed? How could a courthouse possibly allow a bunch of armed vampires inside? I felt distinctly unsafe. What if the vampires from House Salvite were armed?

We went to a large courtroom. There was a jury that seemed to be half-human, half-vampire, and I wondered how they were ready to go so quickly. I had always gotten the impression that jury selection took time. Apparently not. The rows of seats were filled with journalists but none of these shouted questions at us, nor did they take pictures. They weren't allowed to take pictures in here and that was some relief, but there would be several sketch artists. I wondered how they would draw me. I had seen sketches from courts on tv before and the people always looked cartoonish. How would I turn out? Would I ever see how they drew me?

Alaric was at the very front with two other vampires from House Tennison. All of House Elviore was already in the first row directly behind the lawyers, and Adze brought us there. I sat with Dmitri, Dianne, and Margaret in the second row as Adze joined the rest of his house in the front. I could feel people staring and whispering about me. I thought of the reporter outside and wondered how many people knew about the relationship between me and Adze, or suspected. If the press was asking about it, then it was almost certain that the lawyers for House Salvite would ask about it as well.

Alaric was in deep discussion with the others but as we sat down, he came to me and shook my hand, staring into my eyes with an intensity that frightened me.

"Are you going to be able to do this?" he asked. I nodded. I was scared and still didn't want to do this, but I wouldn't disappoint Adze. "Just remember, tell the truth. Even if they ask you something we don't want to share, you have to tell the truth."

I nodded again and he returned his attention to the others, conferring with Lilith and the other vampires. I examined the jury, many of whom were eyeing me curiously. There were an equal number of men and women, and humans and vampires. They were all elegantly dressed and professional and spoke quietly to each other while scanning the room. I looked at the rest of the room as well and my heart skidded. On the opposing side were three vampires who must be the lawyers but in the row behind them were the four vampires who had attacked Adze. I tensed and Adze must have sensed it because he turned to me and followed my gaze.

"They can't hurt you," he said softly. "Try not to let them throw you off."

Then someone new approached from the other side to sit beside them and I gasped as I recognized him. Professor Grayson. Adze leaned close to me.

"You're safe," he repeated in a quiet voice.

Alaric had been watching the other side and glanced at me.

"Is he a problem?" he asked in an equally quiet voice. "Do you know him?"

"He's my professor," I said.

Alaric turned to Dr. Grayson sharply, his eyes narrow. "Did he teach you how to break Salvite's code?"

"Yes."

"That might help us," Alaric said slowly. "Thank you for telling me. We'll be on alert for him."

He returned to the others, as did Adze. I knew Adze couldn't show me too much favor in public but I felt a little abandoned. Dr. Grayson looked over and our eyes met. I flushed. I had betrayed him by working with Elviore. But it was the right thing to do. He wanted me to help House Salvite manipulate and kill people, and run a drug ring. It was far better that I ended up with Adze. How could my favorite professor want such a thing from me? Why would he support vampires who wanted to kill? I had known him for years and he had privately tutored me over a year, and I hadn't suspected anything about him. Even now it was hard to reconcile the sight of him with the vampires who had attacked Adze. We were on different sides now and I regretted it, because he had always been my mentor.

Soon the judge entered the room and we all stood. She was a short, round woman with ebony hair and russet skin, a pretty reddish-brown. She wore glasses halfway down her nose that gave her a sharp, predatory look. I wasn't sure what I had expected, but it wasn't her. The court was called to order and opening statements began. As Alaric laid out the case against House Salvite, there was astonishment from the crowd and the jury. The lawyer from Salvite, Cassius, laid out their defense and it sounded fairly convincing. A lot of it was untrue, but it sounded good. How could they lie so easily in a court of law? Weren't there consequences for lying? It was clear they didn't know about me, though. They were assuming Elviore's actions were based on guesses and hunches and were arguing a longstanding grudge between the houses that was the real cause of this suit, not the very real crimes they had been engaged in.

We took a recess after a while and I realized I was extremely tense. I took a moment to clear my thoughts, but I kept thinking back to that reporter. What if my parents had already seen me in the news? This was likely the biggest story in Redmond in years, if not longer, but would it seep out into the human news? I hoped not. I glanced at my phone. I had turned it off for the trial and I was scared to turn it on and see messages from my family and friends.

"You can turn that on if you want," Margaret said, noticing my attention. "No one will mind. Do you need to call someone?"

"No," I said. "I was just wondering if anyone I know knows about this yet."

"Maybe don't turn it on, then," she said kindly.

"Do you think this will make human news?"

"Maybe," she said, but sounded evasive for some reason. I narrowed my eyes.

"Are you lying to me? About what?"

She hesitated, then smiled cautiously. "Kairos, the premiere ancient house is accusing another house of organizing a drug trade that has killed hundreds of vampires and thousands of humans ever since the war. Everyone in the world is going to be watching this."

I gulped. Everyone in the world? When I took the stand, everyone in the world would be watching me? Suddenly Dmitri's idea of staying silent didn't seem that bad. I hadn't minded talking to the court. I didn't want to do it, but I could. But talking to the entire world? Having to tell everyone in the world about my relationship with Adze, about the attacks, about everything that had been happening? I had only been worried about my immediate family but what about my aunts and uncles, and all of my cousins? What about everyone from my classes, everyone I had ever met? They would all be watching me.

"I don't feel well," I said faintly.

"I shouldn't have said anything," Margaret said, and Dmitri turned to us.

"What's wrong? You're pale, Kairos. Is everything all right?"

"No," I said, panic rising from deep within me.

"Kairos," Adze said, turning to face me. He reached out and touched my shoulder gently. I leaned into the caress. "What happened?"

Margaret blushed. "I just told him how many people would be watching this. I'm sorry."

"I can't talk in front of everyone," I said, trying to keep calm. This was not a good place to freak out. I was in front of too many people and already I was aware of the reporters watching me. They would record every single thing I did and soon the whole world would know.

Adze stood up and gestured for me to stand as well. Alaric came to our side as we went into a small, private room off to one side. There were several chairs and I collapsed into one, taking deep breaths because I felt like I would hyperventilate. My blood was pulsing against my ears and more than anything, I didn't want to be here.

"Kairos, we'll need you to take the stand next," Alaric said, and my panic spiked.

"I can't," I said. "I'm sorry. I can't do this. I can't talk like this where everyone can hear me. I don't want people knowing about this. I can't."

"You can," Adze said firmly, kneeling to face me and taking my face in his hands. The touch soothed me a little and I clutched his wrist with my uninjured hand, needing to feel him. "You won't be talking to everyone. You'll be talking to me. Can you do that? Just answer the questions and focus on me. I'm the only one you need to worry about."

"But they'll be asking about you," I whispered, tears filling my eyes. "I don't want them to know about you."

"Just focus on me when you're up there, no matter what they say," he said. His dark eyes glowed and I took comfort in that. He lifted one hand to stroke through my hair, then leaned forward and kissed my forehead. I shut my eyes and luxuriated in the feel of his lips on my skin. It had been too long since I had gotten to feel him.

"What if I disappoint you?" I asked. His lips curled into a

smile.

"Nothing you say will disappoint me, as long as you tell the truth. Can you do that, Kairos?"

"I guess," I said, trying to draw as much strength from him as possible.

"We can push you back but it's best if you go first," Alaric said. I straightened my shoulders.

"No, I can go," I said. "It's not going to get any easier if I wait. Maybe I'll talk myself out of it again."

"Then I'll call you to the stand as soon as we're back," he said, and I nodded. Adze was counting on me, and all I had to do was talk to him. I would worry about the rest of the world later. For now, he was my only audience.

CHAPTER FORTY-FIVE: TESTIMONY

Alaric asked me questions first. I was tense being in front of everyone. When I first took the stand, I felt the pressure that meant a glamour was being used against me, but then the judge reminded everyone that glamours were forbidden when a human was testifying. The pressure faded and I was grateful. All of the journalists were human but the first three rows on Salvite's side were all vampires. I suspected their entire house was here, which would make sense since their entire house had been accused. I wondered if they were being kept here by force. Vampires from House Tennison were around the edges of the room and they were armed. Was that to prevent anyone from leaving?

Alaric asked for my name first, then asked the question he had warned me he would ask.

"What do you do for House Elviore?"

I took a deep breath and looked at my professor. Alaric had told me to answer this question truthfully, since my job would be obvious soon enough.

"I translate messages for them."

Gasps from Salvite, and the opposing lawyer leapt to his feet.

"Objection," he cried.

"On what grounds?" the judge asked after a moment passed and he didn't clarify his objection.

"He has no qualifications to translate messages," the lawyer said after another pause, clearly trying to think of something. Dr. Grayson was glaring daggers at me and the rest of the house didn't look any happier about it. Clearly none of them had any idea what I was doing. That was a little reassuring, because it meant they wouldn't have had time to prepare a good defense against me, but I was scared at the pure rage in the lawyer's eyes.

"Overruled," the judge said. "House Elviore has the right to use whatever standard they see fit in hiring people."

"We are prepared to provide evidence of his qualifications," Alaric said. "He is trained to decode messages from House Salvite, and I understand you'll want proof of his ability."

The entire audience seemed to draw in a breath at that, then break out into murmurs. The judged banged her gavel. Alaric had told me I would have to prove my abilities but hadn't told me how, and I was nervous. What if I messed up in front of everyone? I looked at Adze and tried to still my heart. All I needed to do was focus on him. Nothing else mattered.

The judge ordered for two documents to be brought and the vampires from House Salvite were seething. Then one of the uniformed men lining the walls between the Tennison vampires approached and handed me a letter.

"Kairos, please translate this."

I opened the letter cautiously. I had never done this in front of so many people. I read the letter and frowned. It didn't seem to make sense. The language was hinting at a message but I couldn't figure out what it said. I looked up at Adze in panic, realizing I was about to disappoint him, when I remembered what he had said. He would only be disappointed if I lied. I would have to tell the truth.

"I don't know what it says," I said, a little frightened by that answer.

The uniformed man took the letter from me and brought it to the judge.

"Let the record show that this was letter 201A from the archives," she said, then gestured for the man to give me the second letter.

This time, the letter made sense and I was relieved. I didn't know why I hadn't been able to understand the first, but I felt confident about this one and explained it to the court. To Adze. The man took the letter and handed it to the judge.

"Let the record show that this was letter 332B from the archives," she said, then smiled at me. "I believe our young human has proven his ability to translate House Salvite's code. You may continue."

That meant I had passed, even if I had only understood one of the letters. Maybe the other letter wasn't from House Salvite. Maybe it was a decoy to see if I actually could recognize their code and translate it, or if I was making guesses about all of the letters. That would mean I hadn't failed but had actually passed. I hoped that was the case. House Salvite certainly didn't look pleased by my results.

Alaric had me explain the cathedral attack, how I had known about it, and what my perception had been when it happened. I was as honest as possible, trying to answer only what he asked and not provide additional information. He asked very direct questions so it was fairly easy. Then we moved on to when I had been attacked while jogging. I again gave my answers as clearly as I could. Finally, we reached the attack of yesterday. It was odd that it was only yesterday. Things were moving so quickly and even though the fear of the attack was fresh in my mind, it was overshadowed by my lingering fear being up here in front of everyone. I looked at Adze again to calm down and it worked, but my arm was beginning to ache. The doctor had said I could ask for him even during the testimony, but was that true? I would hold out a little longer, at least until I finished describing the attack. Alaric was extremely careful not to ask why Adze and I were out in the grounds in the first place. He warned that the opposing counsel might ask, but I should be vague while making sure to tell the truth.

Finally, we were done with the most recent events and I shifted uncomfortably. My arm was really starting to ache.

Alaric returned to his table to confer with the others, probably to make sure they didn't have any final questions for me. Adze leaned forward and said something to him. I was rubbing my arm, I realized, and stopped. But I could feel it burning and the fear of becoming a vampire was overtaking the rest of my fears. Alaric stood and faced the judge.

"May I request a brief recess, your honor? I believe our witness is in need of medical attention."

The judge looked down at me expressionlessly. "Do you need medical attention?"

"Um, if I can," I said uncertainly, not wanting to impose. The judge nodded and called a five minute recess. Opposing counsel would begin the cross examination after that. To my surprise, Lilith stood and brought me to that private room along with the doctor, not Adze. Instead of trying to roll my sleeve up high enough, the doctor had me unbutton the shirt and pull it down so he could inject my shoulder. I was a little embarrassed taking my shirt almost all the way off in a courtroom in front of Lilith, but this was a private room and she had no doubt seen a shirtless human before. I obeyed. Within moments, I felt that burning sensation, then relief. I sighed.

"Did that hurt?" the doctor asked, and I nodded. "How's the lighting in here? Too bright?"

"Not that I noticed," I said. He helped me button my shirt again. Would the lighting be too bright for me if I were turning into a vampire?

"You're doing well," Lilith said. "They're going to try to trip you up and confuse you to catch you in a lie. Take all the time you need to answer, and tell the truth. Even if it makes you uncomfortable, even if you have to expose secrets. Don't rush, but make sure to answer everything."

I nodded, and then they led me back into the courtroom and I resumed my place on the stand. The judge called us to order and the opposing counsel approached. His name was Cassius and he had a wicked gleam in his eye as he turned to the jury.

"Kairos tells a good story, but he's been coached on his answers by his master."

"Objection," Alaric said angrily. "He hasn't been coached by anyone."

"Sustained," the judge said. "Counsel, keep to the facts."

"Kairos, what is your relationship with Adze?"

Exactly what I didn't want. I could feel sweat forming along my hairline and I looked at Adze. He was expressionless. The jury was looking between me and Adze as well. I had to answer, and answer honestly.

"Um, I work for him, and... I've been sleeping with him."

Gasps from the crowd. Cassius looked smug.

"But that's not all, is it? Isn't it true that he's fed from you?"

Another round of gasps and the jury looked horrified. I didn't want to confirm it. I was very aware of the press in the audience who would take my words to the entire world. I looked at Adze again and swallowed hard. I had to tell the truth.

"He fed on me once," I said, and the jury sat back and stared at Adze in disgust. Cassius looked pleased.

"You see, your honor, members of the jury, that his testimony is tainted. We have no reason to believe anything he says because he's been unduly influenced by his master."

"Objection," Alaric said again, rising to his feet. "Request redirect, your honor."

The judge leaned back and I tried to fight the heat sweeping across my cheeks. I was blushing. They had said that I was compromised because of what I had begged Adze to do but I hadn't really believed it. Was everything I had just said going to be thrown out?

"Counsels, approach the bench," she said, and they did. I tried not to be scared. I had gathered my courage and gotten up here and talked about everything. Was it all for nothing? I looked at the jury but they were busy glaring at Adze, who appeared completely impassive. Alaric was insisting on something and Cassius was refusing, but it seemed Alaric won the argument because when they returned to their places, Cassius was scowling.

"Kairos, explain the circumstances under which Adze fed on you," he said. "So the jury can see for themselves that your testimony is tainted."

My blush returned full force and I looked at Alaric in shock. I had to explain what had happened? I couldn't. He just stared at me and I realized that I did have to answer. I was going to have to explain my own lust for Adze in front of everyone here. In front of the world. I focused on Adze. His feelings for me wouldn't change because of this. I had to hold onto that, because everything else was falling apart.

"We were... together," I said, hoping I didn't have to go into any more detail than that. "I wanted him to bite me. I begged him to bite me." This was extremely painful but I had to keep going. "He refused and started to leave but I kept begging him. Finally, he did it. I don't blame him. It's my fault."

"Humans aren't at fault when a vampire feeds on them," Cassius said in a sour voice. I looked at the jury, afraid to see their reactions, but they looked thoughtful now. Except for one human who was still glaring at Adze. "He should have known better and his lack of control reveals the flaws of the entire house. They're out of control."

"Counsel," the judge said sharply, and Cassius managed a smile. I wondered if he was allowed to make statements like that or if the judge was just trying to get him back on track.

Cassius turned to me with a malicious smile.

"Kairos, would you be here right now if it weren't for Adze?"

I frowned. "No."

"So you're obeying his orders in testifying?"

"Well, yes," I said. "But that isn't what I meant."

"Then what did you mean?"

"I meant that if it weren't for him, I wouldn't have this job and I wouldn't be here."

"But it is true that you're testifying on his orders."

"He asked me to do it, yes," I said, mystified as to where this was going.

"So you'll do anything he asks? Without question?"

My mind immediately flew to him leaning over me in the darkness, how desperate I was to do whatever he told me. I started to answer yes, then hesitated.

"No," I said.

"No?" He sounded surprised. "You expect me to believe that you won't do anything your lover and master tells you to do? Name one time when you've defied him."

"He told me to stop asking him to bite me and I ignored him," I said with a blush, not wanting to mention it again but it was the only time I could think of. There were some murmurs from the crowd but I didn't know what that meant.

"But you were under his sway when you said that," Cassius said. "You weren't able to think clearly. He was manipulating you into asking so he could pretend that it wasn't his idea."

"Objection," Alaric said in an annoyed voice, and the judge sounded equally annoyed when she sustained the objection.

Cassius smirked, clearly of the opinion that he had scored a point though I wasn't sure what. Maybe he just wanted to indicate that I wasn't giving this testimony freely, or that Adze was controlling my answers. I was a little angry. Here I was sacrificing everything to tell the truth and he kept trying to cut me down. I wouldn't let him ruin my credibility.

Then Cassius turned to me again and began questioning me about the cathedral attack, trying to get me to admit that it was possible Elviore had done it. I held firm to my perception of events which led me to believe that there was no way they were behind it. Then we moved to the first attack and he was clearly trying to pin the blame for that on Adze for not protecting me. I wasn't entirely sure how to defend against that but kept to the truth. He kept throwing odd questions at me and I struggled not to answer too quickly, because they were obviously designed to provoke me into a lie. I focused on

Adze in the crowd, only Adze, and took my time. I answered everything honestly.

I thought he would turn to the final attack but he didn't. Instead, he returned to my credibility.

"Did anyone tell you what to say today?" he asked.

"Sort of," I said. "I mean, a bunch of people told me to only tell the truth. But that's it."

"No one helped you prepare for this at all?"

"Well, Alaric told me what kinds of questions to prepare for, but all he said about my answers was that they needed to be honest."

"And the rest of Elviore? None of them told you to say anything?"

"They said not to keep any secrets, to share everything," I said uncomfortably. I knew I was answering correctly and I knew my answers were frustrating Cassius, who had clearly hoped that someone had told me something. I didn't like the anger in his eyes and I could tell the rest of the Salvite vampires weren't pleased by the way this had gone. Cassius returned to a quiet conferences with the other lawyers.

"Kairos," he said, coming to face me again. "House Elviore is charging that a vampire they claim was under orders from House Salvite attempted to turn you into a vampire. Is that true?"

"The vampire who attacked me was ordered to do so by the vampires sitting there," I said, pointing at the four vampires who stiffened as if not expecting to be pointed out. "I don't know if I'm going to be a vampire or not." My voice trembled at that. My arm was starting to burn again and I knew it wasn't a good sign.

"This charge is only valid if he becomes a vampire, your honor," Cassius said. "And there's no evidence that House Salvite gave instructions to turn him. Members of the jury, keep in mind when deciding this charge that there is no evidence a crime has even been committed."

"Objection," Alaric said, rising to his feet. "Attempted

crimes are still crimes."

"Duly noted," the judge said.

Cassius glared at me, then bowed to the judge. "No further questions, your honor."

The judge looked at Alaric, who stood up. He hadn't warned me that he would be asking even more questions.

"Kairos, why do you think that the vampire who attacked you was under orders from the vampires from House Salvite?"

"After they shot Master Adze," I said, remembering to use the honorific, "I tried to run. One of them told the vampires to attack me and they all obeyed."

Several of the jurors glared at the Salvite vampires and that made me feel a little better. A few of them were on my side at least. I just hoped the rest of the witnesses persuaded the rest of them. I wasn't sure what would happen if this case fell through. If House Salvite walked free, they would undoubtedly come after me. Probably my family and friends, too. They needed to be found guilty and locked away, but as Alaric and the judge thanked me and I returned to my spot beside Margaret, I wasn't sure if it could happen.

CHAPTER FORTY-SIX: INTIMIDATION

Lilith was called to the stand next in order to flesh out the historic details. I was grateful they had called me first and slunk into the bench. Margaret congratulated me but I felt miserable. What if Salvite won the case? What if the jurors weren't persuaded? Lilith hadn't wanted to bring this case to trial yet. They didn't have all the evidence in. She listed accounts of Elviore's suspicions for the past hundred years of Salvite's participation in the drug trade and explained numerous operations that she assured everyone would be backed up by other vampires from other houses. House Tennison at least would back up her information. I was shocked at how long everything had been going on. The intensity of Salvite's attacks had spiked when Elviore hired me, but they had been killing for decades. And until me, Elviore didn't have many good strategies for dealing with it other than careful reporting and old-fashioned investigations. Even without the convenience of understanding everything, though, they were incredibly good at tracking down corruption.

My arm started aching again as Lilith's testimony dragged on and I looked around for the doctor. Margaret noticed my restlessness and together we slid down the aisle towards where the doctor was patrolling with the rest of Tennison's vampires. He took me to the side room again and gave me another injection. It burned, but with less intensity, and he seemed to take that as a good sign. On the way back to the courtroom, my feet dragged. I didn't want to go back in and hear Cassius cross exam Lilith. I didn't want to hear him try to distort her words and trip her up. I had complete faith in Lilith but just seeing the abuse of power made me sick. What if they won?

"Do you not want to go back?" Margaret asked me. The doctor, who had been about to leave us, paused and looked at me as if waiting for my answer.

"I mean, we have to, don't we?"

"You can go somewhere else to wait," the doctor offered. "Would you prefer that?"

"Is that okay?"

"As long as you remain near the courtroom, you should be safe. Vampires from my house are patrolling the area. You need to return, however," he said to Margaret. "We may need you."

"Of course," she said meekly. "You feel safe enough out here?"

"I guess," I said. I would be on edge, but it would be better than sitting in there listening to everything House Salvite had done that they might get away with. The doctor walked me to a sitting area outside the courtroom. Several vampires were patrolling the area and they all looked at me, then at the doctor. He nodded to them and helped me sit down.

"Do you need something to do?"

"I have my phone," I assured him, and he joined the other vampires. I looked around. There were a dozen benches and it looked more like a train station or an airport than a courthouse. There were seven people scattered around, but none near me. I wondered why they were here. There had to be other court cases going on. Were they here for my case or for other cases? One of them, a friendly looking young woman, caught my eye and smiled at me. I cautiously smiled back, then turned my attention to my phone to indicate that I didn't want any further communication. There were dozens of new messages in my inbox and I didn't feel like dealing it yet. I knew Janae at least was probably trying to get in touch with me, and my parents. From the number of messages, it seemed like everyone I knew was reaching out. I wasn't entirely sure what else to do so I opened my social media. I rarely went online since I started working. I hadn't been very active even before that. Not a single person had commented on the fact that I stopped going on social media when I started the job, not even Janae. She had scolded me for not calling anyone, but not for anything involving social media. She probably hadn't even noticed because she knew how little I cared about it. Today, though, I needed something to do.

I opened the app and blinked. The first thing I saw was a sketch of me surrounded by vampires. It must have been taken when we were entering the courthouse this evening. A chill ran down my spine. It was from a major news organization.

"Bombshell Revelation from House Elviore: Master Adze sleeping with, feeding on servants" read the headline. I shivered and felt violated. Him feeding on me ought to be private. Our whole relationship should be private. I already felt uncomfortable with the fact that Lilith and the others knew, and now the whole world knew? And why were they gossiping about Elviore when it was Salvite who was on trial? I scrolled down and did see some more headlines about the drug trade and the attacks on me, but most of it was about me and Adze and I could feel my cheeks growing hotter and hotter. My face was everywhere. There was no way my family could miss this. Janae was going to kill me. Maybe she was already asleep and was missing this. I could only hope, but it was only a little after midnight. There was no way she was already asleep. The court would be breaking for lunch in an hour. I doubted Lilith would be done by then but I was sure Alaric had planned everything out carefully. If this fell through, then both Elviore and Tennison would lose much of their reputation.

Should I text her? Maybe she was so upset she never wanted to talk to me again. Cautiously, I went to my messages. Sure enough, there were dozens of messages from everyone who had my number. Even the people I barely knew were trying to contact me. I stared at the messages from my mom for a minute, guilt crashing over me. I didn't know what to tell her. I would start with Janae. That was less stressful. She had been sending me messages every half hour or so since the trial started, it looked like. They were all fairly simple messages, just asking to talk to me, asking what was going on, if I was all right. She was clearly worried and I knew my mom was too, but I could only handle my friend right now.

Hi Janae, I wrote, not knowing what else to put.

Silence. I looked around. The young women was still eyeing me every once in a while but no one else was paying me any attention. I really didn't want to go back on social media and see myself exploited by the press. A few minutes passed as I watched the vampires from House Tennison walk around the edges of the room. Then my phone buzzed and I flipped it over.

Shouldn't you be in court?

That wasn't very promising.

I stepped out for a minute. I wanted to talk.

Another silence as I watched her typing her response, wondering what she was saying.

Why didn't you tell me?

A fairly short question for the amount of time she had been typing. I imagined she had written something else first, probably a rant, and then deleted it and sent this instead.

I didn't want you to worry, and I was under orders not to tell.

It wasn't a very good excuse but it was all I had.

Have you talked to your parents about this?

Not yet, I admitted. *You're the first person I'm talking to.*

Another silence, then my phone rang. Janae. I looked around. This was a pretty public place, but there wasn't anyone near the edge of the room except a vampire from Tennison. I headed over there and answered. The instant I accepted the call, Janae was talking.

"I can't believe you lied to me," she hissed. "You've been in danger this whole time. So you stayed because you were sleeping with him? Is that it?"

"That's not the entire reason," I said, though it was in fact the only reason I had stayed. "I was doing important work. They needed me."

"Do you know how many stories there are about you? How many of our friends are calling me to see if I knew any of this? How do you think I feel seeing your face all over the news?"

"How do you think I feel?" I snapped. "I didn't want any of this. Do you know how humiliating it is to have to share my life with all these people?"

"You're never going to escape this, Kairos," she said. "Everyone knows you now. Why didn't you tell me? I could have helped you avoid this."

I gulped. That was probably true. If I had told her I was in danger, or even that I was sleeping with Adze, she would have gotten me out of the situation and insisted I quit my job.

"And Kairos," she continued, then hesitated. "Is it true you might be a vampire now?"

I shut my eyes and winced, feeling my arm. It still burned. But the medicine hadn't hurt as much and the lights weren't too bright for me.

"Adze doesn't think I am," I said. "None of the vampires from House Elviore think I am."

"But you might be?"

"Yeah," I said, unable to hide the tremor in my voice. "I guess we won't know for sure until an entire day has passed."

"How did it happen?"

"I was attacked," I said, then paused. Was I supposed to share how vampires were turned? Probably not. I had never known how it happened. The people here all seemed to know but they lived in Redmond and were probably all dhampir. "It's complicated."

"You're lying again, aren't you?" She sounded skeptical.

"I don't actually know what happened," I said, because that was true. "I just know the basics, but I don't know if I can tell you. I'm sorry."

"You never should have gotten a job with vampires," she

said. "I can't believe I was the one who suggested it."

"I would have ended up working for them no matter what," I said. "Dr. Grayson was training me to work for House Salvite."

"Dr. Grayson?"

"Yeah, he's here too, at the trial," I said. I had been uncomfortably aware of him the entire time I was testifying. "He's with them."

"Is any of what they're saying true? The reporting is all over the place. Some are saying Elviore is bringing serious charges that could bring down House Salvite, some are saying Elviore is lashing out because of the attack last night and lying about prior offenses to get revenge."

"Everything we're saying is true," I said sharply. "My house doesn't lie. We don't need to. We have all the evidence we need to back up our accusations."

"You don't belong to that house, Kairos," Janae said with a hint of displeasure in her voice. "It's not your house. It's their house. You just work for it."

"They are my house now," I said firmly. "I belong to them."

"You don't belong to anyone," she said. "You're an independent person who made a mistake working for them."

"No," I said. "I am an independent person, but they're my house now and I didn't make a mistake."

She sighed.

"At least they're not using your name. Apparently since you're not a public figure, your name isn't being shared. You're just referred to as the human, or the servant."

"That's good," I thought, though it was only temporary. Eventually, someone would match my photo to my records and spill my identity. It was almost inevitable. And then my name would be out there, and as Janae had said, I would forever be tied to this trial. Could I possibly return to my normal life? Would my family suffer?

The young woman was still looking at me, I realized. I was talking quietly and fairly certain no one could hear, except maybe the Tennison vampire nearby, but I probably shouldn't keep talking in public like this.

"Look, Janae, this isn't the best time for me to talk. I just wanted to... to get in touch with you. Can you call my parents and tell them I'm fine? I'll call them as soon as I get home."

"When do you get back?"

"I don't know. At the end of the work day probably, so morning. It might be longer."

"Are we going to hear any more about you tonight?"

"I don't know," I said again. "I'm not saying anything else, but they might talk about me. I helped a lot in this case."

"You shouldn't be in danger," she hissed. "But I'll call your mom. You'd better talk to her in the morning. She and your dad are worried sick."

"I'll call as soon as I can."

We said goodbye and I slid my phone back in my pocket and returned to my seat. The young woman stood up and sat on the bench across from me. I glanced at the nearby vampire, who was watching closely but not coming over. The people here must not be a threat then, though the vampire was clearly keeping an eye on this development. The woman smiled at me.

"I saw your testimony," she said, and I flushed. "That was quite brave. Not many people would testify against House Salvite."

"I was just telling the truth," I said.

"They have a lot of allies, you know," she said, again with that smile. This time it seemed almost sinister. "Even if House Salvite gets taken down, you'll have a target on your back the rest of your life."

"What?" I felt faint again. I had assumed that House Salvite was the only threat, but of course it made sense that they had allies. Allies who might retaliate, who might target the human who helped in the house's collapse. I didn't even know what would happen if Salvite was found guilty. Would they be thrown in jail? I had assumed so. But what if it were just a fine, or some other punishment that left them free? They were going to target me. And Dr. Grayson knew my family and friends. He would know exactly who to target and he wasn't going to jail for any of this. He wasn't in House Salvite, though he was closely associated with them. I shivered. It had never occurred to me that the danger would continue after this, and maybe intensify. I had assumed this was the end of it.

"There is a solution, you know," she said. "Just go to the judge and tell her you were compelled to lie by your house. Tell her everything you said was false, and your testimony should be thrown out. House Elviore doesn't even need to know. You'll be protected from them."

"But that would be a lie," I pointed out, and she laughed.

"A lie that might save your life," she said. "You have a family, don't you? Don't you care about their safety?"

I shivered and looked over at the Tennison vampire. He immediately began heading my way and the woman leaned back, raising her hands as if to indicate that she meant no harm.

"Just think about it," she said. "This trial will last days, most likely, so you have time to consider what's best for you and the ones you love."

"Is there a problem?" asked the vampire, coming to my side.

"I, uh, I'm ready to go back to court," I said, rising to my feet and extremely uncomfortable with what she had said.

"I'll walk you there," the vampire said, and I hurried after him, eager to be away from the woman and her thinly veiled threats. Should I go lie to the judge? Would that really help? Or would it just make things worse for everyone?

CHAPTER FORTY-SEVEN: MIXED BLOOD

The night at court was rough. Lunch was quiet. I stayed with Margaret, Dmitri, and Dianne. And then Lilith finished her testimony and I had to sit through the agony of watching Cassius come at her. Luckily, there wasn't much he could do in the face of her facts. She was calm and emotionless, as she always was, and stated the facts clearly and succinctly no matter what he tried. The jury was clearly swayed. That was good. Her testimony filled the rest of the night. Adze was tomorrow and I worried about that. Cassius actually would have things to accuse him of that he wouldn't be able to defend. The rumors about me, which had faded from the headlines after Lilith's blockbuster revelations of the history of Salvite's crimes, would come to the surface again. Finally, we were headed home. I rode with the other servants, not with Adze this time. I wondered if I would be able to see him at all the rest of the trial. He would want to avoid any further impropriety with me, so I would probably have to deal with this on my own.

There was a crowd at the edge of the estate who slowed our cars down as they clamored for information and tried to take pictures through the darkened windows. I shrank down and wondered how many of them were trying to ask me questions. All I could hear was a murmur of shouts, not distinct questions, and I felt uneasy as we passed through the gates to the manor. I looked back to see guards lining the fence. At least we had some protection. But there was no way I was leaving the house now. I felt more frightened of the reporters than I had about being attacked by vampires.

Adze retreated as soon as we arrived, along with Alessandro and the female vampire who had tailed him last time. I wondered if they were here to protect Adze or to provide surveillance. Probably both. Margaret made us dinner, but though she attempted to smile at all of us, she didn't try to start any conversations. Dmitri and Dianne were both extremely serious. Dmitri would be testifying tomorrow, after Adze. I was finished and I wondered how many days of this I could stand. I had no idea how long it would take but if each of Elviore's vampires took most of a day, and I had to assume they would, then there would be at least five more days. I suspected vampires from House Tennison would be testifying as well, and House Salvite would probably be allowed to call their own witnesses to refute the evidence. This was going to take forever and the woman's words hung on me heavily. What would happen if I went to the judge and told her I had been pressured? It would invalidate my testimony, and it would severely undermine everyone else's as well. Would it be worth it?

My face was already out there. People already knew what Adze and I had done. Going back on my testimony wouldn't change that. Or would it? Maybe I could pretend that all of it had been a lie, even that part. Would people believe that? But then I would be branded a liar. I had sworn to tell the truth and if people thought I had lied, that might even be worse than what people thought about me and Adze together. Still, my family's safety was on the line. I started. My family. I needed to call my mom.

As soon as dinner was over, I excused myself and went to my room. My mom picked up immediately and I could hear tears in her voice. In moments, my dad was also on the line. Then began the painful process of explaining to them everything that had happened. They wanted to know all the details. They had read about what I had said, but they wanted to hear it from me and I winced as I shared the parts I really didn't want to share, the parts about me and Adze, but I knew they had heard the rumors and I couldn't lie to them.

They were horrified and demanded I come home immediately. I tried to explain that I couldn't leave until the trial was over and my mom started crying. My father began yelling and insisting I return immediately and by the time my mom stopped wailing, he had mostly calmed down. The call ended rather abruptly with my father giving an ultimatum: come home immediately after the trial or risk never seeing them again. I didn't know what to say so I agreed. They hung up.

I stared at my phone for a long time, then got into my pajamas. The sun was up and I shut the window, plunging the room into darkness. I waited as my eyes adjusted, just standing there staring into nothingness. I would have to return home the instant the trial was over. Would I be safe there? Would I be there permanently, or could I somehow return here? I wanted to talk to Adze. I needed him right now. But I couldn't go to him. Not today. All because I had begged him to bite me. I cursed that impulse now and got in bed, remembering the ecstasy of the feel of his fangs in my body. I curled around my pillow and buried my head, stroking my neck where his fangs had punctured me, where he had given me such pleasure. Nothing would ever compare to that. I stayed that way a long time until there was a knock at the door.

I opened it and was surprised to see the doctor. I realized a day had passed and felt a flash of relief. I was still a human. He asked to come in and I turned the light on and let him in, realizing after the light was on that he wouldn't need it. He examined me carefully, then took my bandaged arm and squeezed it slightly.

"Does this hurt?"

"Yes," I said, only barely managing to keep it in his hands and not jerk it away from him. It was extremely painful.

"Does it feel numb anywhere? Tingly?"

"I don't think so."

He nodded. "Do you need more medicine to help you sleep?"

"Oh," I said in surprise. "It hasn't really hurt since you gave me some earlier tonight."

"Really," he said. "But it hurts when I put pressure on it?"

"Yes," I said with a trace of fear. Was it bad that it no longer hurt? He sighed.

"Sometimes it takes longer to tell," he said, and my heart sank.

"You don't know if I'm human or not? I thought it just took a day. How can you not know? Can't you do a blood test or something? Aren't vampires different enough from humans that you can test for it?"

"We already did a test for it," he said. "Right after it happened, when you were unconscious. You had a mixed result. Now we just have to wait to see which wins out."

"Wait, so... I'm already part vampire?" I couldn't believe it.

"For the moment," he said. "I'll do another test but I'm sure it'll still be mixed. Being resistant tends to throw all of our calculations off."

"Do another test," I said without hesitation. He agreed and withdrew a syringe and vial, then drew a sample of my blood. "When will you get the results?"

"In a few minutes," he said. "I brought a calibrator. It's just outside. If you'll wait here, I'll have your results shortly."

I nodded and he left, then I collapsed in the bed. So the past day I had had vampire blood inside me? Fighting with my human blood? Adze and Lilith seemed convinced that my human blood would win out, probably because I was resistant, but what if they were wrong? They weren't perfect. They made mistakes. And maybe my resistance wasn't as strong as they thought. What would happen then? Could I go home after the trial if I were a vampire? What would happen to my parents? To Janae? What would happen to Lee and Angie and Scott? All of my friends, all of my relatives, everyone? I shut my eyes and wondered if there were some way I could will myself to be human. Would my body listen to me if I concentrated hard enough?

The doctor came back in with a grim look and I inhaled sharply. He patted me on the shoulder.

"Still mixed," he said. "But the vampire part is dominant. It's unlikely you'll remain human."

I sank into the bed in stunned silence. I was still human for the moment, but it might not last.

"Isn't there anything I can do?"

"There's a chance you might remain human, but it's very slim," the doctor said gently. "You should start preparing for life as a vampire."

"I don't even know what that means," I whispered. "I don't know anything about vampires."

"As soon as the trial is over, I'm sure your house will help you."

"I'll still be in House Elviore?"

"I'm not sure," he admitted. "Probably not. House Elviore is the founding house and no one can really get in. But they might keep you nearby, since you were turned helping them."

My lower lip trembled. I didn't want to be in any house other than Elviore. I didn't belong anywhere else. Would I be able to see Adze if I were in a different house? Would I really have to spend an eternity without him? I wouldn't be able to bear it.

"How do vampires die?"

"Why?" he asked sharply.

"I just don't want to live forever."

"Vampires can't kill themselves," he said firmly.

"Why not?"

"We just can't," he said. "It's impossible. It doesn't work. Many of us have tried. There's no way to do it."

That was a depressing thought. I wondered how many of them had tried. He said "us," so he must have tried. Most of House Tennison had probably tried, since they hadn't wanted to become vampires. But why wouldn't it work? Sunlight could kill vampires, so wouldn't it be easy to just lock yourself somewhere that would be in sunlight? Or maybe sunlight only hurt vampires, not killed them. But couldn't vampires just put themselves in harm's way even if they couldn't do it themselves?

"You shouldn't be thinking of killing yourself," he said. "I know it may seem like the end of your world, but it isn't. It's the start of a new world."

"I can't just throw away my life," I said. "I have family. Friends. What happens to them? My parents will kill me. They've already made me promise to go home after this trial."

"You might not be allowed to return," he said.

"They'll disown me if I don't."

"You might have to accept that," he said gently. "Everyone in House Tennison lost our families when we were turned. There's no good way to retain relationships. But your house will fill that void. They'll become your family, your friends."

I sniffled. I was on the brink of tears. This couldn't be happening. I couldn't become a vampire and lose everything in my life. The doctor patted my shoulder.

"I know this is difficult. Trust me, I know. But you'll survive. I need to go downstairs now. Do you need anything else?"

"No," I whispered. He left. I shut the light off and then got into my bed. I felt stunned. I hadn't really believed I could become a vampire. I supposed there was still a chance I could be human, but not much of one. I was a vampire, and everything had changed.

CHAPTER FORTY-EIGHT: TRANSITION

I didn't see Adze at all that evening or on the way to the courthouse. He was surrounded by four vampires, and the rest of the servants and I were surrounded by eight. The press crowded around us and shouted offensive and intrusive questions that would have shamed me to my core yesterday. Today, though, all I could feel was the lack of pain in my arm and the burning sensation in my belly. The lighting was a little harsh but I ignored it. I didn't want to be a vampire. If there was any way I could avoid it, I would, and right now ignoring the change was the only option I had. The doctor had checked on me but hadn't said a word other than his usual questions. He seemed to know I didn't want to talk about my inevitable fate.

Alessandro was at my side today. He had been guarding Adze yesterday and I wondered why he was with me. I trusted him more than the other vampires, nearly as much as the vampires from my house. He had volunteered more information than any other vampires, and we had spent a lot of casual time together. What did he think about me becoming a vampire? I shivered. He instantly turned to me. We were just entering the courthouse and finally out of sight of the press.

"Is everything all right?" he asked softly enough that no one else would be able to hear.

I nodded, though nothing was all right. But there wasn't any particular reason I was upset. It was the entire situation. We started to go into the courtroom but he pulled me to one side. Everyone else filed in but he brought me to an empty hallway nearby.

"I heard what the doctor said," he said, still very quiet. I shuddered. I didn't want to think about it. If I didn't think about it, maybe it wouldn't be real. "You won't be abandoned, Kairos. I've spoken to Darius. If you do become a vampire, House Tennison will take you."

I looked up at him in surprise. "But I thought you were all generals, all turned by Elviore. I'm not."

"We've made exceptions before," he said. "They all eventually left, and you would be free to leave as well should you find a house that suits you better, but you'll have a home."

I thought of Darius and shivered. He had drunk my blood. Did I really want to be in his house? But he wouldn't ever be able to do it again. I fingered the tattoo on my neck, the mark of House Elviore. I didn't want any other mark. They couldn't take me, though. The doctor had called them the founding house, and all of them were ancients. They had a history. I didn't belong with them, even though I wanted to.

"Will I ever see Adze again?" I asked softly.

"Master Adze," Alessandro corrected. "At least as long as you're human. And yes, you'll see him again. Especially if you become a vampire."

"Really?" That brought some life back into me. I wouldn't be completely cut off from everything in my life. Would becoming a vampire mean I got to keep Adze? Would that be worth losing everything else?

"New vampires are usually mentored by the vampire who turns them. The vampire who turned you is dead, but another will take on that role. I'm sure Adze will volunteer."

"Did he mentor you?"

"Yes," Alessandro said, his fangs flashing as he smiled. "He knows what he's doing."

I took a deep breath and tried to collect myself. So I could still have a relationship with Adze. I would lose everything else, but at least keep that.

"Do you want to spend the day somewhere besides the

courtroom?" Alessandro asked.

"Am I allowed to do that?"

"It might be better if you're not present when Adze testifies," he said. "I'll accompany you."

"Good," I said, thinking of the young woman who had cornered me yesterday with her threats. I had assumed I would be a human when she had threatened my friends and family. Were they still in danger if I was a vampire? Would I still be in danger? She had said that House Salvite had a lot of allies. Would they strike at my family even if I were a vampire?

Alessandro led me to the room where I had encountered the woman yesterday. He sat across from me and relaxed, glancing around. There wasn't anyone nearby.

"Um, is my family safe?" I asked. "You know, in case someone... tries something?"

Alessandro narrowed his eyes. "We can keep an eye on them if you think there's a threat. Is there a threat?"

"Well," I said, considering my options. Should I keep quiet? I could still go to the judge and change my story. If I told Alessandro about the woman, I would completely lose that chance. I would be trapped. If I were a vampire, I didn't want to side with Salvite. They might come after me, but I didn't want to associate with them. What if they slipped me the drug, though? Would I lose control and kill people? I didn't want them as enemies. But I didn't want Elviore as enemies either, and they would become my enemies if I changed my story. Adze would be my enemy. I shivered. I would not let that happen.

I cautiously told Alessandro about the woman who had approached me and what she had said, and he looked shocked and furious.

"Why didn't you say something immediately?" he asked, and I looked away.

"I want to protect my family," I said. "I don't know how best to do that."

"You seriously considered turning on us?"

"I didn't know what to do," I said. "But I'm telling you now. I've decided."

Alessandro let out a sigh. "That's true. You made the right choice, even if it took you too long to do it. But I can't judge. It's been a long time since I had a family to protect and I barely remember the pressure."

Alessandro waved his hand and one of the vampires patrolling the room came to his side. She eyed me curiously. Did she know I was going to be a vampire? Did she know I had been invited into her house? I suddenly realized that joining House Tennison meant I would be a vampire hunter. I didn't want that. Maybe there were other jobs besides killing vampires. I would never be able to kill anyone, no matter how guilty they were.

"Wait here," Alessandro said to me as he got to his feet. "I won't go far."

He and the other vampire went to the edge of the room and spoke quietly. I nervously got out my phone. I didn't want to see what was happening in the news so I went to my messages. My friends were desperately trying to get in touch with me. I knew Janae would have reassured them to some extent, but they needed to hear from me personally. They probably felt betrayed, especially since I hadn't contacted them at the same time I had contacted Janae. I was closest to her but we were all friends and I shouldn't have ignored them. There was just so much going on it was hard to think clearly.

I went through and read their panicked messages, then sent them individual apologies and assurances. I could have sent a group message and gotten it over with all at once, but I wanted them to know I cared about them so they each got something unique. I knew without question that they would be comparing what I told them. I hoped this wasn't making their lives more difficult. Everyone knew they were my friends. Were they getting bombarded? At least the press hadn't shared my name. They were safe from the press for the moment, though it wouldn't be long before my identity got out and everyone linked to me would be pressed for information. Hopefully this would pass quickly. Hopefully the rumors and scandal would die down when the trial ended and I could remain anonymous until then.

Alessandro returned when I was finishing my message to Scott. I was warning all of them that I wouldn't be able to text because I was in and out of court, but I would keep in touch. As I finished, I got a response from Lee followed quickly by Angie. They were grateful to hear from me and clearly freaked out. Scott's response came moments after I sent it. I wondered if they were all together. Were they safe?

"Are my friends safe?" I asked Alessandro.

"We're getting people to watch your parents," he said. "Tell me anyone else you want protected and we'll do it, for as long as it takes."

"Will they know?"

"Only if you tell them. They won't notice our surveillance."

"They're not a night schedule," I pointed out, and his lips curled in a smile.

"We have humans watching them. They'll be safe. House Salvite might have allies, it's true, but House Elviore has more."

"Thank you."

I told him Janae, Lee, Angie, and Scott's names and he entered it into his phone. He didn't ask for anything besides their names and when I offered to give him their addresses, he just smiled and assured me he could find them, and it was best to keep their personal information to myself in public. I didn't want anyone finding out any of their personal information so I kept quiet, but I wondered what resources House Tennison had and if House Salvite had similar resources. When I felt secure that they would be safe, I put my phone away and sighed. Another day at court, and this time I couldn't even distract myself listening to the testimony. The only thing I had to do was try to figure out my life now that everything had fallen apart.

Hours passed as I tried not to think too much about my situation. I kept checking my phone and did start a group chat with my friends to talk a little bit. Their support was necessary. Until Scott asked the question I had been dreading.

There's a rumor you might turn into a vampire, he wrote. I drew in a breath and looked around. There was a couple at the other side of the room but otherwise it was just me and Alessandro. He was reading something on his phone but keeping a close eye on me. He met my gaze.

"Is everything all right?"

"Yeah," I said. "Just talking to my friends."

He watched me a little longer as I returned to the group chat.

It's true, I wrote. I didn't know what else to say. I didn't want to confirm anything because there was still a sliver of a chance I wasn't a vampire.

There was silence. None of them were even typing anything. I suspected they were all together right now as they chatted with me, probably spending the night to watch the trial together. They were probably talking, trying to figure out what to say to me.

I shivered and looked around. It seemed suddenly colder, but there weren't any doors anywhere nearby where a draft might have slipped in. I shaded my eyes and looked for some cause of the temperature shift. My teeth stung in the sudden cold and I ran my tongue along them and froze. My heart skipped a beat. My incisors were fangs. I ran my tongue over my teeth again. There was no question. I reached to feel my teeth with a rising panic and realized Alessandro had moved to sit next to me. He pulled my hands away and held my shoulders tightly.

"Calm down," he said in a soothing voice. "You've transitioned. I'll take you somewhere to recover."

"But-"

I didn't know what to say. I couldn't deny that something had changed. I felt cold in a way I never had before. Not just

341

physically, but something deep within me. He helped me to my feet and I looked around. It was far brighter than it had been a minute ago. Uncomfortably bright. Did it feel this way to Alessandro? Would I always be uncomfortable in ordinary light like this? Alessandro brought me back into the small room where I had been several times now. He examined my eyes, then asked to see my fangs. I shivered at the thought of having fangs but opened my mouth obediently and couldn't help but wonder what my teeth looked like now. Would I be driven to drink blood now?

"Everything looks good so far," Alessandro murmured. "Vladimir will be here soon."

"Who?"

"The doctor who's been looking after you," he said with a smile. "You don't know his name?"

"I guess I never asked. You vampires all seem really similar."

"It should be easier spotting differences between us now," he said, then touched my cheek. "Congratulations. I know you don't see it as a gift, but becoming a vampire is a rare thing. In time you might appreciate it."

"Thanks, I guess," I said, feeling in a daze. I was a vampire. Nothing had changed, but somehow I could tell that something essential about me was different. What would my mom and dad say? I could never go back home now. What was I supposed to do? Part of me wanted to burst into tears but somehow I felt removed. Everything within me wanted to cry but my body wouldn't respond. I thought of how emotionless the vampires always seemed. Did I have that trait now, too? How much of me had just changed? I hadn't expected it to be so sudden. I took a deep breath and tried to think clearly. Everything had just changed. There was no going back.

CHAPTER FORTY-NINE: NEW HOUSE

The doctor came in after several minutes and had me take my shirt off to remove the bandage. I stared at my arm. It was completely healed. Not a trace of an injury. Vladimir tested the area, applying pressure, but it didn't hurt at all. The burning sensation was gone, replaced by a feeling of ice. When I asked if that would go away, he shrugged.

"You learn to live with it. You'll be a little more sensitive to temperatures but nothing significant."

"And the light? Will it always be this bright?" I asked.

"Your eyes will adapt," he said. "That will get better."

He examined my eyes and fangs, then had me put my shirt back on.

"How are you feeling?" he asked.

"Surprisingly good," I admitted. "I thought I'd be freaking out. Part of me still wants to."

"No more suicidal urges?"

I shook my head. My life might be in tatters but I had no desire to die. I felt oddly optimistic, though as I fingered my neck where Elviore's mark was on me, I wondered what would happen to me. Did I even have the mark anymore?

"Darius will be in to talk to you at lunch," Vladimir said. "Has Alessandro told you about our offer?"

"He said House Tennison might take me," I said. "Is that what you mean?"

"You're welcome to choose another house, of course," Vladimir said.

"I don't know any other houses except Elviore and Salvite."

"You really are new to life with vampires," he observed. "Well, in time you'll meet vampires from other houses and you may want to switch. The vampire who turned you was likely from House Avaron, so I'm sure they'll talk to you at some point. Many of the newer houses are based on career so when you find something you like, you might join one of them."

"I don't have to kill vampires if I'm in Tennison, do I?"

Vladimir and Alessandro both smiled.

"No," Alessandro assured me. "You're welcome to keep translating, if you like. We have humans doing it right now but you know how to do it. We'll teach you our code."

"I guess I won't have to translate messages from Salvite anymore, will I?"

I hadn't even thought of that consequence to this trial. If I weren't a vampire, would I still have a job? Maybe not. Maybe Adze would have fired me even if I managed to avoid my family and friends and keep my job.

"We don't know what will happen," Vladimir said. "Elviore is pushing for all of the vampires from Salvite to be executed, or at least removed from power and imprisoned, and all of their allies sanctioned, but it's unlikely they'll get all of that."

"Were you just in there?"

He nodded.

"How is Ad- Master Adze doing?"

"You can call him Adze now," he said. "And he's doing well. He explained his relationship with you well. Cassius will try to focus all the attention on that but it's hard to ignore the rest of what he said."

"I'm sorry," I said. "If I had known all of the problems it would cause..."

My voice faded. I didn't know what to say. Even if I had known, I still would have done it. Being fed on by Adze would always be one of my cherished memories. There was no chance of repeating it now that I was a vampire. A wave of dizziness swept over me and I staggered back a step. Vladimir helped me sit in one of the chairs along the wall.

"It'll take a while for your body to fully adapt," he said.

"What am I supposed to do now? What do I tell everyone?"

"Darius will be able to talk to you about everything," Alessandro said, coming to sit next to me. "I'll stay with you until then. Thanks, Vladimir."

The doctor left me alone with Alessandro and my thoughts. I needed to tell my parents, but I didn't know what to say. We hadn't even discussed the fact that I might be a vampire last time we had talked. There was so much else to say and I hadn't really believed it could happen. I ran my tongue over my fangs. It had definitely happened. This was going to destroy them. They would never be able to brag about their professor son. I wouldn't be going to grad school, wouldn't get a PhD, wouldn't do any of the things they wanted for me. All because I had taken a job with a vampire. What would have happened if Janae hadn't mentioned looking for a job with vampires? What would have happened if Dr. Grayson weren't one of my references, if his recommendation hadn't triggered Adze's curiosity and compelled him to invite me and see if I had really been trained in Salvite's code? What would have happened if I hadn't instantly fallen in love with Adze and been determined to stay with him no matter what? I wouldn't be sitting here now with vampire blood running through my veins, pondering how to tell everyone in my life that things had irrevocably changed. My stomach growled.

"Is it almost lunch?" I asked. "I'm starting to get hungry."

"I've let Lilith's house know to set something aside for you. They should bring it at lunch."

"Didn't Margaret cook us something?"

Alessandro looked at me in amusement. "You're a vampire. You don't eat food anymore. They'll bring you some blood. It may not be to your taste, but we'll administer the taste preferences test soon and get you properly entered into the system."

I shivered. I was now one of the points of information in

the blood allotment system. Instead of giving blood, it would now be allotted to me just as it was to every other vampire. I would probably be at the bottom of the list since I was so new. They did a good job with everyone, but the ancient houses got preference and there was a distinct order after that. I hadn't worked with them enough to know the exact order or how it was determined, but it had to be age. At least everyone got blood. It just might not be their preferred type. I wondered what my preferred type would be, and if I would ever drink blood from anyone I knew. I shivered harder. That ice inside me wasn't going away and thoughts of blood were souring my stomach.

There was a sudden spike of noise outside the small room and then the judge came in. She looked incredibly stern and Alessandro stood up immediately, so I did, too.

"I would like to speak with the witness alone," she said, and Alessandro left without a word. The judge studied me. "I heard you had something to tell me."

My mind flashed to the young woman and what she had said. Had she gotten in touch with the judge in order to force my hand? Well, I had made my decision. I wasn't going back on what I had said.

"No, your honor," I said.

"About witness tampering?" the judge prodded. "Apparently someone is trying to sway your testimony?"

"Oh," I said, a little startled. "Yes. Um, when I was sitting outside yesterday, a young woman came up to me and said I should lie to you and change my story, say that Elviore pressured me to say what I did."

"Did you lie under oath?"

"No," I said firmly. "Everything I said was true."

"Did you consider changing your story?"

I hesitated. "She said my family and friends might be in danger if I didn't, that House Salvite had powerful allies who might hurt them. I thought about it, but I couldn't do it."

"Will you be willing to go back on the stand and explain

that interaction? House Elviore wants to add witness tampering to the charges and I'm allowing it based on this conversation."

I gulped. "Wouldn't that put my family at even greater risk?"

"I understand Houses Elviore and Tennison are taking care of their protection now," the judge said. "I'm sure they'll be safe."

"All right," I said. "I guess I can talk about it."

"Do you know who it was?" she asked, and I shook my head. "Would you recognize her if you saw her again?"

"Probably," I said, not wanting to promise too much. I hadn't really paid attention to her face, only her words. "She had short brown hair and a red dress."

"Good. Now I understand you need to talk to your new house. I won't keep you any longer."

I flinched. So she knew I was a vampire now and needed a house to belong to. At least I had a house. I would feel completely lost if Tennison hadn't offered to take me and Elviore couldn't.

"Thanks," I said, and the judge gestured for me to leave. Alessandro was right outside with Darius at his side. The handsome vampire smiled at me and took my arm to escort me towards the large room where we had eaten yesterday. He pulled me to the side of the room and I was aware of the eyes on us, of Margaret and Dmitri and Dianne, and of the vampires from House Tennison, and those of House Elviore. I was aware of Adze's eyes and I wanted nothing more than to go to his side. I even took a step in that direction but Darius stepped between me and Adze.

"A vampire is drawn to the person who turned them," he said. "Adze may not have turned you, but he's the most closely associated with it. It's natural for you to be drawn to him even if you didn't have the relationship you do. But you won't belong to his house."

"Alessandro said he might... mentor me," I said rather

hopefully.

"I'm sure he will. But not until after the trial and you'll need guidance until then. Have you considered our offer? Are you interested in joining House Tennison?"

"Yes," I said. "I mean, if I can. I don't really know anyone else and I trust you."

"Good," he said with a nod. "Trust is important."

He waved to Lilith, who came over and looked at me with sympathetic eyes. I could feel a buzz from her, an almost physical connection between us.

"I'm sorry," she said. "We felt confident that you wouldn't turn. The vampire who attacked you must have been Akasha, one of the head vampires in House Avaron. She was the most powerful vampire of the ones who attacked you. Her blood would have been enough to overcome even your resistance."

"It's okay," I said.

Lilith reached out and placed her hand over the mark on my neck. A chill swept over me and my skin tingled. The buzz from being near her faded and I realized she had removed me from House Elviore. Sudden loss hit me, but though I was filled with the desire to cry, I didn't. I just felt the sorrow at being severed from a house and suddenly alone. I didn't belong to anyone and I shied back a step. Alessandro took my arm.

"This will only last a moment," he murmured. "I know it's painful being without a house."

Darius placed his hand on the same spot on my neck and narrowed his eyes. Another wave of ice tingled my skin, and then I could feel a reassuring buzz from him, and from Alessandro beside me, and from the other vampires in the room. I belonged to House Tennison and I couldn't believe how relieved I felt to belong. I would have preferred to remain with House Elviore but it wasn't possible. I felt the spot on my neck, wondering if there were a mark. No other vampires had marks, so probably not. Then I felt a pressure on my mind similar to how it had felt when vampires used glamours on me. This pressure was curious, though, and didn't make me short of breath. I realized it was the other vampires in the house reaching out to me, trying to meet me. I looked around and realized all of House Tennison's vampires were staring at me. Normally it would be intimidating being the focus of so many vampires, but it was oddly reassuring. They were my house now. I belonged to them.

"We've always had close ties to House Elviore," Darius said, glancing at Lilith. "For the time being, with your permission, Lilith, Kairos can serve as our ambassador and remain with Adze even after he's finished mentoring him."

I perked up. I would get to stay with Adze? Lilith seemed to consider, then nodded regally.

"It will be Adze's decision, but I will allow it. We value your house and your help in this trial will not be forgotten. Ever. No matter the outcome."

Darius smiled. "As we will never forget the reason for our alliance with you."

Her lips curled in the faintest of smiles and I wondered at the note of almost resentment in his voice. Then I remembered their history. The reason they were allies was because the Elviore vampires had turned House Tennison against their will. There was an odd blend of hatred and respect in their relationship and I would have to learn to navigate that relationship if I wanted to be their ambassador. Lilith returned to the rest of the Elviore vampires and I eyed Adze longingly. He was looking at me with a similar expression. Would he let me stay? I hoped so.

"You'll need someone to guide you these first few days until your mentor can take over," Darius said. "If it weren't for the trial, Adze could take over immediately, but we need to minimize your relationship until a verdict is reached. I apologize. I know it'll make things harder for you."

"It's alright," I said. "I want to win this case. Are my family and friends safe?"

"Far safer than if you had sided with Salvite," he said. "I won't question your motives in considering that offer. But should someone approach you about anything like that again, I expect you to inform me. I'm your leader now, and everything must go through me."

"Of course," I said. I noticed Denise entering with a bag of what had to be blood and placed a hand on my stomach. I was starving, but would I really be able to drink blood? I didn't even know how to do it. Darius's lips twitched.

"I'm sure you're hungry. Let's go somewhere more private and I can show you what to do."

CHAPTER FIFTY:
SHARING NEWS

I don't know what I was expecting, but the blood tasted exactly like I had imagined blood would taste: bitter and coppery. I had tasted blood before when I was hurt, and this was identical. I had thought it would taste different now that I was a vampire and pulled away after just a small taste. Blood dribbled down my cheek as I held the bag. The bags were specially designed to be bitten into without dripping out but having the liquid fill my mouth as I struggled to swallow it was something Darius assured me I would get used to. I wiped my mouth and Denise made a note on the chart she held.

"Apparently this isn't the type of blood for you," she said in amusement.

"It tastes exactly like blood," I said. "Is there actually a difference?"

"You'll know when you find blood you like," she said. "It'll taste different. You'll enjoy it."

"You need to drink all of this," Darius said. "You're new and you must be hungry. I know it might not taste good, but you need the strength."

"I think I'll throw up if I drink all of this," I said skeptically, but I tentatively bit into the bag against and felt the liquid squirt into my mouth. I swallowed and gagged. I had always hated when I bit my lip, or the one time I had gotten into a fight when I was younger and split my lip. I hated the taste of blood. I withdrew and shook my head. "I can't drink this."

Darius sighed. "It takes time to adapt. That should be

enough to keep you going until we can administer the taste test and get you blood you enjoy. Denise, get everything ready for this morning after court."

She nodded and took the bag from me, then scurried away. Darius handed me a towel and I wiped my face, a little embarrassed I was so bad at drinking blood. Luckily, he had recommended I take my shirt off, because otherwise I would have stained it.

"You'll need to remain out of the courtroom until Adze finishes, but then you can return," Darius said. "Alessandro will stay with you until then. If you need anything, tell him. If you feel you can't tell him for some reason, ask him to get me."

"Where will I stay tonight?"

"At Adze's house, but Alessandro will go with you."

My heart leapt. I would see Adze today. Maybe today he would talk to me. I was a vampire now, after all. Wouldn't I have to sleep in his lair now? It was almost certain I could have some time with him.

The thought of seeing him kept me going as everyone returned to court and I went to sit with Alessandro. There were other people out here now, nearly a dozen of them, scattered through the room. They were all on their phones or reading newspapers but they eyed me and Alessandro curiously every once in a while. I tensed every time they did, wondering if they were allies or enemies. Now that I was officially in House Tennison, any of their enemies were now my enemies and with court still in session, I might be attacked because of that alliance. I got out my own phone and stared at the last messages in my group chat. I had gone silent after telling them I might be a vampire. Janae had sent a message after that asking if I was okay, then nothing else. I had warned them that I might have to turn my phone off unexpectedly and that was undoubtedly what they thought had happened. They might figure out that we were breaking for lunch or assumed I had gone back into the courtroom.

I have something to tell you, I wrote, and hesitated before sending it. Should I get advice from Darius before telling my friends? I should probably tell my parents first, I realized. Instead of sending the message, I opened my phone app and stared at my mom's number. She was the first person I needed to tell, along with my dad. They would never forgive me if they found out any other way. I needed to tell them before the press got hold of this. I looked at Alessandro.

"I have to call my parents," I said. "Is there somewhere private I can go?"

"I can see if the judge's office is available," he said. "She's been letting us use it so far to keep an eye on you. I'll have to go with you."

"That's fine," I said, and we went to talk to one of the guards along the wall who didn't belong to Tennison. It was odd. I could sense where the Tennison vampires were without seeing them. I could feel them pass by behind me and they all felt different. I was starting to get used to how Alessandro felt, the tenor of the buzz he emitted, and I knew before long I would recognize all of the vampires like this. They would recognize me, too. Maybe they already did. I was the only one they didn't know so I probably stood out.

The judge must have given permission because we were escorted into the small room I had been in several times already. I hadn't realized it was hers and was grateful she was allowing us to use it. Then I got out my phone and took a deep breath. I had no idea how this call was going to go. Alessandro sat along the edge of the room but I was too nervous to sit. I hit the button to call her and heard it ring. I shut my eyes and wasn't ready when she picked up right away.

"Honey, is everything all right?" she asked. "Let me get your father."

I heard her shouting for my dad to get on the line.

"Kairos, how is everything going?" he asked, sounding incredibly serious.

"Um, something happened, mom, dad," I said. Probably better to just say it. "You know I was attacked. Somehow, the vampire… turned me."

Silence.

"What does that mean?" asked my mom fearfully, though she could probably guess.

"It means, well, I was hoping it didn't mean anything but I just… I'm a vampire now."

Another silence, then his mom's disbelieving laugh.

"You can't be a vampire."

"Why didn't you tell us this earlier?" my father demanded.

"It just happened," I said, already feeling miserable. I could practically feel their fear and desperation and anger through the phone. "I was hoping it wouldn't. But it did."

"Well, we'll take good care of you," my mom said. "We'll move to a night schedule if that's what it takes. What else will you need? We can get you anything."

"You need to come home immediately," my father added. "It's not good for you to be around vampires like that. You need a home to give you stability."

"Mom, dad, I can't… I can't come home," I said. Now I really was miserable. Their first assumption had been that I would still come live with them and they would just have to accommodate a vampire. I was a little touched that they still wanted me, but they couldn't have me and it hurt. "I would love to go home," I added. "But I can't. I have to live with my house now. I might be able to visit," I said, wracking my brain for anything that could make this less painful. Alessandro shook his head and I gulped. I couldn't even do that. "You can come visit me," I amended. "This isn't the end."

"Of course it isn't," my dad said, his voice rising. "You'll come home and that's final."

"I can't," I said desperately. "It's not a matter of not wanting to go home. I want to. But I can't."

"Honey, are those vampires threatening you?" my mom asked. "Are they forcing you to stay there?"

"No," I said. "I do want to stay here. They're my house now. I belong to them."

"You don't belong to anyone," my dad said angrily. "The way the press talks about you, like you're nothing more than a servant, like you don't have free will. You're not an object. You're a human being able to think for himself."

"I'm not human anymore, though," I pointed out. "I'm a vampire. Things are different."

Silence. I heard a muffled conversation. They must be trying to figure out what to say to me. My heart broke for them. They were losing their only son and I didn't know how to soften the blow. When they returned to the call, I could hear the sorrow in their voices.

"We still love you, honey."

"You always have a place here," my dad added gruffly. "And we expect to visit regularly."

"Of course," I said, relieved. They were actually taking this better than I expected. "Look, I want to keep talking but I don't have a lot of time."

"We understand," my mom said. "Stay safe, honey. And call us again when you get a chance."

"I will," I promised, and we ended the call with declarations of love. I did love them. Absolutely. I would try to stay safe for them, and I only hoped House Tennison kept them safe for me. I didn't know what I would do if something happened to them.

As soon as I was done, Alessandro escorted me to the increasingly crowded waiting area. We still had a corner to ourselves but I was uncomfortably aware of everyone watching us. We were the only vampires here and probably stood out quite a bit. I finally sent the message to my friends and explained the situation as simply as possible. There was silence but as I glanced at my watch, I realized they were probably asleep by now. They had stayed up, but might not stay up all night. Since the trial wasn't televised, there probably wasn't a lot of news during the actual testimony. If something exciting happened, reporters probably slipped out to report it, but no cameras were allowed inside and the news would be scarce until court took a recess.

Soon enough, there was a buzz of voices and reporters piled out of the room on their way outside where cameras were allowed. Alessandro brought me inside. Adze's testimony was over and as we approached, he was just sitting down. I sat several rows back with other vampires from House Tennison but he turned and smiled at me, a wider smile than I had ever seen. My heart leapt into a quick tattoo at the sight, but then he turned away and I practically collapsed on the bench. The vampires around me introduced themselves and I struggled to memorize their names. I would have to learn eighteen new people and I struggled with names anyway. I had a feeling they would be patient with me, though. They were my house now. We were linked. It was an odd sensation and I wished I were linked to House Elviore and to Adze, but it was comforting having so many vampires to lean on. I was safe as long as I stuck with them, and they would protect me and mine. It was a good feeling.

CHAPTER FIFTY-ONE: ADAPTATIONS

Dmitri took the stand next and I was amazed at everything he did for the house. I had no idea his job was so complex. He also confirmed everything I had said in my testimony, adding on his own insight into the matter since he had experience and I didn't. There was nothing scandalous about what he said except for the numerous crimes and I could see that the jury – and the audience – were increasingly persuaded by the solid evidence Elviore was providing. They might have wanted to wait longer to bring this to trial but I wasn't sure how much more they would have gotten. It seemed like everything was already in place to bring House Salvite to justice and I just hoped they hadn't manipulated the jury the same way they had tried to manipulate me.

Then the day was over. I drove with Margaret and the others again and they were cautious around me until I started chatting with them like usual. I was in a better mood than I had been since this whole thing had started and knew it was partially because of the way Adze had smiled at me. His feelings for me hadn't changed and I hadn't realized how much of my state of mind relied on that.

When we arrived, Margaret and the others went to eat dinner. My stomach felt a little empty and I was grateful when I saw Denise getting out of one of the other cars along with Kyle. They were each carrying large suitcases. I really wanted something to eat and might tolerate the blood now. Alessandro, still at my side, brought me to one of the formal dining rooms we didn't normally use. Denise and Kyle laid out a variety of small bags of blood and computers, then had me sit down.

"We're going to give you samples to compare," she said. "Just tell us which of the two tastes better."

"Aren't they all going to taste like blood?" I asked skeptically. She just laughed and shook her head, then gave me the first two to try.

To my surprise, all of the bags did taste slightly different. I couldn't always tell which I liked better, but I could distinguish between them. Denise and Kyle made notes on everything and I was slowly getting better about not spilling as I drank. Some of the blood was barely tolerable but some I could handle pretty well. And then I bit into a bag and it tasted like silver moonlight. Almost like Adze. I drained the bag.

"Do you have more of that?"

"You liked it?" She sounded surprised. "That's the first one you've liked. How odd."

"What?"

"Well, it's just that that's your blood type. From when you were a human."

I remembered that they had gotten my blood type when they had ordered blood for the transfusion and stared at the empty bag. Was it unusual to like my own blood? It kind of made sense that I would, didn't it? I was used to having that blood inside me, so I wanted more of it.

"We'll have to see what else you like," she said. "That's probably the most desirable type of blood there is."

I flushed at the thought that my blood was desirable and thought of Adze drinking it. He must have enjoyed it, then. But if I only liked desirable blood, it might be impossible to get. Surely everyone else wanted it, too, and I had to be at the bottom of the list. I kept trying other types of blood and there were several that tasted good, though not as good. I hoped I would be able to get the blood I liked as much as possible.

As soon as we were done and my belly felt full, Alessandro brought me downstairs. One of the windows was open in the hall and I winced as the light from the soon-to-rise sun struck me. The sun wasn't even up yet; how could it hurt this much? Alessandro didn't seem to notice the light, though he hurried me downstairs where it was cool and the light didn't hurt. It was bright, to my surprise. Normally it was pitch black down here. Then I realized it probably was still pitch black and it was just that I could see in the dark. Adze was waiting at the bottom of the stairs and my breath hitched. He held his arms out and without a thought, I threw myself on him. He held me close and I snuggled into him, needing this more than I had ever needed anything else. Even more than I had needed him to bite me.

When we finally parted, he kept me close and patted my head.

"I'm sorry, Kairos," he said. "I had hoped you wouldn't become a vampire. I must have given you false hope."

"It's okay," I said. "I don't mind as much as I thought I would."

"One of the benefits of being a vampire," he said with a slight smile. "Once you're fully transitioned, your fears of it fade. I think you'll enjoy being a vampire before long."

"Alessandro and Darius said you might, um, you might want to mentor me," I said hesitantly, looking into those beautiful glowing eyes.

"I wouldn't let anyone else do it," he said, and pulled me into a hug. I melted into him. We broke apart again and he stroked my cheek. "I've never mentored anyone who doesn't resent me in some way. This should be far more enjoyable."

"I only tried to kill you once," Alessandro said with a half-smile. I blinked. He had tried to kill Adze? But Adze just smiled.

"You always were the easy one. But Kairos has no reason at all to want me dead, do you?" He rubbed his thumb across my lower lip and I felt dizzy. "I'll make sure you're fully prepared to be a vampire." He sighed. "After the trial, that is. I hope you understand why I have to be so distant right now."

"I can stand it for a few days," I assured him.

"The trial will take at least a week, probably longer," he warned. "And we don't know how long the jury will take. This is a very serious crime.They're not going to make this decision lightly."

"As long as I can see you at the end, I can wait," I said confidently.

Adze smiled, that full smile I had only seen once before. Without thinking, I rose on my tiptoes and kissed him. He wrapped his arms around me and held me tight, his lips opening under mine and his tongue winding along mine. I felt him lick my fangs and had a moment of panic and insecurity. Did he still want me like this now that I was a vampire? But he slid his tongue along mine without hesitation and I relaxed into him, leaning into him fully. I loved this. I needed this. Everything else seemed to fade. All of my worries and fears, thoughts of the trial, my parents, my friends, my permanently shifted life, all of it faded into the bliss of the moment and Adze under my eager tongue and hands. I clutched at him, grasping his back and trying to get as close as possible.

We kissed for a long, long time until I finally had to break away or risk begging for more. We probably weren't allowed to have sex until the trial was over and if I didn't stop now, I wouldn't be satisfied until I was in his bed panting under him. Even so, I was gasping for breath as we parted and he stroked my head.

"Far more enjoyable," he murmured, and I blushed. What would he be like as a mentor? How often would he take me to his room? I would be able to see the room now, I realized with a start. I could finally see if it was his private bedroom or something else. Then I became aware of Alessandro standing right there, watching us in amusement.

"We should get you settled," Alessandro said. "Before you do anything we need to avoid. Adze's self-control is questionable around you."

Adze didn't deny that and I blushed deeper.

"Margaret is getting a few of your things," Adze said. "She'll be down shortly and you can sleep."

"So vampires do sleep?"

"We don't have to," he said. "I don't. But you're still in your human habits. You'll probably need to sleep for years."

I nodded, the finality of this hitting me once again. Years. This wasn't a temporary thing. I was going to be like this my whole life, and I was immortal now. I gulped. Adze stroked my head.

"It'll be fine," he murmured reassuringly. "You have a home. You're not alone."

I took a shuddering breath and cuddled him. He kissed my cheek and then pushed me back.

"Alessandro is right," he said. "We shouldn't be too close right now. I'll let him get you settled. I'll see you tonight."

CHAPTER FIFTY-TWO: WAITING

The trial passed quickly. I stayed in court and listened to the testimony from the rest of House Elviore and a few vampires from House Tennison, including Darius and Alessandro. Alessandro testified that I was now a vampire, the first time that had been made public, and I was grateful I had told everyone in advance. I would not have wanted them to find out from the news. I was keeping an eye on social media and most of the attention was now on the meat of the issue, not on me, but a few articles kept popping up about me. Most seemed driven by people sympathetic to House Salvite, as it was usually an argument that Elviore couldn't be trusted because of what had happened to me. I wondered what the rumors would be now that I was a vampire. There had been a lot of online speculation on the topic. Apparently no human had been turned in nearly a hundred years. And now that Alessandro had made it official, the rumors were sure to start up again.

Cassius did his best to undermine everyone who came to the stand, but he seemed unable to trip anyone up. Even I had stood against him pretty well because I was relying on the truth, as was everyone else. We didn't have to make sure our lies lined up or worry about saying the right thing. All we needed to do was tell the truth.

I was called back to the stand on the last day of Elviore's testimony, after Alessandro. I shivered as I took my place, because they all knew I was a vampire now. Alaric asked me to describe what had happened with the young woman and I obeyed. The jury looked disgusted and Cassius's only questions were about whether or not I misinterpreted the woman's comments. After all, she hadn't directly threatened my family, just said they might be in danger. But I knew what she had meant, and what she had wanted. I realized as I stepped down that now my parents and friends would know they were in danger. Court was adjourned after I finished and I quickly texted them to let them know that they were safe.

Communication with everyone had been stilted after telling them I was a vampire. I didn't know if it was something I was doing wrong or if they felt differently about me now, but I didn't push. My relationship with them was changing. Nothing could stop that. If things fell apart naturally, I would let them. I hoped they wouldn't, though. I hoped it was just the craziness of the trial and as soon as this was over, Janae would be pestering me about visiting again. I would let her. There was nothing to hide now. I would even let Scott come because there was no way Adze would be jealous of him.

Every night, Adze and Alessandro escorted me downstairs. Adze embraced me, sometimes kissed me, but nothing else, and I slept in the luxurious bed wanting more. The trial continued, moving into the witnesses for House Salvite. Since most of the evidence was hard to argue, they instead attacked Elviore's credibility and brought up alternate theories that didn't seem to have any basis in reality. I began to read those same theories in the news, though, and knew they were having an effect. People were believing them. Would the jury? And finally, after fifteen nights sitting in the courtroom trying not to worry too much about what the jury was thinking, Alaric and Cassius made their closing arguments and the case went to the jury. Court was adjourned and, as usual, reporters swarmed us on the way out. I had noticed Alaric frequently stopping to talk to them, though no one else did, but today he and Lilith went to the steps and faced the crowd. They made a brief version of their case to the public. Since nothing in the courtroom was televised, this was the only time people could actually see the information being announced. It was extremely abbreviated and didn't go into any details, but it was an outline of their charges against Salvite. I noticed Cassius and the four vampires who had attacked Adze making similar announcements on the other side of the steps, and I caught sight of Dr. Grayson. Our eyes met and I shivered. He made his way over to me and the vampires moved to shield me. Dr. Grayson smiled.

"I'm just here to speak to my student for a moment," he said. Cautiously, I placed my hand on the nearest vampire to pull her back slightly so I could face Dr. Grayson. The vampires remained at my side, a reassuring buzz, but parted so I could see him.

"It's good to see you again," Dr. Grayson said. "I've been worried about you. I see I had reason to worry. You've been getting caught up in all sorts of things you shouldn't have."

"At least I ended up in the right place," I said, feeling far bolder than I usually did around him. Normally I was keenly aware that he was my professor but right now, he was just a human talking to a vampire. I had the power here.

"I hope you'll remember that it was thanks to me that you're here," he said. "I'm sure I'll see you again. Even vampires can go to school, you know."

I was a little surprised as he left. Was that true? Maybe I could still go to grad school and become a professor. Maybe at least a few of my parent's wishes for me could come true. The vampires surrounded me again and escorted me to a nearby building. It was a tall building, at least twenty stories, with classy neon lights proclaiming it the Creston Center. It looked like an ordinary office building and as we entered the nondescript lobby, I wondered why we were here. Alessandro took me and another vampire to the elevator up to the seventh floor, then through an open area filled with cubicles. Some had people in them, some didn't, but the people were mostly humans. He led us to a glassed-in suite at the end of the room with large windows overlooking the city. I went to the window and stared out at the city, far more alive at night than it was during the day. People bustled along the sidewalks, but there were patches where the crowd was noticeably thin and I knew there was a vampire walking there. The female vampire with us came to my side. I was starting to recognize all of them by their feel, but still had trouble with their names. I was pretty sure this was Ambrosia. She had fair blond hair with a hint of red, and the pale white skin I associated with most vampires. Some had darker skin, like Adze, but most were a sunless white. I wondered if my tan skin would fade to that shade after I had lived away from the sun for a while.

"What is this place?" I asked, turning away from the window. "Why are we here?"

"One of our offices," Alessandro said. "We don't know when the jury will reach a verdict. House Elviore is remaining at the courthouse but we wanted to get you away from the press."

"I had to go through them to get here," I pointed out.

"They'll be harassing everyone related to this inside the courthouse," he said. "Now that the trial is over, the rules are a little more lax."

"Oh. Thank you."

I took a deep breath and sat at the long table in the middle of the room. The sun would be rising in a couple of hours and I wondered what would happen then. We couldn't stay here. But the jury might decide at any moment. Would they continue deliberations during the day or take a break to sleep? I could probably ask.

"So what happens now? How does the jury decide?"

"They'll have to go through each count separately, and House Elviore brought over 200 charges against each of them, from extortion to murder to drug trafficking, plus a variety of other charges like witness intimidation and turning you. You're not the only witness they've intimidated," he added. "Having them try to scare you makes Elviore's case that this is a pattern of behavior a lot stronger. But it's going to take time to go through all of them. Even if they don't need discussion,

365

it's a lot to do. It'll likely take a few nights."

"Where will we be during that time? Are we staying here or do I get to go home?"

He smiled. "You'll be allowed to go home, I suspect. We're not really equipped to have vampires sleep here."

"Where will you be?"

"I'll go with you. Ambrosia and the others will stay here."

"I thought you weren't equipped," I said, puzzled.

"For a sleeping vampire," he clarified. "But for vampires who stay awake, we're well suited here. There's a secure basement and Tennison will continue our work. This is our major focus but not our only one."

That made sense, as Adze had said that vampires didn't really need to sleep. I wondered what it would be like to stay up for so long. I needed sleep to break up the time and give me a chance to refresh and reset for the next day. It was hard enough getting used to a night schedule; I couldn't imagine getting used to no schedule at all. Eventually, it would happen. I suspected it would happen slowly, with me needing less and less sleep until I stayed up without realizing it. I shivered. Everything in my life was going to change and the thought of something as essential to my survival as sleep going away made me realize yet again how permanent this change was. At least I wasn't frightened anymore. There was just a sense of dread.

"You'll only be here for about a half hour," he added. "Lilith will come to get you when they're ready. They're handling the press right now."

I got out my phone. My friends seemed to have remembered that I had social media, at least my more distant friends, and now every time I went on, my dms were filled with requests for information. I was ignoring everyone except my closest friends. Maybe eventually I'd have the strength to go through everyone, but maybe not. They all knew I was a vampire now and they'd probably figure out that I wouldn't respond. I skimmed through the headlines. I could basically tell the political leanings of each organization based on what they were focused on. Most were about the vast criminal reach of House Salvite, but some were still about me and Adze. Those were the outlets biased towards House Salvite, trying to proclaim their innocence. I instinctively disliked those sites. I would have blocked them, but I wanted to see what people were saying about me.

The stories had evolved into a lurid sex affair between me and Adze that involved drinking my blood every day. I hated reading about it but I could tell some of my friends believed it because they were the ones liking the stories. And I wanted to know what people thought of me, because I was sure to run into this in my life. People believed this and would judge me accordingly. I needed to know. Alessandro sat beside me and looked over my shoulder.

"You shouldn't be reading that," he said as I paused on an especially explicit story.

"I should know what they're saying about me, shouldn't I?"

"They're not news organizations," he said. "Those are just the gossip pages. They'll stop as soon as a new scandal starts up."

"People think this, though," I said. "They believe these stories."

"Anyone who believes a story like that isn't worth knowing," he said dismissively.

"But they'll still think it. I can't just ignore everyone who thinks this."

"You can," he said. "You're a vampire now. You can choose to ignore anyone you want and no one will question you."

I thought of how the vampires in the streets always moved with a pocket of protection around them. It was true that now that I was a vampire, I would have more control over who I talked to. Maybe I could just ignore everyone I didn't like.

"What app are you using?" Ambrosia asked, coming to sit on my other side and peering to my phone. I tilted it so she could see. "I see. Perhaps you could get a job with our social media staff."

"No, I'm terrible at it," I said. "I never go on, but I wanted to see what everyone's saying. It seems like everyone in the world is talking about this," I added as I scrolled past an article from Japan that was in English.

"This is the largest case in vampire history," Alessandro said. "Before the war, House Elviore would have simply killed House Salvite without a trial and only provided evidence if the other houses challenged them. After the war, though, they have to follow the legal system and take them to trial. Nothing like this has ever happened."

"You called them the founding house," I said cautiously. "What does that mean?"

"You're going to learn a lot of things you can't share now that you're a vampire," he said. "You understand that, don't you? You may still have human friends and family but you can't tell them anything about us."

"I won't," I said. "I'm already not telling them things."

"Good." He looked at Ambrosia, who nodded. I was curious now, as this was clearly a highly-held secret. "House Elviore aren't vampires like the rest of us. All other vampires were human once. They weren't."

"What does that mean?"

"They're the original vampires," he explained. "Every other vampire is descended from them in some way."

"That's impossible," I said, my mind boggling at that. There were original vampires who weren't human? I thought back to their names, to Adze's name. I had assumed he had named himself after an African myth, but what if he *were* the African myth? What if the stories were based on him, not the other way around?

"It's very possible," Alessandro said. "No one knows how old they are. They all came from different parts of the world and eventually found each other and started their house. That's why their house is the premiere house. It's why they led the war. It's why their accusations hold so much weight, and why any smears against them are so incredibly offensive. Every vampire in the world reveres them."

I was stunned. I didn't know what to think. They were the original vampires? They must be thousands of years old, then. And Adze had feelings for me, a mere human? He had risked everything for me? He had lost some of his reputation, and all because of me.

"So you can see why Adze should have refused to bite you," Alessandro added. "He's had humans throw themselves at him before, probably hundreds of times. Before the war there was no need to refrain but ever since then, House Elviore has made it a point of pride that they respect all human laws. If they didn't, no one else would. We only follow the law because they do. Because Adze broke that law, there's going to be a rash of vampires feeding on their servants."

I shivered. I hadn't meant to start something like that. It made sense, though. If the only reason vampires followed the law was because House Elviore did and Adze broke the law, then they could break the law as well and justify it with his actions. I hoped no servants or humans were harmed as a result of my actions. There wasn't much I could do about now, though. I still didn't regret it. I probably should. So many things had happened because of what I had done, but I couldn't bring myself to wish it hadn't happened. I was humiliated that it had become public, worried about the consequences, but there wasn't a trace of regret in my mind.

CHAPTER FIFTY-THREE: LOSS OF CONTROL

The next evening, Alessandro brought me straight to the office building, not to the courthouse. We would go to the courthouse immediately if the jury finished, but he didn't think it would happen tonight. The case was incredibly complex and there were so many charges for so many people. Every single one of House Salvite's vampires was charged with multiple crimes, though the four leaders were charged with considerably more. There were thirty-one of them, so it was a time-consuming process. I wondered if some of them would be found not guilty and what would happen if some but not all of them went to jail. Or were executed. Would their house still exist? Would they start a new house? How would they be monitored? They knew I was translating their messages now so they would undoubtedly shift their code and all of my knowledge would be useless. I needed to learn other codes so I could better decipher messages.

Instead of retreating to the suite, Alessandro walked me around and introduced me to the humans, who all worked for or with House Tennison. I was quickly overwhelmed by names but he assured me no one would judge me for not knowing everyone right away. The other vampires working there were from two other houses, one that specialized in crime and one that focused on cracking codes. They were House Vera, and Alessandro suggested that I might eventually want to join them. The vampires from that house were especially friendly to me, probably knowing I might want to join them. But I was welcome to stay with Tennison for as long as I wanted, he assured me, and House Vera didn't try to pressure me in any way.

I was a little wary of switching to a house I didn't know, since I only had experience with three houses and one was involved in a breath-taking number of crimes. I was worried other houses would be like that, though I suspected a house friendly to Salvite wouldn't be working with Tennison. It had seemed like Tennison and Salvite were the only vampire hunters in the city and everyone else probably sided with one of them. I thought of the woman's threats and hoped I had ended up with the more powerful side, but if I was siding with House Elviore, the founding house, then I should be safe. And so should my friends and family.

I had talked to my parents again, explaining a little more about the house I had joined. They were happy I wasn't still with Adze and I didn't mention that he would be mentoring me and I would remain with him even after that. They were a little wary that my new house was so closely linked to the current case and had done enough research to know they were vampire hunters. I assured them that I wouldn't have to kill anyone and that I would pretty much keep doing my current job. It was hard talking to them, but I had to keep in touch with them. I was less careful with my friends. I was still contacting them through our group chat but they seemed to be waiting for the verdict. I was, too.

The day passed at a crawl. I was given more blood around midnight, a flavor I had liked but not my ideal type. This was probably what I would get from now on and at least it was good. Darius stopped by with the blood and explained that I would likely eat at least once a day until my body stabilized, when I would start eating less often and finally only once a week as they did. I had wondered why no one else seemed to be eating. I was getting better at feeding now that the blood actually tasted decent.

Soon it was time to go home and Alessandro helped me get to the car with minimal interaction with the press. They continued to shout questions but now they were about what I thought the verdict would be, and they were aimed at the Tennison vampires as well. I was with Ambrosia again and she kept repeating no comment to the press as we got in the car. This morning it was just me and the Tennison vampires and their servants and for the first time, I experienced traffic in Redmond. I was so used to be taken everywhere quickly that it was strange having to stop and start and worry that the sun was going to rise while we were trapped in traffic. The windows were practically black but I would need to get from the car to the house when we arrived.

"I didn't know there was this much traffic," I said as we came to another stop. The other vampires smiled.

"Have you never been in it?"

"We always just skip over it," I admitted. "I haven't been in traffic since I got my job."

"You'll have to get used to it," Ambrosia said. "Only ancient houses are allowed to skip it. But we'll get to the manor in time, if that's what you're worried about. We take the traffic into account."

That was good. But as we crawled through the city, I wondered. I remembered my first couple of times out here and how slow everything had gone. I had worried about being late to my job interview but hadn't been driving through at rush hour. I had been through the city at human rush hour but never vampire rush hour and it was noticeably slower. I shifted uncomfortably and hoped I got used to this. I hadn't realized how spoiled I had gotten skipping over the traffic.

We arrived at the estate just as the sky was starting to get light and we went to the garage connected to the house. I hadn't even noticed it, as I parked in a garage farther away. This meant that I wouldn't have to go outside and I was relieved. I was pretty sure it was light enough out that it would hurt. I hoped I stopped being less sensitive to light soon. It didn't seem to bother anyone else but I was mildly uncomfortable in the bright lights of the courtroom and office building. Vladimir had assured me it would get better and I trusted him, but when?

Adze greeted me warmly as we entered, as did everyone else. I was starting to get exhausted but I asked to have dinner with Margaret and the others. The vampires looked surprised and reminded me I couldn't eat anything, but I wanted the company. I couldn't be with my other friends but I could still hold on to these relationships. If I kept living here, I wanted to be on good terms with them and I didn't want to lose the closeness we had gained the past months. I sat and chatted with them as they ate. Dmitri and Dianne seemed a little more formal than usual around me. Margaret started that way, but quickly reverted to her usual friendly self. I was glad. Things had permanently changed between us but I still wanted to be friends. I wondered how much they knew about House Elviore. They knew it was an ancient house, and probably knew it was the premiere house, but did they know it was the founding house? I would never know, because I would never ask. I was bound to keep vampire secrets now and while they could know some things because they were dhampir, there was a lot they still couldn't know.

I spent the night longing for Adze, but I slept soundly. I had been sleeping really well since becoming a vampire: I fell asleep quickly and when I woke up, I was completely refreshed. I wasn't having dreams, at least that I remembered, but maybe that was normal. I wondered if Adze could still enter my dreams as a firefly. There were no fireflies down here so I would probably never find out. I rather suspected he couldn't, though. I was a vampire now and no longer as susceptible to his power.

As we got up in the evening and I left my room, I came face to face with Adze and drew in a sharp breath. There was no one else around. Just us. He seemed to realize the same because without a word, he pulled me into a fierce kiss. I submitted immediately, giving in to his lips on mine and his hand grasping my body and caressing my ass. I moaned softly and gripped his back, the sensations sweeping over me as I gave in to desire. Every part of me sparked on fire as he plundered my lips and took what he wanted. He had never kissed me like this before. It was unbelievably good. And then he released me. Abruptly. I gasped as he pushed me back a step, out of his embrace. He was emotionless again and his eyes were behind me. I turned to see Ambrosia with her arms crossed and a bemused expression on her face. I blushed and tried to cool down, because that kiss had gotten me hot.

"You really have lost control, Adze," she said. "I hope it doesn't extend to anyone else. Your house can't afford any more scandals."

"He's a vampire now," Adze said, reaching out to caress my cheek. I leaned into his touch. My lips still tingled and I wanted nothing more than to grab him the way he had grabbed me. "There's no longer a scandal."

"I suppose it does benefit House Tennison to have such strong favor from Elviore," she said. "But you need to avoid him until the jury reaches a verdict."

"But the testimony is over," I pointed out rather breathlessly. "Why does it matter?"

"The jury is allowed to ask the court basic questions and if they ask if you still have a relationship, we'll have to tell the truth. We want to avoid that," she explained.

"And after that?" I asked, looking to Adze. His lips twitched into a smile and he petted my head.

"After that you're mine," he said quite possessively. I flushed and couldn't help the shiver of pleasure that ran through me. I still couldn't believe that he wanted me. It seemed impossible that one of the original vampires was so taken with me but what Ambrosia had said was true: he had lost control around me. I could tell that even having sex with me violated ethical behavior. He hadn't hesitated to take me like that and while it would have been a scandal if it had come out, I got the impression that it happened frequently, just not in Elviore. It would blow over quickly. But it wasn't just the sex where he had lost control. He had given in when I begged him to bite me, violating one of the core rules that Elviore was sworn to obey.

"But not yet," Ambrosia said, taking my arm and pulling me away. I wanted to resist and stay at his side, but I allowed myself to be drawn away. I didn't want him in any more trouble and I wanted this case to end in convictions, not get thrown out because of my carelessness. Still, he was the one who had grabbed me this time. For once, I wasn't the one initiating it.

Dmitri drove us to the courthouse and we skipped over traffic, then Alessandro and Ambrosia brought me to the nearby office building. The press was just as loud as ever but I was starting to get good at ignoring them. I wondered if this was being streamed live and if any of my friends were watching me go into the building. I realized with a start that I would no longer show up on camera. They would only be seeing sketches. I would have to ask how closely they were following the trial. I knew they were keeping up on it but they might only be reading about it, not watching the gossipy coverage that seemed to dominate the headlines.

Another night passed, then another. Alessandro assured me that it was expected the jury should take this long. No one seemed worried about it. In fact, the few times Darius came to check on me and chat with the others, he warned me that it might take a week before this was settled. The case was just too complex. House Elviore had provided detailed documentation on the involvement of each of the thirty-one members of House Salvite and the jury would need to sort through that, plus take into account the verbal testimony. The jury knew full well how important the case was and how their decision would shape vampire society for decades to come. They were taking it seriously.

If they found House Salvite guilty and they were punished as Elviore wanted, then it was likely the drug trade would come to a virtual stop. There would be a strong precedent for

House Elviore investigating other houses and they would gain even more power in vampire society. But if they ruled in favor of House Salvite, it would deal a deadly blow to House Elviore's reputation and the drug trade would continue. I couldn't help but worry that they believed the fantasies Cassius had spun that placed the blame on Elviore, not Salvite. I kept an eye on those stories in the news but couldn't bring myself to actually read them. It terrified me that people could ignore the obvious evidence and instead believe a bunch of loosely constructed lies just because they wanted to support Salvite. Or maybe the believers were invested in the drug trade, I didn't know. But a lot of people seemed to believe it and that worried me.

Another few nights passed and then, as it was approaching midnight, Alessandro's phone rang. He listened, then gathered all of us and started hustling us out of the building.

"The jury's back," he said. "They'll wait until we're there but we have to hurry."

CHAPTER FIFTY-FOUR: VERDICT

I sat next to Margaret in the second row this time, as I was one of the injured parties in the lawsuit. I was very aware of House Tennison around the edges of the room, ready to jump into action if House Salvite tried anything. If it were decided against them, would they fight? They might. Alessandro had warned on the way here. There were enough of them that they could overwhelm House Tennison even with House Elviore helping them. He said there were plenty of human guards stationed outside the room who would stop anything from happening, but I had to be careful. If they did strike, they might target me specifically. Without my testimony and translations, Elviore's case would have been a lot weaker and more susceptible to Cassius's arguments. I trembled as I sat beside Margaret and she reached over to pat my hand. I smiled at her gratefully. Then the head juror stood up.

"Has the jury reached a verdict?" the judge asked.

"We have, your honor."

The head juror was holding a long piece of paper and he began quickly reading through each count. Guilty. Guilty Guilty. Some of the stress left me as count after count went in our favor. But I looked at House Salvite nervously, wondering how they would react. So far they were tense, but no one had attacked.

The juror paused before giving a not guilty and I saw Adze's eyes narrow. It was a single count for one of the lesser vampires, but that wasn't a good sign. Then more guilty counts were read. They passed in a blur, as I didn't really understand most of the counts. All I knew was that they were being found guilty and the vampires were growing angrier by the minute. They were tense, and so was House Tennison. Several of them had hands on their waists where I assumed their guns were. If anyone tried anything, they probably had permission to kill. Or at least injure, since bullets couldn't actually kill vampires. There were several other not guilty verdicts, but not enough to change the overwhelming number of guilty verdicts.

We finally reached the charges for the four head vampires and the juror paused again. Most of the charges related to the four of them and even though the other vampires in the house had been found mostly guilty, with a couple of not guilty verdicts on lesser charges, this was the main thing everyone was waiting for. The other vampires would accept their sentences, it seemed. Would the main four?

Many of the charges were against all four of them as a group, with only a couple for them individually. Would that strengthen or weaken their case? The juror took a drink of water, as he had been talking for quite a while. The tension in the room was thick and everyone was leaning forward, waiting to hear the verdict for the main charges. The jury looked nervous. Was that a good sign? Or were they about to cross House Elviore? I held my breath.

"On the count of turning Kairos Cross into a vampire," he said, and I tensed. This was one of the two charges that related to me directly. "We find the defendants not guilty."

I gasped, as did several others in the room. Blood pounded in my ears and I tried to stifle my rage. I was a vampire now, and they weren't getting blamed? They had ordered the attack. They had been responsible, and now my life was irrevocably changed. Was no one going to pay for what had been done to me? Margaret squeezed my hand and I tried to relax. The juror was pausing again, looking a little nervous. Were they going to send the lower vampires to jail and spare the four leaders? They couldn't, could they?

"On the count of witness intimidation, we find the defendants guilty," he said, and I let out a sigh. At least that had gone in our direction. I felt a little better that they hadn't ignored me completely. Of course, I wasn't the only witness they had intimidated but it was my testimony that had proven their past actions.

The juror continued to look nervously between House Elviore and House Salvite, then cleared his throat.

"On the count of murder in the first degree," he said, and I noticed Adze draw in a breath. This was one of the major charges. "We find the defendants guilty."

There was deadly silence in the room and I looked at House Salvite. The four leaders looked about to kill but they were still seated, not attacking. The jury had probably been warned they might attack and that was the reason for the juror's fear. He read another count, extortion, again guilty. As he read through the major crimes, they were all guilty and the Salvite vampires were growing more and more on edge. Already they were looking at each other as if wondering whether or not to act. And more counts kept coming in, with the juror pausing nervously between each guilty verdict. Finally, he finished.

There had been only sixteen not guilty verdicts in over three hundred charges and I was a little stunned at the enormity of Elviore's victory. And frightened, because as soon as the final verdict was read, the four leaders stood up in a threatening manner. Cassius tried to persuade them to sit down and looked just as nervous as everyone else. The crowd was still absolutely silent and no one was moving.

Darius stood as well and gestured to the vampires lining the walls, all of whom had their guns out now.

"Don't do anything you regret," he said. "You had a fair hearing. We follow the law."

"We'll appeal," one of them snarled. "This case was biased and you know it. You bribed the jury. Anyone can see."

"You're the ones guilty of witness intimidation," Darius said calmly. "Now sit down and don't try anything."

The vampires looked at each other, then one of them stared straight at me and I went stiff with fear. Surely they weren't going to attack me. Were they? The vampire's hand flew to his waist and I gasped. Did he have a gun? There was an explosion of sound and I ducked as Darius jumped in front of me. I trembled in place, then lifted my head. Darius wasn't injured. Then I noticed the four vampires from House Salvite. All were bleeding and crumpled in the chairs looking furious. House Tennison had opened fire on them. The other twenty-seven members of House Salvite were on their feet now, firing at Tennison, and then Lilith strode to the front of the room. All of my attention concentrated on her. I could feel everything bending towards her, all of my thoughts and emotions and feelings wrapping around her until she was the center of my universe.

"You will obey the law," she said, and the words imprinted on my mind and seared into me. I shivered as they were like ice deep inside me. I would obey. I would always obey her. Then everything seemed to shatter and I jerked back to reality. Lilith was standing at the front of the court and House Salvite looked shaken. All of the other vampires looked equally unbalanced, including the jury. Had they all felt what I had felt? Had Lilith given that unbreakable command to all of us? How much power did she have? My mouth was dry and I looked to Darius, who had jumped in front of me. He turned to me.

"You're safe now," he said, then returned to the front row.

"I apologize," Lilith said to the judge. "I believe you were about to continue."

The judge seemed shocked and looked at House Salvite in fear, but they were sitting down meekly. The four leaders were bleeding but otherwise fine. Bullets couldn't kill them and I suspected all of them were now bound to obey the law because of Lilith's words. If she were so powerful, why didn't she just order them not to drug or kill anyone in the first place? There had to be some limits on her power, but I didn't know what they were. Could Adze do that, too? Could all of them? Or was it because Lilith was the head of the house and she had the most power?

"Thank you," the judge said faintly, then clenched her hand around the gavel and seemed to regain her strength. "Sentencing will be in one month. House Salvite will be remanded to federal custody."

"Your honor," Cassius said, but the judge just narrowed her eyes.

"Federal custody. Thank you all. Court is dismissed."

The vampires from my house immediately surrounded the Salvite vampires, but they weren't resisting. I wondered what federal custody meant for vampires. Clearly something they were unhappy about. I wondered where they had been during this trial. I suspected they had been allowed to remain at their homes, but not anymore. Now they were criminals, even if they were not guilty on a handful of counts. It still stung a little that one of the few counts they weren't guilty of was turning me into a vampire. Someone had to pay for that. Really, though, someone had. Everyone was sure the vampire who had attacked me was Akasha, because none of the other vampires were strong enough to turn me. She had been killed by the vampires from House Tennison in that attack. Tennison had killed all of the vampires in withdrawal. So someone had paid the price, but it didn't make me feel better. She wasn't in control of her actions; they were. And they wouldn't pay for it.

I followed everyone out of the courthouse into a swarm of press. Cameras started flashing and everyone was shouting questions at us. While before Alessandro had shuffled me through everyone quickly, today he pulled me to stand beside House Elviore. I was between Darius and Alessandro with Lilith and the rest of the Elviore vampires a few steps ahead of us. Alaric was with Lilith and the two of them made a statement and then answered questions. I could barely hear their answers over the shouting and jostling going on.

Darius leaned close to me suddenly.

"Do you have any statement you want to give about the not guilty verdict for you?" he asked softly. I shook my head and he said something to Alaric, who I realized was looking at me. The press must be asking about the few not guilty counts. Indeed, they were all staring at me. Darius patted my shoulder and brought me to the microphones, though to one side. I panicked for a moment. Had he not heard me? Was he going to make me talk when I had nothing to say? He pulled me to a stop about a foot away from the microphone and I let out a silent sigh of relief. It didn't seem like I would have to say anything. But they were still going to talk about me. I realized that my name had been said in the verdict. Did that mean it was public knowledge yet, or would the press continue to hide it?

"Our house is pleased to gain a new member," Darius announced to the crowd. "Though his turning was unintentional, he has been vital in bringing House Salvite to justice and he will be honored."

"But how do you feel about his verdict?" one of the woman shouted.

"The court found that House Salvite was not responsible for the attack," Darius said. "But it was still an attack, and still a crime. Just not their crime."

"Are you pressing other charges?" another woman shouted. "Who is to blame?"

"He was attacked by a vampire in withdrawal, as his testimony states, and that vampire is now dead," Darius said. "There is no need for further charges."

A few more questions but he pushed me back to stand with Alessandro and patted my shoulder in a reassuring manner. He hadn't said my name. Maybe I was still anonymous. For now. There were so many cameras on me right now that I knew it wouldn't be long before my identity was leaked. It was amazing no one I knew had gone to the press seeking attention. Maybe they had and the press had refused them since I wasn't a public figure. I wondered if any of my friends would try to profit off their connection to me. Not my true friends –they would never betray me like that – but the casual friends I had, the ones who were messaging me but I hadn't gotten back to yet. Would they sell me out?

The press conference seemed to last forever. Question after question was shouted out and Lilith and Alaric answered most of them. Many of the questions were aimed at Adze, but he didn't answer any. Lilith and Alaric handled everything. Darius occasionally added to one of the answers, but no one else spoke. We just stood there, on display. It was the most uncomfortable I think I had ever been. Everyone was staring at me, shouting at me, cameras were flashing and aimed at me, and I was helpless to stop them. It was all I could do to retain my composure and being a vampire was helping. It helped create a distance from the panic in my heart and my exterior emotions. I wondered if my parents were watching this, if Janae was watching this. I had to be strong for them. If I broke down or showed my anxiety, they would worry. I had to be as emotionless as Lilith as she answered question after question.

After nearly an hour, Lilith thanked the reporters and we moved down the steps as a unit. House Elviore went into their limos and I was brought to a limo with Darius, Alaric, and Alessandro. The others with us went into other cars and soon we were headed into the traffic. I let out a deep breath and tried to relax. The trial was over.

CHAPTER FIFTY-FIVE: NEXT STEPS

"So what happens now?" I asked, looking between Darius and Alaric as we made our way through the thick traffic. Alessandro was at my side looking out the window.

"We'll have to wait for the sentencing," Alaric said. "Since they tried to attack you in the court, I don't think the judge will be lenient. I'm just glad Lilith was willing to use vampiric gaze for us."

"What *was* that?" I asked with a shiver, remembering how her voice had echoed through me and bound me to her words.

"Only House Elviore is capable of it," he said. "Since all vampires are descended from them, they still have quite a bit of power over us. She can order us to do anything and we have to obey."

"Why didn't she stop them from committing crimes in the first place?"

"It's difficult to do, and you have to be close for it to work," Alaric said. "She's never been in a position to address all of House Salvite before."

"They won't be able to commit any crimes anymore," Darius added. "Even if the judge goes easy on some of them. None of us will, at least not for decades until it fades."

"What if I don't know the laws?" I asked. "How can obey what I don't know?"

"Adze will teach you everything you need to know," Darius said. "And you're only bound to obey laws you know about."

"So I can finally see him again?" I asked hopefully.

Alessandro grinned and Darius looked amused. They seemed far more expressive now that I was also a vampire. Either they were more relaxed around me or I was just better at picking up their subtle expressions. Adze's smile had been broader than usual; maybe I was just learning to interpret their expressions better.

"Yes, you can see him freely now," Darius said. "But remember that you're not in his house anymore. You're in ours. You have to represent us well."

"I'll do my best," I promised, though I wasn't exactly sure how to do that.

"Darius and I will be stopping by to keep in touch with you," Alessandro said. "It's not good for a vampire to be isolated from the rest of his house while he's adapting."

"You have the gratitude of our entire house," Alaric added. "We're all indebted to you. You can ask any one of us for help and we'll give it."

"We would help him anyway," Alessandro pointed out. "He's in our house now."

Alaric shrugged. "True. But we'll be even more inclined to help you while you adjust."

"Thanks," I said cautiously. It was strange being so connected to vampires. I could feel a reassuring buzz from all three of them, each one unique but friendly. They were my house now. I belonged to them in a way I had never belonged to anything else. Before, I had called myself part of House Elviore and I had been a part of them, as much as was possible. But there was always a separation, because I wasn't one of their vampires. I was on the outside looking in, belonging but not essential. Now I was one of the vampires and I was at the center of the house.

"In answer to your question, though, there's a lot that happens now," Darius said. "We have to dismantle an entire criminal enterprise. We have the main actors, but they have people all over the world. It'll take a while, and we'll have to

385

prevent others from taking over now that House Salvite is out of power."

"But they can't hurt us, can they?" I asked, thinking of my family and friends.

"We'll protect everyone close to you until everyone is safe," Darius confirmed. "And we'll protect you."

"What's to stop people from just dumping the drug into all of the blood and sending everything into chaos?" I asked fearfully, because that was another thought that had just arisen. House Salvite seemed to addict people purposefully, but what if their allies lashed out against everyone now that their drug trade was being taken down?

There was silence as the others looked at each other, then Darius smiled.

"I didn't expect you to think of that," he said. "But you have nothing to fear. We've been monitoring all blood since the trial started. It's time-consuming and expensive, but we won't allow any vampire to be addicted. It's not public knowledge that the blood is being monitored. If they attack, we'll be able to track them quite easily."

"But what if all the blood is drugged?" I asked. "No one will be able to feed."

"Vampires can go quite a long time without feeding," Darius said. "You're the only one who'll need it regularly, and we'll make sure you get it."

"You'll need to keep translating," Alessandro added. "Even though they know we can break their code, it'll be a while before they figure something else out. You'll be a valuable part of this process."

I nodded, pleased that I would still be able to help. I had worried that with House Salvite gone, I would be useless. I would learn other codes in time, but I wanted to be helpful now and it seemed I would be. I wondered how long it would take, and if we would ever stop the drug trade completely. There was always a war on drugs among humans and it never worked. It just targeted people and punished them unfairly.

Would the vampires be starting a similar campaign, or would they be able to completely remove the drug from their society? If they could figure out how the drug was made and prevent people from making more, it might be possible to stop it completely. If anyone could do it, House Elviore could. I had been amazed at the intellect, resourcefulness, and patience on display in their testimony. I had faith that they could do anything and I was relieved the case had been decided as it was. A few not guilty findings, but a massive victory for Elviore. And for justice. I supposed it wasn't out of question for them to be found not guilty in turning me, even though I wanted someone to pay for what had happened. The longer I was a vampire, though, the less I minded it. I had a feeling I would enjoy it before long. I had worried about immortality and drinking blood, but it wasn't as terrifying as I had thought. It was natural now.

We reached my house, Adze's house, and went through the garage into the house even though it was still safely dark. Alessandro had warned me that I would be exceptionally sensitive to the sun for a while and should be careful to retreat to the basement at the first sign of light. He assured me that I would be able to work from down there if necessary. I thought of Adze's sleek computer that I had envied and wondered if now I would get one. It had the Elviore symbol, so maybe it was reserved for their house only. Did Tennison have equipment just as nice? I hoped so. I suspected a lot of perks I had taken for granted working for House Elviore were about to be taken away now that I was no longer a member, but surely all vampire houses had some comforts. Darius had once said that their house was the premiere vampire hunter house in Redmond so they had to be one of the best houses to work for even if they weren't an ancient house. And maybe I could still get benefits while I lived with Adze, even if I wasn't in his house. I would have to ask.

Instead of retreating to the basement, Darius brought me to my office and I was surprised to see a pile of letters. He smiled at me.

"I told you we still needed you. It looks like they're still using their code. Do you think you could go through these, and some emails as well?"

"Of course," I said. "Do I do everything the same? Report to the same people?"

"You'll forward your results to our house as well, but otherwise the same," he said, showing me who to contact. They had a human dedicated to communications, though I got the feeling their job was not nearly as complex as mine. I doubted anyone was translating as many messages as I had been, and not for the same reason. Their jobs were what I had assumed mine had been at first: checking messages for the vampires in the house to make sure there weren't any human quirks a vampire might miss. Would I still be able to do this job now that I was a vampire?

I sat down and got to work. Alessandro stayed with me and it was just like when I was under surveillance. Everything felt familiar and I relished the feeling. Some of the code was different but not dramatically, and I could figure it all out. Apparently being a vampire didn't impact my ability to translate messages. Why couldn't vampires learn to do this themselves? They had plenty of time to learn, since they didn't have to sleep. They seemed to be experts in everything else. I remembered how good Alessandro was at tennis. Maybe now that I had unlimited time, I could perfect all of my hobbies. Something to look forward to, and a reason to be grateful for immortality.

Court had ended just after midnight and as it started to get towards morning, Alessandro stopped me and brought me downstairs to avoid any risk of me being exposed to sunlight. When I got downstairs, Alessandro looked around and then pulled me to the side of the hall.

"Kairos, do you have any second thoughts about staying here?" he asked. "Any at all?"

"I want to be here," I said, wondering why he was asking.

He reached out and stroked my shoulder.

"Just remember that you're in our house. Darius and I will stop by to see you and make sure you learn our history, but you're going to be alone here. It can be difficult not seeing your house. Remember how anxious you felt when you were between houses?"

I gulped and nodded. It had been a terrifying moment of absolute loneliness. He squeezed my shoulder.

"If you start to feel that way at all, let us know. We'll be here immediately, no matter what time it is, no matter what else is going on."

"Is that going to happen?"

"We should be visiting you enough to prevent it, but it's hard to tell how much you'll need us when you're newly turned. We'll be here for you. You understand?"

"Thank you," I said. "I'll let you know, no matter what. I didn't like feeling that way."

"Good," he said. "And Kairos, if Adze does anything you're uncomfortable with, you have to tell us that as well."

I blushed. "I doubt he will."

Alessandro's lips twitched. "I rather doubt it as well, but just know you have our absolute protection, even against him."

"Thank you," I said again. "I know which house I belong to, and I trust you. If I need your help for anything, I'll tell you."

He nodded and squeezed my arm again.

"Then I'm leaving you here. I'll be returning to my house. From now on, you'll be under Adze's care."

I couldn't help but smile and he looked amused.

"Just remember that he's in charge of mentoring you," he said. "There are a lot of things he has to teach you. Make sure you learn as much as you can. I look forward to working with you on translating as we figure out how to dismantle everything Salvite has built. I'm sure you'll do your best to help."

"I will," I promised. "Will I see you in a month when the

sentencing happens? Or do we not have to go to that?"

"I'll be there, as will Adze. Since they weren't found guilty of turning you, there's no real reason for you to be there unless you want to be. It might be a good chance for you to see us, so maybe you'd want to. Seeing one of us helps, but you might want to be surrounded by your house. Whatever you're comfortable with."

"Thank you, Alessandro," I said shyly. "You've really helped me a lot. Even before I was in your house."

"You're valuable," Alessandro said. "You've always been valuable, but now you're in my house. I'll do everything in my power to protect you. Don't forget that."

"I won't," I said, and Alessandro looked around and sighed.

"I'm sure you're eager for me to leave, but it might be more difficult for you than you imagine. If you need us-"

"I'll tell you," I finished, and he smiled.

"Good. I'll see you soon."

He retreated up the stairs and I looked around. It was odd having everything so well lit down here. The door to the office opened and my heart leapt. Adze stood in the doorway with a soft smile on his face.

"Are you ready to live here, without your house, under my care?" he asked.

"Yes," I said, shyly approaching him. I held out my hand and he took it, then raised it to his lips. My heart stuttered. He had never made a romantic gesture like this before. I met his gaze and that beautiful smile strengthened.

"Then let's get started."

CHAPTER FIFTY-SIX: TOGETHER

Adze held my hand in his and led me to the door across from where I had been sleeping. My heart hitched. It had to be the room where he took me when we had sex. Every other time I had been here, it had been pitch black and I was unable to see. I was intensely curious about what it was like and I would finally be able to see it. Adze paused with his hand on the door.

"You seem excited," he said, and I realized I was starting to get hard just at the thought of what we usually did in this room. I blushed deeply and he stroked my cheek. "Good."

He opened the door and pushed me inside. I came to a halt as my eyes widened. The only thing I had known about this room was that there was a bed and there was, in the center of the room. It had black silk sheets with blood red trim. That wasn't what caught my attention, though. The rest of the room was wildly beyond anything I had imagined and even looking at it, I couldn't believe something like this existed in real life.

The walls were lined with racks of various types of whips and there were chains hanging from the ceiling. There were oddly shaped benches in several places, and a swing in one corner. There was a display case with a variety of dildos and I gulped. Other aspects of the room flashed through my mind and then everything went black as something soft covered my eyes. I drew in a sharp breath.

"I think you've seen enough," Adze said in my ear as he secured the blindfold.

"Does everyone know what this room is?" I whispered, heat flooding through me at the thought of Alessandro and the others knowing exactly how Adze took me.

Talking about my relationship with Adze during the trial had been difficult but at least I hadn't been forced to share what exactly I did with him. I would have been humiliated. I might have refused to answer those questions, as Dmitri had suggested I had the right to do.

"Many vampires have a room like this, or at least the ancients do," he said, his breath tickling my neck as he kissed me. "We enjoy bringing humans down here."

"I thought it was a scandal that you were sleeping with me."

"You're my servant," he said. "That is a scandal. Now, if you were just a human who caught my eye and I used for a short period of time... that would be an entirely different story."

"Have you ever brought a vampire here before?" I wasn't sure if I wanted the answer. I wanted to be the only one he had ever brought here but it sounded like he had brought quite a few humans over the years. I couldn't compete there. But maybe he was pickier about vampires.

"Vampires are not always as... submissive... as humans," he said, kissing my neck again. "I couldn't force one to come here, and none have ever come voluntarily. Are you having second thoughts?"

His hand wrapped around my waist to cup my crotch right as he asked that and I moaned softly. He could feel exactly how into this I was. The sight of the room, rather than put me off, had turned me on. I wanted him to use those things on me, to whip me and tie me up and force me to do his bidding. I wanted him to control me. I might be a vampire now, but the desire to obey was stronger than ever. I needed him.

"I'll never have second thoughts," I murmured, and tilted my head to kiss him.

A brush of his lips against mine and I wondered if he were smiling. Then he locked on, stroking my body with his hands as his mouth opened and he invaded me. I shivered and grabbed his shoulders, turning in his arms to face him. He kissed me thoroughly, then released me and gently pushed me back a few steps. Even though I couldn't see anything – as usual – I felt more confident than usual. Maybe it was because I had seen the room and understood the basic layout or maybe it was because I was a vampire and had more confidence in general, but I didn't worry about my footing as I let him steer me backwards to the bed. It hit the back of my legs we paused.

Did I want this? I said I did, and part of me did, but was I wholeheartedly into this as I usually was? I felt some resistance deep down in my heart, some half-felt protest that I shouldn't allow this, that I shouldn't submit to him. Was it because I was a vampire now and not supposed to submit like this? He gently shoved me back until I was lying on the bed.

"Are you positive?" he asked, as if he could read my sudden hesitation.

"I want you, but," I started, then stopped. I didn't know what to say. How could I explain that feeling, especially when it contradicted my heart's desire? I wanted him, I did. There was just this hesitation now and I didn't know what to do about it. "I want to see you smile," I said cautiously. "Just that, just once, then I'm yours."

I heard a low chuckle and my heart twinged. I was desperate to see him. His hand brushed against my cheek and he lifted the blindfold. A wide smile lit his face and I nearly gasped at the sight. He was beautiful. His lips curled upward, exposing a flash of white teeth with his fangs just visible. The corners of his eyes crinkled in a way I'd never seen before and there were lines between his nose and the outside of his lips. He was really, truly smiling and I'd never seen anything as perfect or lovely. I let out a sigh of admiration and his smile widened. I reached out to stroke his face, to feel those lovely lips. He opened his mouth and caught my fingers, twirling his tongue around them. I felt an instant response in my groin.

"You're perfect," I whispered. "I want to be yours."

I did. That resistance in my heart faded away. I wanted to belong to him with the desperation of months of longing. He had taken me in those months, played with me body and soul and driven me to desire time and time again, but it had never been like this, equally sharing in his pleasure. That was what I craved. The sight of him enjoying me, the knowledge that I made him feel the way he made me feel.

He let my fingers go and lifted the blindfold in one hand. It dangled above me as I lay on the bed.

"Would you feel better without this?"

"No," I whispered. "But I always want to see you smile."

His lips curved again and my heart throbbed with desire. The rest of me throbbed, too. I had rarely been this turned on without him even touching me. He glanced down at my body and let his hand stroke down my chest. I shivered and when he reached my cock, I gasped. Then he reached back up to secure the blindfold.

"I enjoy you blind," he said. "I enjoy controlling you. But only if you want it. Can you submit, now that you're a vampire?"

I considered again, but it didn't take long. All resistance had melted away at the sight of those beautiful lips curved in a smile, those lovely teeth, those little crinkles by his eyes. It was everything I had wanted since I saw him for the first time months ago. Ever since then, I had wondered what it would be like. I had caught glimpses of a faint smile in that time, and more open smiles since becoming a vampire, but nothing like that. If he could look at me like that, then he could do whatever he wanted to me and nothing in me opposed it.

"I want to submit to you," I said softly. "I want to belong to you. I want to know I please you."

"You do," he said, with humor in his voice. "Did you not know that? I wouldn't have sacrificed so much for you if I didn't want you."

"I know," I said. "It's just… nice to see you smile."

"If that's the only price I have to pay to get you, I'm more than willing to pay it," he said, leaning down to peck my cheeks and run his hand down my side. "If you weren't a vampire, you wouldn't see my emotions the way you do now."

My breathing was short and quick as his hand tingled across my hips but didn't come anywhere near my cock. I desperately wanted him. Why wasn't he touching me? His words barely registered, then I thought about how open he had been since I became a vampire. All of them had become more open. Maybe it wasn't that were more expressive but that I could finally see their true emotions. Maybe humans just weren't capable of seeing it. I wondered if I was now as impassive as them even though I felt just as expressive. Maybe that explained the distance between me and the other servants, even though Margaret had seemed willing to overcome that distance. I was different now, in more ways than one, and felt a flash of regret. What would my parents think? But I pushed that away hastily. I did not want to think of them, not when my body was singing like this.

"Please," I murmured, arching my body against his hands. He laughed softly again and I knew he was smiling. Then his hand made contact and I sighed in relief. He stroked me slowly, firmly, until I could barely stand it anymore, then pulled me off the bed into his arms. I went willingly, though I wondered what exactly he would do to me. He turned me in his arms and pushed me forward until my hands were against the bed and I was bent over. I quivered in anticipation, that tiny resistance long forgotten. This was everything I needed.

"Stay," he said, and I obeyed. I shifted slightly, longing for physical contact, for relief, but it would be a long time until he gave me that. I heard him moving around the room and heard something catch. I longed to know what it was and thought of all the toys and devices I had so briefly seen. I shivered again, wondering what he was getting.

His hands caressed my hips, then moved to touch me. I enjoyed the touch but he wasn't stroking me, he was securing something around me. A cockring, I realized with a start. We hadn't ever played with that before. The tight sensation was cool and arousing, and I shifted again, longing for even more pressure. Then his hand traced to my ass.

He stopped touching me and I ached from the loss of his hand, then something rushed by and I gasped as a thread of pain lashed across my bare ass. It was like when he had spanked me but more concentrated and stung in a pleasurable way I had never felt before. Again, and again, until I leaned forward and rested my head against my arms and moaned and swayed and longed for more. I began begging for more before long and he gave it, but right when I couldn't stand it anymore, right when the pain began to outweigh the pleasure and my cock felt like it would explode, his hand touched me and caressed my swollen skin.

"You're beautiful," he murmured. My heard skipped a beat. His hands slid to my hips and pulled me backwards until I felt him right against my opening. I tried not to tense in anticipation, coaxing myself to relax and enjoy what was about to happen.

He thrust into me quickly, his hands yanking me back as my sore ass stung at the sudden pressure of his body against mine. I gasped and cried out, but he gave me no time to adapt before he started pulsing into me. I pressed my forehead into my arm and moaned, shifting in time to his thrusts and feeling like my cock couldn't bear it anymore. He kept going as I grew harder and harder, my pleasure threatening to overtake me no matter what was around my cock. Then, finally, his hand slid from my hips to my cock and he released me. I had one moment of relief before pleasure swamped through my senses. I nearly screamed as my orgasm hit me and I could feel him explode inside me at the same time. Waves of heat and tingling pleasure washed through me, over and over again as a thread of pure bliss spewed from me.

My high seemed to last forever, then I slowly came down, panting and still moaning and writhing against Adze as he pulled out of me. I had never felt anything like that, not in any of our times together. No matter how earth-shattering my previous orgasms with him had been, nothing compared. I didn't know if it was the cockring stifling my pleasure until the last possible moment, or the fact that I was now a vampire, or just seeing him smile at the beginning, but something about that was completely different. It was just as good as when he had fed on me. He helped me into the bed and got in next to me, cradling me and stroking my head as I lay limply against him. I felt sticky, but in a pleasant way, and he didn't seem to mind. He kept stroking me and I felt a flicker of pleasure, a flicker deep down in my belly that stirred me once again. Adze chuckled.

"You have different stamina now," he said in a low voice. "Are you already wanting more?"

I blushed and snuggled against him. Did I want more? Yes. A very large part of me wanted to experience that again, and again, until I couldn't breathe and couldn't think from the bliss. But I also wanted to hold him like this. He rarely held me; normally it was limited to sex with very little before or after. I wanted to curl against him, to be held in his arms, to have my hair stroked and played with. So I shook my head.

"Can I see you again?" I asked, and he pulled the blindfold from my eyes. He was smiling and I reached up to stroke his face. He was so incredibly beautiful. Was this worth losing everything else in my life?

A twinge of sorrow as I thought of my parents, of Janae, of everything I had lost. I would never be the same, never have the same dreams and opportunities. Everything was gone, and I had to rebuild my life from scratch. But I had him. I finally had Adze. There wasn't anything stopping us from being together.

Was it worth it? I leaned forward and kissed him. Yes, it was worth it. I wanted him more than I wanted anything else. Oh, I wouldn't have chosen this. If given the choice, I would have stayed human and risked losing him. But now that he was mine, now that I was irrevocably in his world and a vampire, I didn't regret it. If I had to lose everything, at least I kept him.

It was going to be a hard road adapting to be a vampire, I already knew. There was so much I didn't know, so much I had to learn. I had to completely alter not only my lifestyle but my outlook on life. I was immortal now and needed to adjust how I viewed time. I fed on blood and had to adjust my feeding habits. I thrived in darkness and even though I had been on a night schedule for a while now, it would still be a drastic difference now that sunlight actually hurt me. So many changes and I felt completely unprepared and unready.

But he would help me. He would stay at my side and teach me, and protect me until I was able to protect myself. And even after that, I could stay with him. I was grateful that my house was allowing me to stay here. I was an ambassador now and I would do my best, because that gave me access to the vampire I loved.

It was odd to think of love and I paused. That emotion had crossed my mind before but never this clearly. He couldn't love me before. I was human, and his servant. Now we were equals. Well, maybe not equals – he was an ancient vampire, and a founding vampire at that – but we were on a more level playing field. Love could actually enter the picture. Could vampires love each other? I wasn't sure.

I didn't see any reason they couldn't, except that no vampires I had ever met seemed to have romantic attachments. But there were the dhampir. There wouldn't be vampire-human hybrids unless vampires fell in love and wanted to have children with humans. So the emotion was available to them even if they didn't take it often. And I felt love for Adze. It had never crystallized like this but I knew in that moment that I did love him, and if I loved him, it was perfectly possible he loved me.

I wouldn't ask. Not yet, maybe not for a long time. But eventually I would ask him how he felt about me and he would tell me the truth. I looked up at him, at those twinkling eyes I had only imagined before, and stroked his cheek again. Yes, I loved him, and someday, he would love me too.

THE END

ABOUT THE AUTHOR

Elizabeth James

Elizabeth James hails from Portland, Oregon and spent many hours of her childhood tucked away in the Gold Room of Powell's Books, reading science fiction and fantasy masterpieces and hidden treasures. She writes romance with strong elements of science fiction and fantasy as a result, focusing on LGBT characters.

THRALL OF DARKNESS

*science fiction and fantasy
romance publisher*

Thrall of Darkness was founded because there is a shortage of good, quality literature featuring gay protagonists that does not reduce gay characters to stereotypes or dismiss them as secondary characters. Every story seeks to challenge the status quo by focusing on gay characters and combining drama, action, and sex into an addicting blend of fun-filled narrative.

You can find more information on Thrall of Darkness novels and short stories at thrallofdarkness.com.

BOOKS BY THIS AUTHOR

Bride Of Albis

An mm science fiction novella. Sam and his crew are kidnapped and Sam is sold as a slave in exchange for the freedom of his crew. But when the pirates lie and sell his crew as well, he vows vengeance. Sam falls in love with his new master as they search for his enslaved crew members and seek to free them, but will it be too late?

Dark Offering

An mm science fiction novella. Humans have struggled to survive on an alien world for centuries, fed on by creatures spawned from their nightmares. As the planet quiets for the annual peace where humans can roam freely for five days, one man sets out into the woods and finds a creature he doesn't expect who brings almost certain death but offers hope as well.

Demon Season

An mm urban fantasy novel. Taylor just wanted to bond with an ordinary demon during his first demon season, but he ends up with the Prince of Demons: an incubus. But his dark past slows his initial bonding with his demon and dangers from the demon's past threaten their safety in the present. Will their love succeed, or will the demon hunters and shadowed memories prevail?

Dragon Tamer

An mm urban fantasy novel. After a troubled youth, Luke has come to terms with his role as the dragon tamer of his clan. But when a rival clan kidnaps him, Luke learns that he has been misled about his life and his purpose. Will he adapt to his new reality, or will he return to the safety of the past?

Eve Of Eternity

An mm, mf space opera series. Sabine is a young woman searching for her identity while fleeing the powerful man trying to steal her heart and mind. She is almost under his control when she is kidnapped by a man with conflicting loyalties and a mysterious past who claims to kidnap her in order to rescue her. As they flee from the forces gathering against them, they encounter handsome fighters and charming smugglers who complicate their mission, and soon it becomes clear that Sabine's fate will determine the fate of the galaxy as her kidnapping sparks the Second Galactic War. Is Sabine strong enough to fight the man hunting her and overcome her fears, or will she succumb to temptation and allow him to rule her life once more?

First Prince

An mm dark fantasy novel. Wren, the beautiful yet rebellious first prince of Fontain, will do anything to protect his home even after his nation has been conquered by the Empire. Upon arriving in the Imperial Palace, however, he realizes that his stay will be fraught with drama and danger even as he finds love in an unexpected place. As his relationship expands into his first true love, politics bring his relationship into question and he is forced to choose between love and loyalty or face the ultimate price.

Prisoner Of Love

An mm dark fantasy novella. When Prince Tristan is captured in battle, he fully expects to be tortured and killed. But the torture turns to erotic pleasure as he learns that his enemy, Prince Ryan, is in love with him and has been planning his capture with meticulous care for years. Will Tristan hold firm to his principles, or will Ryan's forceful seduction overpower his senses?

Sagent

An mm science fiction novel. Gabriel is a sagent at the start of his career, but he is already scarred by his previous agency. When he is sent on a dangerous mission to the underbelly of Destiny, everything starts to fall apart for him. Isolated from his agency and not knowing where to go, Gabriel must choose between returning to safety and Destiny, or staying and forging his own path.

Seeking More

Seeking More is a collection of eight contemporary gay romance stories that range from the deeply emotional to action-packed, from hapless MFA students to couples on the brink of a new relationship. Each story is focused not only on steamy romance, of which there is plenty, but also on character development and an emotional connection between reader and character.

Tarragon Academy

An mm urban fantasy series. Tarragon Academy is a college at the foot of a smoldering volcano surrounded in mist and mystery. Graduates of the college are virtually guaranteed success in any field they pursue, but the first year exam can be a real killer. First-year student Jamie Wendell made it into the college, but is having a hard time adapting to the teachers and other students until he meets an upperclassman named Scott. Will Scott help him thrive in his new school, or does Scott have his own reasons for helping the beautiful young freshman?

Treacherous A Dragon's Love

An mf fantasy adventure novella. In the middle of the final battle against the great dragon Arostrath, a woman appears bound in golden chains. The King claims her as his reward but the youngest son has an unusual fondness for her that could cast the kingdom into ruin. Will his love for the beautiful and mysterious woman destroy the kingdom, or does her mystery hide the answer to all of their prayers?

CPSIA information can be obtained
at www.ICGtesting.com
Printed in the USA
LVHW082133080622
720856LV00027B/769